W9-BVM-112

Many Bloody Returns

Many Bloody Returns

Edited by
Charlaine Harris
and Toni L. P. Kelner

ACE BOOKS, NEW YORK

THE BERKLEY PUBLISHING GROUP
Published by the Penguin Group
Penguin Group (USA) Inc.
375 Hudson Street, New York, New York 10014, USA
Penguin Group (Canada), 90 Eglinton Avenue East, Suite 700, Toronto, Ontario M4P 2Y3, Canada
(a division of Pearson Penguin Canada Inc.)
Penguin Books Ltd., 80 Strand, London WC2R 0RL, England
Penguin Group Ireland, 25 St. Stephen's Green, Dublin 2, Ireland (a division of Penguin Books Ltd.)
Penguin Group (Australia), 250 Camberwell Road, Camberwell, Victoria 3124, Australia
(a division of Pearson Australia Group Pty. Ltd.)
Penguin Books India Pvt. Ltd., 11 Community Centre, Panchsheel Park, New Delhi—110 017, India
Penguin Group (NZ), 67 Apollo Drive, Rosedale, North Shore 0745, Auckland, New Zealand
(a division of Pearson New Zealand Ltd.)
Penguin Books (South Africa) (Pty.) Ltd., 24 Sturdee Avenue, Rosebank, Johannesburg 2196, South Africa

Penguin Books Ltd., Registered Offices: 80 Strand, London WC2R 0RL, England

This book is an original publication of The Berkley Publishing Group.

A complete listing of individual copyrights can be found on page 356.
Text design by Kristin del Rosario.

First edition: September 2007

Library of Congress Cataloging-in-Publication Data

Many bloody returns / edited by Charlaine Harris and Toni L. P. Kelner.—1st ed.
p. cm.
ISBN 978-0-441-01522-1
1. Vampires—Fiction. I. Harris, Charlaine. II. Kelner, Toni L. P.

PS648.V35M356 2007
813'.087308—dc22

2007011450

PRINTED IN THE UNITED STATES OF AMERICA

10 9 8 7 6 5 4 3 2 1

This is dedicated to
Joss Whedon,
who may never read it,
and his enthusiastic fans known as the
Buffybuds, who will.

We thank Marty and John at Tekno Books for their inspiration, encouragement, and full-service smoothing of the way; our agents, Joshua Bilmes (Charlaine) and Joan Brandt (Toni); and finally, Ginjer Buchanan at Ace, who agreed this might be a good idea. We also want to thank the authors who contributed their stories to this anthology though they knew their editors were novices. That's trust for you.

CONTENTS

A Few Words

When we were approached about editing this anthology, we were like two kids with a new toy. We had some wonderful planning sessions about the theme. We decided to pick two apparently unrelated concepts—vampires (the dead) and birthdays (celebrations of life)—and see what different ways some very talented writers could combine the two.

After the great fun of drawing up a dream list of contributors and receiving their stories, we had to buckle down to the actual work of editing. We imagined the work would be tedious, or nerve-wracking, or possibly (horrors) boring. But it wasn't. Every day a new story arrived was like—well, like a birthday.

It's amazing what creative minds can do with the same theme. None of these stories are the same. Some of them are funny, and some of them are tragic, but all of them are fascinating. Read and enjoy.

Charlaine Harris
Toni L. P. Kelner

Dracula Night

Charlaine Harris

Charlaine Harris, New York Times *bestselling author of the Sookie Stackhouse series, also writes books about Harper Connelly, a lightning-struck corpse locator. Charlaine has won the Anthony, the Sapphire, and two Romantic Times Reviewers' Choice awards. She lives in a small town in Arkansas with her husband, a duck, three dogs, and three children. Her website is simply www.charlaineharris.com, and she tries real hard to keep it up-to-date.*

I found the invitation in the mailbox at the end of my driveway. I had to lean out of my car window to open it, because I'd paused on my way to work after remembering I hadn't checked my mail in a couple of days. My mail was never interesting. I might get a flyer for Dollar General or Wal-Mart, or one of those ominous mass mailings about pre-need burial plots.

Today, after I'd sighed at my Entergy bill and my cable bill, I had a little treat: a handsome, heavy, buff-colored envelope that clearly contained some kind of invitation. It had been addressed by someone who'd not only taken a calligraphy class but passed the final with flying colors.

I got a little pocketknife out of my glove compartment and slit open the envelope with the care it deserved. I don't get a lot of invitations, and when I do, they're usually more Hallmark than watermark. This was something to be savored. I pulled out the stiff folded paper carefully, and opened it. Something fluttered into my lap: an enclosed sheet of tissue. Without absorbing the revealed words, I ran my finger over the embossing. Wow.

I'd strung out the preliminaries as long as I could. I bent to actually read the italic typeface.

Eric Northman
and the Staff of Fangtasia

request the honor of your presence
at Fangtasia's annual party
to celebrate the birthday of
the Lord of Darkness

Prince Dracula

On February 8, 10:00 p.m.
music provided by the Duke of Death
Dress Formal RSVP

I read it twice. Then I read it again.

I drove to work in such a thoughtful mood that I'm glad there wasn't any other traffic on Hummingbird Road. I took the left to get to Merlotte's, but then I almost sailed right past the parking lot. At the last moment, I braked and turned in to navigate my way to the parking area behind the bar that was reserved for employees.

Sam Merlotte, my boss, was sitting behind his desk when I peeked in to put my purse in the deep drawer in his desk that he let the servers use. He had been running his hands over his hair again, because the tangled red-gold halo was even wilder than usual. He looked up from his tax form and smiled at me.

"Sookie," he said, "how are you doing?"

"Good. Tax season, huh?" I made sure my white T-shirt was tucked in evenly so the "Merlotte's" embroidered over my left breast would be level. I flicked one of my long blond hairs off my black pants. I always bent over to brush my hair out so my ponytail would look smooth. "You not taking them to the CPA this year?"

"I figure if I start this early, I can do them myself."

He said that every year, and he always ended up making an appointment with the CPA, who always had to file for an extension.

"Listen, did you get one of these?" I asked, extending the invitation.

He dropped his pen with some relief and took the sheet from my hand. After scanning the script, he said, "No. They wouldn't invite many shifters, anyway. Maybe the local packmaster, or some supe who'd done them a significant service . . . like you."

"I'm not supernatural," I said, surprised. "I just have a . . . problem."

"Telepathy is a lot more than a problem," Sam said. "Acne is a problem. Shyness is a problem. Reading other peoples' minds is a gift."

"Or a curse," I said. I went around the desk to toss my purse in the drawer, and Sam stood up. I'm around five foot six, and Sam tops me by maybe three inches. He's not a big guy, but he's much stronger than a plain human his size, since Sam's a shapeshifter.

"Are you going to go?" he asked. "Halloween and Dracula's birthday are the only holidays vampires observe, and I understand they can throw quite a party."

"I haven't made up my mind," I said. "When I'm on my break later, I might call Pam on my cell." Pam, Eric's second-in-command, was as close to a friend as I had among the vampires.

I reached her at Fangtasia pretty soon after the sun went down. "There really was a Count Dracula? I thought he was made up," I said after telling her I'd gotten the invitation.

"There really was," Pam said. "Vlad Tepes. He was a Wallachian king whose capital city was Târgovişte, I think." Pam was quite matter-of-fact about the existence of a creature I'd thought was a joint creation of Bram Stoker and Hollywood. "Vlad III was more ferocious and bloodthirsty than any vampire, and this was when he was a live human. He enjoyed executing people by impaling them on huge wooden stakes. They might last for hours."

I shuddered. Ick.

"His own people regarded him with fear, of course. But the local vamps admired Vlad so much they actually brought him over when he was dying, thus ushering in the new era of the vampire. After monks buried him on an island called Snagov, he rose on the third night to become the first modern vampire. Up until then, the vampires were like . . . well, disgusting. Completely secret. Ragged, filthy, living in holes in cemeteries, like animals. But Vlad Dracul had been a ruler, and he wasn't going to dress in rags and live in a hole for any reason." Pam sounded proud.

I tried to imagine Eric wearing rags and living in a hole, but it was almost impossible. "So Stoker didn't just dream the whole thing up based on folktales?"

"Just parts of it. Obviously, he didn't know a lot about what Dracula, as he called him, really could or couldn't do, but he was so excited at meeting the prince that he made up a lot of details he thought would give the story zing. It was just like Anne Rice meeting Louis: an early *Interview with the Vampire*. Dracula really wasn't too happy afterward that Stoker caught him at a weak moment, but he did enjoy the name recognition."

"But he won't actually be there, right? I mean, vampires'll be celebrating this all over the world."

Pam said, very cautiously, "Some believe he shows up somewhere every year, makes a surprise appearance. That chance is so remote, his appearance at our party would be like winning the lottery. Though some believe it could happen."

I heard Eric's voice in the background saying, "Pam, who are you talking to?"

"Okay," Pam said, the word sounding very American with her slight British accent. "Got to go, Sookie. See you then."

As I returned the phone to my purse, Sam said, "Sookie, if you go to the party, please keep alert and on the watch. Sometimes vamps get carried away with the excitement on Dracula Night."

"Thanks, Sam," I said. "I'll sure be careful." No matter how many vamps you claimed as friends, you had to be alert. A few years ago the Japanese had invented a synthetic blood that satisfies the vampires' nutritional requirements, which has enabled the undead to come out of the shadows and take their place at the American table. British vampires had it pretty good, too, and most of the Western European vamps had fared pretty well after the Great Revelation (the day they'd announced their existence, through carefully chosen representatives). However, many South American vamps regretted stepping forward, and the bloodsuckers in the Muslim countries—well, there were mighty few left. Vampires in the inhospitable parts of the world were making efforts to immigrate to countries that tolerated them, with the result that our Congress was considering various bills to limit undead citizens from claiming political asylum. In consequence, we were experiencing an influx of vampires with all kinds of accents as they tried to enter America under the wire. Most of them came in through Louisiana, since it was notably friendly to the Cold Ones, as *Fangbanger Xtreme* called them.

It was more fun thinking about vampires than hearing the thoughts of my fellow citizens. Naturally, as I went from table to table, I was doing my job with a big smile, because I like good tips, but I wasn't able to put my heart into it tonight. It had been a warm day for February, way into the fifties, and people's thoughts had turned to spring.

I try not to listen in, but I'm like a radio that picks up a lot of signals. Some days, I can control my reception a lot better than other days. Today, I kept picking up snippets. Hoyt Fortenberry, my brother's best friend, was thinking about his mother's request that he put in about ten new rosebushes in her already extensive garden. Gloomy but obedient, he was trying to figure out how much time the task would take. Arlene, my longtime friend and another waitress, was wondering if she could get her latest boyfriend to pop the question, but that was pretty much a perennial thought for Arlene. Like the roses, it bloomed every season.

As I mopped up spills and hustled to get chicken strip baskets on the tables (the supper crowd was heavy that night), my own thoughts were centered on how to get a formal gown to wear to the party. Though I did have one ancient prom dress, handmade by my aunt Linda, it was hopelessly outdated. I'm twenty-six, but I didn't have any bridesmaid dresses that might serve. None of my few friends had gotten married except Arlene, who'd been wed so many times that she never even thought of bridesmaids. The few nice clothes I'd bought for vampire events always seemed to get ruined . . . some in very unpleasant ways.

Usually, I shopped at my friend Tara's store, but she wasn't open after six. So after I got off work, I drove to Monroe to Pecanland Mall. At Dillard's, I got lucky. To tell the truth, I was so pleased with the dress I might have gotten it even if it hadn't been on sale, but it had been marked down to twenty-five dollars from a hundred and fifty, surely a shopping triumph. It was rose pink, with a sequin top and a chiffon bottom, and it was strapless and simple. I'd wear my hair down, and my gran's pearl earrings, and some silver heels that were also on major sale.

That major item taken care of, I wrote a polite acceptance note and popped it in the mail. I was good to go.

Three nights later, I was knocking on the back door of Fangtasia, my garment bag held high.

"You're looking a bit informal," Pam said as she let me in.

"Didn't want to wrinkle the dress." I came in, making sure the bag didn't trail, and hightailed it for the bathroom.

There wasn't a lock on the bathroom door. Pam stood outside so I wouldn't be interrupted, and Eric's second-in-command smiled when I came out, a bundle of my more mundane clothes rolled under my arm.

"You look good, Sookie," Pam said. Pam herself had elected to wear a tuxedo made out of silver lamé. She was a sight. My hair has some curl to it, but Pam's is a paler blond and very straight. We both have blue eyes, but hers are a lighter shade and rounder, and she doesn't blink much. "Eric will be very pleased."

I flushed. Eric and I have a History. But since he had amnesia when we created that history, he doesn't remember it. Pam does. "Like I care what he thinks," I said.

Pam smiled at me sideways. "Right," she said. "You are totally indifferent. So is he."

I tried to look like I was accepting her words on their surface level and not seeing through to the sarcasm. To my surprise, Pam gave me a light kiss on the cheek. "Thanks for coming," she said. "You may perk him up. He's been very hard to work for these past few days."

"Why?" I asked, though I wasn't real sure I wanted to know.

"Have you ever seen 'It's the Great Pumpkin, Charlie Brown'?"

I stopped in my tracks. "Sure," I said. "Have *you*?"

"Oh, yes," Pam said calmly. "Many times." She gave me a minute to absorb that. "Eric is like that on Dracula Night. He thinks, every year, that this time Dracula will pick *his* party to attend. Eric fusses and plans; he frets and stews. He sent the invitations back to the printer twice so they were late going out. Now that the night is actually here, he's worked himself into a state."

"So this is a case of hero worship gone crazy?"

"You have such a way with words," Pam said admiringly. We were outside Eric's office, and we could both hear him bellowing inside.

"He's not happy with the new bartender. He thinks there are not enough bottles of the blood the count is said to prefer, according to an interview in *American Vampire*."

I tried to imagine the Vlad Tepes, impaler of so many of his own countrymen, chatting with a reporter. I sure wouldn't want to be the one holding the pad and pencil. "What brand would that be?" I scrambled to catch up with the conversation.

"The Prince of Darkness is said to prefer Royalty."

"Ew." Why was I not surprised?

Royalty was a very, very rare bottled blood. I'd thought the brand was only a rumor until now. Royalty consisted of part synthetic blood and part real blood—the blood of, you guessed it, people of title. Before you go thinking of enterprising vamps ambushing that cute Prince William, let me reassure you. There were plenty of minor royals in Europe who were glad to give blood for an astronomical sum.

"After a month's worth of phone calls, we managed to get two bottles." Pam was looking quite grim. "They cost more than we could afford. I've never known my maker to be other than business-wise, but this year Eric seems to be going overboard. Royalty doesn't keep forever, you know, with the real blood in it . . . and now he's worried that two bottles might not be enough. There is so much legend attached to Dracula, who can say what is true? He has heard that Dracula will only drink Royalty or . . . the real thing."

"Real blood? But that's illegal, unless you got a willing donor."

Any vampire who took a human's blood—against the human's will—was liable to execution—by stake or sunlight, according to the vamp's choice. The execution was usually carried out by another vamp, kept on retainer by the state. I personally thought any vampire who took an unwilling person's blood deserved the execution, because there were enough fangbangers around who were more than willing to donate.

"And no vampire is allowed to kill Dracula, or even strike him," Pam said, chiming right in on my thoughts. "Not that we'd want to strike our prince, of course," she added hastily.

Right, I thought.

"He is held in such reverence that any vampire who assaults him must meet the sun. And we're also expected to offer our prince financial assistance."

I wondered if the other vampires were supposed to floss his fangs for him too.

The door to Eric's office flew open with such vehemence that it bounced right back. It opened again more gently, and Eric emerged.

I had to gape. He looked positively edible. Eric is very tall, very broad, very blond, and tonight he was dressed in a tuxedo that had not come off any rack. This tux had been made for Eric, and he looked as good as any James Bond in it. Black cloth without a speck of lint, a snowy white shirt, and a hand-tied bow at his throat, and his beautiful hair rippling down his back . . .

"James Blond," I muttered. Eric's eyes were blazing with excitement. Without a word, he dipped me as though we were dancing and planted a hell of a kiss on me: lips, tongue, the entire osculant assemblage. Oh boy, oh boy, oh boy. When I was quivering, he assisted me to rise. His brilliant smile revealed glistening fangs. Eric had enjoyed himself.

"Hello to you too," I said tartly, once I was sure I was breathing again.

"My delicious friend," Eric said, and bowed.

I wasn't sure I could be correctly called a friend, and I'd have to take his word for it that I was delicious. "What's the program for the evening?" I asked, hoping that my host would calm down very soon.

"We'll dance, listen to music, drink blood, watch the entertainment, and wait for the count to come," Eric said. "I'm so glad you'll be here tonight. We have a wide array of special guests, but you're the only telepath."

"Okay," I said faintly.

"You look especially lovely tonight," said Lyle. He'd been standing right behind Eric, and I hadn't even noticed him. Slight and narrow-faced, with spiked black hair, Lyle didn't have the presence Eric had acquired in a thousand years of life. Lyle was a visiting vamp from Alexandria, interning at the very successful Fangtasia because he wanted to open his own vampire bar. Lyle was carrying a small cooler, taking great care to keep it level.

"The Royalty," Pam explained in a neutral voice.

"Can I see?" I asked.

Eric lifted the lid and showed me the contents: two blue bottles (for the blue blood, I presumed), with labels that bore the logo of a tiara and the single word *Royalty* in gothic script.

"Very nice," I said, underwhelmed.

"He'll be so pleased," Eric said, sounding as happy as I'd ever heard him.

"You sound oddly sure that the—that Dracula will be coming," I said. The hall was crowded, and we began moving to the public part of the club.

"I was able to have a business discussion with the Master's handler," he said. "I was able to express how much having the Master's presence would honor me and my establishment."

Pam rolled her eyes at me.

"You bribed him," I translated. Hence Eric's extra excitement this year, and his purchase of the Royalty.

I had never suspected Eric harbored this depth of hero worship for anyone except himself. I would never have believed Eric would spend good money for such a reason, either. Eric was charming and enterprising, and he took good care of his employees; but the first person on Eric's admiration list was Eric, and his own well-being was Eric's number one priority.

"Dear Sookie, you're looking less than excited," Pam said, grinning at me. Pam loved to make trouble, and she was finding fertile ground tonight. Eric swung his head back to give me a look, and Pam's face relaxed into its usual bland smoothness.

"Don't you believe it will happen, Sookie?" he asked. From behind his back, Lyle rolled his eyes. He was clearly fed up with Eric's fantasy.

I'd just wanted to come to a party in a pretty dress and have a good time, and here I was, up a conversational creek.

"We'll all find out, won't we?" I said brightly, and Eric seemed satisfied. "The club looks beautiful." Normally, Fangtasia was the plainest place you could imagine, besides the lively gray-and-red paint scheme and the neon. The floors were concrete, the tables and chairs basic metal restaurant furnishings, the booths not much better. I could not believe that Fangtasia had been so transformed. Banners had been hung from the club's ceiling. Each banner was white with a red bear on it: a sort of stylized bear on its hind legs, one paw raised to strike.

"That's a replica of the Master's personal flag," Pam said in answer to my pointed finger. "Eric paid an historian at LSU to research it." Her expression made it clear she thought Eric had been gypped, big-time.

In the center of Fangtasia's small dance floor stood an actual throne on a small dais. As I neared the throne, I decided Eric had rented it from a theater company. It looked good from thirty feet away, but up close . . . not so much. However, it had been freshened up with a plump red cushion for the Dark Prince's derriere, and the dais was placed in the exact middle of a square of dark red carpet. All the tables had been covered with white or dark red cloths, and elaborate flower arrangements were in the middle of each table. I had to laugh when I examined one of the arrangements: in the explosion of red carnations and greenery were miniature coffins and full-size stakes. Eric's sense of humor had surfaced, finally.

Instead of WDED, the all-vampire radio station, the sound system was playing some very emotional violin music that was both scratchy and bouncy. "Transylvanian music," said Lyle, his face carefully expressionless. "Later, the DJ Duke of Death will take us for a musical journey." Lyle looked as though he would rather eat snails.

Against one wall by the bar, I spied a small buffet for beings who ate food, and a large blood fountain for those who didn't. The red fountain, flowing gently down several tiers of gleaming milky glass bowls, was surrounded by crystal goblets. Just a wee bit over the top.

"Golly," I said weakly as Eric and Lyle went over to the bar.

Pam shook her head in despair. "The money we spent," she said.

Not too surprisingly, the room was full of vampires. I recognized a few of the bloodsuckers present: Indira, Thalia, Clancy, Maxwell Lee, and Bill Compton, my ex. There were at least twenty more I had only seen once or twice, vamps who lived in Area Five under Eric's authority. There were a few bloodsuckers I didn't know at all, including a guy behind the bar that must be the new bartender. Fangtasia ran through bartenders pretty quickly.

There were also some creatures in the bar who were not vamps and not human, members of Louisiana's supernatural community. The head of Shreveport's werewolf pack, Colonel Flood, was sitting at a table with Calvin Norris, the leader of the small community of werepanthers who lived in and around Hot Shot, outside of Bon Temps. Colonel Flood, now retired from the air force, was sitting stiffly erect in a good suit, while Calvin was wearing his own idea of party clothes—a western shirt, new jeans, cowboy boots, and a black cowboy hat. He tipped it to me when he caught my eye, and he gave me a nod that expressed admiration. Colonel Flood's nod was less personal but still friendly.

Eric had also invited a short, broad man who strongly reminded me of a goblin I'd met once. I was sure this male was a member of the same race. Goblins are testy and ferociously strong, and when they are angry their touch can burn, so I decided to stay a good distance away from this one. He was deep in conversation with a very thin woman with mad eyes. She was wearing an assemblage of leaves and vines. I wasn't going to ask.

Of course, there weren't any fairies. Fairies are as intoxicating to vampires as sugar water is to hummingbirds.

Behind the bar was the newest member of the Fangtasia staff, a short, burly, man with long, wavy dark hair. He had a prominent nose and large eyes, and he was taking everything in with an air of amusement while he moved around preparing drink orders.

"Who's that?" I asked, nodding toward the bar. "And who are the strange vamps? Is Eric expanding?"

Pam said, "If you're in transit on Dracula Night, the protocol is to check in at the nearest sheriff's headquarters and share in the celebration there. That's why there are vampires here you haven't met. The new bartender is Milos Griesniki, a recent immigrant from the Old Countries. He is disgusting."

I stared at Pam. "How so?" I asked.

"A sneaker. A pryer."

I'd never heard Pam express such a strong opinion, and I looked at the vampire with some curiosity.

"He tries to discover how much money Eric has, and how much the bar makes, and how much our little human barmaids get paid."

"Speaking of whom, where are they?" The waitresses and the rest of the everyday staff, all vampire groupies (known in some circles as fangbangers), were usually much in evidence, dressed in filmy black and powdered almost as pale as the real vampires.

"Too dangerous for them on this night," Pam said simply. "You will see that Indira and Clancy are serving the guests." Indira was wearing a beautiful sari; she usually wore jeans and T-shirts, so I knew she had made an effort to dress up for the occasion. Clancy, who had rough red hair and bright green eyes, was in a suit. That was also a first. Instead of a regular tie, he wore a scarf tied into a floppy bow, and when I caught his eye he swept his hand from his head to his pants to demand my admiration. I smiled and nodded, though truthfully I liked Clancy better in his usual tough-guy clothes and heavy boots.

Eric was buzzing from table to table. He hugged and bowed and talked like a demented thing, and I didn't know if I found this endearing or alarming. I decided it was both. I'd definitely discovered Eric's weak side.

I talked to Colonel Flood and Calvin for a few minutes. Colonel Flood was as polite and distant as he always was; he didn't care much for non-Weres, and now that he had retired, he only dealt with regular people when he had to. Calvin told me that he'd put a new roof on his house himself, and invited me to go fishing with him when the weather was warmer. I smiled but didn't commit to anything. My grandmother had loved fishing, but I was only good for two hours, tops, and then I was ready to do something else. I watched Pam doing her second-in-command job, making sure all the visiting vampires were happy, sharply admonishing the new bartender when he made a mistake with a drink order. Milos Griesniki gave her back a scowl that made me shiver. But if anyone could take care of herself, it was Pam.

Clancy, who'd been managing the club for a month, was checking every table to make sure there were clean ashtrays (some of the vampires smoked) and that all dirty glasses and other discarded items were removed promptly. When DJ Duke of Death took over, the music changed to something with a beat. Some of the vampires turned out onto the dance floor, flinging themselves around with the extreme abandon only the undead show.

Calvin and I danced a couple of times, but we were nowhere in the vampire league. Eric claimed me for a slow dance, and though he was clearly distracted by thoughts of what the night might hold—Dracula-wise—he made my toenails quiver.

"Some night," he whispered, "there's going to be nothing else but you and me."

When the song was over, I had to go back to the table and have a long, cold drink. Lots of ice.

As the time drew closer to midnight, the vampires gathered around the blood fountain and filled the crystal goblets. The non-vamp guests also rose to their feet. I was standing beside the table where I'd been chatting with Calvin and Colonel Flood when Eric brought out a table-top hand gong and began to strike it. If he'd been human, he'd have been flushed with excitement; as it was, his eyes were blazing. Eric looked both beautiful and scary, because he was so intent.

When the last reverberation had shivered into silence, Eric raised his own glass high and said, "On this most memorable of days, we stand together in awe and hope that the Lord of Darkness will honor us with his presence. O Prince, appear to us!"

We actually all stood in hushed silence, waiting for the Great Pumpkin—oh, wait, the Dark Prince. Just when Eric's face began to look downcast, a harsh voice broke the tension.

"My loyal son, I shall reveal myself!"

Milos Griesniki leaped from behind the bar, pulling off his tux jacket and pants and his shirt to reveal . . . an incredible jumpsuit made from black, glittery, stretchy stuff. I would have expected to see it on a girl going to her prom, a girl without much money who was trying to look unconventional and sexy. With his blocky body and dark hair and mustache, the one-piece made Milos look more like an acrobat in a third-rate circus.

There was an excited babble of low-voiced reaction. Calvin said, "Well . . . shit." Colonel Flood gave a sharp nod, to say he agreed completely.

The bartender posed regally before Eric, who after a startled instant bowed before the much shorter vampire. "My lord," Eric said, "I am humbled. That you should honor us . . . that you should actually be here . . . on this day, of all days . . . I am overcome."

"Fucking poser," Pam muttered in my ear. She'd glided up behind me in the hubbub following the bartender's announcement.

"You think?" I was watching the spectacle of the confident and regal Eric babbling away, actually sinking down on one knee.

Dracula made a hushing gesture, and Eric's mouth snapped shut in midsentence. So did the mouths of every vamp in the place. "Since I have been here incognito for a week," Dracula said grandly, his accent harsh but not unattractive, "I have become so fond of this place that I propose to stay for a year. I will take your tribute while I am here, to live in the style I enjoyed during life. Though the bottled Royalty is acceptable as a stopgap, I, Dracula, do not care for this modern habit of drinking artificial blood, so I will require one woman a day. This one will do to start with." He pointed at me, and Colonel Flood and Calvin moved instantly to flank me, a gesture I appreciated. The vampires looked confused, an expression which didn't sit well on undead faces; except Bill. His face went completely blank.

Eric followed Vlad Tepes's stubby finger, identifying me as the future Happy Meal. Then he stared at Dracula, looking up from his kneeling position. I couldn't read his face at all, and I felt a stirring of fear. What would Charlie Brown have done if the Great Pumpkin wanted to eat the little red-haired girl?

"And as for my financial maintenance, a tithe from your club's income and a house will be sufficient for my needs, with some servants thrown in: your second-in-command, or your club manager, one of them should do. . . ." Pam actually growled, a low-level sound that made my hair stand up on my neck. Clancy looked as though someone had kicked his dog.

Pam was fumbling with the centerpiece of the table, hidden by my body. After a second, I felt something pressed into my hand. I glanced down. "You're the human," she whispered.

"Come, girl," Dracula said, beckoning with a curving of his fingers. "I hunger. Come to me and be honored before all these assembled."

Though Colonel Flood and Calvin both grabbed my arms, I said very softly, "This isn't worth your lives. They'll kill you if you try to fight. Don't worry," and I pulled away from them, meeting their eyes, in turn, as I spoke. I was trying to project confidence. I didn't know what they were getting, but they understood there was a plan.

I tried to glide toward the spangled bartender as if I was entranced. Since that's something vamps can't do to me, and Dracula obviously never doubted his own powers, I got away with it.

"Master, how did you escape from your tomb at Târgovişte?" I asked, doing my best to sound admiring and dreamy. I kept my hands down by my sides so the folds of rosy chiffon would conceal them.

"Many have asked me that," the Dark Prince said, inclining his head graciously as Eric's own head jerked up, his brows drawn together. "But that story must wait. My beautiful one, I am so glad you left your neck bare tonight. Come closer to me . . . ERRRK!"

"*That's* for the bad dialogue!" I said, my voice trembling as I tried to shove the stake in even harder.

"And *that's* for the embarrassment," Eric said, giving the end a tap with his fist, just to help, as the "Prince" stared at us in horror. The stake obligingly disappeared into his chest.

"You dare . . . you dare," the short vampire croaked. "You shall be executed."

"I don't think so," I said. His face went blank, and his eyes were empty. Flakes began to drift from his skin as he crumpled.

But as the self-proclaimed Dracula sank to the floor and I looked around me, I wasn't so sure. Only the presence of Eric at my side kept the assemblage from falling on me and taking care of business. The vampires from out of town were the most dangerous; the vampires that knew me would hesitate.

"He wasn't Dracula," I said as clearly and loudly as I could. "He was an impostor."

"Kill her!" said a thin female vamp with short brown hair. "Kill the murderess!" She had a heavy accent, I thought Russian. I was about tired of the new wave of vamps.

Pot calling the kettle black, I thought briefly. I said, "You all really think this goober was the Prince of Darkness?" I pointed to the flaking mess on the floor, held together by the spangled jumpsuit.

"He is dead. Anyone who kills Dracula must die," said Indira quietly, but not like she was going to rush over and rip my throat out.

"Any *vampire* who kills Dracula must die," Pam corrected. "But Sookie is not a vampire, and this was not Dracula."

"She killed one impersonating our founder," Eric said, making sure he could be heard throughout the club. "Milos was not the real Dracula. I would have staked him myself if I had had my wits about me." But I was standing right by Eric, my hand on his arm, and I knew he was shaking.

"How do you know that? How could she tell, a human who had only a few moments in his presence? He looked just like the woodcuts!" This from a tall, heavy man with a French accent.

"Vlad Tepes was buried at the monastery on Snagov," Pam said calmly, and everyone turned to her. "Sookie asked him how he'd escaped from his tomb at Târgovişte."

Well, that hushed them up, at least temporarily. I began to think I might live through this night.

"Recompense must be made to his maker," pointed out the tall, heavy vampire. He'd calmed down quite a bit in the last few minutes.

"If we can determine his maker," Eric said, "certainly."

"I'll search my database," Bill offered. He was standing in the shadows, where he'd lurked all evening. Now he took a step forward, and his dark eyes sought me out like a police helicopter searchlight catches the fleeing felon on *Cops*. "I'll find out his real name, if no one here has met him before."

All the vamps present glanced around. No one stepped forward to claim Milos/Dracula's acquaintance.

"In the meantime," Eric said smoothly, "let's not forget that this event should be a secret amongst us until we can find out more details." He smiled with a great show of fang, making his point quite nicely. "What happens in Shreveport, stays in Shreveport."

There was a murmur of assent.

"What do you say, guests?" Eric asked the non-vamp attendees.

Colonel Flood said, "Vampire business is not pack business. We don't care if you kill each other. We won't meddle in your affairs."

Calvin shrugged. "Panthers don't mind what you do."

The goblin said, "I've already forgotten the whole thing," and the madwoman beside him nodded and laughed. The few other non-vamps hastily agreed.

No one solicited my answer. I guess they were taking my silence for a given, and they were right.

Pam drew me aside. She made an annoyed sound, like "Tchk," and brushed at my dress. I looked down to see a fine spray of blood had misted across the chiffon skirt. I knew immediately that I'd never wear my beloved bargain dress again.

"Too bad, you look good in pink," Pam said.

I started to offer the dress to her, then thought again. I would wear it home and burn it. Vampire blood on my dress? Not a good piece of evidence to leave hanging around someone's closet. If experience has taught me anything, it's to dispose instantly of bloodstained clothing

"That was a brave thing you did," Pam said.

"Well, he was going to bite me," I said. "To death."

"Still," she said.

I didn't like the calculating look in her eyes.

"Thank you for helping Eric when I couldn't," Pam said. "My maker is a big idiot about the prince."

"I did it because he was going to suck my blood," I told her.

"You did some research on Vlad Tepes."

"Yes, I went to the library after you told me about the original Dracula, and I Googled him."

Pam's eyes gleamed. "Legend has it that the original Vlad III was beheaded before he was buried."

"That's just one of the stories surrounding his death," I said.

"True. But you know that not even a vampire can survive a beheading."

"I would think not."

"So you know the whole thing may be a crock of shit."

"Pam," I said, mildly shocked. "Well, it might be. And it might not. After all, Eric talked to someone who said he was the real Dracula's gofer."

"You knew that Milos wasn't the real Dracula the minute he stepped forth."

I shrugged.

Pam shook her head at me. "You're too soft, Sookie Stackhouse. It'll be the death of you some day."

"Nah, I don't think so," I said. I was watching Eric, his golden hair falling forward as he looked down at the rapidly disintegrating remains of the self-styled Prince of Darkness. The thousand years of his life sat on him heavily, and for a second I saw every one of them. Then, by degrees, his face lightened, and when he looked up at me, it was with the expectancy of a child on Christmas Eve.

"Maybe next year," he said.

The Mournful Cry of Owls

Christopher Golden

Christopher Golden is the author of novels including The Myth Hunters, Wildwood Road, *and* Of Saints and Shadows, *and the Body of Evidence series of teen thrillers. With Thomas E. Sniegoski, he is the coauthor of the dark fantasy series The Menagerie, the young readers fantasy series OutCast, and the comic book miniseries Talent. Golden was born and raised in Massachusetts, where he still lives with his family. He is currently collaborating with Hellboy creator Mike Mignola to write* Baltimore, or, the Steadfast Tin Soldier and the Vampire. *Please visit him at www.christophergolden.com.*

On a warm, late summer's night, Donika Ristani sat on the roof outside her open window—fat-bellied acoustic guitar in her hands—and searched for the chords that would bring life to the music she knew lay within her. The shingles were warm from the sun, though an hour had passed since dusk, and the smell of tar and cut grass filled her with a pleasant summery feeling that kept her normally flighty spirit from drifting into fancy.

The radio played in her room, competing with the music of the woods around the house—the crickets and owls and rustling things—which grew to a crescendo as though attempting to draw her down amongst the trees. Her fingers plucked and strummed, for she despised the use of a pick, and she discovered a third melody that created a kind of balance between the radio and the woods, the inside and outside.

Joe Jackson sang "Is She Really Going Out with Him?" Donika liked the song well enough, but her thoughts were elsewhere, thinking about inside and outside—about the person she was for her mother's sake, and the person that all of her instincts told her she ought to be. She found herself strumming Harry Chapin's "Taxi," lost in her head, and singing along to the weird bridge in the middle of the tune.

I've been letting my outside tide me over 'til my time runs out.

The truth frustrated the hell out of her and she brought her right hand down on the strings to stop herself playing another note of that song. Her gaze drifted down her driveway to the darkened ribbon of Blackberry Lane, searching for headlights, for some sign of her mother's return. Without so much as a glimmer from the road, she looked out across the thick woods north of the house, impatient to be down there, following the path to Josh Orton's house. He'd be waiting already, and she could practically feel his arms around her, his face nuzzling her throat.

Donika laughed softly at herself; or perhaps she sighed. She couldn't tell the difference sometimes.

The DJ did his cool voice and introduced the next tune. Donika smiled and started playing the first notes on her acoustic before it even started on the radio. Bad Company. "Rock and Roll Fantasy." Good song. Her bedroom walls were covered with posters for Pink Floyd, Zeppelin, and Sabbath, but she liked a little bit of everything. Most of her girlfriends would have laughed at some of the stuff she sang along to on the radio. Or maybe not. Hell, most of them thought Donna Summer the pinnacle of musical achievement.

Now she wished she'd listened more closely to the Joe Jackson tune. She might have to break into her babysitting stash to buy that album.

Her fingers moved up and down the frets, playing Bad Company by ear. She'd never played the song before, but the guitar was like an extension of herself and picking out the notes presented no greater difficulty than singing along. The crickets had gotten louder, but she managed not to hear them. The radio crackled a bit; some kind of interference, maybe the weather or a passing jet. She didn't understand such things very well. Turn on the box, the music came out. What else did she need to know?

The heat of the day still lingered in her skin the same way it did in the shingles. No more sticky humidity, so that was nice. She felt comfortably warm up there in her spaghetti strap tank top and cutoff jeans, as if the sun had gotten down inside her instead of setting over the horizon, and it would hide there until morning.

Owls cried out in the woods, and Donika glanced up, searching the trees as though she might spot one, the strings of her guitar momentarily forgotten. Other people thought they were funny birds, but she had always heard something else in their hooting, a terrible sadness that she wanted to answer with her own frustrations.

A flash of light came from the road. She watched the headlights move along Blackberry Lane and her breath caught as she thought of Josh again. When the car drove by without slowing, she sighed and lay against the slanted roof, the shingles rough and hot against her back. She hugged the guitar and wondered if Josh was sitting outside, waiting for her, or if he was up in his room listening to music on his bed. Both images had their appeal.

Somehow she missed the sound of an approaching engine and looked up only as light washed across the trees and she heard tires rolling up the driveway. Donika sat forward as her mother's ancient Dodge Dart putted up to the house. When she turned off the engine, it ticked and popped, and then the door creaked open.

"Get off that roof, 'Nika!"

The girl laughed. The woman had eyes like a hawk, even in the dark.

She slipped in through her bedroom window and put away her guitar before going downstairs. Her mother stood in the kitchen, looking through the day's mail. Qendressa Ristani had lush black hair like her daughter, but streaked with gray. She wore it pulled back tightly. Though her mother was nearly fifty, Donika thought her hairstyle too severe, more appropriate for a grandmother. Her clothes reflected the same sensibility, which probably explained why she never dated. Though she'd given up wearing black a decade or so back, Donika's mother still saw herself as a widow. Men might flirt with her—she was prettier than most women her age—but Qendressa would not encourage them. She'd been widowed young, and had no desire to replace the only man she had ever loved.

Her life was the seamstress shop where she worked in downtown Jameson, and the home she'd made for herself and her daughter upon coming to America a dozen years before. But her Old World upbringing still persisted in many ways, not the least of which was her insistence on using herbs and oils as homegrown remedies for all sorts of ills, both physical and spiritual.

"How was your day, Ma?"

"Eh," the woman said, "is the same."

Donika grabbed her sandals and sat down at the table, slipping one on. Her mother dropped the mail on the table. As she slipped on her sandals, she looked up to find her mother staring at her.

"Where you going?"

"Josh's. Sue and Carrie and a couple of Josh's friends are there already waiting for me. We're going to walk into town for pizza."

"You going to hang around those boys dressed like that?"

Donika flushed with anger and stood up, the chair scraping backward on the floor.

"Look, Ma, you need to get off this stuff. This is 1979, not 1950, and we're in Massachusetts, not Albania. You want me to be home when you get back from work so you won't worry about me? Okay, I sort of understand that. I don't like it, but I get it. But look around.

I don't dress differently from other girls. Turn on the TV once in a while—"

"TV," her mother muttered in disgust, averting her eyes.

"I'm going to be sixteen tomorrow," Donika protested.

Qendressa Ristani sniffed. "This is supposed to make me less worried? This is *why* I worry!"

"Well, don't! I'm fine. Just let me enjoy being sixteen, okay?"

The woman hesitated, taking a long breath, and then she nodded slowly and waved her daughter away. "Go. Be a good girl, 'Nika. Don't make me shamed."

"Have I ever?"

Finally, her mother smiled. "No. Never." Her expression turned serious. "Tomorrow, we celebrate, though. Yes? Just the two of us, all the things you love for dinner. You can have your friends over on Friday and we have a cake. But, tomorrow, just us girls."

Donika smiled. "Just us girls."

The path emerged from the woods in the backyard of an older couple who were known to shout at trespassers from their screened-in back porch. Donika had never experienced their wrath and wondered if they didn't mind so much when a girl crossed their yard—maybe thinking girls didn't cause as much trouble as boys—or if they simply didn't see her. As she left the comfortable quiet of the woods and strolled across the back lawn and then alongside the house, she watched the windows, wondering if either of the old folks were looking out. Nothing stirred inside there. It hadn't been dark for long, but she wondered if they were already asleep, and thought how sad it must be to get old.

When she reached the street, she saw Josh sitting on the granite curb at the corner, smoking a cigarette. Her sandals slapped the pavement as she walked and he looked up at the sound. One corner of his mouth lifted in a little smile that made her heart flutter. He flicked his cigarette away and stood to meet her, cool as hell in his faded jeans and Jimi Hendrix T-shirt.

"Hey," he said.

Donika smiled, feeling strangely shy. "Hey."

Josh pushed his shoulder-length blond hair away from his eyes. "Your mom kept you waiting."

"Sorry. Sometimes I think she stays late on purpose. Maybe she figures if she keeps me waiting long enough, I won't go out."

"So much for that plan."

"I'm glad you didn't give up on me," Donika said.

They'd been standing a couple of feet apart, just feeling the static energy of the distance between them. Now Josh reached out and touched her face.

"Never happen."

A shiver went through her. Josh did that to her, just by standing there, and the way he looked at her.

His hand slipped around to the back of her neck and he bent to kiss her. Donika tilted her head back and closed her eyes, letting the details of the moment wash over her, the feel of him so near, the softness of his lips, the strange, burnt taste of nicotine as his tongue sought hers.

Only when they broke apart, a giddy little thrill rushing through her, did she look around and remember where they were. Lights were on in some of the houses along Rolling Lane, and anyone could be watching them.

She felt pleasantly buzzed, as though she'd had a few beers, but she slid her hand along his arm and tangled her fingers in his.

"We shouldn't be doing this out here. I told my mother Sue and Carrie and those guys were gonna be here and we were going to get pizza. If anyone ever saw us and told her, she'd have a fit."

"She doesn't think you've ever kissed me?"

"I don't know, and I don't plan to ask," Donika said. "God, she already thinks I'm slutty just for wearing cutoffs and hanging around with boys."

Josh arched an eyebrow and took out another cigarette. "Boys? Are there others?"

She hit him. "You know what I mean."

"Your mom's pretty Old World."

Donika rolled her eyes. "You have *no* idea. She burns candles for me and puts little bunches of dried herbs and stuff under my bed, tied in little ribbons. Pretty sure they're supposed to ward off boys."

"How's that going?"

Donika only smiled.

Josh kissed her forehead. "So, do you want to go get pizza?"

"Only if you're hungry."

Josh laughed softly, unlit cigarette in his hand. His blue eyes were almost gray in the nighttime. "I could eat. I could always eat. But I'm good. We could just hang out. Why don't we walk downtown, get an ice cream or something?"

"Or we could just go for a walk in the woods. I love those paths. Especially at night."

"You're not afraid?" Josh asked as he thumbed his lighter, the little flame igniting the tip of his cigarette. He drew a lungful of smoke and stared at her.

"Why would I be?" Donika said. "I've got you with me."

She led him by the hand back across the street and through the yard of the belligerent old couple. Josh's cigarette glowed orange in the dark. The moon and stars were bright, but as they passed alongside the house and into the backyard of that old split-level house, with the canopy of the woods reaching out above them, the darkness thickened and little of the celestial light filtered through.

"Goddamn you kids!" a screechy voice shouted from the porch. "You're gonna burn the whole damn forest down with those cigarettes!"

Donika started and looked at the darkened porch anxiously. Josh put a hand up to try to keep himself from laughing, and that started Donika grinning as well. The voice was faintly ridiculous, like something out of a cartoon or a movie. On the porch, in the dark, another pinprick of burning orange glowed. The old man was smoking, too.

Josh paused to drop the butt and grind it out with his heel. Then, laughing, they ran into the trees, following the path that had been worn there by generations.

Hand in hand, they followed the gently curving path through the woods and talked about their friends and families, and about music.

"I love talking about music with you," Josh told her. "The way your eyes light up . . . I don't know, it's like you feel it inside you more than most people because you can make music with your guitar."

Donika shuddered at that. No one had ever understood that part of her the way that Josh did. He liked the sad songs best, the tragic ones, just as she did. Their conversation meandered, but she didn't mind. All she wanted was his company. Mostly, they just walked.

The paths had been there forever, or so it seemed. There were low stone walls, centuries-old property markers that had been built up by hand and ran for miles. Old, thick roots crossed the path and small animals rustled in the branches above them and in the underbrush on either side. An entire system of paths ran through the woods. They reached a fork and followed the right-hand path. The left would have taken them up the hill toward her house, and that was the last place she wanted to go.

"You seem far away," Josh said as they passed through a small clearing where someone had built a fire pit. Charred logs lay in the pit and the stones around it had been blackened by flames.

Donika squeezed his hand and looked up at him. "Nope. Just happy. I love the woods. Being out here . . . it's so peaceful. So far away from other people. I walk through here all the time, but having you here with me makes it so much better."

Josh stopped walking and gazed down at her. The moon and stars illuminated the clearing, and she saw the mischief in his eyes.

"Better how?" he asked.

She gave him a shy little shrug. "Just feels right."

He kissed her again and she could hear music in her head. Or maybe it was her heart. His hands slid down her back, pulling her close, so that their bodies pressed together. She liked the feel of him against her, his strong arms wrapped around her. Through his jeans she could feel his hardness pressing into her, and she liked that very much. Just knowing that she had that effect on him made her catch her breath.

His hands roamed, fingers tracing along her arms, and then he stepped back just slightly so that he could reach up and touch her breasts through the thin cotton of her tank top.

"Josh," she rasped, enjoying it far too much.

"Yeah."

Donika took his hands in hers and kissed him quickly. "I think maybe I want ice cream after all."

"But it's beautiful right here."

He grinned and ducked his head, kissing her again. Their fingers were still intertwined and he made no attempt to pull his hands away, to touch her again. Donika felt her body yearning toward him, missing the weight and warmth of him.

This is it, she thought. *This is what frightens Ma so much.*

Donika pulled her hands from his and slid her arms around him, breaking off the kiss. She lay her head on his chest and just held herself against him, nuzzling there. Josh stroked her hair.

Deep in the woods, she heard an owl hoot sadly, and then another joined in. A chorus.

"I *am* far away," she confessed. "But you're with me. I wish we could be even farther away, together. I love feeling lost in the woods, like something wild. When I'm out here alone, I like to just run. You'll laugh, but sometimes I imagine I'm running naked through the forest, like I'm some kind of fairy queen or something."

Josh didn't laugh. "Hmm. I like the sound of that," he said. "What's stopping you?"

She blushed deeply and stepped back, trying not to smile. One hip outthrust, she pointed at him.

"You are bad."

"Only in good ways. Seriously, I dare you."

Donika's breath came in shallow sips as she regarded him, lips pressed together, corners of her mouth upturned. The mischief in his eyes seemed to have gotten inside of her somehow. Her skin tingled all over. Nodding her head, she crossed her arms.

"You first."

Without hesitation, he stripped off his T-shirt and dropped it at the edge of the path. He arched an eyebrow and looked at her expectantly.

A rush went through her, a kind of freedom she'd never felt before. It was as though she had just woken from some strange slumber. She grabbed the bottom hem of her tank top and slid it up over her head, then unhooked her bra and let it drop to the ground. The night breeze brushed warmly against her, but she shivered.

Josh stared at her, all the mischief and archness gone from his face, replaced by sheer wonderment. He'd never seen her breasts before—Donika didn't know if he'd ever seen this much of *any* girl.

She didn't wait for him to make the next move. Their gazes locked as she kicked her sandals off and then moved her hand down, unbuttoning her cutoffs. She slid them and her panties down together and stepped out of them, tossing them on top of her tank.

"Jesus, you're beautiful," he whispered.

The breeze picked up, rustling leaves. Somewhere close by, the owls cried again. For once, the sound did not seem sad. Josh stepped toward her and she knew how badly he wanted to touch her. She could already imagine his hands on her, the way she had so many times at home in her bed.

She shook her head, smiling, and stepped backward. "Uh-uh. Not so fast, mister. We're going to run, remember. And you're not quite ready."

For a moment he only stared at her, his mouth hanging open. Donika laughed at how silly he looked, but thrilled to know that she'd beguiled him so completely.

Staggering around, hopping on one foot, Josh pulled off one sneaker and then the other. He shucked his jeans and then paused for a second before slipping off his underwear.

Donika trembled at the sight of him. She'd seen an older boy from the neighborhood skinny-dipping in Bowditch Pond one time, but this was something else entirely.

"Oh," she said.

Josh walked toward her. Donika backed up and then turned, giggling, and began to run as swiftly as she dared, watching the roots and rocks and fallen branches in her path. Josh pursued her, laughing even as he called for her to wait for him. As she ran, the thrill of it all rushed through her—her nakedness, his nakedness and nearness, and the forest around them. In her whole life, she had never felt as wonderful as she did there in the woods, running wild, full of passion and laughter.

The heat rose from deep inside her, desire unlike anything she'd ever known. Flushed with abandon, she slowed her pace, and let Josh catch up. He nearly crashed into her and they slid together on the path. His lips were on hers and their tongues met. His hands were rough and caressing in equal turns, touching her everywhere, and she let him.

A small part of her—the part that remained her mother's daughter—knew that she would not let him make love to her. But, oh, how she wanted to. Anything else he wished would be his, only not that.

In the branches above them, the owls sighed.

Tangled in her sheets, drifting in that limbo between sleep and wakefulness, Donika knew morning had come. She loved how long the summer days lasted; she just wished they didn't start so damned early. Dimly aware of the bedroom around her, she squeezed her eyes tightly closed and admonished herself for not having drawn the shades the night before. She rolled over to face the other direction, twisting the sheets even more. For a moment she remembered her walk in the woods with Josh the night before and the way his hands had felt on her. A contented moan escaped her lips as she slipped back into blissful oblivion.

Drifting.

Somewhere, lost in sleep, she sensed a presence enter the room and began to stir. Then someone started to sing, loudly and horribly, and Donika sat up in bed, drawing a sharp breath, eyes wide.

Her mother sang "Happy Birthday" in a silly, overly dramatic fashion, gesturing with her hands as though onstage. She wore an enormous grin and Donika couldn't help laughing. Her mother always seemed so grim, and seeing her like this gave the girl such pleasure.

When the song finished, Qendressa bowed deeply. Donika applauded, shaking her head. During her childhood, it had not been quite so uncommon for her mother to clown around for Donika's amusement. They'd shared so many wonderful times together. Now that she was older and their desires and morals clashed so often, it had become hard for Donika to remember those times.

Not this morning, however. This morning, all the laughter came back to her. Her mother would be off to work in moments, decked out in her usual sensible skirt and blouse and dark shoes, and her hair was tied back severely, but for a few minutes, it felt like Donika was a little girl again.

"Thank you, thank you," Qendressa said, her accent almost unnoticeable as she mimicked performers she had seen on television. "And for my next trick, I leave work early to come home and make all your favorites."

She ticked the parts of the birthday meal off on her fingers. "Tavë kosi, Tirana furghes with peppers, and kadaif for dessert. With candles and more bad singing."

Donika's stomach rumbled just thinking about dinner. The main course was baked lamb and yogurt, which she'd always loved. But the dessert—she could practically taste the walnuts and cinnamon of the kadaif now.

"Can we have dinner for breakfast instead?" she asked, stretching, extricating herself from her sheets.

Her mother shook a finger at her. "The birthday girl gets what she wants, but not until tonight. Breakfast, you make your own. Toast, I bet. You going out today?"

"Maybe to the mall if Gina can borrow her mom's car."

"All right. Back by three o'clock, please. We'll cook together?"

Donika smiled. "Wouldn't miss it."

That was the truth, too. There were times her mother drove her crazy with all her Old World stodginess, but on her birthday and on holidays, she loved nothing better than to spend hours in the kitchen, cooking with her mom. She could practically smell all the wonderful aromas that would fill the house later.

"What about the girls? You talk to them?" Qendressa asked.

"Tomorrow night. They're going to come by to celebrate. We can just have pizza, though."

"Pizza, again?" her mother said. "You going to turn into pizza."

Donika didn't argue. She wasn't about to confess that she and Josh had never gotten around to having pizza last night. Maybe that was the reason she felt so hungry this morning. Her belly growled and she felt a gnawing there, as if she hadn't eaten in weeks instead of half a day.

"We love pizza," she said, shrugging.

"I promised birthday cake tomorrow night, too. And if you are lucky, maybe some good singing."

"Chocolate cake?" Donika asked, propping herself up on one arm, head still muzzy with sleep.

"Of course," her mother replied, as though any other kind would be unthinkable.

"Excellent!"

A flutter of wings came from the open window and a scratching upon the screen. Mother and daughter turned together to see a dark-eyed owl perched on the ledge outside the window, imperious and wise. Brown and white feathers cloaked the owl and it tucked its wings behind it.

"What the . . . ? That's freaky," Donika said, sitting up in bed. "I hear them in the woods all the time, but I've never seen one during the day. Do you think it's sick or some—"

"Away!" her mother shouted. She rushed at the window and banged her open palm against the screen. A string of curses in her native tongue followed.

The owl cocked its head as if to let them know it wasn't troubled by Qendressa's attack, then spread its wings and took flight again. Through the window, Donika caught a glimpse of it gliding back toward the woods.

She stared at her mother. The woman had completely wigged out and now she stood by the window, arms around herself as though a frigid wind had just blown through the room. She had her back to her daughter.

"Ma?"

Qendressa turned, a wan smile on her face. Donika studied her mother and realized that the birthday morning silliness was over. A strange sadness had come over her, as though the bird's arrival had forced her to drop some happy mask she'd been wearing. "I should go to work," she said, but she seemed torn.

"What is it, Ma?"

"Nothing," she said with a wave of her hand, averting her gaze. "Just . . . sixteen. You're not a girl anymore, 'Nika. Soon, you leave me."

Donika kicked aside the sheet that still covered the bottom of her legs and climbed out of bed. She went to her mother. Even with no shoes on, she was the taller of the Ristani women.

"I'm not going anywhere, Ma."

It didn't sound true, even when she said it. There had been many days when Donika had dreamed of nothing but leaving Jameson, finding a life of her own, making her own decisions, and not having to live in the shadow of the old country anymore. Her body still weighted down by some secret sadness, Qendressa reached out and brushed Donika's unruly hair away from her eyes.

"Tonight, we talk about the future. And the past."

Donika blinked. What did that mean? She would have asked but saw her mother stiffen. The woman's eyes narrowed as she stared at her daughter's bed.

"What is that?"

The girl turned. Specks of dirt, a small leaf, and a few pine needles were scattered at the foot of the bed, revealed when Donika had whipped the sheet off of her. A shiver went through her, some terrible combination of elation and guilt. She tried to stifle it as best she could.

"We cut through the woods to get downtown. I always go that way. I took off my sandals. I like going barefoot out there. It's nice. It's all . . . it's wild."

Donika couldn't read the look on her mother's face. If the woman suspected anything, she would have been angry or disappointed. Maybe those emotions were there—maybe Donika read her mother's expression wrong—but the look in her eyes and the way she took a harsh little breath seemed like something else. Weird as it was, in that moment, Donika thought her mother seemed afraid.

The woman turned, all grim seriousness now. At Donika's bedroom door she paused and looked back at her daughter, taking in the whole room—the guitar, the stereo, the records and posters, and the clothes she would never approve of that were hung from the back of her chair and over the end of her bed.

"No boys here while I'm gone. No boys, 'Nika."

"I know, Ma. You think I'm stupid?"

"No," her mother said, shaking her head, the sadness returning to her gaze. "No, you my baby girl, 'Nika. I don't think you are stupid."

With that, Qendressa left. Donika stood and listened to her go down the stairs and out the door. She heard the car start up outside and the sound of tires on the driveway, and then all was silent again except for the birds singing outside the window and the drone of a plane flying somewhere high above the house.

She wasn't sure what her mother suspected or feared, didn't know what had caused her to behave so oddly or why she'd freaked out so completely at the sight of the owl. But Donika had the feeling it was going to be a very weird birthday.

Gina couldn't get the car, so the trip to the mall was off. Donika knew that she ought to have been bummed out, but she couldn't muster up much disappointment. She'd be seeing her friends tomorrow night, and today she wasn't in the mood to window-shop at the mall. The idea of wandering around Jordan Marsh or going to Orange Julius for a nasty cheese dog for lunch didn't have much appeal. If it had been raining, maybe she would have felt differently. But the day was beautiful, and in truth, she wanted to be on her own for a while.

All kinds of different thoughts were swirling in her head, and she wanted to make sense of them if she could. Her mother's strange behavior that morning troubled her, but she was still looking forward to the afternoon of them cooking together. The lamb in the fridge was fresh, not frozen. It had come from the butcher the day before. They'd put some music on—something her mother liked, the Carpenters, maybe, or Neil Diamond—and work side by side at the counter. Normally, that kind of music made Donika want to stick pencils in her eyes, but somehow with her mother whipping up the yogurt sauce for the lamb or slicing peppers as she hummed along, it seemed perfect.

At lunchtime she sat on the front porch with a glass of iced tea and a salami sandwich. A fly buzzed around the plate and then sat on the lip of her glass. Donika ignored it, more interested in the droplets of moisture that slid down the sides of the cup. She stared at them as she strummed her acoustic, singing a Harry Chapin song. Harry was one of the only musicians she and her mother could agree on.

"All my life's a circle," she sang softly, "sunrise and sundown."

Her fingers kept playing, but she faltered with the words and then stopped singing altogether. Despite her concerns about her mother, she could not focus on anything for very long without her thoughts returning to the previous night.

Pausing for a moment in the song, she leaned over to pick up the iced tea, pressing the glass against the back of her neck. The icy condensation felt wonderful on her skin. Donika took a long sip, liking the sound the melting ice made as it clinked together. Then she set the glass down and grabbed half of the salami sandwich. All morning she had been ravenously hungry, yet when she'd eaten breakfast—Trix cereal, an indulgence left over from when she'd been very small—it hadn't filled her at all. Later in the morning she'd had a nectarine and some grapes, and that hadn't done anything for her either.

Now, even though she still felt as hungry as before—hungrier, in fact, if that was possible—the idea of eating her sandwich held very little appeal. She took an experimental bite, and then another. The salami tasted just as good as it always did, salty and a little spicy. But for some reason she simply did not want it.

She set the sandwich down and took another swig of iced tea to wash away the salt. Her fingers returned to the guitar and started playing chords she wasn't even paying attention to. Whatever song she might be drawing from her instrument, it came from her subconscious. Her conscious mind was otherwise occupied.

"You're a crazy girl," she said aloud, and then she smiled. Talking to herself sort of proved the point, didn't it? Her mother had always been a little crazy, and now Donika knew she shared the trait.

Her hunger didn't come only from her stomach. Her whole body felt ravenous. Her skin tingled with the memory of Josh's hands—on her belly, her breasts, the small of her back, the soft insides of her thighs—and of his kisses, which touched nearly all of the places his hands had gone.

She squeezed her legs together and trembled at the thought of stripping off her clothes, of running through the woods, and then Josh, his body outlined in moonlight, catching up to her. She'd felt, in those moments when she raced along the rutted path and he pursued her, as though she could spread her arms and take wing . . . as though she could have flown, and taken Josh with her.

Touching him, kissing him, that had been a little like flying.

"God," she whispered to herself. "What's wrong with you?"

Her fingers fumbled on the strings and she stopped playing, a sly smile touching her lips. Nothing was wrong with her. It all felt so amazingly good. How could anything be wrong with that?

But that was a lie. There was one thing wrong.

Her hunger. She yearned for Josh so badly that it gnawed at her insides. She wondered if her mother had seen it in her eyes this morning, had sensed it, had *smelled* it on her.

Donika needed to have his hands on her again, to taste his lips and the salty sweat on his fingers and his neck. She felt as though she couldn't get enough of him. She wanted him completely, yearned to consume him, and the only way to do that was to do the one thing she promised herself she would not do.

She had to have him inside her.

Only that could satisfy her hunger.

Her certainty thrilled and terrified her all at once.

With the smell of cinnamon filling the kitchen, her mother leaned back in her chair, hands over her stomach as though she had some voluminous belly.

"I don't think I ever eat again."

Donika smiled, but it felt forced. They had followed the same recipes they had always used, brought over from Albania with her mother years ago, passed down for generations. Somehow, though, the food had tasted bland. Even the cinnamon had seemed stale in her mouth. The smell of dessert had been tantalizing, but its taste had not delivered on that promise. She had eaten as much as she did mainly because she hadn't wanted to hurt her mother's feelings. And the hunger remained.

How she could still feel hungry after such a meal—particularly when nothing seemed to taste good to her—Donika didn't know. She chalked it up to hormones. Today was her sixteenth birthday. According to her mother, she had become a woman all of a sudden, like flipping a switch.

She had never believed it really worked that way, but given the way she felt, maybe it did. Maybe that was exactly how it worked. She always craved chocolate right before she got her period—could have eaten gallons of ice cream if she'd given in—so this might be similar.

Or maybe it's love. The thought skittered across her mind. She'd heard of people not being able to eat when they were in love. It occurred to her that this could be another symptom.

She tasted the idea on the back of her tongue. Did she love Josh?

Maybe.

She hungered for him, certainly. Longed for him. Could that be love? No. Donika had seen enough movies and read enough books to know that desire and love might not be mutually exclusive, but they weren't the same thing either.

But desire like this? It hurts. It burns.

"—you listening to me, 'Nika?"

"What?" she asked, blinking.

Her mother studied her, concern etched upon her face. "You okay? You feel sick?"

"No. Sorry, Ma. Just tired, I guess."

A lame excuse. She expected her mother to call her on it, maybe to make some insinuating comment about her walk in the woods the night before, about how maybe if she wasn't always out talking to boys and running around with her friends, she wouldn't be so tired. Her mother didn't let her do very much, and she'd been hanging around the house all day playing guitar, and then cooking, but logic never stopped her mother from suspicion or judgment.

But Qendressa didn't say anything like that.

"You like dinner, though, right?" she asked, and just then it seemed the most important question in the world to her. "Your sixteenth birthday the sweetest. You should be happy today. Celebrate."

Donika felt such love for her mother then. Sometimes she became so angry and frustrated with the woman's Old World traditions, but always she knew that beneath all of that lay nothing but adoration and worry, a mother's constant companions. She thought she understood fairly well for a fifteen-year-old girl.

Sixteen, she reminded herself. *Sixteen, today.*

"I love you, Ma."

They both seemed surprised she'd said it out loud. It had never been common to speak of love, though they both felt it all the time.

Her mother smiled, took a long, shuddering breath, and then began to cry. Donika stared at her in confusion. Qendressa turned her face away to hide her tears and raised a hand to forestall any questions.

After a moment, she wiped her eyes. "You all grown, now, 'Nika. Walk with me. Tonight, I tell you the story of how you were born."

"What do you mean, how I was born?"

Her mother smiled and slid her chair back. It squeaked on the kitchen floor. "Walk with me," she said as she stood. "In the woods. How you like. And maybe you learn why you like it so much."

Donika got up, dropping her napkin on the table. Bewildered, she tried to make sense of her mother's words and behavior, doing her best to push away the hunger inside her and to not think about the fact that Josh had said he'd be out on the corner later, waiting for her if she could manage to get out tonight.

Her mother took her hand. "Come."

Together they left the house. The screen door slammed shut behind them as if in emphasis, the house happy to have them gone. The porch steps creaked underfoot. When her mother led her across the driveway toward the path, Donika hesitated a moment. The woods were hers. She might see other people in there, but something about going into the forest with her mother troubled her. Much as Donika loved her, she didn't want to share.

"Ma," she said, hesitating.

"It won't take long," Qendressa said. "But you need to know the story. Should have told you long time ago. I am selfish."

Donika shook her head. What the hell was her mother talking about?

They walked into the trees. The summer sun had fallen low on the horizon. Soon dusk would arrive. For now, wan daylight still filtered through the thick trees, slanted and pale, shadows long.

"My mother, she knew things," Qendressa began. Her grip on Donika's hand tightened. "How to make two people love. How to heal sickness in body and heart. How to keep spirits away."

Donika tried not to smile. This was what their big talk was about? Old World superstition?

"She was a witch?"

Her mother scowled. "Witch. Stupid word. She was smart. Clever woman. She used herbs and oils—"

"So she was the village wise woman or whatever," Donika said, and it wasn't a question this time. She thought it was kind of adorable the way her mother said *herbs*—with a hard *H*, like the man's name. But this talk of potions and evil spirits made her impatient, too. "I get that she taught you all of that stuff, but how can you still believe it after living in America so long?"

Her mother stopped and pulled her hand away. "Will you be quiet and listen?"

The anguish in her mother's voice stopped her cold. Donika had never heard her mother speak that way. The daylight had waned further and now the slices of sky that could be seen through the thatch of branches had grown a deeper blue. Not dusk yet, but soon. It seemed to be coming on fast.

"I'll listen," she said.

Her mother nodded, then turned and continued along the path. Donika watched the ground, stepped over roots and rocks. The woods were strangely quiet as the dusk approached, with the night birds and nocturnal animals not yet active and the other beasts of the forest already making their beds for the evening.

"She knew things, my mother. And so she taught me these things, just as I teach you to cook the old way. When I married, I made a good wife. Even then, I made money as a seamstress, just like now. But always my husband knew that one day the people in our town would start to come to me with their troubles the way they came to my mother. The ones who believed in superstitions."

Donika couldn't help but hear the admonishment in those words. Her mother wanted her to know she wasn't the only one who still believed in such things.

"There were spirits there, in the hills and the forest. Always, there were spirits, some of them good and some terrible. Other things, too. Believe if you want, or don't believe. But still I will tell you.

"I loved my husband. He had strong hands, but always gentle with me. Some people, they acted strange around my mother and me, but not him. He was so kind and smiled always, and when he laughed, all the women in our town wanted to take him home. But it was me he loved. We talked all the time about babies, about having a little boy to look just like him, or a little girl with my eyes.

"And then he dies. Such a stupid death. Fixing the roof, he slips and falls and breaks his neck. No herbs or oils could raise the dead. He was gone, Donika. Always his face lit up when he talked of babies and now he was dead and the worst part was there wouldn't be any babies."

The patches of sky visible up through the branches had turned indigo. The dusk had come on, and full darkness was only a heartbeat away. It had happened almost without Donika realizing, and now she heard rustling in the underbrush and in the branches above. A light breeze caressed her bare arms and legs and only then did she realize how warm she'd been.

She halted on the path and stared at her mother, eyes narrowed. "What are you talking about, Ma? What the hell are you . . . you had *me.*"

Qendressa slid her hands into the pockets of her skirt as though fighting the urge to reach out and take her daughter's hand. Her features were lost in the gathering darkness.

"No, 'Nika. You came later."

"How could I—"

"Hush now," her mother said. "Just hush. You want to know. You need to know. So hush."

Something shifted in the branches right above them and an owl hooted softly, sadly. Her mother glanced up sharply and scanned the trees as though the mournful cry of that night bird presented some threat.

Donika shook her head, more confused than ever. "Ma?"

Qendressa narrowed her eyes and took a step away from her daughter, casting herself in shadows again. "You know the word *shtriga*?"

"No."

"No." Her mother sighed, and the sound was enough to break Donika's heart. "I was so much like you, 'Nika. Still very young, though already I was a widow. So many questions in my head. I walked in the forest always, cold and grieving and alone. I knew I had to have a baby, to be a mother. I would never love another, but a child I could love. I could have what my husband and I dreamed of . . . even if part of it is *only* a dream.

"One night I am in the forest, walking and dreaming, and I hear voices. Some men and some women. I hear a laugh, and I do not like the way it sounds, that laugh. So I walk quietly, slowly, and go through the trees, following the voices. I walked in the forest so much that I learned to make almost no noise at all. From the trees, I see them, two women and three men, all with no clothes. I felt ashamed to spy on them like that. I would have gone, but could not look away.

"They looked up at the sky and reached up to their mouths and they slipped off their skins, like they were only jackets. Inside were shtriga. They looked like owls, but they were not. I could not breathe and just watched, praying not to be seen. They flew away. I stood there until I could not hear the wings anymore and then I could breathe again."

Qendressa paused. Donika realized that she had been holding her breath, just the way her mother had described. As the story unfolded, she had pictured it all in her mind, so simple to imagine because of all of the hours she had spent walking these woods by herself and because, just last night, she and Josh had been naked beneath the trees and the night sky. But this . . . her imagination could only go so far.

"Ma, you must have been dreaming. You said you were dreaming, right? You fell asleep. That couldn't have been real."

Her mother approached her, stepping into the moonlight, and Donika saw the tears streaking her face. Sorrow weighed on her and made her look like an old woman.

"No?" Qendressa said.

Somewhere in the trees, an owl hooted. Donika flinched and looked up, searching the branches, just as her mother had done. A second owl replied, sharing the sad song.

"Even when they were gone, I could not go away. I should have run. I did not know when they would be back for their skins, the shtriga, but I knew that they *would* be back. The shtriga went 'round the town and through the forest and they hunted the lustful and licentious. They had the scent of those whose lust was strongest, and the shtriga drank their blood to sate their own hungers."

"Sounds like a vampire," Donika said.

Qendressa frowned, shaking her head. "No, 'Nika. Vampires are make-believe. The shtriga are real. But the power they have, it has rules. The shtriga must come back to its skin by morning.

"My mother had told me many stories of them. How they grow.

How to stop them. And I dreamed of a baby, 'Nika. It hurt my heart, I wanted it so much.

"I knew I only had till morning, and maybe not even that long. I ran into the clearing and I took the skin of one of the women, with her beautiful black hair. I carried it home, hurrying and falling, and I locked the door behind me. I took my scissors and sat at my worktable and I cut the skin of the shtriga. I cut away large pieces and later I burned them.

"And then I started to sew. With the shtriga's black hair for my thread, I patched the skin back together, only now it was not the skin of a grown woman, but the skin of a baby girl."

Donika shivered and hugged herself, staring at her mother's eyes shining in the moonlight, tears glistening on her face.

"No," the girl said.

When her mother spoke again, her voice had fallen to the whisper of confession.

"I sat and waited in the corner of the room, in a chair that my husband had loved so much. A little before dawn, the shtriga came looking for her skin. I left the window open and the owl flew in and landed on my worktable. It spread its wings and ducked its head down to pick at the skin it had left behind. The owl pushed itself into the skin.

"When the sun rose, a baby girl lay on my worktable and she cried, so sad, so lonely. I took her in my arms and rocked her and I sang to her an old song that my mother loved, and my baby loved it, too. She didn't cry anymore."

Qendressa bit her lip and gazed forlornly at her daughter. Through her tears, she began to sing that same old song, a lullaby that Donika knew so well. Her mother had been singing it to her all her life.

"I don't believe you."

But then the owls began to cry their mournful song again, hooting softly, not only one or two but four or five of them now. Donika saw the fear in her mother's eyes as the woman searched the trees. Qendressa put out a hand to her.

"Come, 'Nika. We go home."

Donika stared at her.

"I don't believe you," she said again.

But she could taste the salt of her own tears and feel them warm upon her cheeks. She backed away from her mother's outstretched hand, shaking her head. Denials rose up in her heart and mind but somehow would not reach her lips.

She knew. The hunger churned in her gut, gnawing at her, and she knew.

"Why did you tell me?"

Qendressa sobbed. "Because you are not my baby anymore, 'Nika. You're sixteen. Sixteen years since that night. I know the stories. You are shtriga now."

Donika felt something break inside her. She spun on one heel and ran. Low branches whipped at her face and she raised her arms to protect herself. She stumbled over roots and rocks that she'd always avoided before. The owls hooted above her, and now she could hear their wings flapping as they moved through the trees, keeping pace.

In her life, she had never felt so cold. No matter how fast she ran, no matter how her pulse quickened, she could not get warm. Her sobs were words, denials that felt as hollow as her own stomach. The hunger clutched at her belly and a yearning burned in her. Desire.

Josh. She summoned an image of him in her mind and focused on it. They could run together. He would hold her. He could touch her, and maybe, for a little while, the madness and hunger would fade.

A numbness came over her, but Donika began to get control of herself. She still wept, but silently now. Her feet were surer on the path. She saw the stone wall to one side and the fire pit ahead and the memory of last night gave her something to hold on to.

Soon, she found herself at the end of the path, stepping out into the backyard of the bitter old couple. An owl hooted, back in the woods, and she hurried away from the trees, wanting to leave the forest behind for the first time in her life.

She strode across the back lawn unnoticed. A dog barked nearby, the angry yip of a canine scenting the presence of an enemy. Donika made her way between houses, but as she came in sight of the corner where Josh would be waiting, she paused.

Hidden in the night-black shadows of those homes, she watched him. Josh sat on the curb, smoking a cigarette, content to be by himself. He waited for her and didn't mind. In the golden glow of a nearby streetlamp, he was beautiful to her. They would run through the dark woods together once again, but this time she would give herself to him.

Desire clawed at her insides. She ran her tongue out to wet her lips. She could almost taste the salt of his skin, and the urge to do so, to taste him, tugged at her.

A smile touched her lips and she almost called out.

Donika's smile faded.

No, she thought. *It isn't love. Desire isn't love. Hunger isn't.*

She understood hunger now. Donika fled silently back into the woods, where she belonged. The owls cried and flew with her. Loneliness clutched at her until she realized that she wasn't alone at all. She had never been alone.

The woods received her with love. She could never go back to her mother's house. Not now.

She hurtled along the path and then left the trail, breaking off into rough terrain. She raced through the woods, leaped fallen branches, and exulted in the night wind whispering around her. Her tears continued to fall but they were no longer merely tears of sorrow. Her mind whirled in a storm of emotions, but beneath them all, the hunger remained.

Surrendering to the forest and the night, she stripped her clothes off as she ran, paying no attention to where she left them. The moonlight and the breeze caressed her naked flesh and now the warmth returned to her at last. She felt herself burning with want. With need. And then she could feel her skin hanging on her the same way that clothes did, and she reached up to the edges of her mouth and pulled it wide like a hood, slipping it back over her head.

Donika slid from her skin and, at last, took flight, returning to the night sky after sixteen very long years. Reborn.

She flew through the trees, thinking again of the boy she desired, thinking that maybe he would be inside her tonight after all, and they would both get what they wanted.

Her mouth opened in a low, mournful cry. It was a tune she'd always known, a night song that had been in her heart all along.

I Was a Teenage Vampire

Bill Crider

Bill Crider is the author of fifty published novels and numerous short stories. He won the Anthony Award for best first mystery novel in 1987 for Too Late to Die *and was nominated for the Shamus Award for best first private-eye novel for* Dead on the Island. *He won the Golden Duck award for best juvenile science fiction novel for* Mike Gonzo and the UFO Terror. *He and his wife, Judy, won the best short story Anthony in 2002 for their story "Chocolate Moose." His latest novel is* Murder Among the OWLS. *Check out his home page at www.billcrider.com.*

If you really want to hear about it, which a lot of people do, being naturally curious, you probably want to know where I was born, and what I was like as a kid, and how I wound up living (in a manner of speaking) under a bridge, and all that *Catcher in the Rye* kind of crap, but I just don't feel like talking about any of that right now, and anyway it's not all that interesting, to tell you the truth.

I'll tell you how I got to be a goddam vampire, though. *That's* pretty interesting. It was all because of my sister, Kate, who you'd think would know better, for Crissake, because she was practically a high school graduate, but then there aren't a lot of geniuses in my family, including me, although I did make a pretty good grade in a civics class one year.

Kate can't take all the blame. If she'd never seen those movies, it might have been different. It wasn't my fault, though. I was just an innocent bystander.

Anyway, being a vampire isn't as much fun as you might think it is. I mean, you probably think it's all about the cape and the gleaming white fangs and the ripping good times you could have after the goddam sun goes down. Or maybe you don't think that, but that's what *I* thought, which shows how much I knew because I was wrong. Dead wrong, just to throw in a little vampire humor there.

What happened is that my sister was planning this big party for her eighteenth birthday, which happened to be on Halloween, and she wanted it to be really special. My crummy parents said she could do whatever she pleased, which is what they always said when she asked for anything because they liked her best. You probably think that's just sour grapes, but it's not that. It's just the way it was, and it never bothered me because I was used to it, after all.

What she wanted was a vampire.

"Like Christopher Lee," Kate said. She has this way of brushing her hair back out of her eyes when she talks, which is frankly pretty irritating, but she thinks it's cute and that the boys like it. I don't know about other boys, but it just seems phony to me. "Like that movie we saw last year, *Horror of Dracula.*"

She went to a lot of movies like that. *I Was a Teenage Werewolf. I Was a Teenage Frankenstein.* But she liked stuff with vampires best. They'd never made one called *I Was a Teenage Vampire* or she would have been first in line.

"You know," Kate said. "Remember what the ads said? 'The chill of the tomb won't leave your blood for hours.' "

She tried to say the last part in a deep, creepy voice but it wasn't deep, and it wasn't creepy. It was just phony.

"You don't have to *laugh,*" she said, because I couldn't help it. "It's your stupid friend Binky who says he knows a real vampire."

"Binky wouldn't know a vampire if it bit him in the ass," I said, which I knew was a pretty crude thing to say, even to my sister, but I was getting tired of the way she was brushing at her hair. Besides, I was wrong, as it turned out. "And he's not my friend."

"Well, he's certainly not *my* friend," she said. "And you don't have to use that kind of language."

Binky wasn't really anybody's friend. He was just this guy that was always coming around, *wanting* to be somebody's friend and making cracks like he thought they were jokes, but nobody ever laughed at them. He had a pointy nose that was always dripping, and big sad eyes, and hair that he needed to wash a whole lot more often than he did. He hardly ever smiled because he had pretty dingy teeth and he didn't use his tube of Ipana any too regularly, at least as far as I could tell.

He'd told me about this vampire that he'd met. It was supposed to be this big hairy secret just between me and him because we were such good friends. That's what *he* thought, anyway. But Kate had wormed it out of me. She has a way of doing that. I never should have told her, but I did, and there was nothing I could do to change that.

"I guess if anybody knows a *real* vampire, it's Binky," Kate said. Her name's really Katherine, but she thinks Kate is sophisticated or something. "Anyway, he *says* he does, and that's what I need to make the party perfect."

She should never have gone to see that movie, is what I think. Now she had the idea that a party with the girls dressed up in filmy nightgowns and guys looking like Igor or whatever his name was would be just the ticket. But she said it just wouldn't work unless she had a vampire to liven things up.

"Maybe Dad could be the vampire," I said. "He likes to dress up and stuff. He even has a tuxedo."

"That's so passé," she said, brushing back her hair. I thought what she ought to do was cut off her bangs, but nobody ever asked me about stuff like that. "And Dad would make a *terrible* vampire."

She was right about that. He was more the Mr. Peepers type, and he seemed to be getting more that way all the time, which might have been because our mother was a lot like Rip Van Winkle's wife in that story we had to read at school.

"So that's why you have to talk to Binky," Kate said. This time she flipped her hair out of her eyes by tossing her head, which was even more irritating than if she'd used her hand. "If there's a real vampire around, it would make the party just perfect. Will you do it?"

"A real vampire would be pretty dangerous," I said. I didn't even believe in vampires, and I thought Binky was full of crap. I was just trying to get her to shut up. I should have known better. Nobody could get Kate to shut up.

"We'll have garlic and crosses and holy water," she said. "It won't be dangerous."

"That stuff never works in the movies."

"You don't know anything. You don't really like those movies. You think they're not intellectual."

"I never said that," I told her, and it was the truth, even if she was right about what I thought.

"You didn't *have* to say it. You sit around and *observe* everybody, like you think you're better than us. But you're not. You just like to think so."

I couldn't remember ever winning an argument with Kate, and I knew she'd never let up (she was a lot like our mother that way) so I finally said I'd talk to Binky if she'd do my geometry problems for a week. Not that I couldn't do them myself, which I could, but I had to get something from her or she'd think she had the upper hand on me, which she didn't, not really.

She thought she was a whiz at geometry, so she said she'd do the problems, and of course that meant I had to talk to Binky whether I wanted to or not.

* * *

Our high school was a big redbrick two-story building, and it smelled like that red stuff the janitors throw on the wooden floors before they sweep them. I've never figured out how that stuff is supposed to clean the floors, but I kind of liked the smell of it. I actually even liked the school. It's just most of the students and faculty that I couldn't stand.

When I went to school the next morning, not long before the first bell, the girls were all talking about how they'd seen Frankie Avalon sing "Venus" on *American Bandstand* the day before. That was their intellectual level, for Crissake, watching *American Bandstand* and liking Frankie Avalon. The guys were mostly farting and picking their noses, which was about *their* intellectual level. They didn't like Frankie Avalon any more than I did, though; I'll say that for them.

I couldn't find Binky until Fred Burley told me that he was shut in his locker. Binky was small and weak, so some wit was always doing that to him.

"Who did it this time?" I asked. "Harry Larrimore?"

Harry was usually the one who did it. He'd done a few things to me, too, including giving me a terrific wedgie just before geometry class one day. Harry was a lot bigger than I was, so there was nothing I could do to him. I just went on into the class. I had trouble walking into the room, and everybody got a big laugh out of it, even Mrs. Delaney, the teacher, though she tried to hide it.

"I don't think anybody put Binky in his locker," Fred told me. "I think he just likes it in there."

I didn't see how that was possible. Who could like being closed up in a little dark space like that? There was no use in trying to explain that to Fred, though. If it didn't have something to do with a ball, Fred had trouble figuring it out.

I eluded the teachers and sneaked up to the second floor where the sophomore lockers were lined up along the wall across from the study hall. The lockers were about four feet tall and painted gunmetal gray.

They had little louvers at the top. I think the louvers were put there as a safety measure in case somebody left his stinky gym shoes inside but those vents were a lifesaver for some of the kids who got locked inside.

Nobody else was in the hall because we weren't supposed to go up on the second floor before the bell. We might get into all kinds of unsupervised trouble. Anyway, it was very quiet in the hall, but I heard a noise coming from locker number 146, which was Binky's. It wasn't loud. It sounded as if someone might be reading a book in there and flipping the pages. That couldn't be it, though. Binky was weird, but not weird enough to try to read in the dark.

I stood in front of the locker for a few seconds and listened. "Binky?" I said.

"Carleton?"

That's my crummy name, Carleton, and I try to get people to call me Carl, which isn't so bad, but nobody will do it, the bastards. They'll call my sister *Kate*, but they won't even give me the time of day.

"Yeah," I said. "It's me." I know I should have said, "It is I," because old Mrs. Shanklin, our English teacher, keeps telling us how we should use correct grammar at all times if we want people to respect us, but I think it sounds phony as hell to tell you the truth, so I never do it. "Were you expecting somebody else?"

He couldn't have been because nobody else ever came by to let him out of his locker. I didn't come by because he was my friend, though, because he wasn't. It's just that I couldn't treat anybody like the rest of the morons did him.

"What do you want?" he said.

"I need to ask you a favor."

"I'm busy right now, Carleton. I have a test in first period."

"You're studying in the locker?"

"That's right. Go away and leave me alone."

That's the thanks I got for being the one who tried to look out for him. I started to tell him what an ungrateful bastard he was, but I thought better of it.

"It's about the vampire," I said. I figured that would get his attention.

There was a dull thud, like a book being slammed shut. "You know I can't talk about him, Carleton. I told you that. Now go away. I need to study, and I can't be late for class. If I get another tardy, Old Man Harkness will give me detention for a month."

Binky got a lot of tardies, mainly because he was shut up in his locker so much. I did my best to help, but I couldn't remember to go by and let him out every single day.

"I'm going to open the door, Binky. Just don't run off."

"I wish you'd just go away."

"Well, I'm not going anywhere. And you better not, either."

I'd let Binky out so many times that he didn't even have to tell me the combination to his lock. I'd memorized it long ago. But this time, I didn't need the combination because the lock was missing. All anybody needed to do was lift up on the handle and the door would come open. Binky could have jiggled it from inside easily enough. He must have been dumber than I thought.

I opened the door and Binky stepped out into the hall. He was so short and so skinny that he hadn't even been very cramped. For a change his nose wasn't dripping, which I have to admit was an improvement. He was holding his civics book in one hand with his finger in it like he was marking his place.

He ran the other scrawny hand, the one without the book, through his lank blondish hair and said, "I have to go to class, Carleton."

"You're welcome," I said.

He looked at me like I was nuts. "Very funny. I didn't ask you to let me out."

He tried to edge to the side and slip around me, but I moved in front of him.

"The vampire," I said.

"What about the vampire?"

"I need to talk to him."

The first bell rang, and people started coming up the stairs and milling around. I could tell that Binky was going to make a run for it, so I grabbed the front of his shirt. He looked up at me with his sad black eyes and said, "I don't think that would be a good idea, Carleton."

"I know it's not a good idea," I told him. "It's my sister's idea, so it's obviously pretty stupid."

I explained the situation in a low voice so nobody could hear me talking about a vampire in the hall. They'd think I was as crazy as Binky if they did.

I told Binky about the party. While I was talking, I held on to Binky's shirt. He might make a break at any second, even though there was plenty of time for him to get to class before the second bell.

"That's really dumb, Carleton," he said when I was finished telling him Kate's plan. "Even for your sister, it's dumb. You shouldn't mess with a vampire. It's dangerous."

"Yeah, but she's going to do my geometry problems for a week, so we have to talk to the vampire."

"That wasn't the deal you made with Kate."

I asked him what he meant by that. I was the one who made the deal, after all, so I should know what it was.

"She said she'd do the problems if you talked to me. Well, you talked to me. Case closed."

I thought about it, and he was right, technically speaking. Except that Kate's mind didn't work that way. She didn't go in for loopholes and technicalities. She'd never do the geometry problems if I didn't try to get the vampire for the party. Not that I needed her help. I can do geometry. It was just the principle of the thing.

I was still trying to explain that to Binky when he noticed that the hall had just about cleared out. He gave a sudden jerk and pulled away from me. I guess he wasn't as weak as I thought, and he was quicker than I'd have guessed. Before I could do anything about it, he was gone, escaping into Mr. Harkness's classroom. The ungrateful little bastard would be lucky if I ever let him out of his locker again.

Binky tried to make things right during lunch period by offering me his pudding, as if anybody would want pudding that he'd been sniffling over for ten minutes, not that he was sniffling today. Nobody would have wanted it anyway because there were lumps in it. I knew that for sure because there were always lumps in the pudding they served in the cafeteria. There were plenty of rumors that explained what the lumps were, and all of them were unpleasant, to say the least.

"I've been thinking things over," he said. "I'm sorry I ran off this morning."

He put a couple of thin cafeteria napkins on top of his chili to soak up the grease. He's probably the only one who does that. For that matter, he's probably the only one who actually eats the chili. He kills me; he really does.

I wished he hadn't come to sit at my table, but I couldn't do anything about it, and the fact was that there was plenty of room there, and he knew nobody else was likely to be joining me. To tell you the truth, I wasn't a whole lot more popular than Binky was, but at least I was too big to be stuffed into a locker.

"That's okay," I said, hoping he wouldn't say anything else. "I know you had to get to class." But I was pretty cheesed off at him if you want to know the truth.

"I should never have told you about the vampire," he said. "That was a mistake."

"Too late," I said.

"Yeah. So I guess I'll take you to him."

I stopped stirring my chili. That's what I do: I stir it. But I never eat more than a couple of bites. If I do, I'll have gas all during fourth period. I don't eat much of the pudding, either. I just stick the spoon in it and stir that around, too, checking for lumps.

"So now you'll take me to him?"

Binky nodded.

"What do you want from me, Binky?"

"Who says I want anything?"

I didn't bother to answer that. Everybody wants something, and Binky was no different. After a couple of seconds he said, "I want to come to the party."

Well, there it was. He was just a goddam sophomore, and he wanted to go to a party thrown by a senior.

"Binky," I said, "even *I* might not be invited to the party."

"No party, no vampire."

"Okay, I'll ask my sister. But no guarantees."

He thought it over. "I guess that'll have to do."

"So we'll go invite the vampire?"

"Yeah."

"You better not be kidding me, Binky," I said.

He gave me a hurt look. "Meet me outside the north door after sixth period."

"I'll be there," I said.

"You want my chili?" he said. "I soaked the grease off."

First it was the pudding, and now the chili.

"What's the matter with you?" I said.

"I guess I'm not hungry."

I looked down at my own chili, and I couldn't really blame him.

See, the fact of the matter is that like I said, I didn't really believe in vampires. *Now*, it's a different story. Boy, do I believe in vampires now. But this was *then*.

Anyway, I need to tell you about the house where the vampire lived. Back in the nineteenth century sometime, a guy who had more dollars than sense, as my father liked to say, had an old manor house dismantled over in England. The workers numbered the pieces and rebuilt the place outside our little town.

I wasn't around in those days, of course, and neither was my father, but he knew about stuff like that, local history and all. He said they put the house together like some kind of 3-D jigsaw puzzle. The guy even had the plans for the grounds, and he had gardens and all that kind of thing fixed just the way they'd been over in England.

That's the way the story went, anyway. I never saw any of that myself because after a while, the guy died. He didn't have any kin that anybody knew about except some cousins in New York. They inherited the house and property, and they kept right on paying the taxes year after year, but they never even came to visit. The house was abandoned, and vines grew up all over the walls. The gardens and the shrubbery overgrew the grounds, and then the trees closed in.

Eventually the place got a kind of a reputation. You probably know the kind of thing I'm talking about: funny lights, strange noises, ghosts. I didn't believe in any of that kind of crap myself, but I didn't ever go out there to see if any of it was true. It wasn't that I was scared. I just didn't want to go. Hardly anybody else ever went out that way, either.

Except for Binky, who was, as I think I've said already, weird. He *liked* hanging around places like that. That's how he found the vampire.

* * *

I met Binky after school, and we rode our bikes out of town for about two miles and turned down a little dirt road for another half mile. It's hard going on dirt, and I was hot and sweaty. Binky didn't seem bothered. He was wearing a long-sleeved shirt and a cap pulled down low. I could hardly even see his eyes.

"I hope this guy's not a real vampire," I said when we stopped to rest. "I think it would be a big mistake to invite some guy to a party and have him rip open our throats and drink the blood of virgins and stuff. I don't think it's what Kate has in mind. That wouldn't be any fun at all."

"Speak for yourself," Binky said. "All that sounds pretty good to me."

He sounded almost wistful, like he really believed it. He was weird, all right, but I didn't think he meant it. He'd nearly passed out in biology class when we were dissecting the frogs.

"It sounds messy," I said, trying to make a joke of it. I did that sometimes when things made me nervous. "My parents would have a snit fit if the house got all messed up."

Binky took me seriously, though. "It wouldn't be like that. Vampires are pretty fastidious."

I wasn't surprised that Binky knew a word like *fastidious*. He read a lot, and besides being weird he had what you might call a well-developed imagination. He read magazines with titles like *Amazing* and *Astounding* and *Fantastic*, the kind that had stuff like flying saucers and giant bugs on the covers. Sometimes on the same cover. Vampires, too, probably.

"How well do you know this vampire?" I asked.

Binky ducked his head. "I didn't say I knew him."

I'd figured as much.

"I just said I thought he was a vampire. You're the one who wanted to come out here."

I looked up the road. The trees grew right up to both sides, and their branches hung over it and joined in the middle, so it looked like a green and gold and orange tunnel. It was so shady that it was almost dark under there. The house was at the end of the road, and it looked kind of spooky, to tell you the truth, like one of those houses you see in the posters for my sister's favorite movies. Maybe it even looked like the house in the Dracula movie she liked so much. I wasn't at all sure going to the house was a good idea now that I'd had a better look at it, but we'd come this far. I pushed my bike on down the dirt road. Binky followed along.

When we got closer to the house, something flew out of an upstairs window. It looked a little like a bat, but I didn't really know what it was. It was too early for bats to be flying around, I thought, not that it mattered. I got this kind of a chill on the back of my neck like somebody had touched me there with a cold hand. I looked at my watch. It was only four-thirty, but it got dark kind of early at that time of year. The dirt road was covered with fallen leaves, and a little breeze came up from somewhere and blew them along in front of us.

"Probably nobody's home," I said. "Maybe we should just go on back."

"We're already here," Binky said. "You might as well see if anybody's home."

That sounded like a bad idea to me, but I didn't want to chicken out. My crummy sister would never let up if she found out. Neither would Binky, probably, and he was just the type to spread it all around school. If that happened, I'd get crammed into a locker more often than even Binky did. So I kept on going.

The house didn't look any better when we got to what had once been the front yard. It looked worse, to tell you the truth. There was no glass in any of the windows that I could see, and I think there were holes in the roof. I for sure saw a couple of holes in the stone walls where they weren't covered by the vines and bushes. Trees grew all over the place, but they weren't very tall.

The front door of the house didn't look too bad. It was made of heavy wood, and it didn't look as old as the rest of the house, which looked older than a hundred years. It even smelled old and moldy. If there was ever a place a vampire might pick to hide out, this would be it, all right.

The breeze had brought some clouds from somewhere, not storm clouds, but big puffy ones with black bottoms, and they blocked out most of the late afternoon sun. We might as well have been standing out on some old English moor somewhere.

Neither one of us made a move to get any closer to the house. I thought Binky should go knock on the door. He didn't agree.

"You're the one with the invitation," he said.

"He wouldn't answer, anyway," I said. "Not if he's a vampire. It's not nighttime yet."

Binky gave me a disgusted look. "You don't know much about vampires, do you?"

"I saw *Horror of Dracula*," I said, which was a lie, but Binky didn't know that.

"Big deal. So did I. Have you ever read *Dracula*? The book, I mean."

"I've read a lot of stuff," I said.

"But not *Dracula*. If you had, you'd know the difference between the movies and real life."

"You're going to tell me that some made-up book is real life?"

"Bram Stoker knew what he was talking about," Binky said, as positive as if he had a clue, which I was pretty sure he didn't. "Anyway, *his* Dracula could come out in the daylight." He pointed at the house. "I saw this guy in the daylight. So are you going to knock?"

"Why don't you do it?"

"You have to give him the invitation. It's your party, and it's your house you're inviting him to."

It was my sister's crummy party, and it was my parents' house, but I had a feeling Binky wasn't interested in fine distinctions like that. I laid my bike down on the ground and went up to the door. I didn't exactly rush. I wasn't feeling too good about things if you really want to know the truth about it. I mean, if the guy was really a goddam vampire, I could be in big trouble.

The wood of the door was dark and old, but solid. There was no bell, not even a knocker. Maybe whoever lived there wasn't expecting any guests. Or maybe nobody lived there. Binky might not have even seen anybody. He could have just made it all up to get attention.

While I stood there trying to bring myself to knock, I heard something shriek up above me. It was the bat, or whatever it was, and it flew back into the house through one of the windows on the second story.

I got that chill again, and I almost turned around and went back. I didn't, though. I wish I had, but I didn't. I knocked on the door. Nobody came, so I knocked again. Nobody came that time, either. Maybe the vampire was shut up in his coffin and couldn't hear me. Or maybe he was flying around the attic like a bat. I looked over my shoulder at Binky, who shrugged. I was about to leave, and I'd turned halfway around when I heard something. I turned back. The door started to open.

It didn't open very much, just a crack, but there was somebody there, all right. Or I thought there was. I couldn't hear anybody breathing, and I couldn't see into the dark interior of the house.

I didn't know what to say. I mean, I couldn't just say, "Are you the vampire?" So I just stood there, feeling like an idiot.

Finally whoever was behind the door got tired of waiting for me to say something and decided he'd go first. He said, "Yes?" Except he didn't say it quite like that. It was more like "Yessssss?"

I didn't jump when he said it, but that was just because I was kind of paralyzed and could hardly move at all. I tried to talk, but my mouth was too dry. I swallowed a couple of times and said, "I wanted to invite you to a party."

There was no answer for a while. Then, "You are quite sssure?" Like he couldn't believe anybody would actually invite him somewhere.

I couldn't believe it, either. I wished I was at home, even if it meant watching Frankie Avalon pantomiming to a song on *American Bandstand* or something just as lame. But I stayed right where I was and got the invitation out of my pocket. I'd written it out in study hall while old Mr. Garber sat at his desk in the front of the room and pulled on the hairs growing out of his ears while he pretended to read something in his history text. The invitation said, "You are invited to a Birthday Party!", and it had the date and time and address and everything on it.

I held it out, and a hand reached out from behind the door and took it. It wasn't a hand like any I'd ever seen before. It was pale white, and the nails were thick and long and yellow and sharp. That was what bothered me, how sharp they were.

The hand disappeared with the invitation in it, and after a second or two the voice said, "Thisss isss very nissse. I will be there. Will you be at the door to invite me in?"

He already had the invitation, so I didn't see why I had to do any more inviting, but I said, "If I'm not, my sister will be."

"That isss sssatisssfactory."

And then the door closed. I stood there a minute, blinking like I'd just come out of a dream, and then I walked back to where Binky stood waiting.

"What about *my* invitation?" he said.

"I'll ask my sister."

"She'd better invite me."

"We'll see," I said, because knowing my sister, I was sure she wouldn't want Binky hanging around the way he did. She only liked the popular kids, who were all a bunch of phonies. Binky was weird, but at least he wasn't phony, which was about all I could say for him.

A funny thing happened at school the next day. Somebody stuffed Harry Larrimore into a locker. I wasn't the one who let him out, but I heard about it from Fred Burley, who did. He said he asked Harry who put him in there, but Harry didn't want to talk about it, like he was scared or something. I didn't think that was right since Harry wasn't scared of anybody, not even the teachers.

Harry and Fred both got tardy slips because it took awhile to get Harry out of the locker. He was a lot bigger than Binky, and nobody would have believed you could get him into a locker if Fred hadn't seen it himself and described it.

I told Binky about it at lunch, but he didn't seem to think it was funny. All he said was, "Sometimes things come back on you."

I had a feeling he wasn't talking about the cafeteria food. We had fish that day because it was Friday, but Binky wouldn't eat any. He looked interested when I poured ketchup all over mine, and I thought for a minute he'd give it a try, but he said he just wasn't hungry.

My sister surprised me when I told her that Binky had demanded an invitation to the party. She didn't even argue. She pushed her hair back and said, "All right, Binky can come, as long as he stays out of the way."

She meant, "as long as he stays out of sight of my phony friends," which also meant that he'd be hanging out in my room, since that's where I'd be staying. I didn't like Binky any better than she did. I just put up with him because I felt sorry for him, but I didn't want him in my room during the party. There wasn't anything I could do about it, though.

"Did you see the vampire?" Kate said. "Is he the real thing?"

Like I would know a vampire if I saw one, and I hadn't really seen this one, mostly just his hand, which I have to admit looked real enough to satisfy me, so I said, "He's the real thing, all right, and if I were you, I wouldn't want him coming to the party."

She just laughed. "You don't have to worry about a thing. We'll take plenty of precautions, and there aren't any real vampires, anyway, no matter what you think."

"If you say so."

She could believe it was all a big joke if she wanted to, but it so happened that I didn't agree with her, not that it made any difference.

"I *do* say so, and I want you and your pal Binky to stay out of the way."

I didn't bother to remind her that Binky wasn't my pal. I asked if she'd told our parents about the vampire, and she gave me this condescending look.

"I don't tell them a lot of things," she said, as if she had these big secrets to keep, but I knew she didn't because I'd sneaked into her room and read her diary one day. "And you'd better not tell them, either, if you know what's good for you, buster."

I told her I wouldn't cause any trouble and handed her my geometry book.

"Oh, no, you don't," she said. "I'm not doing any problems until after the party and after the vampire shows up."

I wished I'd never said anything to her about the vampire. Binky had warned me not to, but I had. There was nothing I could do about it. I took my geometry book upstairs and got to work.

Halloween was pretty dreary. It rained most of the day, and the thick clouds stayed dark and low all afternoon. By the time of the party, it was inky black outside, with no sign of the moon or stars.

Kate's friends started to arrive, and our parents went next door to play canasta with our neighbors. Our parents were very liberal that way, not pushing in where they weren't wanted. My mother said to be sure to call if there were any problems, and Kate told her not to worry about a thing. I wasn't so sure, myself, but I kept my mouth shut. I knew what was good for me, buster.

When Binky got there, Kate invited him in. He had on a black plastic rain jacket with the hood pulled over his head, like it might've still been raining, and he didn't seem to like the wreath of garlic hanging around Kate's neck. I couldn't blame him. It smelled pretty bad, but Kate thought it was just the right touch. She had a crucifix, too, not just a cross but the real thing with an image of Jesus on it, which was pretty funny considering nobody in our family had been to church in the last ten or fifteen years as far as I knew.

After Binky got inside, he wanted to hang around the way he always does, but I told him we had to go up to my room.

"I want to be here when he comes," Binky said, and I didn't have to ask who he meant. I told him we could slip back down later, and he said he guessed that would have to do.

"That crucifix won't do any good," Binky said when we got to the top of the stairs. "You have to believe in it."

"I don't guess it matters," I said. "There's all that garlic."

"Yeah. That might help."

I didn't like it that he said *might*, but I didn't believe in the vampire anyway, or that's what I kept telling myself.

The doorbell rang exactly at eight-thirty, which is when the invitation I gave the vampire had said for him to come. Kate wanted all her friends to be there first.

Binky and I slipped to the head of the stairs and looked down. Binky still had that dumb hood over his head, but I guess he could see all right. Kate went to the front door and opened it. She said something, and then the vampire stepped inside.

He was tall and pale, and his hair was slicked back. From where I was standing, it looked as if he had pointed ears and red eyes. A bunch of Kate's friends came into the room and stared.

The vampire looked them over like they were buffet items at the smorgasbord restaurant downtown. They all took a step back, even Kate, who usually didn't back away from anything.

I looked at Binky. He pushed the hood of the rain jacket off his head, and I saw the tips of his ears.

"Binky," I said.

He smiled. I wished he hadn't. His teeth weren't bad anymore. They were white and shiny, and his incisors were pointed and sharp.

"Binky," I said.

His eyes looked as if they were lit from the inside with red lanterns.

"Binky," I said.

I thought of a lot of things all at once: Binky studying in the dark locker, wearing long sleeves when it was so warm, Harry Larrimore. I remembered a lot of other things, too, things that I should have thought about before.

"Binky," I said.

There was some screaming from downstairs now, but I didn't look to see what was happening. I couldn't take my eyes off those red eyes, Binky's eyes. I wanted to look away, but I couldn't.

"Binky," I said.

The screaming was louder, and I wondered if anybody had called next door, but I was pretty sure they hadn't been able to get to a phone.

"Binky," I said. "For Crissakes, Binky."

And then he was on me.

* * *

I never went back to school after that. Somehow I couldn't see trying to fit in with a bunch of people whose blood I wanted to suck. After what must have happened downstairs at my house, they probably wouldn't have been real glad to see me, anyway.

Binky didn't go back, either, now that he had a "friend" to keep him company. That just goes to show what can happen if you let somebody sit with you at lunch. They start thinking you like them, and then they turn you into a vampire.

Binky says he and the other vampire never did get friendly. Binky had found him out at the old house, where he'd moved after having a close call with some Van Helsing type in the Boston area. He'd told Binky that he was trying to kick the bloodsucking habit, but Binky had pleaded to be turned into a vampire. I blame all those nutty magazines that Binky read. Anyway the guy finally gave in.

"Nobody liked me anyway," Binky said. "I'm still not with the in-crowd, but at least this way I get to live forever, or at least until somebody stakes me. So do you."

If you could call it living. It wasn't anything I wanted to thank him for.

"Too bad the Master had to leave town," Binky said. "You would have liked him."

As if I could ever like anybody called "the Master." If there was ever a phony name, that was it. I'd rather be called Carleton than "the Master." I'd have liked him about as much as I liked living in that broken-down old house, which is where Binky and I had gone after we left the party by the back door. I never knew much about what happened in my own house that night, and never tried to find out. I guess I didn't want to know. You probably think that's hard-hearted of me, since my sister was there and all, but she wasn't my sister anymore, not now that I'd been changed.

"I don't think he made any of them into vampires," Binky said. "He thinks it would be a bad idea to have too many of us around, and he prefers just to drink the blood."

I said I thought he was trying to break the goddam habit.

"He was," Binky said. "But living on mice and rabbits and stuff like that got pretty boring after a while, I guess."

Come to think of it, it was getting pretty boring to me, too. I mean, they were all right if you couldn't get anything else, but before long I was going to have to go for something bigger and more substantial. More nourishing.

"Even blood from a mouse beats that cafeteria chili, though, right?" Binky said.

"Yeah," I said, "I guess it does, at that."

All that was a long time ago. For the last few years Binky and I have been hanging out (a little more vampire humor there) under a bridge in Austin, Texas. When you're surrounded by thousands of Mexican free-tailed bats, nobody's going to notice you, not if you're a bat, too, even if you're a lot bigger than they are. Being bigger works out fine, since they don't try to push us around.

It's a pretty boring way to have to spend your time, though, to tell you the truth. Like I said at the beginning, being a vampire's not all capes and fangs and ripping times. When the highlight of your day is flying out from under a bridge and seeing how many tourists' mouths you can crap into before they get wise and shut their mouths, you can be pretty sure you're not living the high life.

It's actually even worse than that. Bats have parasites. Maybe you didn't know that. Fleas, mites, ticks. They can be pretty irritating sometimes. I don't know how living on me affects them. I don't even care. All I know is that they make me itch.

I think about the old days now and then, and sometimes around her birthday I wonder if Kate survived her party, and if she did, whether she got married to one of her phony friends and had a bunch of kids who were just as phony as their parents. And I wonder if she ever thought about any of those crummy movies she used to like so much. They were pretty much to blame for the whole thing, after all.

"It's nearly sundown," Binky squeaked.

The children of the night, such music they make. You probably couldn't understand Binky even if you heard him, but I could.

"Time to give the tourists a thrill," he said. "I'll bet I can hit more open mouths this evening than you can!"

"Sure, Binky," I said.

"Some fun!" he said.

"Sure, Binky," I said. "Some fun."

There's nothing like being a teenage vampire. I should know. I've been one for forty-five years now, so I figured it was time to let the world know.

Maybe somebody will make a movie.

Twilight

Kelley Armstrong

Kelley Armstrong is the author of the Women of the Otherworld paranormal suspense series. A former computer programmer, she's now escaped her corporate cubicle, but she puts her old skills to work on her website at www.Kelley Armstrong.com.

Another life taken. Another year to live.

That is the bargain that rules our existence. We feed off blood, but for three hundred and sixty-four days a year, it is merely that: feeding. Yet on that last day—or sometime before the anniversary of our rebirth as vampires—we must drain the lifeblood of one person. Fail and we begin the rapid descent into death.

As I sipped white wine on the outdoor patio, I watched the steady stream of passersby. Although there was a chill in the air—late autumn coming fast and sharp—the patio was crowded, no one willing to surrender the dream of summer quite yet. Leaves fluttering onto the tables were lauded as decorations. The scent of a distant wood fire was willfully mistaken for candles. The sun, almost gone despite the still early hour, only added romance to the meal. All embellishments to the night, not signs of impending winter.

I sipped my wine and watched night fall. At the next table, a lone businessman eyed me. He was the sort of man I often had the misfortune to attract: middle-aged and prosperous, laboring under the delusion that success and wealth were such irresistible lures that he could allow his waistband and jowls to thicken unchecked.

Under other circumstances, I might have returned the attention, let him lead me to some tawdry motel, then taken *my* dinner. He would survive, of course, waking weakened, blaming it on too much wine. A meal without guilt. Any man who took such a chance with a stranger—particularly when he bore a wedding band—deserved an occasional bout of morning-after discomfort.

He did not, however, deserve to serve as my annual kill. I can justify many things, but not that. Yet I found myself toying with the idea more than I should have, prodded by a niggling voice that told me I was already late.

I stared at the glow over the horizon. The sun had set on the anniversary of my rebirth, and I hadn't taken a life. Yet there was no need for panic. I would hardly explode into dust at midnight. I would weaken as I began the descent into death, but I could avoid that simply by fulfilling my bargain tonight.

I measured the darkness, deemed it enough for hunting, then laid a twenty on the table and left.

A bell tolled ten. Two hours left. I chastised myself for being so dramatic. I loathe vampires given to theatrics—those who have read too many horror novels and labor under the delusion that that's how they're supposed to behave. I despise any sign of it in myself and yet, under the circumstances, perhaps it could be forgiven.

In all the years that came before this, I had never reached this date without fulfilling my obligation. I had chosen this vampiric life and would not risk losing it through carelessness.

Only once had I ever neared my rebirth day, and then only due to circumstances beyond my control. It had been 1867 . . . or perhaps 1869. I'd been hunting for my annual victim when I'd found myself tossed into a Hungarian prison. I hadn't been caught at my kill—I'd never made so amateurish a mistake even when I'd been an amateur.

The prison sojourn had been Aaron's fault, as such things usually were. We'd been hunting my victim when he'd come across a nobleman whipping a servant in the street. Naturally, Aaron couldn't leave well enough alone. In the ensuing confusion of the brawl, I'd been rousted with him and thrown into a pest-infested cell that wouldn't pass any modern health code.

Aaron had worked himself into a full-frothing frenzy, seeing my rebirth anniversary only days away while I languished in prison, waiting for justice that seemed unlikely to come swiftly. I hadn't been concerned. When one partakes of Aaron's company, one learns to expect such inconveniences. While he plotted, schemed, and swore he'd get us out on time, I simply waited. There was time yet and no need to panic until panic was warranted.

The day before my rebirth anniversary, as I'd begun to suspect that a more strenuous course of action might be required, we'd been released. I'd compensated for the trouble and delay by taking the life of a prison guard who'd enjoyed his work far more than was necessary.

This year, my only excuse for not taking a victim yet was that I hadn't gotten around to it. As for why, I was somewhat . . . baffled. I am nothing if not conscientious about my obligations. Yet, this year, delays had arisen, and somehow I'd been content to watch the days slip past and tell myself I would get around to it, as if it was no more momentous than a missed salon appointment.

The week had passed and I'd been unable to work up any sense of urgency until today, and even now, it was only an oddly cerebral concern. No matter. I would take care of it tonight.

As I walked, an old drunkard drew my gaze. I watched him totter into the shadows of an alley and thought: "There's a possibility. . . ." Perhaps I could get this chore over with sooner than expected. I could be quite finicky—refusing to feed off sleeping vagrants—yet as my annual kill, this one was a choice I could make.

Every vampire deals with our "bargain" in the way that best suits his temperament and capacity for guilt and remorse. I cull from the edges—the sick, the elderly, those already nearing their end. I do not fool myself into thinking this is a just choice. There's no way to know whether that cancer-wracked woman might have been on the brink of remission or if that elderly man had been enjoying his last days to the fullest. I make the choice because it is one I can live with.

This old drunkard would do. As I watched him, I felt the gnawing in the pit of my stomach, telling me I'd already waited too long. I should follow him into that alley, and get this over with. I *wanted* to get it over with—there was no question of that, no possibility I was conflicted on this point. Other vampires may struggle with our bargain. I do not.

Yet even as I visualized myself following the drunk into the alley, my legs didn't follow through. I stood there, watching him disappear into the darkness. Then I moved on.

A block farther, a crowd poured from a movie theater. As it passed, its life force enveloped me. I wasn't hungry, yet I could still feel that tingle of anticipation, of hunger. I could smell their blood, hear the rush of it through their veins. The scent and sound of life.

Twenty steps later, and they were still passing, an endless stream of humanity disgorged by a packed theater. How many seats were inside? Three hundred, three fifty? As many years as had passed since my rebirth?

One life per year. It seems so moderate a price . . . until you looked back and realized you could fill a movie theater with your victims. A sobering thought, even for one not inclined to dwell on such things. No matter. There wouldn't be hundreds more. Not from this vampire.

Contrary to legend, our gift of longevity comes with an expiry date. Mine was drawing near. I'd felt the signs, the disconnect from the world, a growing disinterest in all around me. For me, that was nothing new. I'd long since learned to keep my distance from a world that changed while I didn't.

After some struggle with denial, I'd accepted that I had begun the decline toward death. But it would be slow, and I still had years left, decades even. Or I would if I could get past this silly bout of ennui and make my rebirth kill.

As the crowd dwindled, I looked over my shoulder to watch them go and considered taking a life from them. A random kill. I'd done it once before, more than a century ago, during a particularly bleak time when I hadn't been able to rouse enough feeling to care. Yet later I'd regretted it, having let myself indulge my darkest inclinations simply because I'd been in a dark place myself. Unacceptable. I wouldn't do it again.

I wrenched my gaze from the dispersing crowd. This was ridiculous. I was no angst-ridden cinema vampire, bemoaning the choices she'd made in life. I was no flighty youngster, easily distracted from duty, abhorring responsibility. I was Cassandra DuCharme, senior vampire delegate to the interracial council. If any vampire had come to me with this problem—"I'm having trouble making my annual kill"—I'd have shown her the sharp side of my tongue, hauled her into the alley with that drunk, and told her, as Aaron might say, to "piss or get off the pot."

I turned around and headed back to the alley.

I'd gone only a few steps when I picked up a sense of the drunkard. Excitement swept through me. I closed my eyes and smiled. That was more like it.

The quickening accelerated as I slid into the shadows. My stride smoothed out, each step taken with care, rolling heel to toe, making no sound.

That sense of my prey grew stronger with each step, telling me he was near. I could see a recessed emergency exit a dozen feet ahead. A shoe protruded from the darkness. I crept forward until I spotted a dark form crumpled inside.

The rush of his blood vibrated through the air. My canines lengthened and I allowed myself one shudder of anticipation, then shook it off and focused on the sound of his breathing.

A gust whipped along the alley, scattering candy wrappers and leaflets, and the stink of alcohol washed over me. I caught the extra notes in his breathing—the deep, almost determined rhythm. Passed out drunk. He'd probably stumbled into the first semi-sheltered place he'd seen and collapsed.

That would make it easier.

Still, I hesitated, telling myself I needed to be sure. But the rhythm of his breathing stayed steady. He was clearly asleep and unlikely to awake even if I bounded over there and shouted in his ear.

So what was I waiting for? I should be in that doorway already, reveling in the luck of finding so easy a victim.

I shook the lead from my bones and crossed the alley.

The drunkard wore an army jacket, a real one if I was any judge. I resisted the fanciful urge to speculate, to imagine him as some shell-shocked soldier turned to drink by the horrors of war. More likely, he'd bought the jacket at a thrift shop. Or stolen it.

His hair was matted, so filthy it was impossible to tell the original color. Above the scraggly beard, though, his face was unlined. Younger than I'd first imagined. Significantly younger.

That gave me pause, but while he was not the old drunkard I'd first imagined, he was certainly no healthy young man. I could sense disease and wasting, most likely cirrhosis. Not my ideal target, but he would do.

And yet . . .

Almost before I realized it, I was striding toward the road.

He wasn't right. I was succumbing to panic, and that was unnecessary, even dangerous. If I made the wrong choice, I'd regret it. Better to let the pressure of this ominous date pass and find a better choice tomorrow.

I slid into the park and stepped off the path. The ground was hard, so I could walk swiftly and silently.

As I stepped from the wooded patch, my exit startled two young men huddled together. Their gazes tripped over me, eyes glittering under the shadows of their hoods, like jackals spotting easy prey. I met the stronger one's gaze. He broke first, grumbling deep in his throat. Then he shuffled back and waved his friend away as he muttered some excuse for moving on.

I watched them go, considering . . . then dismissing.

It was easy to separate one victim from a group. Not nearly so simple when the "group" consisted of only two people. As the young men disappeared, I resumed my silent trek across the park.

My goal lay twenty paces away. Had I not sensed him, I likely would have passed by. He'd ignored a park bench under the light and instead had stretched along the top of a raised garden, hidden under the bushes and amidst the dying flowers.

He lay on his back with his eyes closed. His face was peaceful, relaxed. A handsome face, broad and tanned. He had thick blond hair and the healthy vitality of a young man in his prime. A big man, too, tall and solid, his muscular arms crossed behind his head, his slim hips and long denim-clad legs ending in work boots crossed at the ankles.

I circled north to sneak up behind his head. He lay completely motionless, even his chest still, not rising and falling with the slow rhythm of breathing. I crossed the last few feet between us and stopped just behind his head. Then I leaned over.

His eyes opened. Deep brown eyes, the color of rich earth. He snarled a yawn.

“ ’Bout time, Cass,” he said. “Couple of punks been circling to see if I’m still conscious. Another few minutes, and I’d have had to teach them to let sleeping vamps lie.”

“Shall I go away then? Let you have your fun?”

Aaron grinned. “Nah. They come back? We can both have fun.” He heaved his legs over the side of the garden wall and sat up, shaking off sleep. Then, catching a glimpse of my face, his grin dropped into a frown. “You didn’t do it, did you?”

“I couldn’t find anyone.”

“Couldn’t find—?” He pushed to his feet, towering over me. “Goddamn it, what are you playing at? First you let it go until the last minute, then you ‘can’t find anyone’?”

I checked my watch. “It’s not the last minute. I still have ten left. I trust that if I explode at midnight, you’ll be kind enough to sweep up the bits. I would like to be scattered over the Atlantic but, if you’re pressed for time, the Charleston River will do.”

He glowered at me. “A hundred and twenty years together, and you never got within a week of your rebirth day without making your kill.”

“Hungary. 1867.”

“Sixty-eight. And I don’t see any bars this time. So what was your excuse?”

“Among others, I was busy researching that council matter Paige brought to my attention. I admit I let things creep up on me this year, and a century ago that would never have happened, but while we were apart, I changed—”

“Bullshit. You never change. Except to get more imperious, more pigheaded, and more cranky.”

“The word is ‘crankier.’ ”

He muttered a few more descriptors under his breath. I started down the path.

“You’d better be going off to find someone,” he called after me.

"No, I'm heading home to bed. I'm tired."

"Tired?" He strode up beside me. "You don't get tired. You're—"

He stopped, mouth closing so fast his teeth clicked.

"The word is 'dying,'" I said. "And, while that is true, and it is equally true that my recent inability to sleep is a symptom of that, tonight I am, indeed, tired."

"Because you're late for your kill. You can't pull this shit, Cassandra, not in your condition."

I gave an unladylike snort and kept walking.

His fingers closed around my arm. "Let's go find those punks. Have some fun." A broad, boyish grin. "I think one has a gun. Been a long time since I got shot."

"Another day."

"A hunt then."

"I'm not hungry."

"Well, I am. Maybe you couldn't find someone suitable, but I can. I know what you look for. We'll hunt together. I'll get a snack; you'll get another year. Fair enough?"

He tried to grin, but I could see a hint of panic behind his eyes. I felt an answering prickle of worry, but told myself I was being ridiculous. I'd simply had too much on my mind lately. I was tired and easily distracted. I needed to snap out of this embarrassing lethargy and make this kill, and I would do so tomorrow, once Aaron had gone back to Atlanta.

"It's not the end of the world—or *my* world—if I don't take a life tonight, Aaron. You've been late yourself when you couldn't find someone suitable. I haven't—and perhaps I'd simply like to know what that's like." I touched his arm. "At my age, new experiences are few and far between. I take them where I can."

He hesitated, then nodded, mollified, and accompanied me from the park.

* * *

Aaron followed me home. That wasn't nearly as exciting a prospect as it sounds. These days we were simply friends. His choice. If I had my way, tired or not, I would have found the energy to accommodate him.

When I first met Aaron, less than a year after his rebirth, he'd accused me of helping him in his new life because he looked like something to "decorate my bed with." True enough.

Even as a human, I had never been able to rouse more than a passing interest in men of my own class. Too well mannered, too gently spoken, too *soft.* My tastes had run to stable boys and, later, to discreet working men.

Finding Aaron as a newly reborn vampire, a big strapping farm boy with hands as rough as his manners, I will admit that my first thought was indeed carnal. He was younger than I liked, but I'd decided I could live with that.

So I'd trained him in the life of a vampire. In return, I'd received friendship, protection . . . and endless nights alone, frustrated beyond reason. It was preposterous, of course. I'd never had any trouble leading men to my bed and there I'd been, reduced to chasing a virile young man who strung me along as if he were some coy maiden. I told myself it wasn't his fault—he was English. Thankfully, when he finally capitulated, I discovered he wasn't nearly as repressed as I'd feared.

Over a hundred years together. It was no grand romance. The word "love" never passed between us. We were partners in every sense—best friends, hunting allies, and faithful lovers. Then came the morning I woke, looked over at him, and imagined *not* seeing him there, tried to picture life without him. I'd gone cold at the thought.

I had told myself I'd never allow that again. When you've lost everyone, you learn the danger of attachments. As a vampire, you must accept that every person you ever know will die, and you are the only constant in your life, the only person you can—and should—rely on. So I made a decision.

I betrayed Aaron. Not with another man. Had I done that, he'd simply have flown into a rage and, once past it, demanded to know what was really bothering me. What I did instead was a deeper betrayal, one that said, more coldly than I could ever speak the words, "I don't want you anymore."

After over half a century apart, happenstance had brought us together again. We'd resisted the pull of that past bond, reminded ourselves of what had happened the last time and yet, gradually, we'd drifted back into friendship. Only friendship. Sex was not allowed—Aaron's way of keeping his distance. Given the choice between having him as a friend and not having him in my life at all, I'd gladly choose the former . . . though that didn't keep me from hoping to change his mind.

That night I slept. It was the first time I'd done more than catnapped in over a year. While I longed to seize on this as some sign that I wasn't dying, I knew Aaron's assessment was far more likely—I was tired because I'd missed my annual kill.

Was this what happened, then, when we didn't hold up our end of the bargain? An increasing lethargy that would lead to death? I shook it off. I had no intention of exploring the phenomenon further. Come sunset, I would end this foolishness and take a life.

As I entered my living room that morning, I heard a dull slapping from the open patio doors. Aaron was in the yard, building a new retaining wall for my garden.

When he'd been here in the spring, he'd commented on the crumbling wall and said, "I could fix that for you." I'd nodded and said, "Yes, I suppose you could." Three more intervening visits. Three more hints about the wall. Yet I refused to ask for his help. I had lost that right when I betrayed him. So yesterday, he'd shown up on my doorstep, masonry tools in one hand, suitcase in the other, and announced he was building a new wall for my rebirth day.

That meant he had a reason to stay until he'd finished it. Had he simply decided my rebirth day made a good excuse? Or was there more than that? When I'd spoken to him this week, had something in my voice told him I had yet to take my annual victim? I watched Aaron through the patio doors. The breeze was chilly, but the sun beat down and he had his shirt off as he worked, oblivious to all around him. This was what he did for a living—masonry, the latest in a string of "careers." I chided him that, after two hundred years, one should have a healthy retirement savings plan. He only pointed the finger back at me, declaring that I too worked when I didn't need to. But I was self-employed, and selling art and antiques was certainly not in the same category as the physically demanding jobs he undertook. Yet another matter on which we disagreed—with vigor and enthusiasm.

I watched him for another minute, then headed for the kitchen to make him an iced tea.

I went out later to check a new shipment at an antique shop. When I got home, Aaron was sitting on the couch, a pile of newspapers on the table and one spread in his hands.

"I hope you didn't take those from my trash."

"I wouldn't have had to if you'd recycle." He peered around the side of the paper. "That blue box in the garage? That's what it's for, not holding garden tools."

I waved him off. "Three hundred and fifty years and I have never been deprived of a newspaper or book by want of paper. I'm not going to start recycling now. I'm too old."

"Too stubborn." He gave a sly grin. "Or too lazy."

He earned a glare for that one. I walked over and snatched up a stray paper from the carpet before it stained.

"If you're that desperate for reading material, just tell me, and I'll walk to the store and buy you a magazine."

He folded the paper and laid it on the coffee table, then patted the spot next to him. I hesitated, sensing trouble, and took a place at the opposite end, perched on the edge. He reached over, his hand going around my waist, and dragged me until I was sitting against him.

"Remember when we met, Cass?"

"Vaguely."

He laughed. "Your memory isn't *that* bad. Remember what you did for me? My first rebirth day was coming, and I'd decided I wasn't doing it. You found me a victim, a choice I could live with." With his free hand, he picked up a paper separated from the rest and dropped it onto my lap. "Found you a victim."

I sighed. "Aaron, I don't need you to—"

"Too late." He poked a calloused finger at the top article. "Right there."

The week-old story told of a terminally ill patient fighting for the right to die. When I looked over at Aaron, he was grinning, pleased with himself.

"Perfect, isn't it?" he said. "Exactly what you look for. She wants to die. She's in pain."

"She's in a palliative-care ward. How would I even get in there, let alone kill her?"

"Is that a challenge?" His arm tightened around my waist. "Because if it is, I'm up for it. You know I am."

He was still smiling, but behind it lurked a shadow of desperation. Again, his worry ignited mine. Perhaps this added incentive was exactly what I needed. It wouldn't be easy, but it could be interesting, particularly with Aaron's help.

Any other time, I'd have pounced on the idea, but now, even as I envisioned it, I felt only a spark of interest, buried under an inexplicable layer of lethargy, even antipathy, and all I could think was "Oh, but it would just be so much *work*."

My hackles rose at such indolence, but I squelched my indignation. I *was* determined to take a life tonight. I would allow nothing to stand in the way of that. Therefore, I could not enter into a plan that might prove too difficult. Better to keep this simple, so I would have no excuse for failure.

I set the paper aside. "Are you hungry?"

A faint frown.

"Last night, you said you were hungry," I continued. "If you were telling the truth, then I presume you still need to feed, unless you slipped out last night."

"I thought we'd be hunting together later. So I waited."

"Then we'll hunt tonight. But not—" A wave at the paper. "—in a hospital."

We strolled along the sidewalk. It was almost dark now, the sun only a red-tinged memory along the horizon. As I watched a flower seller clear her outdoor stock for the night, Aaron snapped his fingers.

"Flowers. That's what's missing in your house. You always have flowers."

"The last arrangement wilted early. I was going to pick up more when I was out today, but I didn't get the chance."

He seemed to cheer at that, as if reading some hidden message in my words.

"Here then," he said. "I'll get some for you now."

I arched my brows. "And carry bouquets on a hunt?"

"Think I can't? Sounds like a challenge."

I laughed and laid my fingers on his forearm. "We'll get some tomorrow."

He took my hand and looped it through his arm as we resumed walking.

"We're going to Paris this spring," he said after a moment.

"Are we? Dare I ask what prompted that?"

"Flowers. Spring. Paris."

"Ah. A thoughtful gesture, but Paris in the spring is highly overrated. And overpriced."

"Too bad. I'm taking you. I'll book the time off when I get home and call you with the dates."

When I didn't argue, he glanced over at me, then grinned and quickened his pace, launching into a "remember when" story of our last spring in Paris.

We bickered over the choice of victim. Aaron wanted to find one to suit my preference, but I insisted we select his type. Finally, he capitulated.

The fight dampened the evening's mood, but only temporarily. Once Aaron found a target, he forgot everything else.

In the early years, Aaron had struggled with vampiric life. He'd died rescuing a stranger from a petty thug. And his reward? After a life spent thinking of others, he'd been reborn as one who fed off them. Ironic and cruel.

Yet we'd found a way for him to justify—even relish—the harder facts of our survival. He fed from the dregs of society, punks and criminals like those youths in the park. For his annual kill, he condemned those whose crimes he deemed worthy of the harshest punishment. And so he could feel he did some good in this parasitic life.

As he said, I'd found his first victim. Now, two hundred years later, he no longer scoured newspapers or tracked down rumors but seemed able to locate victims by intuition alone, as I could find the dying. The predatory instinct will adapt to anything that ensures the survival of the host.

Tonight's choice was a drug dealer with feral eyes and a quick switchblade. We watched from the shadows as the man threatened a young runner. Aaron rocked on the balls at his feet, his gaze fixed on that waving knife, but I laid my hand on his arm. As the runner loped toward the street, Aaron's lips curved, happy to see him go, but even happier with what the boy's safe departure portended—not a quick intervention but a true hunt.

We tracked the man for over an hour before Aaron's hunger won out. With no small amount of regret, he stopped toying with his dinner and I lured the drug dealer into an alleyway. An easy maneuver, as such things usually were with men like this, too greedy and cocksure to feel threatened by a middle-aged woman.

As Aaron's fangs sank into the drug dealer's throat, the man's eyes bugged in horror, unable to believe what was happening. This was the most dangerous point of feeding, that split second where they felt our fangs and felt a nightmare come to life. It is but a moment, then the sedative in our saliva takes hold and they pass out, those last few seconds wiped from memory when they wake.

The man lashed out once, then slumped in Aaron's grasp. Still gripping the man's shirtfront, Aaron began to drink, gulping the blood. His eyes were closed, face rapturous, and I watched him, enjoying the sight of his pleasure, his appetite.

He'd been hungrier than he'd let on. Typical for Aaron, waiting that extra day or two, not to practice control or avoid feeding, but to drink heartily. Delayed gratification for heightened pleasure. I shivered.

"Cass?"

He licked a fallen drop from the corner of his mouth as he held the man out for me.

This was how we hunted—how Aaron liked it, not taking separate victims but sharing. He always made the disabling bite, drank some, then let me feed to satiation. If I took too much for him to continue feeding safely, he'd find a second victim. There was no sense arguing that I could find my own food—he knew that, but continued, compelled by a need to protect and provide.

"You go on," I said softly. "You're still hungry."

He thrust the man to me. "Yours."

His jaw set and I knew his insistence had nothing to do with providing sustenance.

As Aaron held the man up for me, I moved forward. My canines lengthened, throat tightening, and I allowed myself a shudder of anticipation.

I lowered my mouth to the man's throat, scraped my canines over the skin, tasting, preparing. Then, with one swift bite, my mouth filled with—

I jerked back, almost choking. I resisted the urge to spit, and forced—with effort—the mouthful down, my stomach revolting in disgust.

It tasted like . . . blood.

When I became a vampire, I thought this would be the most unbearable part: drinking blood. But the moment that first drop of blood touched my tongue, I'd realized my worries had been for naught. There was no word for the taste; no human memory that came close. I can only say that it was so perfect a food that I could never tire of it nor wish for something else.

But this tasted like *blood*, like my human memory of it. Once, before I'd completed the transition to vampire, I'd filled a goblet with cow's blood and forced it down, preparing for my new life. I could still taste the thick, metallic fluid that had coated my mouth and tongue, then sat in my stomach for no more than a minute before returning the way it had gone down.

Now, after only a mouthful of this man's blood, I had to clamp my mouth shut to keep from gagging. Aaron dropped the man and grabbed for me. I waved him aside.

"I swallowed wrong."

I rubbed my throat, lips curving in a moue of annoyance, then looked around and found the man at my feet. I steeled myself and bent. Aaron crouched to lift the man for me, but I motioned him back and shielded my face, so he wouldn't see my reaction. Then I forced my mouth to the man's throat.

The bleeding had already stopped. I bit his neck again, my nails digging into my palms, eyes closed, letting the disgusting taste fill my mouth, then swallowing. Drink. Swallow. Drink. Swallow. My nails broke my skin, but I felt no pain. I wished I could, if only to give me something else to think about.

It wasn't just the taste. That I could struggle past. But my whole body rebelled at the very sensation of the blood filling my stomach, screaming at me to stop, as if what I was doing was unnatural, even dangerous.

I managed one last swallow. And then . . . I couldn't. I simply couldn't. I hung there, fangs still in the man's neck, willing myself to suck, to fill my mouth, to finish this, mentally screaming, raging against the preposterousness of it. I was a vampire; I drank blood. And even if I didn't want to, by God, I would force every drop down my throat—

My stomach heaved. I swallowed hard.

I could sense Aaron behind me. Hovering. Watching. Worrying.

Another heave. If I took one more sip, I'd vomit and give Aaron reason to worry, to panic, and give *myself* reason to panic.

It was the victim. God only knew what poisons this drug dealer had swimming through his veins and, while such things don't affect vampires, I am a delicate feeder, too sensitive to anomalies in the blood. I've gone hungry rather than drink anything that tastes "off." There was no sense asking Aaron to confirm it—he could swill week-old blood and not notice.

That was it, then. The victim. Just the victim.

I sealed the wound with my tongue and stepped back.

"Cass . . ." Aaron's voice was low with warning. "You need to finish him."

"I—" The word "can't" rose to my lips, but I swallowed it back. I couldn't say that. Wouldn't. This was just another temporary hurdle. I'd rest tonight and find a victim of my own choosing tomorrow.

"He isn't right," I said, then turned and headed down the alley.

After a moment, I heard Aaron pitch the unconscious man into a heap of trash bags and storm off in the opposite direction.

Any other man would have thrown up his hands and left me there. I arrived at my car to find Aaron waiting by the driver's door. I handed him the keys and got in the passenger's side.

At home, as I headed toward my room, Aaron called after me. "I hope you're not going to tell me you're tired again."

"No, I'm taking a bath to scrub off the filth of that alley. Then, if you aren't ready to retire, we could have a glass of wine, perhaps light the fire. It's getting cool."

He paused, still ready for a fight, but finding no excuse in my words.

"I'll start the fire," he said.

"Thank you."

No more than ten minutes after I got into the tub, the door banged open with such a crash that I started, sloshing bubbles over the side. Aaron barreled in and shoved a small book at me. My appointment book.

"I found this in your desk."

"Keen detective work. Practicing for your next council investigation?"

"*Our* next council investigation."

I reached for my loofah brush. "My mistake. That's what I meant."

"Is it?"

I looked up, trying to understand his meaning, but seeing only rage in his eyes. He was determined to find out what had happened in that alley, and somehow this was his route there. My stomach clenched, as if the blood was still pooled in it, curdling. I wouldn't have this conversation. I wouldn't.

Ostensibly reaching for the loofah brush, I rose, letting the bubbles slide from me. Aaron's gaze dropped from my face. I tucked my legs under, took hold of the side of the tub and started to rise. He let me get halfway up, then put his hand on my head and firmly pushed me down.

I reclined into the tub again, then leaned my head back, floating, breasts and belly peeking from the water. Aaron watched for a moment before tearing his gaze away with a growl.

"Stop that, Cass. I'm not going to run off and I'm not going to be distracted. I want to talk to you."

I sighed. "About my appointment book, I presume."

He lifted it. "Last week. On the day marked 'birthday.' The date you must have planned to make your kill. There's nothing else scheduled."

"Of course not. I keep that day open—"

"But you said you were busy. That's why you didn't do it."

"I don't believe I said that. I said things came up."

"Such as . . . ?"

I raised a leg onto the rim and ran the loofah brush down it. Aaron's eyes followed, but after a second, he forced his gaze back to mine and repeated the question.

I sighed. "Very well. Let's see. On that particular day, it was a midnight end-of-season designer clothing sale. As I was driving out of the city to make my kill, I saw the sign and stopped. By the time I left, it was too late to hunt."

He glowered at me. "That's not funny."

"I didn't say it was."

The glower deepened to a scowl. "You postponed your annual kill to *shop*? Bullshit. Yeah, you like your fancy clothes, and you're cheap as hell. But getting distracted by a clothing sale?" He snorted. "That's like a cop stopping a high speed chase to grab doughnuts."

I went quiet for a moment, then said, as evenly as I could, "Perhaps. But I did."

He searched my eyes, finding the truth there. "Then something's wrong. Very wrong. And you know it."

I shuttered my gaze. "All I know is that you're making too big a deal of this, as always. You take the smallest—"

"Cassandra DuCharme skips her annual kill to go *shopping*? That's not small. That's apocalyptic."

"Oh, please, spare me the—"

He shoved the open book in my face. "Forget the sale. Explain the rest of it. You had nothing scheduled all week. You had no excuse. You didn't forget. You didn't get distracted." His voice dropped as he lowered himself to the edge of the tub. "You have no intention of taking a life."

"You . . . you think I'm trying to kill myself?" I laughed, the sound almost bitter. "Do you forget how I became what I am, Aaron? I *chose* it. I risked everything to get this life, and if you think I'd throw away one minute before my time is up—"

"How you came into this life is exactly why you're hell-bent on leaving it like this." He snagged my gaze and held it. "You cheated death. No, you *beat* it—by sheer goddamned force of will. You said 'I won't die.' And now, when it's coming around again, you're damned well not going to sit back and let it happen. You chose once. You'll choose again."

I paused, looked away, then back at him. "Why are you here, Aaron?"

"I came to fix your wall—"

"At no prompting from me. No hints from me. You came of your own accord, correct?"

"Yeah, but—"

"Then, if I'd planned to let myself die, presumably you wouldn't have seen me again." I met his gaze. "Do you think I would do that? Of everyone I know in this world, would I leave you without saying goodbye?"

His jaw worked, but he said nothing. After a moment, he pushed to his feet and walked out.

I lay in bed, propped on my pillows, staring at the wall. Aaron was right. When the time came, I would leave this vampiric life as I'd come into it: by choice. But this was not that time. There was no doubt of that, no possibility that I was subconsciously trying to end my life. That was preposterous. I had no qualms about suicide. Fears . . . perhaps. Yet no different than my fear of death itself.

When the time came, yes. But I would never be so irresponsible as to end my life before my affairs were in order. My estate would need to be disposed of in advance, given to those I wished to see benefit. Of equal concern was the discovery and disposal of my body. To leave that to chance would be unforgivably irresponsible.

I would make my peace with Aaron and make amends for my betrayal or, at the very least, ensure he understood that whatever I had done to him, the reason for it, the *failing* behind it, had been mine.

Then there was the council. Aaron was already my co-delegate, but I had to ready him to take my senior position and ready the vampire community to accept that change. Moreover, as the senior overall council member, it was my duty to pass on all I knew to Paige, the keeper of records, something I'd been postponing, unwilling to accept that my time was ending.

Ending.

My stomach clenched at the thought. I closed my eyes and shuddered.

I had never lacked for backbone and never stood for the lack of it in others. Now I needed to face and accept this reality. I was dying. Not beginning a lengthy descent, but at the end of the slope.

I now knew how a vampire died. A rebirth date came and we discovered, without warning, that we could not fulfill our end of the bargain. Not *would* not, but *could* not.

If I couldn't overcome this, I would die. Not in decades, but days.

Panic surged, coupled with an overwhelming wave of raw rage. Of all the ways to die, could any be more humiliating in its sublime ridiculousness? Not to die suddenly, existence snuffed out as my time ended. Not to die, beheaded, at the hands of an enemy. Not to grow ill and fade away. Not even to pass in my sleep. Such deaths couldn't be helped, and while I would have raged against that, the injustice of it, such a fate was nothing compared to this—to die because I inexplicably lacked the will to do something I'd done hundreds of times before.

No, that wasn't possible. I wouldn't *let* it be possible.

I would get out of this bed, find a victim, and force myself to drain his blood if I vomited up every mouthful.

I envisioned myself standing, yanking on clothing, striding from the room. . . .

Yet I didn't move.

My limbs felt leaden. Inside, I was spitting mad, snarling and cursing, but my body lay as still and calm as if I'd already passed.

I pushed down the burbling panic.

Consider the matter with care and logic. I should have taken Aaron's victim, while I still had the strength, but now that I'd missed my opportunity, I couldn't chance waiting another day. I'd rest for an hour or so, until Aaron had retired.

Better for him not to know. I wouldn't let him pity and coddle me simply because it was in his nature to help the sick, the weak, the needy. I would not be needy.

I'd stay awake and wait until the house grew quiet. Then I'd do this—alone.

I fixed my gaze on the light, staring at it to keep myself awake. Minutes ticked past, each feeling like an hour. My eyes burned. My body begged for sleep. I refused. It threatened to pull me under even with my eyes wide. I compromised. I'd close them for a moment's rest and then I'd leave.

I shut my eyes and all went dark.

I awoke to the smell of flowers. I usually had some in the house, so the smell came as no surprise, and I drowsily stretched, rested and refreshed.

Then I remembered I hadn't replaced my last flowers, and I was seized by the sudden vision of my corpse lying on my bed, surrounded by funeral wreaths. I bolted upright and found myself staring in horror at a room of flowers . . . before realizing that the fact I was sitting upright would suggest I was not dead.

With a deep sigh, I looked around. Flowers did indeed fill my room. There were at least a dozen bouquets, each a riot of blooms, with no unifying theme of color, shape, or type. I smiled. Aaron.

My feet lit on the cool hardwood as I crossed to a piece of paper propped against the nearest bouquet. An advertisement for flights to France. Beside another was a list of hotels. A picture of the Eiffel Tower adorned a third. Random images of Parisian travel littered the room, again with no obvious theme, simply pages hurriedly printed from websites. Typically Aaron. Making his point with all the finesse of a sledgehammer wielded with equal parts enthusiasm and determination.

Should I still fail to be swayed, he'd scrawled a note with letters two inches high, the paper thrust into a bouquet of roses. Paige had called.

She was still working on that case and needed my help. In smaller letters below, he informed me that today's paper carried another article on the palliative-care patient who wanted to die.

I dressed, then tucked two of the pages into my pocket, and slipped out the side door.

I didn't go to the hospital Aaron had suggested. It was too late for that. If I was having difficulty making this kill, I could not compound that by choosing one that would itself be difficult.

So I returned to the alley where I'd found—and dismissed—my first choice two nights ago. The drunkard wasn't there, of course. No one was. But I traversed the maze of alleys and back roads in search of another victim. I couldn't wait for nightfall. I couldn't risk falling asleep again or I might not wake up.

When an exit door swung open, I darted into an alley to avoid detection and spotted my victim. A woman, sitting in an alcove, surrounded by grocery bags stuffed with what looked like trash but, I presumed, encompassed the sum of her worldly belongings. Behind me, whoever opened that door tossed trash into the alley and slammed the door shut again. The woman didn't move. She stared straight ahead, gaze vacant. Resting before someone told her to move on.

Even as I watched her, evaluated her, and decided she would do, something deep in me threw up excuses. Not old enough. Not sick enough. Too dangerous a location. Too dangerous a time of day. Keep looking. Find someone better, someplace safer. But if I left here, left *her*, I would grow more tired, more distracted, and more disinterested with every passing hour.

She would do. She had to. For once, not a choice I could live with, but the choice that would let me live.

There was no way to approach without the woman seeing me. Unlike Aaron, I didn't like to let my victims see the specter of death approach, but today I had no choice. So I straightened and started toward her, as if it was perfectly natural for a well-dressed middle-aged woman to cut through alleyways.

Out of the corner of my eye, I saw her look up as I passed. She tensed, then relaxed, seeing no threat. I turned, as if just noticing her. Then with a brisk nod, I took a twenty from my wallet.

A cruel ruse? Or making her last memory a pleasant one? Perhaps both. As expected, she smiled, her guard lowering even more. I reached down, but let go of the bill too soon. As it fluttered to the ground, I murmured an apology and bent, as if to retrieve it, but she was already snatching it up. I kept bending, still apologizing . . . and sank my fangs into the back of her neck.

She gave one gasp before the sedative took effect and she fell forward. I tugged her into the alcove, propped her against the wall, and crouched beside her still form.

As my fangs pierced her jugular, I braced myself. The blood filled my mouth, as thick, hot, and horrible as the drug dealer's the night before. My throat tried to seize up, rejecting it, but I swallowed hard. Another mouthful. Another swallow. Drink. Swallow. Drink. Swallow.

My stomach heaved. I pulled back from the woman, closed my eyes, lifted my chin, and swallowed the blood. Another heave, and my mouth filled, the taste too horrible to describe. I gritted my teeth and swallowed.

With every mouthful now, some came back up. I swallowed it again. Soon my whole body was shaking, my brain screaming that this wasn't right, that I was killing myself, drowning.

My stomach gave one violent heave, my throat refilling. I clamped my hand to my mouth, eyes squeezed shut as I forced myself to swallow the regurgitated blood.

Body shaking, I crouched over her again. I opened my eyes and saw the woman lying there. I couldn't do this. I couldn't—

One hand still pressed to my mouth, I tugged the pages from my pocket. I unfolded them and forced myself to look. Paris. Aaron. Paige. The council. I wasn't done yet. Soon . . . but not yet.

I squeezed my eyes shut, then slammed my fangs into the woman's throat and drank.

Her pulse started to fade. My stomach was convulsing now, body trembling so hard I could barely keep my mouth locked on her neck. Even as I pushed on, seeing the end in sight, I knew this wasn't success. I'd won only the first round of a match I was doomed to lose.

The last drops of blood filled my mouth. Her heart beat slower, and slower, then . . . stopped.

Another life taken. Another year to live.

It's My Birthday, Too

Jim Butcher

Jim Butcher is the author of The Dresden Files and the Codex Alera series. A martial arts enthusiast, Jim enjoys fencing, singing, bad science fiction movies, and live-action gaming. He lives in Missouri with his wife, son, and a vicious guard dog.

"Hey, Miyagi-san," my apprentice said. Her jeans still dripped with purple-brown mucus. "You think the dry cleaners can get this out?"

I threw my car keys down on my kitchen counter, leaned my slimed, rune-carved wooden staff next to them, and said, "The last time I took something stained by a slime golem to a cleaner, the owner burned his place down the next day and tried to collect on the insurance."

Molly, my apprentice, was just barely out of her teens, and it was impossible not to notice what great legs she had when she stripped out of her trendily mangled jeans. She wrinkled her nose as she tossed them into the kitchen trash can. "Have I told you how much I love the wizard business, Harry?"

"Neither of us is in the hospital, kid. This was a good day at work." I took my mantled leather duster off. It was generously covered in splatters of the sticky, smelly mucus as well. I toted it over to the fireplace in my basement apartment, which I keep going during the winter. Given that I have to live without the benefits of electricity, it's necessary. I made sure the fire was burning strongly and tossed the coat in.

"Hey!" Molly said. "Not the coat!"

"Relax," I told her. "The spells on it should protect it. They'll bake the slime hard and I'll chisel it off tomorrow."

"Oh, good. I like the coat." The girl subsided as she tossed her secondhand combat boots and socks into my trash after her ruined jeans. She was tall for a woman and built like a schoolboy's fantasy of the Scandinavian exchange student. Her hair was shoulder length and the color of white gold, except for the tips, which had been dyed in a blend of blue, red, and purple. She'd lost a couple of the piercings she'd previously worn on her face, and was now down to only one eyebrow, one nostril, her tongue, and her lower lip. She went over to the throw rug in the middle of my living room floor, hauled it to one side, and opened the trapdoor leading down to my lab in the subbasement. She lit a candle in the fire, wrinkling her nose at the stink from the greasy smoke coming up from my coat, and padded down the stepladder stairs into the lab.

Mouse, my pet Sabertoothed Retriever, padded out of my bedroom and spread his doggy jaws in a big yawn, wagging his shaggy gray tail. He took one step toward me, then froze as the smell of the mucus hit his nose. The big gray dog turned around at once and padded back into the bedroom.

"Coward!" I called after him. I glanced up at Mister, my tomcat, who drowsed upon the top of my heaviest bookshelf, catching the updraft from the fireplace. "At least you haven't deserted me."

Mister glanced at me, and then gave his head a little shake as the pungent smoke from the fireplace rose to him. He flicked his ears at me, obviously annoyed, and descended from the bookshelf with gracefully offended dignity to follow Mouse into the relative aromatic safety of my bedroom.

"Wimp," I muttered. I eyed my staff. It was crusty with the ichor. I'd have to take it off with sandpaper and repair the carvings. I'd probably have to do the blasting rod, too. Stupid freaking amateurs, playing with things they didn't understand. Slime golems are just disgusting.

Molly thumped back up the stairs, now dressed in her backup clothes. Her experiences in training with me had taught her that lesson about six months in, and she had a second set of clothing stored in a gym bag underneath the little desk I let her keep in the lab. She came up in one of those black broomstick skirts that's supposed to look wrinkled and Doc Martens, inappropriate for the winter weather but way less inappropriate than black athletic panties. "Harry, are you going to be able to drive me home?"

I frowned and checked the clock. After nine. Too late for a young woman to trust herself to Chicago's public transportation. Given Molly's skills, she probably wouldn't be in any real danger, but it's best not to tempt fate. "Could you call your folks?"

She shook her head. "On Valentine's Day, are you kidding? They'll have barricaded themselves upstairs and forced the older kids to wear the little ones out so that they'll sleep through the noise." Molly shuddered. "I'm not interrupting them. Way too disturbing."

"Valentine's Day," I groaned. "Dammit."

"What?"

"Oh, I forgot, what with the excitement. It's, uh, someone's birthday. I got them a present and wanted to get it to them today."

"Oh?" Molly chirped. "Who?"

I hesitated for a minute, but Molly had earned a certain amount of candor—and trust. "Thomas," I said.

"The vampire?" Molly asked.

"Yeah," I said.

"Wow, Harry," she said, blue eyes sparkling. "That's odd. I mean, why would you get *him* a birthday present?" She frowned prettily. "I mean, you didn't get my dad one, and you're friends with him, and he's a Knight of the Sword and one of the good guys, and he's saved your life about twenty times and all."

"More like four times," I said testily. "And I do Christmas for hi—"

Molly was looking at me, a smug smile on her face.

"You figured it out," I said.

"That Thomas was your brother?" Molly asked innocently. "Yep."

I blinked at her. "How?"

"I've seen you two fight." She lifted both pale eyebrows. "What? Have you *seen* how many brothers and sisters I have? I know my sibling conflicts."

"Hell's bells," I sighed. "Molly—"

She lifted a hand. "I know, boss. I know. Big secret; safe with me." Her expression turned serious, and she gave me a look that was very knowing for someone so young. "Family is important."

I'd grown up in a succession of orphanages and foster homes. "Yeah," I said, "it is."

She nodded. "So you haven't given family presents much. And your brother doesn't exactly have a ton of people bringing him presents on his birthday, does he?"

I just looked at her for a second. Molly was growing up into a person I thought I was going to like.

"No," I said, quietly. "I haven't and he doesn't."

"Well then," she said, smiling. "Let's go give him one."

I frowned at the intercom outside Thomas's apartment building and said, "I don't get it. He's always home this time of night."

"Maybe he's out to dinner," Molly said, shivering in the cold—after all, her backup clothing had been summer wear.

I shook my head. "He limits himself pretty drastically when it comes to exposing himself to the public."

"Why?"

"He's a White Court vampire, an incubus," I said. "Pretty much every woman who looks at him gets ideas."

Molly coughed delicately. "Oh. It's not just me, then."

"No. I followed him around town once. It was like watching one of those campy cologne commercials."

"But he *does* go out, right?"

"Sure."

She nodded and immediately started digging into her backpack. "Then maybe we could use a tracking spell and run him down. I think I've got some materials we can use."

"Me, too," I said, and produced two quarters from my pocket, holding them up between my fingers with slow, ominous flair, like David Blaine.

Then I took two steps to the pay phone next to the apartment building's entrance, plugged the coins in, and called Thomas's cell phone.

Molly gave me a level look and folded her arms.

"Hey," I told her as it rang. "We're wizards, kid. We have trouble using technology. Doesn't mean we can't be smart about it."

Molly rolled her eyes and muttered to herself, and I paid attention to the phone call.

"'Allo," Thomas answered, the word thick with the French accent he used in his public persona.

"Hello, France?" I responded. "I found a dead mouse in my can of French roast coffee, and I've called to complain. I'm an American, and I refuse to stand for that kind of thing from you people."

My half brother sighed. "A moment, please," he said in his accent. I could hear music playing and people talking behind him. A party? A door clicked shut and he said, without any accent, "Hey, Harry."

"I'm standing outside your apartment in the freaking snow with your birthday present."

"That won't do you much good," he said. "I'm not there."

"Being a professional detective, I had deduced that much," I said.

"A birthday present, huh?" he said.

"I get much colder and I'm going to burn it for warmth."

He laughed. "I'm at the Woodfield Mall in Schamburg."

I glanced at my watch. "This late?"

"Uh-huh. I'm doing a favor for one of my employees. I'll be here until midnight or so. Look, just come back tomorrow evening."

"No," I said stubbornly. "Your birthday is today. I'll drive there."

"Uh," Thomas said. "Yeah. I guess, uh. Okay."

I frowned. "What are you doing out there?"

"Gotta go." He hung up on me.

I traded a look with Molly. "Huh."

She tilted her head. "What's going on?"

I turned and headed back for the car. "Let's find out."

Woodfield Mall is the largest such establishment in the state, but its parking lots were all but entirely empty. The mall had been closed for more than an hour.

"How are we supposed to find him?" Molly asked.

I drove my car, the beat-up old Volkswagen Bug I had dubbed the Blue Beetle, around for a few minutes. "There," I said, nodding at a white sedan parked among a dozen other vehicles, the largest concentration of such transport left at the mall. "That's his car." I started to say something else but stopped myself before I wasted an opportunity to Yoda the trainee. "Molly, tell me what you see."

She scrunched up her nose, frowning, as I drove through the lot to park next to Thomas's car. The tires crunched over the thin dusting of snow that had frosted itself over scraped asphalt, streaks of salt and ice melt, and stubborn patches of ice. I killed the engine. It ticked for a few seconds, and then the car filled with the kind of soft, heavy silence you only get on a winter night with snow on the ground.

"The mall is closed," Molly said. "But there are cars at this entrance. There is a single section of lights on inside when the rest of them are out. I think one of the shops is lit inside. There's no curtain down over it, even though the rest of the shops have them."

"So what should we be asking?" I prompted.

"What is Thomas doing, in a group, in a closed mall, on Valentine's Day night?" Her tone rose at the end, questioning.

"Good; the significance of the date might mean something," I said. "But the real question is this: Is it a coincidence that the exterior security camera facing that door is broken?"

Molly blinked at me, then frowned, looking around.

I pointed a finger up. "Remember to look in all three dimensions. Human instincts don't tend toward checking up above us or directly at our own feet, in general. You have to make yourself pick up the habit."

Molly frowned and then leaned over, peering up through the Beetle's window to the tall streetlamp pole above us.

Maybe ten feet up, there was the square, black metal housing of a security camera. Several bare wires dangled beneath it, their ends connected to nothing. I'd seen it as I pulled the car in.

My apprentice drew in a nervous breath. "You think something is happening?"

"I think that we don't have enough information to make any assumptions," I said. "It's probably nothing. But let's keep our eyes open."

No sooner had the words left my mouth than two figures stepped out of the night, walking briskly down the sidewalk outside the mall toward the lighted entrance.

They both wore long black capes with hoods.

Not your standard wear for Chicago shoppers.

Molly opened her mouth to stammer something.

"Quiet," I hissed. "Do not move."

The two figures went by only thirty or forty feet away. I caught a glimpse of a very, very pale face within one of the figure's hoods, eyes sunken into the skull like pits. They both turned to the door without so much as glancing at us, opened it as though they expected it to be unlocked, and proceeded inside.

"All right," I said quietly. "It might be something."

"Um," Molly said. "W-were those v-vampires?"

"Deep breaths, kid," I told her. "Fear isn't stupid, but don't let it control you. I have no idea what they were." I made sure my old fleece-lined heavy denim coat was buttoned up and got out of the car.

"Uh. Then where are you going?" she asked.

"Inside," I said, walking around to the Beetle's trunk. I unwrapped the wire that had held it closed ever since a dozen vehicular mishaps ago. "Whatever they are, Thomas doesn't know about them. He'd have said something."

I couldn't see her through the lifted hood, but Molly rolled down the window enough to talk to me. "B-but you don't have your staff or blasting rod or coat or anything. They're all back at your apartment."

I opened the case that held my .44 revolver and the box that held my ammunition, slipped shells into the weapon, and put it in my coat pocket. I dropped some extra rounds into the front pocket of my jeans and shut the hood. "They're only toys, Padawan." Familiar, capable, proven toys that I felt naked without, but a true wizard shouldn't absolutely rely on them—or teach his apprentice to do so. "Stay here, start up the car, and be ready to roll if we need to leave in a hurry."

"Right," she said, and wriggled over into the driver's seat. Give Molly credit, she might be nervous, but she had learned the job of wheelman—sorry, political correctioners, wheel*person*—fairly well.

I kept my right hand in my coat pocket, on the handle of my gun, hunched my shoulders against a small breath of frozen wind, and hurried to the mall entrance, my shoes crunching and squeaking on the little coating of snow. I walked toward the doors like I owned them, shoved them open like any shopper, and got a quick look around.

The mall was dark, except for the entrance and that single open shop—a little bistro with tinted windows that would have been dimly lit even when all the lights were on. I could see figures seated at tables inside and at a long dining counter and bar. They wore lots of black, and none of them looked much older than Molly, though the dim lights revealed few details.

I narrowed my eyes a bit, debating. Vampires gave off a certain amount of energy that someone like me could sense, but depending on which breed you were talking about, that energy could vary. Sometimes my sense of an approaching vampire was as overtly creepy as a child's giggle coming from an open grave. Other times there was barely anything at all, and it registered on my senses as something as subtle as a simple, instinctive dislike for the creature in question. For White Court vamps like my half brother, there was nothing at all, unless they were doing something overtly vampiric. From outside the shop, I couldn't tell anything.

Assuming they were vampires at all—which was a fairly large assumption. They didn't meet up in the open like this. Vampires don't apologize to the normal world for existing, but they don't exactly run around auditioning for the latest reality TV shows, either.

One way to find out. I opened the door to the bistro, hand on my gun, took a step inside, holding the door open in case I needed to flee, and peered around warily at the occupants. The nearest was a pair of young men, speaking earnestly at a table over two cups of what looked like coffee and . . .

And they had acne. Not like disfiguring acne, or anything, just a few zits.

In case no one's told you, here's a monster-hunting tip for free: vampires have little to no need for Clearasil.

Seen in that light, the two young men's costumes looked like exactly that. Costumes. They had two big cloaks, dripping a little meltwater, hung over the backs of their chairs, and I caught the distinctive aroma of weed coming from their general direction. Two kids, slipping out from the gathering to toke up and come back inside. One of them produced a candy bar from a pocket and tore into it, to the reassurance of the people who make Clearasil, I'm sure.

I looked around the room. More people. Mostly young, mostly with the thinness that goes with youth, as opposed to the leanly cadaverous kind that goes with being a bloodsucking fiend. They were mostly dressed in similar costume-style clothing, unless there had been a big sale at Goth-R-Us.

I felt my shoulders sag in relief, and I slipped my hand out of my pocket. Any time one of my bouts of constructive paranoia didn't pan out was a good time.

"Sir," said a gruff voice from behind me. "The mall is closed. You want to tell me what you're doing here?"

I turned to face a squat, blocky man with watery blue eyes and no chin. He'd grown a thick, brown gold walrus mustache that emphasized rather than distracted from the lack. He had a high hairline, a brown uniform, and what looked like a cop's weapon belt until you saw that he had a walkie-talkie where the sidearm would be, next to a tiny can of mace. His name tag read: *Raymond.*

"Observing suspicious activity, Raymond," I said, and hooked my chin vaguely back at the bistro. "See that? People hanging around in the mall after hours. Weird."

He narrowed his eyes. "Wait. Don't I know you?"

I pursed my lips and thought. "Oh, right. Six, seven years ago, at Shoegasm."

He grunted in recognition. "The phony psychic."

"Consultant," I responded. "And from what I hear, their inventory stopped shrinking. Which hadn't happened before I showed up."

Raymond gave me a look that would have cowed lesser men. Much,

much lesser men. Like maybe fourth graders. "If you aren't with the group, you're gone. You want to leave, or would you rather I took care of it for you?"

"Stop," I said, "you're scaring me."

Raymond's mustache quivered. He apparently wasn't used to people who didn't take him seriously. Plus, I was much, much bigger than he was.

"'Allo, 'Ah-ree," came my brother's voice from behind me.

I turned to find Thomas there, dressed in tight black pants and a blousy red silk shirt. His shoulder-length hair was tied back in a tail with a matching red ribbon. His face didn't look much like mine, except around the eyes and maybe the chin. Thomas was good looking the way Mozart was talented. There were people on the covers of magazines and on television and on movie screens who despaired of ever looking as good as Thomas.

On his arm was a slim young girl, quite pretty and wholesome-looking, wearing leather pants that rode low on her hips and a red bikini top, her silky brown hair artfully mussed. I recognized her from Thomas's shop, a young woman named Sarah.

"Harry!" she said. "Oh, it's nice to see you again." She nudged Thomas with her hip. "Isn't it?"

"Always," Thomas said in his French accent, smiling.

"Hello, Mr. Raymond!" Sarah said, brightly.

Raymond scowled at me and asked Sarah, "He with you?"

"But of course," Thomas said, in that annoying French way, giving Raymond his most brilliant smile.

Raymond grunted and took his hand away from the radio. Lucky me. I had evidently been dismissed from Raymond's world. "I was going to tell you that I'm going to be in the parking lot, replacing a camera we've got down, if you need me."

"*Merci,*" Thomas said, still smiling.

Raymond grunted. He gave me a sour look, picked up a toolbox from where he'd set it aside, along with his coat and a stepladder, and headed out to the parking lot.

"'Ah-ree, you know Say-rah," Thomas said.

"Never had the pleasure of an introduction," I said, and offered Sarah my hand.

She took it, smiling. "I take it you aren't here to play Evernight?"

I looked from her to the costumed people. "Oh," I said. "*Oh*, it's a . . . game of some kind, I take it?"

"A larp," she said.

I looked blank for a second. "Is that like a lark?"

She grinned. "Larp," she repeated. "Live action role play."

"Live action . . . vampire role play, I guess," I said. I looked at Thomas. "And this is why you are here?"

Thomas gave me a sunny smile and nodded. "She asked me to pretend to be a vampire, just for tonight," he said. "And straight."

No wonder he was having a good time.

Sarah beamed at me. "Thomas *never* talks about his, ah, personal life. So you're quite the man of mystery at the shop. We all speculate about you, all the time."

I'll just bet they did. There were times when my brother's cover as a flamingly gay hairdresser really grated. And it wasn't like I could go around telling people we were related—not with the White Council of Wizards at war with the Vampire Courts.

"How nice," I told Sarah. I was never getting out of the role people had assumed for me around Thomas. "Thomas, can we talk for a moment?"

"*Mais oui*," he said. He smiled at Sarah, took her hand, and gave her a little bow over it. She beamed fondly at him, and then hurried back inside.

I watched her go, in her tight pants and skimpy top, and sighed. She had an awfully appealing curve of back and hip, and just enough bounce to make the motion pleasant, and there was no way I could ever even think about flirting with her.

"Roll your tongue back up into your mouth before someone notices," Thomas said, sotto voce. "I've got a cover to keep."

"Tell them I'm larping like I'm straight," I said, and we turned to walk down the entry hall, a little away from the bistro. "Pretending to be a vampire, huh?"

"It's fun," Thomas said. "I'm like a guest star on the season finale."

I eyed him. "Vampires aren't fun and games."

"I know that," Thomas said. "You know that. But *they* don't know that."

"You aren't doing them any favors," I said.

"Lighten up," Thomas said. The words were teasing, but there were serious undertones to his voice. "They're having fun, and I'm helping. I don't get a chance to do that very often."

"By making light of something that is a very real danger."

He stopped and faced me. "They're *innocent*, Harry. They don't know any better. They've never been hurt by a vampire, lost loved ones to a vampire." He lifted his eyebrows. "I thought that was what your people were fighting for in the first place."

I gave him a sour look. "If you weren't my brother, I'd probably tell you that you have some awfully nerdy hobbies."

We reached the front doors. Thomas studied himself in the glass and struck a pose. "True. But I look gorgeous doing them. Besides, Sarah worked eleven Friday to Mondays in a row without a complaint. She earned a favor."

Outside, the snow was thickening. Raymond was atop his ladder, fiddling with the camera. Molly was watching him. I waved until I got her attention, then made a little outline figure of a box with my fingers, and beckoned her. She nodded and killed the engine.

"I came in here expecting trouble. We're lucky I didn't bounce a few of these kids off the ceiling before I realized they weren't something from the dark side."

"Bah," Thomas said. "Never happen. You're careful."

I snorted. "I hope you won't mind if I just give you your present and run."

"Wow," Thomas said. "Gracious much?"

"Up yours," I said, as Molly grabbed the present and hurried in through the cold, shivering all the way. "And Happy Birthday."

He turned to me and gave me a small, genuinely pleased smile. "Thank you."

There was a click of high heels in the hall behind us, and a young woman appeared. She was pretty enough, I suspected, but in the tight black dress, black hose, and with her hair slicked back like that, it was sort of threatening. She gave me a slow, cold look and said, "So. I see that you're keeping low company after all, Ravenius."

Ever suave, I replied, "Uh. What?"

"'Ah-ree," Thomas said.

I glanced at him.

He put his hand flat on the top of his head and said, "Do this."

I peered at him.

He gave me a look.

I sighed and put my hand on the top of my head.

The girl in the black dress promptly did the same thing and gave me a smile. "Oh, right, sorry. I didn't realize."

"I will be back in one moment," Thomas said, his accent back. "Personal business."

"Right," she said, "sorry. I figured Ennui had stumbled onto a subplot." She smiled again, then took her hand off the top of her head, reassumed that cold, haughty expression, and stalked clickety-clack back to the bistro.

I watched her go, turned to my brother while we both stood there with our hands flat on top of our heads, elbows sticking out like chicken wings, and said, "What does this mean?"

"We're out of character," Thomas said.

"Oh," I said. "And not a subplot."

"If we had our hands crossed over our chests," Thomas said, "we'd be invisible."

"I missed dinner," I said. I put my other hand on my stomach. Then, just to prove that I could, I patted my head and rubbed my stomach. "Now I'm out of character—and hungry."

"You're always hungry. How is that out of character?"

"True," I said. I frowned, and looked back. "What's taking Molly—"

My apprentice stood with her back pressed to the glass doors, faced away from me. She stood rigid, one hand pressed to her mouth. Thomas's birthday present, in its pink and red Valentine's Day wrapping paper, lay on its side among grains of snowmelt on the sidewalk. Molly trembled violently.

Thomas was a beat slow to catch on to what was happening. "Isn't that skirt a little light for the weather? Look, she's freezing."

Before he got to "skirt," I was out the door. I seized Molly and dragged her inside, eyes on the parking lot. I noticed two things.

First, that Raymond's ladder was tipped over and lay on its side in the parking lot. Flakes of snow were already gathering upon it. In fact, the snow was coming down more and more heavily, despite the weather forecast that had called for clearing skies.

Second, there were droplets of blood on my car and the cars immediately around it, the ones closest to Raymond's ladder. They were rapidly freezing and glittered under the parking lot's lamps like tiny, brilliant rubies.

"What?" Thomas asked, as I brought Molly back in. "What is—" He stared out the windows for a second and answered the question for himself. "Crap."

"Yeah," I said. "Molly?"

She gave me a wild-eyed glance, shook her head once, and then bowed it and closed her eyes, speaking in a low, repetitive whisper.

"What the hell?" Thomas said.

"She's in psychic shock," I said quietly.

"Never seen you in psychic shock," my brother said.

"Different talents. I blow things up. Molly's a sensitive, and getting more so," I told him. "She'll snap herself out of it, but she needs a minute."

"Uh-huh," Thomas said quietly. He stared intently at the shuddering young woman, his eyes shifting colors slightly, from deep gray to something paler.

"Hey," I said to him. "Focus."

He gave his head a little shake, his eyes gradually darkening again. "Right. Come on. Let's get her a chair and some coffee and stop standing around in front of big glass windows making targets of ourselves."

We did, dragging her into the bistro and to the table nearest the door, where Thomas could stand watching the darkness while I grabbed the girl some coffee from a dispenser, holding my hand on top of my silly head the whole while.

Molly got her act together within a couple of minutes after I sat down. It surprised me: despite my casual words to Thomas, I hadn't seen her that badly shaken up before. She grabbed at the coffee, shaking, and slurped some.

"Okay, grasshopper," I said. "What happened?"

"I was on the way in," she replied, her voice distant and oddly flat. "The security man. S-something killed him." A hint of something desperate crept into her voice. "I f-felt him die. It was horrible."

"What?" I asked her. "Give me some details to work with."

Molly shook her head rapidly. "D-didn't see. It was too fast. I sensed something moving behind me—m-maybe a footstep. Then there was a quiet sound and h-he *died*. . . ." Her breaths started coming rapidly again.

"Easy," I told her, keeping my voice in the steady cadence I'd used when teaching her how to maintain self-control under stress. "Breathe. Focus. Remember who you are."

"Okay," she said, several breaths later. "Okay."

"This sound. What was it?"

She stared down at the steam coming up off her coffee. "I . . . a thump, maybe. Lighter."

"A snap?" I asked.

She grimaced but nodded. "And I turned around, fast as I could. But he was gone. I didn't *see* anything there, Harry."

Thomas, ten feet away, could hear our quiet conversation as clearly as if he'd been sitting with us. "Something grabbed Raymond," he said. "Something moving fast enough to cross her whole field of vision in a second or two. It didn't stop moving when it took him. She probably heard his neck breaking from the whiplash."

Not much to say to that. The whole concept was disturbing as hell.

Thomas glanced back at me and said, "It's a great way to do a grab and snatch if you're fast enough. My father showed me how it was done once." His head whipped around toward the parking lot.

I felt myself tense. "What?"

"The streetlights just went out."

I sat back in my chair, thinking furiously. "Only one reason to do that."

"To blind us," Thomas said. "Prevent anyone from reaching the vehicles."

"Also keeps anyone outside from seeing what is happening here," I said. "How are you guys using this place after hours?"

"Sarah's uncle owns it," Thomas said.

"Get her," I said, rising to take up watching the door. "Hurry."

Thomas brought her over to me a moment later. By the time he did, the larpers had become aware that something was wrong, and their awkwardly sinister role-playing dwindled into an uncertain silence as Sarah hurried over. Before, I had watched her and her scarlet bikini top in appraisal. Now I couldn't help but think how slender and vulnerable it made her neck look.

"What is it?" Sarah asked me.

"Trouble," I said. "We may be in danger, and I need you to answer a few questions for me, right now."

She opened her mouth and started to ask me something.

"First," I said, interrupting her, "do you know how many security men are present at night?"

She blinked at me for a second. Then she said, "Uh, four before closing, two after. But the two who leave are usually here until midnight, doing maintenance and some of the cleaning."

"Where?"

She shook her head. "The security office, in administration."

"Right," I said. "This place have a phone?"

"Of course."

"Take me to it."

She did, back in the little place's tiny kitchen. I picked it up, got a dial tone, and slammed Murphy's phone number across the numbers. If the bad guys, whoever or whatever they were, were afraid of attracting attention from the outside world, I might be able to avoid the entire situation by calling in lots of police cars and flashy lights.

The phone rang once, twice.

And then it went dead, along with the lights, the music playing on the speakers, and the constant blowing sigh of the heating system.

Several short, breathy screams came from the front of the bistro, and I heard Thomas shout for silence and call, "Harry?"

"The security office," I said to Sarah. "Where is it?"

"Um. It's at the far end of the mall from here."

"Easy to find?"

"No," she said, shaking her head. "You have to go through the administrative hall and—"

I shook my head. "You can show me. Come on." I stalked out to the front room of the bistro. "Thomas? Anything?"

All the larpers had gathered in close, herd instinct kicking in under the tension. Thomas stepped closer to me so that he could answer me under his breath.

"Nothing yet," Thomas said. "But I saw something moving out there."

I grunted. "Here's the plan. Molly, Sarah, and me are going to go down to the security office and try to reach someone."

"Bad idea," Thomas said. "We need to get out of here."

"We're too vulnerable. They're between us and the cars," I said. "Whatever they are. We'll never make it out all the way across the parking lot without getting caught."

"Fine," he said. "You fort up here and I'll go."

"No. Once we're gone, you'll try to get through to the cops on a cell phone. There's not a prayer of getting one to work if Molly and me are anywhere nearby—not with both of us this nervous."

He didn't like that answer, but he couldn't refute it. "All right," he said, grimacing. "Watch your back."

I nodded to him and raised my voice. "All right, everyone. I'm not sure exactly what is going on here, but I'm going to go find security. I want everyone to stay here until I get back and we're sure it's safe."

There was a round of halfhearted protests at that, but Thomas quelled them with a look. It wasn't an angry or threatening look. It was simply a steady gaze.

Everyone shut up.

I headed out with Molly and Sarah in tow, and as we stepped out of the bistro, there was an enormous crashing sound, and a car came flying sideways through the glass wall of the entranceway about eight feet off the ground. It hit the ground, broken glass and steel foaming around it like crashing surf, bounced with a shockingly loud crunch, and tumbled ponderously toward us, heralded by a rush of freezing air.

Molly was already moving, but Sarah only stood there staring incredulously as the car came toward us. I grabbed her around the waist and all but hauled her off her feet, dragging her away. I ran straight away from the oncoming missile, which was not the smartest way to go—but since a little perfume kiosk was blocking my path, it was the *only* way.

I was fast, and we got a little bit lucky. I pulled Sarah past the kiosk just as the car hit it. Its momentum was almost gone by the time it hit, and it crashed to a halt, a small wave of safety glass washing past our shoes. Sarah wobbled and nearly fell. I caught her and kept going. She started to scream or shout or ask a question—but I clapped my hand over her mouth and hissed, "Quiet!"

I didn't stop until we were around the corner and the crashing racket was coming to a halt. Then I stopped with my back against the wall and got Sarah's attention.

I didn't speak. I raised one finger to my lips with as much physical emphasis as I could manage. Sarah, trembling violently, nodded at me. I turned to give the same signal to Molly, who looked pale but in control of herself. She nodded as well, and we turned and slipped away from that arm of the mall.

I listened as hard as I could, which is actually quite hard. It's a talent I seem to have developed, maybe because I'm a wizard, and maybe just because some people can hear really well. It was difficult to make out anything at all, much less any kind of detail, but I was sure I heard one thing—footsteps, coming in the crushed door of the mall, crunching on broken glass and debris.

Something fast enough to snap a man's neck with the whiplash of its passage and strong enough to throw that car through a wall of glass had just walked into the mall behind us. I figured it was a very, very good idea not to let it know we were there and sneaking away.

We got away with it, walking slowly and silently out through the mall, which yawned all around us, three levels of darkened stores, deserted shops, and closed metal grates and doors. I stopped a dozen shops later, after we'd gone past the central plaza of the mall and were far enough away for the space to swallow up quiet conversation.

"Oh my God," Sarah whimpered, her voice a strangled little whisper. "Oh my God. What is happening? Is it terrorists?"

I probably would have had a more suave answer if she hadn't been pressed up against my side, mostly naked from the hips up, warm and lithe and trembling. The adrenaline rush that had hit me when the car nearly smashed us caught up to me, and it was suddenly difficult to keep from shivering, myself. I had a sudden, insanely intense need to rip off the strings on that red bikini top and kiss her, purely for the sake of how good it would feel. All things considered, though, it would have been less than appropriate. "Uh," I mumbled, forcing myself to look back the way we'd come. "They're . . . bad guys of some kind, yeah. Are you hurt?"

"No," Sarah said.

"Molly?" I asked.

"I'm fine," my apprentice answered.

"The security office," I said.

Sarah stared at me for a second, her eyes still wide. "But . . . but I don't understand why—"

I put my hand firmly over her mouth. "Sarah," I said, meeting her eyes for as long as I dared. "I've been in trouble before, and I know what I'm doing. I need you to trust me. All right?"

Her eyes widened for a second. She reached up to lightly touch my wrist, and I let her push my hand gently away from her mouth. She swallowed and nodded once.

"There's no time. We have to find the security office now."

"A-all right," she said. "This way."

She led us off and we followed her, creeping through the cavernous dimness of the unlit mall. Molly leaned in close to me to whisper, "Even if we get the security guards, what are they going to do against something that can do *that*?"

"They'll have radios," I whispered back. "Cell phones. They'll know all the ways out. If we can't call in help, they'll give us the best shot of getting these people out of here in one—"

Lights began flickering on and off. Not blinking, not starting up and shutting down in rhythm, but irregularly. First they came on over a section of the third floor for a few seconds. Then they went out. A few seconds later, it was a far section of the second floor. Then they went out. Then light shone from one of the distant wings for a moment and vanished again. It was like watching a child experiment with the switches.

Then the PA system let out a crackle and a little squeal of feedback. It shut off again and came back on. "Testing," said a dry, rasping voice over the speakers. "Testing one, two, three."

Sarah froze in place, and then backed up warily, looking at me. I stepped up next to her, and she pressed in close to me, shivering.

"There," said the voice. It was a horrible thing to listen to—like Linda Blair's impression of a demon-possessed victim, only less melodious. "I'm sure you all can hear me now."

And I'd heard such a voice before. "Oh, hell," I breathed.

"This is Constance," continued the voice. "Constance Bushnell. I'm sure you all remember me."

I glanced at Molly, who shook her head. Sarah looked frightened and confused, but when she caught my look, she shook her head, too.

"You might also remember me," she continued, "As Drulinda." And then the voice started singing "Happy Birthday." The tune wasn't even vaguely close to the actual song, but the lyrics, sung "to me," were unmistakable.

Sarah's eyes had widened. "Drulinda?"

"Who the hell is Drulinda?" I asked.

Sarah shook her head. "One of our characters. But her player ran away from home or something."

"And you didn't recognize her actual name?"

Sarah gave me a slightly guilty glance. "Well. I never played with her much. She wasn't really very, you know. Popular."

"Uh-huh," I said. "Tell me whatever you can about her."

She shook her head. "Um. About five four, sort of . . . plain. You know, not ugly or anything, but not really pretty. Maybe a little heavy."

"Not that," I sighed. "Tell me something *important* about her. People make fun of her?"

"Some did," she said. "I never liked it, but . . ."

"Crap." I looked at Molly and said, "Code Carrie. We're in trouble."

The horrible, dusty song came to an end. "It's been a year since I left you," Drulinda's voice said. "A year since I found what all you whining losers were looking for. And I decided to give myself a present." There was a horrible pause and then the voice said, "You. All of you."

"Code what?" Molly asked me.

I shook my head. "Sarah, do you know where the announcement system is?"

"Yes," Sarah said. "Administration. Right by—"

"The security office," I sighed.

Drulinda's voice continued. "The entrances are closed and watched. But you should feel free to run for them. You all taste *so* much better when you've had time to be properly terrified. I've *so* been looking forward to seeing your reaction to the new me."

With that, the PA system shut off, but a second later, it started playing music: "Only You," by the Platters.

"Molly," I hissed, suddenly realizing the danger. "Veil us, *now.*"

She blinked at me, then nodded, bowed her head with a frown of concentration, and folded her arms across her chest. I felt her gather up her will and release it with a word and a surge of energy that made the air sparkle like diamond dust for a half second.

Inside the veil, the air suddenly turned a few degrees cooler, and the area outside it seemed to become even more dim than it had been a second before. I could sense the delicate tracery of the veil's magic in the air around us, though I knew that, from the other side, none of that would be detectable—assuming Molly had done it correctly, of course. Veils were one of her strongest areas, and I was gambling our lives that she had gotten it right.

Not more than a breath or two later, there was a swift pattering sound and a dim blur in the shadows—which ceased moving abruptly maybe twenty feet away and revealed the presence of a vampire of the Black Court.

Drulinda, or so I presumed her to be, was dressed in dark jeans, a red knit sweater, and a long black leather coat. If she'd been heavy in life, death had taken care of that problem for her. She was sunken and shriveled, as bony and dried up as the year-old corpse she now was. Unlike the older vamps of her breed, she still had most of her hair, though it had clearly not been washed or styled. Most of the Black

Court that I'd run into had never been terribly body conscious. I suppose once you'd seen it rot, there just wasn't much more that could happen to sway your opinion of it, either way.

Unlike the older vampires I'd faced, she stank. I don't mean that she carried a little whiff of the grave along with her. I mean she smelled like a year-old corpse that still had a few juicy corners left and wasn't entirely done returning to the earth. It was noxious enough to make me gag—and I'd spent my day tracking down and dismantling a freaking slime golem.

She stood there for a moment, while the Platters went through the first verse, looking all around her. She'd sensed something, but she wasn't sure what. The vampire turned a slow circle, her shriveled lips moving in time with the music coming over the PA system, and as she did, two more of the creatures, slower than Drulinda, appeared out of the darkness.

They were freshly made vampires—so much so that for a second, I thought them human. Both men wore brown uniforms identical to Raymond's. Both were stained with blood, and both of them had narrow scoops of flesh missing from the sides of their throats—at the jugular and carotid, specifically. They moved stiffly, making many little twitching motions of their arms and legs, as if struggling against the onset of rigor mortis.

"What is it?" slurred one of them. His voice was ragged but not the horrible parody Drulinda's was.

Her hand blurred, too fast to see. The newborn vampire reacted with inhuman speed, but not nearly enough of it, and the blow threw him from his feet to land on the floor, shattered teeth scattering out from him like coins from a dropped purse. "You can talk," Drulinda rasped, "when I say you can talk. Speak again and I will rip you apart and throw you into Lake Michigan. You can spend eternity down there with no arms, no legs, no light, and no blood."

The vampire, his nose smashed into shapelessness, rose as if he'd just slipped and fallen on his ass. He nodded, his body language twitchy and cringing.

Drulinda's leathery lips peeled back from yellow teeth stained with drying, brownish blood. Then she turned and darted ahead, her footsteps making that light, swift patter on the tiles of the floor. She was gone and around the corner, heading for the bistro, in maybe two or three seconds. The two newbie vampires went after her, if far more slowly.

"Crap," I whispered as they vanished. "Dammit, dammit, dammit."

"What was that, Harry?" Molly whispered.

"Black Court vampires," I replied, trying not to inhale too deeply. The stench was fading, but it wasn't gone. "Some of the fastest, strongest, meanest things out there."

"Vampires?" Sarah hissed, incredulous. She didn't look so good. Her face was turning green. "No, this is, no, no, no—" She broke off and was violently sick. I avoided joining in by the narrowest of margins. Molly had an easier time of it than me, focused as she was on maintaining the veil over us, but I saw her swallow very carefully.

"Okay, Molly," I said quietly. "Listen to me."

She nodded, turning abstracted eyes to me.

"Black Court vampires," I told her. "The ones Stoker's book outed. All their weaknesses—sunlight, garlic, holy water, symbols of faith. Remember?"

She nodded. "Yes."

"Most of the strengths, too. Strong, fast. Don't look them in the eyes." I swallowed. "Don't let them take you alive."

My apprentice's eyes flickered with both apprehension and a sudden, fierce fire. "I understand. What do you want me to do?"

"Keep the veil up. Take Sarah here. Find a shady spot and lay low. This should be over in half an hour, maybe less. By then, there's going to be a ruckus getting people's attention, one way or another."

"But I can—"

"Get me killed trying to cover you," I said firmly. "You aren't in this league, grasshopper. Not yet. I have to move fast. And I have friends here. I won't be alone."

Molly stared at me for a moment, her eyes shining with brief, frustrated tears. Then she nodded once and said, "Isn't there anything I can do?"

I peered at her, then down at her Birkenstocks. "Yeah. Give me your shoes."

Molly hadn't been my apprentice in the bizarre for a year and a half for nothing. She didn't even blink, much less ask questions. She just took off her shoes and handed them to me.

I put a gentle hand on her shoulder, then touched Sarah's face until she lifted her eyes to me. "I don't understand what's happening," she whispered.

"Stay with Molly," I told Sarah. "She's going to take care of you. Do whatever she says. All right?" I frowned down at her expensive black heels. "Gucci?"

"Prada," she said in a numb voice.

Being all manly, I know dick about shoes, but hopefully it wouldn't blow my cover as Thomas's mystery man. "Give them to me."

"All right," she said, and did, too shocked to argue.

Thomas had been right about the larpers. The corpse of Sarah's innocence lay on the floor along with her last meal, and she was taking it pretty hard.

I fought down a surge of anger and rose without another word, padding out from the protection of Molly's veil, shoes gripped in one hand, my gun in the other. The .44 might as well have been Linus's security blanket. It wouldn't do a thing to help me against a vampire of the Black Court—it just made me feel better.

I went as fast as I could without making an enormous racket and stalked up the nearest stairs—a deactivated escalator. Once I'd reached the second level, I took a right and hurried toward Shoegasm.

It was a fairly spacious shop that had originally occupied only a tiny spot, but after ironing out some early troubles, the prosperous little store had expanded into the space beside it. Now, behind a steel mesh security curtain, the store was arranged in an oh-so-trendy fashion and sported several huge signs that went on with a thematically appropriate orgasmic enthusiasm about the store's quality money-back guarantee.

"I am totally underappreciated," I muttered. Then I raised my voice a little, forcing a very slight effort of will, of magic, into the words as I spoke. "Keef! Hey, Keef! It's Harry Dresden!"

I waited for a long moment, peering through the grating, but I couldn't see anything in the dim shadows of the store. I took a chance, slipping the silver pentacle amulet from its chain around my neck, and with a murmur willed a whisper of magic through the piece of jewelry. A soft blue radiance began to emanate from the silver, though I tried to keep the light it let out to a minimum. If Drulinda or her vampire buddies were looking even vaguely in my direction, I was going to stand out like a freaking moron holding the only light in an entire darkened shopping mall.

"Keef!" I called again.

The cobb appeared from an expensive handbag hung over the arm of a dressing dummy wearing a pair of six-hundred-dollar Italian boots. He was a tiny thing, maybe ten inches tall, with a big puff of fine white hair like Albert Einstein. He was dressed in something vaguely approximating nineteenth-century urban European wear—dark trousers, boots, a white shirt, and suspenders. He also wore a leather work belt thick with tiny tools and had a pair of odd-looking goggles pushed up over his forehead.

Keef hopped down from the dressing dummy and hurried across the floor to the security grate. He put on a pair of gloves, pulled out a couple of straps from his work belt, and climbed up the metal grate using a pair of carabiners, nearly as nimble as a squirrel, being very careful not to touch the metal with his bare skin. Keef was a faerie, one of the little folk who dwelled within the shadows and hidden places of our own world, and the touch of steel was painful to him.

"Wizard Dresden," he greeted me in a Germanic accent as he came level with my head. The cobb's voice was pitched low, even for someone as tiny as he. "The market this night danger roams. Here you should not be."

"Don't I know it," I replied. "But there are people in danger."

"Ah," Keef said. "The mortals whom you insist to defend. Unwise that battle is."

"I need your help," I said.

Keef eyed me and gave me a firm shake of his head. "The walking dead very dangerous are. My people's blood it could cost. That I will risk not."

"You owe me, Keef," I growled.

"Our living. Not our lives."

"Have it your way," I said. Then I lifted up one of Sarah's shoes and, without looking away from the little cobb, snapped the heel off.

"Ach!" Keef cried in horror, his little feet slipping off the metal grate. "*Nein!*"

There was a chorus of similar gasps and cries from inside Shoegasm.

I held up the other shoe and did it again.

Keef wailed in protest. All of a sudden, thirty of the little cobbs, male and female, pressed up to the security mesh. All of them had the same frizzy white hair, all of them dressed like something from Oktoberfest, and all of them were horrified.

"*Nein!*" Keef wailed again. "Those are Italian leather! Handmade! What are you doing?"

I took a step to my left and held the broken shoes over a trash can.

The cobbler elves gasped, all together, and froze in place.

"Do not do this," Keef begged me. "Lost all is not. Repaired they can be. Good as new we can fix them. Good as new! Do not throw them away."

I didn't waver. "I know things have been hard for your people since cobblers have gone out of business," I said. "I got you permission for your clan to work here, fixing shoes, in exchange for taking what you need from the vending machine. True?"

"True," Keef said, his eyes on the broken shoes in my hand. "Wizard, over the trash you need not hold them. If dropped they are, trash they become, and touch them we may not. Lost to all will they be. Anything we both will regret let us not do."

Anxious murmurs of agreement rose from the other cobbs.

Enough of the stick. Time to show them the carrot. I held up Molly's battered old Birkenstocks. The sight made several of the more matronly cobbs cluck their tongues in disapproval.

"I helped set you up with a good deal here at Shoegasm," I said. "But I can see you're getting a little crowded. I can get you another good setup—a family, seven kids, mom and dad, all of them active."

The cobbs murmured in sudden excitement.

Keef coughed delicately and said, staring anxiously at the broken heels in my hand, "And the shoes?"

"I'll turn them over to you," I said. "If you help me."

Keef narrowed his eyes. "Slaves to you we are," he snapped. "Threatened and bribed."

"You know the cause I fight for," I said. "I protect mortals. I've never tried to hide that, and I've never lied to you. I need your help, Keef. I'll do what it takes to get it—but you know my reputation by now. I deal fairly with the little folk, and I always show gratitude for their help."

The leader of the cobbs regarded me steadily for a moment.

Nobody likes being strong-armed, not even the little folk, who are used to getting walked on, but I didn't have time for diplomacy.

Keef's gaze kept getting distracted by the shoes, dangling over the trash can, and he made no answer. The other cobbs all waited, clearly taking their cue from Keef.

"Show of good faith, Keef," I said quietly. I took the broken shoes and set them gently on the ground in front of the shop. "I'll trust you and your people to repair them and return them. And I'll pay in pizza."

The cobbs gasped, staring at me as if I'd just offered them a map to El Dorado. I heard one of the younger cobbs exclaim, "*True*, it is!"

"Fleeting, pizza is," Keef said sternly. "Eternal are shoes and leather goods."

"Shoes and leather goods," the rest of the cobbs intoned, tiny voices solemn.

"Few mortals to the little folk show respect, these days," Keef said quietly. "Or trust. True it is that beneath this roof we are crowded. And unto the wizard, debt is owed." He gave the shoes a professional glance and nodded once. "Under your terms, and within our means, our aid is given. Your need unto us speak."

"Scouts," I said at once. "I know there are Black Court vampires in the mall. I need to know exactly how many and exactly where they are."

"Done it will be," Keef barked. "Cobbs!"

There was a little gust of wind, and I was suddenly alone. Oh, and both Sarah's expensive heels and Molly's clunky sandals were gone, the latter right out of my hands and so smoothly that I hadn't even noticed them being taken. I checked, just to be careful, but my own shoes remained safely on my feet, which was a relief. You can't ever be certain with cobbs. The little faeries, at times, could get awfully fixated upon whatever their particular area of concern might be, and messing around with it was more dangerous than most realized. Despite the metal screen between the cobbs and me, I'd been playing with fire when I held those Pradas over the trash can.

Another thing that most folks don't realize is just how much the little folk can learn, and how fast they can do it—especially when things are happening on their own turf. It took Keef and his people about thirty seconds to go and return.

"Four, there are," Keef reported. "Three lesser, who of late this place did guard. One greater, who gave them not-life."

"Four," I breathed. "Where?"

"One outside near the group of cars waits and watches," Keef said. "One outside the bistro where the mortals hide stands watch. One beside his mistress stands within."

I got a sick little feeling in my stomach. "Has anyone been hurt?"

Keef shook his head. "Taunt them, she does. Frighten them." He shrugged. "It is not as their kind often is."

"No. She's there for vengeance, not food." I frowned. "I need you to get me something. Can you?"

I told him what I needed, and Keef gave me a mildly offended look. "Of course."

"Good. Now, the one outside," I said. "Can you show me a way I could get close to him without being seen?"

Keef's eyes glittered with a sudden ferocity that was wholly at odds with his size and appearance. "This way, wizard."

I went at what was practically a run, but the tiny cobb had no trouble staying ahead of me. He led me through a service access door that required a key to open—until it suddenly swung open from the other side, a dozen young male cobbs dangling from the security bar and cheering. My amulet cast the only light as Keef led me down a flight of stairs and through a long, low tunnel.

"Access to the drains and watering system, this passage is," Keef called to me. We stopped at a ladder leading up. A small paper sack sat on the floor by the ladder. "Your weapons," he said, nodding at the bag. He pointed at the ladder. "Behind the vampire, this opens."

I opened the bag and found two plastic cylinders. I didn't want the crinkling paper, so I put one of them in my jacket pocket, kept the other in hand, and crept up the ladder. At the top was a hatch made out of some kind of heavy synthetic, rather than wood or steel, and it opened without a sound. I poked my head up and looked cautiously around the parking lot.

The lights were out, but there was enough snow on the ground to bounce around plenty of light, giving the outdoors an oddly close, quiet quality, almost as if someone had put a roof overhead, just barely out of sight. Over by the last group of cars in the mall parking lot, next to the Blue Beetle in fact, stood the vampire.

It was little more than a black form, and though it was human in shape, it was inhumanly still, every bit as motionless as the other inanimate objects in the parking lot. Snow had begun to gather on its head and shoulders, just as it had on the roofs and hoods of the parked cars. It stood facing the darkened mall, where snow blew into the hole left by the thrown car. It was watching, I supposed, for anyone who might come running out, screaming.

A newborn vampire might not be anywhere near as dangerous as an older one, but that was like saying a Mack truck was nowhere near as dangerous as a main battle tank. If you happened to be the guy standing in the road in front of one, it wouldn't much matter to you which of them crushed you to pulp. If I'd had my staff and rod with me, I might have chanced a stand-up fight. But I didn't have my gear, and even if I had, my usual magic would have made plenty of noise and warned the vampire's companions.

Vampires are tough. They take a lot of killing. I had to take this one out suddenly and with tremendous violence without making any noise. If I had to face it openly, I'd have no chance.

Which is why I had used the cobbs' intelligence to get sneaky.

I drew in my will, the magic I had been born with and that I had spent a lifetime exercising, practicing, and focusing. As the power came into me, it made the skin of my arms ripple with goose bumps, and I could feel a strange pressure at the back of my head and pressing against the *inside* of my forehead. Once I had the power ready, I started shaping it with my thoughts, focusing my will and intent on the desired outcome.

The spell I worked up wasn't one of my better evocations. It took me more than twenty seconds to get it together. For fast and dirty combat magic, that's the next best thing to forever.

For treacherous, backstabbing, sucker-punch magic, though, it's just fine.

At the very last second, the vampire seemed to sense something. It turned its head toward me.

I clenched my fist as I released my will and snarled, "*Gravitus!*"

The magic lashed out into the ground beneath the vampire's feet, and the steady, slow, immovable power of the earth suddenly stirred, concentrating, reaching up for the vampire standing upon it. In technical terms, I didn't actually *increase* the gravity of the earth beneath it. I only concentrated it a little. In a circle fifty yards across, for just a fraction of a second, gravity vanished. The cars all surged up against their shock absorbers and settled again. The thin coat of snow leapt several inches off the parking lot and fell back.

In that same fraction of a second, all of that gravity from all of that area concentrated itself into a circle, maybe eighteen inches across, directly at the vampire's feet.

There was no explosion, no flash of light—and no scream. The vampire just went down, slammed to the earth as suddenly and violently as if I'd dropped an anvil on him. There was a rippling, crackling sound as hundreds of bones shattered all together, and a splatter of sludgy liquid that splashed all over the cars around the vampire—mostly upon the Beetle, really.

The effort of gathering and releasing so much energy left me gasping. I was out of shape when it came to earth magic. It had never been my strongest suit—too slow, most of the time, to seem like it would have been worth the bother. As I hauled myself out of the ground, though, I had to admit that when there was enough time to actually use it, it sure as hell was impressive.

I padded to the car, watching the mall entrance, but there was no outcry and no sudden appearance of Drulinda or the other vampires of her scourge.

The vampire was still alive.

Un-alive. Whatever. The thing was still trying to move.

It was mostly just a mass of pulped, squishy meat. In the cold, at least, it hadn't begun to rot, so that cut down on the smell. One eye rolled around in its mashed skull. Muscles twitched, but without a solid framework of bone to work with, they didn't accomplish much beyond an odd, pulsing motion. It could probably put itself back together, given blood and time, but I didn't feel like letting it have either. I held the plastic cylinder over it.

"Nothing personal," I told the vampire. Then I dumped powdered garlic from the pizzeria in the mall's food court all over it.

I can't say that the vampire screamed, really. It died the way a salted slug does, in silent, pulsing agony. I had to fight to keep my stomach from emptying itself, but only for a second. Absolutely disgusting demises are par for the course when fighting vampires. A few wisps of smoke rose up, and after a few seconds, the mass of undead flesh became simple dead flesh again.

One down.

Three to go.

I stalked toward the mall, moving with all the silence I could manage. After years working as a private investigator, and more years fighting a magical war against the vampires in the shadows, I know how to be quiet. I slipped up to within thirty feet of the entrance and spotted the second vampire before he noticed me, right where Keef's people said he was.

He stood facing the door of the bistro, apparently intent on what was happening within. I could hear voices inside, though I could make out no details over the continued, repeated playing of "Only You," beyond that one of the voices was Drulinda's leathery rasp. There were no sounds of fighting, which wasn't good. Thomas certainly wouldn't have allowed them to hurt anyone without putting up a struggle, and given the mutual capabilities of everyone involved, it would have been noticeable.

A second's thought told me that it might also be a good sign. If they'd killed him, they would have made a big mess doing it. Assuming he hadn't gone down without getting to put up much of a fight—and I refused to assume anything else: I knew my brother too well—something else had to be happening.

My brother could go toe to toe with a vampire of the Black Court, if he had to, but the last time he'd done it the effort had nearly killed both him and the woman he'd had to feed from in order to recover. There were two of them inside, and though Thomas was as combat-capable as any of the White Court's best, he wasn't going to start a slugfest if he thought he could get a better fight by biding his time, doing what the White Court did—looking human and using guile. My instincts told me that Thomas was stalling, choosing his moment. Hell, he was probably waiting for me to show up and help.

I looked down and found his birthday present, untouched by the flying debris, lying in its bright red and pink paper where Molly had dropped it on the sidewalk outside the doors.

I found myself smiling.

Twenty seconds or so later, I tossed the present underhand. It tumbled through the air and landed on the floor directly outside the bistro's entrance. The head of the vampire on guard jerked around, focusing on the present. It tilted its head to one side. Then it whipped around toward me, baring its teeth in a snarl.

"*Gravitus!*" I thundered, releasing a second earthcrafting.

Once again, everything jumped up—but this time, it wasn't quiet. The circle of nullified gravity embraced every shop nearby in the mall, sending merchandise and shelves and dishes and furniture and cash registers and dressing dummies and God knew what other sundry objects flying up, to come crashing back down to the floor again. A great crashing rose up from the floors above us as well.

Once again, the circle of supergravity crushed a brown-shirted vampire flat to the floor—only I'd forgotten about the levels above. There was a shriek of tortured metal and a great crashing rain of debris came down in a nearly solid column as floors and ceilings gave way under the sudden, enormous stress. It all thundered down on the pulped vampire.

There was a second of shocked silence, while objects continued falling from their shelves and bins and who knew what else. Evidently, the damage to the ceiling had torn through some plumbing; a steady stream of water began to patter down from overhead onto the mound of rubble, along with occasional bits of still-falling material.

Then two things happened, almost at the same time.

First, my brother chose his moment.

The front wall of the bistro exploded outward. I saw the flying form of another vampire security guard hurtle across the hallway into the opposite wall with no detectable loss of altitude, and it smashed against a metal security grate with terrifying force.

Second, Drulinda let out an eerie howl of fury. It was a horrible sound, nasty and rasping and somehow spidery, for all that it was of inhuman volume. There was a crash from inside the bistro. Young men and women started screaming.

There wasn't any time to waste. I ran for the vampire my brother had thrown from the bistro. It had bounced off and fallen on the ground and was still gathering itself up. I had hoped it would take it a moment to recover from the blow, to give me time to get close enough to act.

It didn't work out that way.

The vampire was on its feet again before I could get halfway there, one of its shoulders twisted and deformed by the impact, one arm hanging loosely. It spun toward me with no sense of discomfort evident in its expression or posture, and it let out a very human-sounding scream of fury and flung itself at me.

I reacted with instant instinct, raising my right hand, with my will, and calling, "*Fuego!*"

Fire kindled from my open palm and rushed out in a furious torrent, spewing raggedly across the tile floor in a great, slewing cone. It splashed against the floor, up onto the metal grate, and all over the vampire in question, a sudden, if clumsy, immolation.

But without my blasting rod to help me focus the attack, it was diffused; the heat was spread out over a broad area instead of focused into a single, searing beam. Though I'm sure it hurt like hell, and though it set the security guard vampire's uniform on fire, it didn't cripple him. It might have sent up an older, more withered vampire like a torch, but the newbie was still too . . . juicy. It didn't burn him up so much as broil him a bit.

Pretty much, it just pissed him off.

The vampire came at me with another, higher-pitched scream, and swung a flaming arm at me. Maybe the fire had disoriented him a little, because I was able to get out of the way of the blow—sort of. It missed my head and neck and instead slammed into my left shoulder like a train wreck.

Pain flooded through me, and the canister of garlic went flying. The force of the blow spun me around, and I fell to the floor. The vampire came down on top of me, teeth bared, still on freaking *fire* as he leaned in with his non-pointy, still-white teeth, which were plenty strong enough to rip my throat open.

"Harry!" Thomas screamed. There was a rushing sound, and a tremendous force pulled the vampire off me. I sat up in time to see my brother drive his shoulder into the vampire's chest, slamming the undead thing back against the concrete wall between two stalls. Then Thomas whipped out what looked like a broken chair leg and drove the shattered end of the wood directly into the vampire's chest, a couple of inches below the gold, metallic security badge on his left breast, slightly off center.

The vampire's mouth opened, too-dark blood exploding from it in a gasp. The creature reached for the chair leg with its remaining arm.

Thomas solved that problem in the most brutal way imaginable. His face set in fury, my brother ignored the flames of the vampire's burning clothing, seized the remaining arm with both of his hands, and with a twist of his hips and shoulders ripped it out of the socket.

More blood splashed out, if only for a second—without a heartbeat to keep pumping it, blood loss is mostly about leakage—and then the mortally crippled vampire fell, twitching and dying as the stake of wood through its heart put an end to its unlife.

I felt Drulinda coming, more than I saw it happen, the cold presence of a Black Court vampire in a fury rubbing abrasively against my wizard's senses. "Thomas!"

My brother turned in time to duck a blow so swift I didn't even *see* it. He returned it with one of his own, but Drulinda, though new to the trade, was a master vampire, a creature with its own terrible will and power. Thomas had fought other Black Court vamps before—but not a master.

He was on the defensive from the outset. Though my brother was unthinkably strong and swift when drawing upon his vampiric nature, he wasn't strong or swift enough. I lay sprawled on the ground, still half-paralyzed by the pain in the left half of my body, and tried to think of what to do next.

"Get out!" I screamed at the bistro. "Get out of here, people! Get the hell out now!"

While I screamed, Drulinda slammed my brother's back into a metal security grate so hard that it left a broad smear of his pale red blood on its bars.

People started hurrying out of the bistro, running for the parking lot.

Drulinda looked over her shoulder and let out another hissing squall of rage. At this opening, Thomas managed to get a grip on her arm, set his feet, and swing her into the wall, sending cracks streaking through the concrete. On the rebound, he swung her up and around and then down, smashing her down onto the floor, then up from that and into a security mesh again, crushing tile and bending metal with every impact.

I heard a scream and looked up to see Ennui fall from her impossibly high black heels in her tiny, tight black dress, as she tried to flee the bistro.

A horribly disfigured hand had reached out from the rubble over the crushed vampire, and now held her.

I ran for the girl as my brother laid into Drulinda. My left arm wasn't talking to me, and I fumbled the second canister out of my left jacket pocket with my right arm, then dumped garlic over the outstretched vampire's hand.

It began smoking and spasming. Ennui screamed as the crushing grip broke her ankle. I stood up in frustration and started stomping down on the vampire's arm. Supernaturally strong it might be, but its bones were made of bone, and it couldn't maintain its grip on the girl without them.

It took a lot of stomping, but I was finally able to pull the girl free. I tried to get her to her feet, but her weight came down on her broken ankle, and from there it came down on my wounded shoulder. I went down to one knee, and it was all I could do not to fall.

I almost didn't notice when my brother flew through the air just over my head, smashed out what had to be the last remaining pane of glass at the mall entrance, and landed limply in the parking lot.

I felt Drulinda's presence coming up behind me.

The vampire let out a dusty laugh. "I thought it was just some poor pretty boy to play with. Silly me."

I fumbled with the canister for a second, and then whirled, flinging its contents at Drulinda in a slewing arc.

The vampire blurred to one side, dodging the garlic with ease. She looked battered and was covered with dust. Her undead flesh was approximately the consistency of wood, and so it wasn't cut and damaged so much as chipped and crushed. Her clothes were torn and ruined—and none of that mattered. She was just as functional, just as deadly as she had been before the fight.

I dropped the canister and drew forth my pentacle amulet, lifting it as a talisman against her.

The old bit with the crucifix works on the Black Court—but it isn't purely about Christianity. They are repelled not by the holy symbol itself, but by the faith of the one holding it up against them. I'd seen vampires repulsed by crosses, crucifixes, strips of paper written with holy symbols by a Shinto priest—once even a Star of David.

Me, I used the pentacle, because that's what I believed in. The five-pointed star, to me, represented the five elements of earth, air, water, fire, and spirit, bound within the solid circle of mortal will. I believed that magic was a force intended to be used to create, to protect, and to preserve. I believed that magic was a gift that had to be used responsibly and wisely—and that it especially had to be used against creatures like Drulinda, against literal, personified *evil*, to protect those who couldn't protect themselves. That's what I thought, and I'd spent my life acting in accordance with it.

I *believed.*

Pale blue light began to spill from the symbol—and Drulinda stopped with a hiss of sudden rage.

"You," she said after a few seconds. "I have heard of you. The wizard. Dresden."

I nodded slowly. Behind her, the fire from my earlier spell was spreading. The power was out, and I had no doubt that Drulinda and her former security-guard lackeys had disabled the alarms. It wouldn't take long for a fire to go insane in this place, once it got its teeth sunk in. We needed to get out.

"Go," I mumbled at Ennui.

She sobbed and started crawling for the exit, while I held Drulinda off with the amulet.

The vampire stared steadily at me for a second, her eyes all milky white, corpse cataracts glinting in the reflected light of the fire. Then she smiled and moved.

She was just too damned fast. I tried to turn to keep up with her, but by the time I did, Ennui screamed, and Drulinda had seized her hair and dragged her back, out of the immediate circle of light cast by the amulet.

She lifted the struggling girl with ease, so that I could see her mascara-streaked face. "Wizard," Drulinda said. Ennui had been cut by flying glass or the fall at some point, and some blood had streaked out of her slicked-back hair, over her ear, and down one side of her throat. The vampire leaned in, extending a tongue like a strip of beef jerky, and licked blood from the girl's skin. "You can hide behind your light. But you can't save her."

I ground my teeth and said nothing.

"But your death will profit me, grant me standing with others of my kind. The feared and vaunted Wizard Dresden." She bared yellowed teeth in a smile. "So I offer you this bargain. Throw away the amulet. I will let the girl go. You have my word." She leaned her teeth in close and brushed them over the girl's neck. "Otherwise . . . well. All of my new friends are gone. I'll have to make more."

That made me shudder. Dying was one thing. Dying and being made into one of *those* . . .

I lowered the amulet. I hesitated for a second, and then dropped it.

Drulinda let out a low, eager sound and tossed Ennui aside like an empty candy wrapper. Then she was on me, letting out rasping *giggles*, for God's sake, pressing me down. "I can smell your fear, wizard," she rasped. "I think I'm going to enjoy this."

She leaned closer, slowly, as she bared her teeth, her face only inches from mine.

Which is where I wanted her to be.

I reared up my head and spat out a gooey mouthful of powdered garlic directly into those cataract eyes.

Drulinda let out a scream, bounding away in a violent rush, clawing at her eyes with her fingers—and getting them burned, too. She thrashed in wild agony, swinging randomly at anything she touched or bumped into, tearing great, gaping gashes in metal fences, smashing holes in concrete walls.

"Couple words of advice," I growled, my mouth burning with the remains of the garlic I'd stuffed it with as she'd come sneaking up on me. "First, any time I'm not shooting my mouth off to a clichéd, two-bit creature of the night like you, it's because I'm up to something."

Drulinda howled more and rushed toward me—tripping on some rubble and sprawling on the ground, only to rush about on all fours like some kind of ungainly and horrible insect.

I checked behind me. Ennui was already out, and Thomas was beginning to stir, maybe roused by the snow now falling on him. I turned back to the blinded, pain-maddened vampire. We were the only ones left in that wing of the mall.

"Second," I spat. "Never touch my brother on his fucking birthday."

I reached for my will, lifted my hand, and snarled, *"Fuego!"*

Fire roared out to eagerly engulf the vampire.

What the hell. The building was burning down anyway.

"Freaking amateur villains," I muttered, glowering down at the splatters on my car.

Thomas leaned against it with one hand pressed to his head, a grimace of pain on his face. "You okay?"

I waved my left arm a little. "Feeling's coming back. I'll have Butters check me out later. Thanks for loaning Molly your car."

"Least I could do. Let her drive Sarah and Ennui to the hospital." He squinted at the rising smoke from the mall. "Think the whole thing will go?"

"Nah," I said. "This wing, maybe. They'll get here before too much more goes up. Keef and his folk should be all right."

My brother grunted. "How they going to explain this one?"

"Who knows," I said. "Meteor, maybe. Smashed holes in the roof, crushed some poor security guard, set the place on fire."

"My vote is for terrorists," Thomas said. "Terrorists are real popular these days." He shook his head. "But I meant the larpers, not the cops."

"Oh," I said. "Probably, they won't talk to anyone about what they saw. Afraid people would think they were crazy."

"And they would," Thomas said.

"And they would," I agreed. "Come tomorrow, it will seem very unreal. A few months from now, they'll wonder if they didn't imagine some of it or if there wasn't some kind of gas leak or something that made them hallucinate. Give it a few more years, and they'll remember that Drulinda and some rough-looking types showed up to give them a hard time. They drove a car through the front of the mall. Maybe they were crazy people dressed in costumes who had been to a few too many larps themselves." I shook my head. "It's human nature to try to understand and explain everything. The world is less scary that way. But I don't think they'll be in any danger, really. No more so than anyone else."

"That's good," Thomas said quietly. "I guess."

"It's the way it is." In the distance, sirens were starting up and coming closer. I grunted and said, "We'd better go."

"Yeah."

We got into the Beetle. I started it up and we headed out. I left the lights off. No sense attracting attention.

"You going to be all right?" I asked him.

He nodded. "Take me a few days to get enough back into me to feel normal, but . . ." He shrugged. "I'll make it."

"Thanks for the backup," I said.

"Kicked their freaky asses," he said, and held out his fist.

I rapped my knuckles lightly against it.

"Nice signal. The birthday present."

"I figured you'd get it," I said. Then I frowned. "Crap," I said. "Your present."

"You didn't remember to bring it?"

"I was a little busy," I said.

He was quiet for a minute. Then he asked, "What was it?"

"Rock'em Sock'em Robots," I said.

He blinked at me. "What?"

I repeated myself. "The little plastic robots you make fight."

"I know what they are, Harry," he responded. "I'm trying to figure out why you'd give me them."

I pursed my lips for a minute. Then I said, "Right after my dad died, they put me in an orphanage. It was Christmastime. On television, they had commercials for Rock'em Sock'em Robots. Two kids playing with them, you know? Two brothers." I shrugged. "That was a year when I really, really wanted to give those stupid plastic robots to my brother."

"Because it would mean you weren't alone," Thomas said quietly.

"Yeah," I said. "Sorry I forgot them. And happy birthday."

He glanced back at the burning mall. "Well," my brother said. "I suppose it's the thought that counts."

Grave-Robbed

P. N. Elrod

P. N. Elrod has sold more than twenty novels and as many short stories and is best known for The Vampire Files series, featuring undead detective Jack Fleming. She's cowritten three novels with actor/director Nigel Bennett, has edited and coedited several genre collections, and is an incurable chocoholic. More news on her toothy titles may be found at www.vampwriter.com.

CHICAGO, FEBRUARY 1937

When the girl draped in black stepped in to ask if I could help her with a séance, Hal Kemp's version of "Gloomy Sunday" began to murmur sadly from the office radio.

Coincidences annoy me. A mournful song for a dead sweetheart put together with a ceremony that's supposed to help the dead speak with the living made me uneasy—and I was annoyed it made me uneasy.

I should know better, being dead myself.

"You sure you're in the right place?" I asked, taking in her outfit. Black overcoat, pocketbook, gloves, heels, and stockings—she was a walking funeral. Along with the mourning weeds she wore a brimmed hat with a chin-brushing veil even I couldn't see past.

"The Escott Agency—that's what's on the door," she said, sitting on the client chair in front of the desk without an invitation. "You're Mr. Escott?"

"I'm Mr. Fleming. I fill in for Mr. Escott when he's elsewhere." He was visiting his girlfriend tonight. I'd come over to his office to work on his books since I was better at accounting.

"It was Mr. Escott who was recommended to me."

"By who?"

"A friend."

I waited, but she left it at that. Much of Escott's business as a private agent came by word of mouth. Call him a private eye and you'd get a pained look and perhaps an acerbic declaration that he did not undertake divorce cases. His specialty as an agent was carrying out unpleasant errands for the unable or unwilling, not peeking through keyholes, but did a séance qualify? He was interested in that kind of thing, but mostly from a skeptic's point of view. I had to say *mostly* since he couldn't be a complete skeptic what with his partner—me—being a vampire.

And nice to meet you, too.

Hal Kemp played on in the little office until the girl stood, went to the radio, and shut it off.

"I hate that song," she stated, turning around, the veil swirling lightly. Faceless women annoy me as well, but she had good legs.

"Me, too. You got any particular reason?"

"My sister plays it all the time. It gets on my nerves."

"Does it have to do with this séance?"

"Can't you call Mr. Escott?"

"I could, but you didn't make an appointment for this late or he'd be here."

"My appointment is for tomorrow, but something's happened since I made it, and I need to speak with him tonight. I came by just in case he worked late. The light was on and a car was out front. . . ."

I checked his appointment book. In his precise hand he'd written *10 am, Abigail Saeger.* "Spell that name again?"

She did so, correct for both.

"What's the big emergency?" I asked. "If this is something I can't handle, I'll let him know, but otherwise you'll find I'm ready, able, and willing."

"I don't mean to offend, but you look rather young for such work. Over the phone I thought Mr. Escott to be . . . more mature."

Escott and I were the same age but I did look younger by over a decade. On the other hand if she thought a man in his midthirties was old, then she'd be something of a kid herself. Her light voice told me as much, though you couldn't tell by her mannerisms and speech, which bore a finishing school's not so subtle polish.

"Miss Saeger, would you mind raising your blinds? I like to see who's hiring before I take a job."

She went still a moment, then lifted her veil. As I thought, a fresh-faced kid who should be home studying, but her eyes were red-rimmed, her expression serious.

"That's better. What can I do for you?"

"My older sister, Flora, is holding a séance tonight. She's crazy to talk with her dead husband, and there's a medium taking advantage of her. He wants her money, and more."

"A fake medium?"

"Is there any other kind?"

I smiled, liking her. "Give me the whole story, same as you'd have told to Mr. Escott."

"You'll help me?"

"I need to know more first." I said it in a tone to indicate I was interested.

She plunged in, talking fast, but I had good shorthand and scribbled notes.

Miss Saeger and her older sister, Flora, were alone; their parents long dead. But Flora had money in trust and married into more money by getting hitched to James Weisinger Jr., who inherited a tidy fortune some years ago. The Depression had little effect on them. Flora became a widow last August when her still-young husband died in a sailing accident on Lake Michigan.

I'd been killed on that lake. "Sure it was an accident?"

"A wind shift caused the boom to swing around. It caught him on the side of the head and over he went. I still have nightmares about the awful thud when it hit him and the splash, but it's worse for Flora—she was at the wheel at the time. She blames herself. No one else does. There were half a dozen people aboard who knew sailing. That kind of thing can happen out of the blue."

I vaguely remembered reading about it in the paper. Nothing like some rich guy getting killed while doing rich-guy stuff to generate copy.

"Poor James never knew what hit him; it was just that fast. Flora was in hysterics and had to be drugged for a week. Then she kept to her bed nearly a month, then she read some stupid article in a magazine about using a Ouija board to talk to spirits and got it into her head that she had to contact James, to apologize to him."

"That opened the door?"

"James is dead, and if he did things right, he's in heaven and should stay there—in peace." Miss Saeger growled in disgust. "I've gotten Flora's pastor to talk to her, but she won't listen to him. I've talked to her until we both end up screaming and crying, and she won't see sense. I'm just her little sister and don't know anything, you see."

"What's so objectionable?"

"Her obsession. It's not healthy. I thought after all this time she'd lose interest, but she's gotten worse. Every week she has a gaggle of those creeps from the Society over, they set up the board, light candles, and ask questions while looking at James's picture. It's pointless and sad and unnatural and—and . . . just plain *disrespectful.*"

I was really liking her now. "Society?"

"The Psychical Society of Chicago."

Though briefly tempted to ask her to say it three times fast, I kept my yap shut. The group investigated haunted houses and held sittings—their word for séances—writing their experiences up for their archives. Escott was a member. For a buck a year to cover mailing costs, he'd get a pamphlet every month and read the more oddball pieces out to me.

"The odious thing is," said Miss Saeger, "they're absolutely *sincere*. When one has that kind of belief going, then of course it's going to produce results."

"What kind of results?"

"They've spelled out the names of all the people who ever died in the house, which is stupid because the house isn't that old. The man who supervises these sittings says that's because the house was built over the site of another, so the dead people are connected to *it*, you see. There's no way to prove or disprove any of it. He's got an answer for everything and always sounds perfectly reasonable."

"Is he the medium?"

"No, but he brought him in. Alistair Bradford." She put plenty of venom in that name. "He looks like something out of a movie."

"What? Wears a turban like Chandu the Magician?"

Her big dark eyes flashed, then she choked, stifling a sudden laugh. She got things under control after a moment. "Thank you. It's so good to talk with someone who sees things the way I do."

"Tell me about him."

"No turban, but he has piercing eyes, and when he walks into a room, everyone turns around. He's handsome . . . for an old guy."

"How old?"

"At least forty."

"That's ancient."

"Please don't make fun of me. I get that all the time from him, from all of them."

"I'm sorry, Miss Saeger. Are you the only one left in the house with any common sense?"

"Yes." She breathed that out, and it almost turned into a sob, but she headed it off. The poor kid looked to be only barely keeping control of a truckload of high emotion. I heard her heart pound fast, then gradually slow. "Even the servants are under his spell. I have friends, but I can't talk to them about this. It's just too embarrassing."

"You've been by yourself on this since August?"

She nodded. "Except for our pastor, but he can't be there every day. He tells me to keep praying for Flora, and I do, and still this goes on and just gets worse. I miss James, too. He was a nice man. He deserves better than this—this—"

"What broke the camel's back to bring you here?"

"Before Alistair Bradford came, all they did was play with that stupid Ouija board. I'd burn it but they'd just buy another from the five and dime. After *he* was introduced, they began holding real séances. I don't like any of that stuff and don't believe in it, but he made it scary. It's as though he gets taller and broader and his voice changes. With the room almost totally dark it's easy to believe him."

"They let you sit in?"

"Just the once—on sufferance so long as I kept quiet. When I turned the lights on in the middle of things, Flora banished me. She said my negative thoughts were preventing the spirits from coming through and that I was endangering Bradford's life. You're not supposed to startle a medium out of a trance or it could kill him. I wouldn't mind seeing that, but he was faking. While they were all yelling I had my eye on him, and the look he gave me was pure hate . . . and he was *smiling*. He wanted to scare me and it worked. I've kept my door locked and haven't slept much."

"I don't blame you. No one believes you?"

"Of course not. I'm not in their little club and to them I'm just a kid. What do I know?"

"Kids have instinct, a good thing to follow. Is he living in the house?"

"He mentioned it, but Flora—for once—didn't think that was proper."

"Is he romancing her?"

Miss Saeger's eyes went hard. "Slowly. He's too smart to rush things, but I see the way he struts around, looking at everything. If he lays a finger on Flora I'll—"

I raised one hand. "I get it. You want Flora protected and him discredited."

"Or his legs broken and his big smirking face smashed in."

That was something I could have arranged. I know those kind of people. "It's better if Flora gets rid of him by her own choice, though."

"I don't see how; I may have left it too late. I called here on Saturday to make the appointment, but—" She went red in the face. "I could just *kill* him."

"What'd he do?"

"The last séance—they have one every Sunday and that's just *wrong* having it on a Sunday—something horrible happened. They all gathered in the larger parlor at the table as usual, lighted candles, and put out the lights. Soon as it went dark, I slipped in while they were getting settled. There's an old Chinese screen in one corner, and I hide behind it during their séances. Negative feelings, my foot; no one's noticed me yet, not even Bradford, so I saw the whole thing."

"Which was?"

"He put himself in a trance right on time. It usually takes five minutes, and by then everyone's expecting something to happen; you can feel it. He starts out with a low groan and breathing loudly, and in the dark it's spooky, and that's when his spirit guide takes over. His voice gets deeper and he puts on a French accent. Calls himself *Frère* Lèon. He's supposed to have been a monk who traveled with Joan of Arc."

"Who speaks perfect English?"

"Of course. No one's ever thought of talking to him in French. I doubt Bradford knows much more than *mon Dieu* and *sang sacré*."

She'd attended a good finishing school, speaking with the right kind of pronunciation. I'd heard it when I'd been a doughboy in France during the last year of the war, and had picked up enough to get by. Much of that was too rough for Miss Saeger's tender ears, though.

"And the horrible thing that happened?"

"It was at the end. He pretends to have *Frère* Lèon pass on messages from James. He can't have James talk directly to Flora or he'd trip himself up. He doesn't pass too many messages, either, just general stuff about how beautiful it is on the other side. She tries to talk to him and ask him things and she's so desperate and afterwards she always cries and then she goes back for *more*. It's cruel. But this time he said he was giving her a sign of what she should do."

"Do?"

"I didn't know what that meant, until . . . well, Bradford finished just then and pretended to be waking from his trance. That's when they found what he'd snuck on the table. It was James's wedding ring, the one he was buried with."

I gave that the pause it deserved. "Not a duplicate?"

She shook her head, a fast, jerky movement. Her voice was thick. "Inside it's engraved with *To J. from F.—Forever Love*. He never took it off and it had some hard wear: two distinct parallel scratches, and it wasn't a perfect circle. Flora showed it to me as proof that Alistair Bradford was genuine. She didn't want to hear my idea that . . . that he'd dug up and robbed James's grave. I thought she'd slap me. She's gone crazy, Mr.—"

"Fleming. Call me Jack."

"Jack. Flora's never raised a hand to me, even when we were kids and I was being bratty, but this has her all turned around. I thought Mr. Escott could find something out about Bradford that would prove him a fake or come to a séance and do something to break it up, but I don't think she'd listen now. The last thing Bradford said before his trance ended was 'You have his blessing.' Put that with the ring and I know it means if he asks Flora to marry him, she'll say yes because she'll think that's what James would want."

"Come on, she can't be that—"

"Stupid? Foolish? Under a spell? She is! That's what's driving *me* crazy. She should be *smarter* than this."

"Grief can make you go right over the edge. Guilt can make it worse, and I bet she's lonely, too. She should have gone to a head doctor but picked up a Ouija board instead. Does this Bradford ask for money?"

"*He* calls it a donation. She's given him fifty dollars every time. He gets that much for all his sittings—and he does thirty to forty a month. My sister's not the only dope in town."

My mouth went dry. Fifty a week was a princely income, but that much times forty? I was in the wrong business. I'd gotten twenty-five a week back in New York as a reporter and counted myself lucky. "Well. It's safer than robbing banks. Your sister can give him more by marriage?"

"Yes, her trust money and the estate from James. Bradford would have it, the house, never have to work again. Please, can you help me stop him?"

I thought of the people I knew who broke bones for a sawbuck and could make a man disappear for twice that. "I need to check this, you know. I only have your side of things."

"And I'm just a kid."

"Miss Saeger, I'd say the same thing to Eleanor Roosevelt if she was in that chair. Lemme make a phone call. Anyone going to be worried you're gone?"

"I snuck out and got a taxi. Flora and I had a fight tonight and she thinks I'm sulking in my room. She's busy, anyway—the new séance."

"Uh-huh." I dialed Gordy at the Nightcrawler Club and asked if he had any dirt on an Alistair Bradford, professional medium.

"Medium what?" asked Gordy in his sleepy-sounding voice.

"A swami; you know, séances, fortune-telling. It's for a case. I'm filling in for Charles."

He grunted, and he sounded amused. "You at his office? Ten minutes." He hung up. As the Nightcrawler was a longer than ten-minute drive away I took him to mean he'd phone back, not drop by.

"Ten minutes," I repeated to Miss Saeger. "What's with the black getup? You still in mourning for your brother-in-law?"

"It was the only way I could think of to cover my face. I'm full grown, but soon as anyone looks at me, they think I'm fifteen or something."

"And you're really . . . ?"

"Sixteen."

"Miss Saeger, you are one brave and brainy sixteen-year-old, so I'm sure you're aware that this is a school night."

"My sister is more important than that, but thank you for the reminder." There was a dryness in her tone that would have done credit to Escott. A couple years from now and she'd be one formidable young woman.

"What time is this séance?"

"Nine o'clock. Always."

"Not at midnight?"

"Some of the older Society members get too sleepy if things go much past ten."

"Why tonight instead of next Sunday?"

"James's birthday. Bradford said that holding a sitting on the loved one's birthday always means something special."

"Like what?"

"He won't say; he just *smiles.* It makes my skin crawl. I swear, if he's not stopped, I'll get one of James's golf clubs and—" She went red in the face again, stood up, and paced. I did that when the pent-up energy got to be too much.

I tried to get more from her on tonight's event, but she didn't have anything else to add, though she had plenty of comments about Bradford's antics. Guys like him I'd met before: they're always the first to look you square in the eye and assure you they're honest long before you begin to wonder.

The phone rang in seven minutes. Abigail Saeger halted midword and midstride and sat, leaning forward as I put the receiver to my ear. Gordy was like a library for all that was crooked in the great city of Chicago, with good reason: if he wasn't behind it himself, he knew who was and where to find them. He gave me slim pickings about Bradford, but it was enough to confirm that the guy was trouble. He'd done some stage work as a magician, Alistair the Great, until discovering there was more cash to be had conjuring dead relatives from thin air instead of live rabbits. He preferred to collect as much money as possible in the shortest time, then make an exit. The wealthy widow Weisinger was too good a temptation to a man looking for an easy way to retire.

"You need help with this bo'?" Gordy asked.

"I'll let you know. Thanks."

"No problem."

"Well?" asked Miss Saeger.

I hung up. "Count me in, ma'am."

"That sounds so old. My name's Abby."

"Fine, you can sign it here." I pulled out one of Escott's standard contracts. It was short and vague, mostly a statement that the Escott Agency was retained for services by, with a blank after that and room for the date.

"How much will this be?"

"Five bucks should do it."

"It has to be more than that. I read detective stories."

"Special sale, tonight only. Anyone walking in here named Abby pays five bucks, no more, no less."

For a second I thought she'd kiss me, and I was prepared to duck out of range. If my girlfriend found out I'd canoodled, however innocently or briefly, with a mere pippin of sixteen, I would find myself dead for real and for ever after.

Abby signed, fished a five-dollar bill from her pocketbook, and took my receipt in exchange. I put the money and the contract in Escott's top desk drawer along with my shorthand notes. He'd have a fine time trying to figure things out when he came in tomorrow morning. I harvested my overcoat and fedora from the coat tree in the corner, and ushered my newest client out, locking up. She made it to the bottom of the stairs, then pulled the veil back over her face.

"Afraid someone will recognize you?" I asked. The street was empty.

"No sense in taking chances."

Now I really liked her. I opened my new Studebaker up and handed her in, checking the sky. It had been threatening to sleet since before I got up tonight; I hoped it would hold off.

"Nice car," she said.

The nicest I'd ever owned. My faithful '34 Buick had come to a bad end, but this sporty replacement helped ease the loss. I got the motor purring, remembered to turn the headlights on, and put it in gear, pulling slowly from the curb. "Where's your brother-in-law buried?" As Abby's chin was just visible, I could see her jaw drop.

"Why do you need to know that?"

"I want to pay my respects."

"The cemetery will be closed."

"Which one? And where?"

She told me, finally, and I made a U-turn and got us on our way. Chicago traffic was no worse than usual as we headed toward Lincolnwood. Following Abby's directions we ended up driving slowly along North Ravenswood Avenue. A railroad track on our left obscured the view of the cemetery grounds. When a cross street opened, I took the turn under the tracks. A pale stone building with crenellations, Gothic windows, and a square, two-storied tower with a number of slender, round towers at the corners and along the front wall looked back at us. It had too much dignity to be embarrassed. The gates that blocked its arched central opening were, indeed, closed.

"Told you," said Abby.

"Is Mr. Weisinger anywhere near the front?" This place looked huge. They only put fancy stone buildings like that in front of the really large cemeteries.

"Go back south and turn on Bryn Mawr. I'll tell you when to stop."

What the lady said. It took awhile to find a sufficiently secluded place to park, then Abby provided very specific directions to the grave, which was not too far from the boundary wall.

"What are you going to do?" she asked.

I was about to say she didn't want to know, but decided that would get me an observation about not treating her like an adult. "I'm going to check to see if the grave has been disturbed enough to bring in the law."

"But the police, the papers—"

"A necessary evil. If they show up asking Bradford how he got that wedding ring, how long do you think he'll stick around?"

"Would they put him in jail?" She looked hopeful.

"We'll see. You gonna be warm enough? Good. I'll be quick."

"Don't you want me along?"

"I'll bet you're good at it, but you're not exactly dressed for getting around fences."

She looked relieved.

I slammed the door, opened the trunk, and drew out a crowbar from the toolbox I kept there. Since Abby didn't need to see it and try to guess why I'd want one, I held it out of sight while approaching the cemetery's boundary. It was made of iron bars with points on top, an easy climb if you were nimble.

I had the agility, but slipped between the bars instead. Literally. One of my happier talents acquired after my death was being able to vanish and float just about anywhere I liked, invisible as air. Since it was dark and there was some distance between me and the car, I figured Abby wouldn't see much if I partially vanished, eased through, and went solid again. Blink of an eye and it was done.

The cemetery grounds were covered with a thick layer of mostly undisturbed snow. Trees, bushes, and monuments of all shapes showed black against it. I made my way to one of the wide paths that had been shoveled clear, looking out for the landmark of an especially ornate mausoleum with marble columns in front. Weisinger's grave marker was just behind it. The dates on the substantial granite block told me he'd been born this day and was only a few years younger than I, the poor bastard. Another, identical block sprouted right next to it with his widow's name and date of birth already in place.

The snow lay differently over his plot, clumped and broken, dirtier than the stuff in the surrounding area. Footprints were all over, but not being an Indian tracker I couldn't make much from them, only that someone had recently been busy here and worn galoshes.

I poked the long end of the crowbar into the soil, and it went in far too easily. Ground that had had seven months to settle and freeze in the winter weather would have put up more resistance. Bradford or someone working for him had dug down, opened the coffin, grabbed the wedding ring, and put the earth back. Then he'd taken the trouble to dump shovelfuls of snow on top so a casual eye wouldn't notice. He was probably hoping there'd be another fall soon to cover the rest of the evidence.

The ghoulishness of the robbery appalled me; the level of greed behind it disgusted me. I knew some tough customers who worked for Gordy, and even they would have balked at this level of low.

The moment Abigail Saeger told me about Weisinger's death on the lake, I'd signed myself onto the job. Something twinged inside me then, connecting that death to my own and to that damned "Gloomy Sunday" song playing on the radio. I didn't want to believe in coincidences of the weird kind; signs and portents were strictly for the fortune-teller's booth at the midway.

But still . . . I got a twinge.

It was different from the gooseflesh creep that means someone's walking over your grave. When it came down to it, I didn't have a grave, just that lake. The people who'd murdered me had also robbed me of a proper burial. Weisinger had gotten one but Bradford had violated it.

That was just *wrong*.

And just as that thought crossed my mind the wind abruptly kicked up, rattling the bare branches as though the trees were waking up around me. They scratched and clacked and I tried to not imagine bones making a similar noise, but it was too late.

"All right, keep your shirt on," I said to no one in particular, stepping away from the grave. It sure as hell felt like someone was listening.

I was dead (or undead), surrounded by acres of the truly dead. The wind sent snow dust skittering along the black path. My imagination gave it form and purpose as it swept by. A sizable icicle from high up broke away and dropped like a spear, making a pop as loud as a gunshot when it hit a stone marker and shattered not two yards away. If my heart had been beating, it would have stopped then and there.

It's easy to be calm about weird coincidence when one is *not* in a cemetery at night. I decided it was time to leave. That I winked out quick and sped invisibly over the ground toward the fence faster than a scalded cat was my own business. Anyway, I went solid again as soon as I was on the other side.

Abby and I needed to get to her house before nine.

That's what I told myself while quick-marching to the car, consciously not looking over my shoulder.

* * *

Rich people live in some damned oddball houses. The Weisinger place started out with Frank Lloyd Wright on the ground floor, lots of glass and native stone, then the rest looked like a Tudor mansion straight from *The Private Life of Henry VIII.* I could almost see Charles Laughton waving cheerily from an upper window, framed by dark wood crosspieces set into the plaster.

"It's awful, but roomy," said Abby as I parked across the street to indulge in a good long stare.

"You okay for going back without getting caught?"

"Yes, but aren't you coming in?"

"This is the part where I do some sneaking around."

"They'll catch you; they'll think you're a burglar!"

"You hired an expert. Look, we can't go through the front so you can introduce me to everyone. It'll put Bradford on his guard, and your sister will be within her rights to kick me out."

"What will you do?"

"Exactly what's needed to get rid of him—and for that *you* need an alibi so they'll know you aren't involved. This means you can't hide behind that screen as usual. You said there're servants? Do they eavesdrop? Perfect. Think you can eavesdrop with them?"

"It wouldn't be the first time."

"Good for you. Whatever happens I want them to truthfully vouch that you were with them the whole time. This keeps you off the hook with Flora. I'm going to do my best to make Bradford look bad, so you have to be completely clear. Can you look innocent? Never mind, you're a natural." I checked my watch: twenty to nine. "I need a sketch of the floor plan."

I pulled a shorthand pad from the glove compartment and gave her a pencil. A streetlamp on the corner bled just enough light to work by as she plotted out an irregular shape, dividing it into squares and rectangles, putting a big X in to mark the parlor.

"That's the ground floor." She handed the pad over. "Kitchen, dining room, card room, music room, small parlor, large parlor: that's where they have the séances. How will you—"

"Trade secret. You'll get your money's worth and then some. Now beat it. Shuck those weeds and keep some witnesses around you. Don't be alone for a minute." She got out of the car quickly, coming around to the driver's side. I rolled the window down. "One more thing . . ."

She bent to be at eye level. "Yes?"

"When the dust settles, don't give your sister any 'I told you so's,' okay?"

Abby got a funny look, and I thought she'd ask one more time about what I'd be doing, and I'd have to put her off, not being sure myself. Instead, she pecked me a solid one right on the mouth, and honest to God, I did *not* see it coming.

"Good luck!" she whispered, then scampered off.

No point in wiping away the lip color; she wasn't wearing any. Dangerous girl. I felt old.

I took the car around the block once and found a likely place to leave it, close behind another that had just parked along the curb. A line of vehicles of various makes and vintages led to the Weisinger house. Partygoers, I thought. A well-bundled couple emerged and stalked carefully along the damp sidewalk toward the lights. Slouching down, I waited until five to nine, then got out and followed.

Not as many lights showed around the curtains now, but I could hear the noise of a sizable gathering within the walls. The possibility of sneaking in to blend with the crowd occurred, but I decided against it. Groups like the Psychical Society tended to be close-knit and notice outsiders. With his membership card Escott could get away with bluffing himself in (his English accent didn't hurt, either), but I was a ready-made sore thumb. Better that they never see my face at all.

I took the long way around the house to compare it to Abby's sketch. She'd not marked the windows, not that I needed to open any to get inside; they were just easier to go through than lath and plaster. Picking a likely one above the larger parlor, I vanished, floated up the wall, and seeped through by way of the cracks.

Bumbling around in the space on the other side, I regretted not getting a sketch of the second story as well. The room was big and I sensed furniture shapes filling it. Though my hearing was muffled, I determined no one else was there and cautiously re-formed, taking it slow. An empty, dark bedroom, and laid out on the bed was a man's dressing gown. Neatly together on the floor were his slippers. The rest of the room was in perfect order, personal items set out on a bureau, no dust anywhere, and yet it didn't feel lived in. No one is ever this tidy when they're actually using such things.

The hair went up on the back of my neck.

This stuff was too high quality to belong to the butler. The *J. W.* engraved into the back of a heavy silver hairbrush confirmed it—the room was a shrine. I concluded that Flora Weisinger was in sore need of real help to deal with her grief and guilt, not well-meaning morons with Ouija boards.

The upstairs seemed to be deserted, but I crept softly along the hall, ready to vanish again if company came. The downstairs noise was loud from several conversations going at once, the same as for any party, but no music, no laughter.

Nosy, I opened doors. The one nearest Weisinger's room led to Flora's, to judge by the furnishings and metaphysical reading matter. I never understood why it was that rich couples sometimes went in for separate bedrooms, even when they really liked each other.

Her closet was stuffed with dark clothing, all the cheerful print dresses and light colors shoved far to either side. Women wore dark things in the winter, but this was too much. There was an out of place–looking portable record player on a table by the bed. The only record on the spindle was Kemp's "Gloomy Sunday."

Enough already. I got out before I had another damn twinge.

One of the hall doors opened to a sizable linen cupboard. I stepped in and put on the light. With my vision the night is like day to me if there's any kind of illumination, but not so much in interior rooms with no windows. This place reminded me of the hidden room under Escott's kitchen where I slept while the sun was up. I took off my overcoat and hat, putting them out of sight in the back on an upper shelf. I wanted to be able to move around quick if required.

Sheets and towels filled other shelves, along with some white, filmy material that I figured out were spare curtains. When I was a kid my mom drafted me twice a year to help change the winter curtains to summer and back again. No matter that it was women's work, I was the youngest and available.

I held the fabric up and it was just like what Mom used. In a lighted room you could see through it, but in a dark place with only a candle burning and imaginations at a fever pitch—yeah, I could make good use of it. The widest, longest piece folded up small, and I easily pushed it into the gap between my belt and shirt in the back.

But I wanted something more spectacular than a fun house spook. The items in Weisinger's room would do it.

From his bureau I pocketed the hairbrush, a pipe, a comb, and some keys, and checked out a bottle of aftershave cologne. Aqua Velva was good enough for me, but rich guys had to be different. I shook some into my hands and gave myself a thorough slapping down, face, neck, hands, and lapels. Fortunately, it smelled pretty nice.

Downstairs, things suddenly went quiet. The séance must be starting.

No time for further refinements, I vanished and sank straight through the floor until I'd cleared its barrier and was sure it was now a ceiling. I hovered high, listening.

They sang "Happy Birthday."

I could have done without that.

The mostly in-key singing ended, then a man gently urged, "Blow them out and make a wish for him, Flora."

The soft applause that followed indicated success, then there was a general shuffling and scraping as they took seats. No one spoke, which was odd. People talked at parties.

Silence now, a long stretch of silence. I took the pause as an opportunity to explore the edges of the room. Certainly I bumped and brushed into people, and they'd shiver in reaction, because in this form I'd feel like a cold draft to them, but the silence held. Without too much trouble I found a corner and determined this was where Abby hid herself. She was absent, so I gradually re-formed.

The Chinese screen—and I didn't have much experience with them—was seven feet tall and wide enough to conceal a sizable serving area. When holding formal receptions, you didn't have to see the servants messing with the dishes. There were spaces between the painted panels that I could peer through, though. Each sliver of space provided a different angle on things.

The large parlor was much bigger than I expected. A long table was set up in the middle and seated eight to a side. Each chair had an occupant, and they were a motley group: some wore formal clothes, others were artistically Bohemian.

An older, more polished, more somber version of Abby sat at one end on the side opposite me: Flora Weisinger. Behind her was a framed portrait of a young man in his prime: her late husband. In front of her was a large birthday cake, its candles dead. She clutched a wadded handkerchief in one hand; in the other, pinched between thumb and forefinger and held up like an offering, was a gold ring. I could guess whose. Her posture was tense, expectant, her big dark gaze fixed on the tall man next to her.

At the head of the table, clearly in charge, stood Alistair Bradford. Having seen a few mediums in the course of my checkered life, I knew they ran to all types, from self-effacing, lace-clad ladies, to suave young lounge lizards with Vaseline-slicked hair. Bradford was lofty and distinguished, his own too-long hair swept back like that of an orchestra maestro. It suited his serious features. He was handsome, if you liked that brand of it, and his slate blue eyes did look piercing as they took in the disciples at the table.

"Now, dear friends," he said in a startlingly soft, clear, beautiful voice, "please let us bow our heads in sincere prayer for a safe and enlightening spiritual journey on this very, *very* special night."

Such was the influence of that surprising voice that I actually followed through with the rest of them. I had to shake myself and remember he'd been happy to dig up a grave to get to that ring in Flora Weisinger's fingers. The wave of disgust snapped me out of it. The next time he spoke, saying *amen*, I had my guard up.

Down the whole length of that big, bare table there were only two candles burning, leaving the rest of the room—to their eyes—dark. It was as good as daylight to me.

"And now I ask that everyone remain utterly quiet, and I will attempt to make contact," he said, smiling warmly.

I expected them to hold hands, touch fingers, or something like that. So much for how things were done in the movies.

Bradford sat, composed himself with his palms flat on the table, and shut his eyes. He drew in a deep breath, audibly releasing it. In contrast, no one else seemed able to move. Flora looked at him with an intense and heartbreaking hope that was terrible to see.

His stertorous breathing gradually got louder. The man knew how to play things to raise the suspense.

And I knew how to bust it.

His noises got thicker with more throat behind them, so I could guess he was ready to turn it into a good long groan so *Frère* Lèon could make his entrance.

I went invisible, floated until I was exactly behind his chair, went solid while crouched down, and drew a big breath of my own. During the brief silence between his puffings I cut loose with loudest, juiciest Bronx cheer I could manage, then vanished.

In a tense, emotion-charged room it had a predictable effect. I slipped behind the screen to watch.

His rhythm abruptly shattered, Bradford looked around in confusion, as did the others. Some seemed scandalized, a couple were amused, and one guy suggested that perhaps there was a playful spirit in the room already. A more practical man got up to check my corner, which was the only hiding place, and announced it to be empty.

A few of them noticed the cologne and mentioned it. Much to their delight, Flora finally confirmed that it was James's scent hanging in the air. She sounded awful. Bradford made no comment.

After some excited discussion that didn't go anywhere, they settled down, and Bradford started his breathing routine again. I watched and waited.

Frère Lèon eventually began to speak through Bradford, and to give him credit, it was a damned well-done French accent. His voice was rougher, deeper in pitch, very effective in the dark.

I ventured forth again, keeping low while he gave them a weather report for the other side, and went solid just long enough to call out a handy bit of French I'd learned while on leave in Paris. The loose translation was *How much for an hour of love, my little cabbage?*

Or something like that; it had usually been enough to get my face slapped.

Then I clocked him sharp on the back of the noggin with the hairbrush, dropped it, and vanished.

I was back to the screen, going solid in time to see things fall apart. A few in the room had understood what I'd said and were either flabbergasted or trying not to laugh. Bradford's trance was thoroughly broken; he launched from his chair to look behind it, startled as the rest. He remembered himself, though, and flopped down again, apparently in a state of collapse. They fussed over him, and the electric chandelier was switched on.

Somewhere in the middle of it Flora spotted the hairbrush. She froze, screamed, and sat down fast, sheet white and pointing to where it lay on the floor.

It took attention away from Bradford, and I was betting he was none too pleased. The knock he'd taken bothered him—his hand kept rubbing the spot—but I'd hit to hurt, not cause permanent damage. He'd earned it. I kept myself out of sight for the duration, going solid in the next room over, which was empty. Vanishing took it out of me. I'd have to stop at the stockyards before dawn for some blood or I'd feel like hell tomorrow night.

Some guy who seemed to be the one in charge of the Psychical Society was for canceling the sitting, but Bradford assured everyone that he was fine. Sometimes mischievous spirits delighted in disrupting things—unless, of course, there was a more earthly explanation. With Flora's permission the ground floor was searched for uninvited guests. I had to not be there for a few minutes but didn't mind.

Elsewhere in the house, probably the distant kitchen, I heard strident voices denying any part of the business. Abby's was in that chorus, her outrage genuine. Good girl.

This time it took longer for everyone to settle. Though the hour inched toward ten, none showed signs of being sleepy enough to leave. The entertainment was too interesting.

The hour struck and they assembled in the parlor again. On the long table fresh candles were substituted for the ones that had expired. The chandelier was switched off.

From my vantage point at the screen I tried to get a sense of Flora's reaction to things. She had the silver-backed hairbrush square in front of her and kept looking at it. She had to be the gracious hostess, but her nerves were showing in the way she played with that handkerchief. She'd rip it apart before too long. As she took her seat again close to Bradford, she held the wedding ring out as before, but her fingers shook.

Third time's the charm, I thought, and waited.

Bradford did his routine without a hitch, and before too long good old *Frère* Lèon was back and in a thick accent offered them greetings and a warning against paying mind to dark spirits who could lead them astray from the True Path.

That's what *he* called it. I just shook my head, assembling my borrowed weapons quietly on the serving table, a napkin scrounged from a stack at one end to nix the noise.

Flora gave *Frère* Lèon a formal greeting and asked if her husband was present.

"He is, *ma petit*. 'E shines like the sun and speaks of 'is love for you."

She released a shaky sigh of relief and it sounded too much like a sob. "What else does he say? James? Are you sure? Tell me what to do!"

Bradford's old monk tortured her a little longer, not answering. He said he could not hear well for the dark spirits trying to come between, then: "Ah! 'E is clear at last. 'E says 'is love is deep, and 'e wants you to be 'appy on this plane. You are to open your 'eart to new love. Ah—the 'appiness that awaits you is great. 'E smiles! Such joy for you, sweet child, such joy!"

Flora shook her head a little. Some part of her must have known this was all wrong.

Time to confirm it.

I'd pulled out the curtain material and draped it over my head, tying one of the napkins kerchieflike around my neck to keep the stuff from slipping off. It looked phony as hell, I was sure, but in the darkness with this crowd it would lay 'em in the aisles.

Picking up Weisinger's things, I eased from behind the screen. Everyone was looking at Bradford. He might have seen me in the shadows beyond the candle glow, but his eyes were shut.

Made to order, I thought, and accurately bounced the keys off his skull. It was a damned good throw, and I followed quickly with the other things. The comb landed square in the cake, the pipe skidded along the table and slid into Flora's lap. She shrieked and jumped up.

If *Frère* Lèon had a good entrance, that was nothing to compare to that of Jack Fleming, fake ghost-for-hire.

I vanished and reappeared but only just, holding to a mostly transparent state—standing smack-dab in the middle of the table. The top half of my body was visible, beautifully obscured by the pale curtain. The bottom half went right into the wood.

It didn't feel good but was pretty spectacular. The screaming helped.

With some effort I pressed forward, moving right *through* the table, candles and all, down its remaining length, working steadily toward Bradford. His eyes were now wide open, and it was a treat to see him shed the trance to see some real supernatural trouble. When I raised a pale, curtain-swathed hand to point at him, I thought he'd swallow his tongue.

Then I willed myself higher, rising until I was clear of the table and floating free. I made one swimming circuit of the room, then dove toward Bradford, letting myself go solid as I dropped.

I took in enough breath to fill the room with a wordless and hopefully terrifying bellow and hit him like bowling ball taking out one last stubborn pin. It was a nasty impact for us both, but I had the advantage of being able to vanish again. So far as I could tell he was sprawled flat and screaming with the rest.

Remaining invisible was uphill work for me now, but necessary. I clung close to Bradford so he could enjoy my unique kind of cold. I'd been told it was like death's own breath from the Arctic. Through chattering teeth he babbled nonsense about dark spirits being gathered against him and that he had to leave before they manifested again. He got some argument and a suggestion they all pray to dispel the negative influences, but he was already barreling out the door.

I stuck with him until he got in his car, then slipped into the backseat and went solid. He screeched like a woman when I snaked one arm around his neck in a half nelson. I'm damned strong. He couldn't break free. When he stopped making noise, I noticed him staring at the rearview mirror. It was empty, of course.

Leaning in, my mouth close to his ear, in my best imitation of the Shadow, I whispered, "Game's over, Svengali. Digging up that grave pissed off the wrong kind of *things*. We're on to you and we're *hungry*. You want to see another dawn?"

He whimpered, and the sound of his racing heart filled the car. I took that as a yes.

"Get out of town. Get out of the racket. Go back to the stage. Better a live magician than a dead medium. Got that? *Got that?*"

Not waiting for a reply, I vanished, exiting fast. He gunned the motor to life and shot away like Barney Oldfield looking to make a new speed record.

As the wrecked evening played itself out to the survivors in the parlor, I made it back to the linen closet, killed the light, and parked my duff on an overturned bucket to wait in the dark. I needed the rest.

The house grew quiet. The last guests departed with enough copy from tonight to fill their monthly pamphlets for years to come. Escott would have some interesting reading to share. I got the impression Flora was not planning another sitting, though a few people assured her that tonight's events should be continued.

The residents finished and came upstairs one by one. Flora Weisinger went into James's room and stayed there for a long time, crying. Abby found her, they talked in low voices for a time, and Flora cried some more. I wasn't sorry. Better now than later, married to a leech. Apparently things worked out. The sisters emerged, each going to her own room. Some servant made a last round, checking the windows, then things fell silent.

I'd taken off the spook coverings, folding the curtain and napkin, slipping them in with similar ones on a shelf. Retrieving my coat and hat I was ready to make a quiet exit until catching the faint sound of "Gloomy Sunday" seeping through the walls.

Damn.

This night had been a flying rout for Bradford, but Flora was still stuck in her pit. She might dig it even deeper until it was a match for her husband's grave.

Someone needed to talk sense into her. I felt the least qualified for the job, but soon as I recognized the music I got that twinge again.

I did my vanishing act and went across to Flora's room.

The music grew louder as I floated toward it, just solid enough to check the lay of the land. The lights were out, only a little glow from around her heavy curtains, enough to navigate and not be seen.

Quick as I could I re-formed, flicked the phonograph's needle arm clear, and pulled out the record. It made a hell of a crunch when I broke it to pieces.

There was a feminine gasp from the bed, and she fumbled the light on. By then I was gone, but sensed her coming over. Another gasp, then . . .

"James?" Her voice quavered with that heartbreaking hope, now tinged with anguish. "James? Oh, please, darling, talk to me. I know you're here."

She'd picked up on the cologne.

"James? *Please* . . ."

This would be tough. I drifted over to a wall and gradually took shape, keeping it slow so she had time to stare, and if not get used to me, then at least not scream.

Hands to her mouth, eyes big, and her skin dead white, she looked ready to faint. This was cruel. A different kind from Bradford's type of torture, but still cruel.

"James sent me," I said, keeping my voice soft. "Please don't be afraid."

She'd frozen in place and I wasn't sure she understood.

I repeated myself and she finally nodded.

"Where is he?" she demanded, matching my soft tone.

"He's with God." It seemed best to keep things as simple as possible. "Everything that man told you was a lie. You know that now, don't you?"

She nodded again, the jerky movement very similar to Abby's mannerism. "Please, let me speak to James."

"He knows already. He said to tell you it wasn't your fault. There's nothing to forgive. It was just his time to go, that's all. *Not* your fault."

"But it *was*."

"Nope." I raised my right hand. "Swear to God. And I should know."

That had her nonplussed. "What . . . who are you?"

"Just a friend."

"That cologne, it's *his*."

"So you'd know he sent me. Flora, he loves you and knows you love him. But this is not the way to honor his memory. He wants you to give it up before it destroys you. He's dead and you're alive. There's a reason you're here."

"What? Tell me!"

"Doesn't work like that, you have to find out for yourself. You won't find answers in a Ouija board, though."

Flora had tentatively moved closer to me. "You look real."

"Thanks, I try my best. I can't stay long. Not allowed. I have to make sure you're clear-headed on this. No more guilt—it wasn't your fault—get rid of this junk and live your life. James wants you to be happy again. If not now, then someday."

"That's all?"

"Flora . . . that's a lifetime. A good one if you choose it."

"I'll . . . all right. Would you tell James—"

"He knows. Now get some sleep. New day in the morning. Enjoy it." I was set to gradually vanish again, then remembered— "One last thing, Flora. James's wedding band." I held my hand out.

"Oh, no, I couldn't."

"Yes, you can. It belongs with him and you know it. Come on."

Fresh tears ran down her face, but maybe this time there would be healing for her. She had his ring on a gold chain around her neck and reluctantly took it off. She read the inscription one more time, kissed the ring, and gave it over.

"Everything will be fine," I said. "This is from James." I didn't think he'd mind. I leaned over and kissed her on the forehead, very lightly, and vanished before she could open her eyes.

For the next few hours I drove around Chicago, feeling like a prize idiot and hoping I'd not done even worse damage to Flora than Alistair Bradford. I didn't think so, but the worry stuck.

Eventually I found my way back to that big cemetery and got myself inside, walking quickly along the path to the fancy mausoleum and the grave behind it.

I was damned tired, but had one last job to do to earn Abby Saeger's five bucks.

Pinching the ring in my fingers as Flora had done at the séance, I extended my arm and disappeared once more, this time sinking into the earth. It was the most unpleasant sensation, pushing down through the broken soil, pushing until what had been my hand found a greater resistance.

That would be James Weisinger's coffin.

I'd never attempted anything like this before but was reasonably sure it was possible. This was a hell of a way to find out for certain.

Pushing just a little more against the resistance, it suddenly ceased to be there. Carefully not thinking what that meant, I focused my concentration on getting just my hand to go solid.

It must have worked, because it hurt like a Fury, felt like my hand was being sawed away at the wrist. Just before the pain got to be too much I felt the gold ring slip from my grasp.

One instant I was six feet under with my hand in a coffin and the next I was stumbling in the snow, clutching my wrist and trying not to yell too much.

My hand was still attached. That was good news. I worked the fingers until they stopped looking so clawlike, then sagged against a tree.

What a night.

I got back in my car just as the sleet began ticking against the windows, trying to get in. It was creepy. I wanted some sound to mask it but hesitated turning on the radio, apprehensive that "Gloomy Sunday" might be playing again.

What the hell. Music was company, proof that there were other people awake somewhere. I could always change the station.

When it warmed up, Bing Crosby sang "Pennies from Heaven." Someone at the radio station had noticed the weather, perhaps, and was having his little joke.

I felt that twinge again, but now it raised a smile.

The First Day of the Rest of Your Life

Rachel Caine

Rachel Caine is known for the bestselling Weather Warden series, as well as her hot new young adult series, The Morganville Vampires. She's also written novels for the Silhouette Bombshell line, and has numerous other books and short stories to her credit. Visit her website at www.rachelcaine.com for news and updates.

Eighteenth birthdays in Morganville are usually celebrated one of two ways: getting totally wasted with your friends or making a terrifying life-or-death decision about your continued survival.

Not that there can't be some combination of the two.

My eighteenth birthday party was held in the back of a rust-colored '70s-era Good Times van, and the select guest list included some of Morganville's Least Wanted. Me, for instance—Eve Rosser. Number of people who'd signed my yearbook: five. Two of them had scrawled C YA LOSER. (Number of people I'd wanted to sign my yearbook? Zero. But that was just me.)

And then there was my best friend, Jane, and her sister, Miranda. I'd invited Jane, not Miranda. Jane was okay—kind of dull, but seriously, with a name like Jane? Cursed from birth. She did like some cool things, other than me of course. Wicked '80s make-out music, for instance. BPAL—Black Phoenix Alchemy Lab—perfume, particularly from the Dark Elements line, although I personally preferred the Funereal Oils. Jane wasn't Goth—more Preppy Nerd Girl than anything else—but she had *some* style.

Miranda, the uninvited one, was a kid. Well, Miranda was a *weird* kid who'd convinced a lot of people she was some kind of psychic. I didn't invite her to the party, because I didn't think she'd be loads of fun, and also she wasn't likely to bring beer. Her BPAL preferences were unknown, mainly because she didn't live on Planet Earth.

Which left Guy and Trent, my two excellent beer-buying buddies. They were my buddies mostly because Guy had a fake ID that he'd made in art class, and Trent owned the party bus in which we were ensconced. Other than that, I didn't know either one of them that well, but they were smart-ass, funny, and safe to get drunk with. Guy and Trent were the only gay couple I actually knew, gaydom being sort of frowned upon in the Heartland of Texas that was Morganville.

We were all about the ironic family values.

The evening went pretty much the way such things are supposed to go: guys buy cheap-ass beer, distribute to underage females, drive to a deserted location (in this case, the creepy-cool high school parking lot) to play loud headbanger music and generally act like idiots. The only thing missing was the make-out sessions, which was okay by me; most of the guys of Morganville were gag worthy, anyway. There were one or two I would have gladly crawled over barbwire to date, but Shane Collins had left town, and Michael Glass . . . well, I hadn't seen Michael in a while. Nobody had.

Jane brought me a birthday present, which was kind of sweet, especially since it was a brand-new mix CD of songs about dead people. Jane knows what I like.

I was still a mystery to Guy and Trent, though. Granted, Morganville's a small town, and all us loser outcast freaks had a nodding acquaintance. The pecking order goes something like this: geeks, freaks, nerds, druggies, gays, and Goths. Goths were on the bottom because the undead think wannabes are disgusting if they're serious about it, or dangerously smart-assed if they aren't. Which I wasn't. Mostly.

Oh, I forgot to mention: vampires. Town's run by them. Full of them. Humans live here on sufferance, heavy on the "suffer."

See what I mean about the ironic family values?

I could tell that Guy had been trying to think of a way to ask me all night, but thanks to consuming over half a case of beer with his Significantly Wasted Other, he finally just blurted out the question of the day. "So, are you signing or what?" he asked. Yelled, actually, over whatever song was currently making my head hurt. "I mean, tomorrow?"

Was I signing? That was the Big Question, the one all of us faced at eighteen. I looked down at my wrist, because I was still wearing my leather bracelet. The symbol on it wasn't anything people outside of Morganville would recognize, but it identified the vampire who was the official Protector for my family. However, as of that morning, I was no longer in that select little club of people who had to kiss Brandon's ass to continue to draw breath.

I also would no longer have any kind of deal or Protection from any vampire in Morganville.

What Guy was asking was whether or not I intended to pick myself a Protector of my very own. It was traditional to sign with your family's hereditary patron, but no way in hell was I letting Brandon have power over me. So I could either shop around to see if any other vampire could—or would—take me, or go bare . . . live without a contract.

Which was attractive but seriously risky. See, Morganville vampires don't generally kill off their own humans, because that would make life difficult for everybody, but free-range, unProtected humans? Nobody worries much what happens to them, because usually they're alone, and they're poor, and they disappear without a trace.

Just another job opening at the Chicken Shack fry machine.

They were all looking at me now. Jane, Miranda, Guy, and Trent, all waiting to hear what Eve Rosser, Professional Rebel, was going to do.

I didn't disappoint them. I tipped back the beer, belched, and said,

"Hell, no, I'm not signing. Bareback all the way, baby! Let's live fast and die young!"

Guy and I did drunken high fives. Trent rolled his eyes and clicked beer bottles with Jane. "They all say that," he said. "Right up until the AIDS test comes back. Then there's the wailing and the weeping. . . ."

"Jesus, Trent, you're the laugh of the party."

"That's *life* of the party, honey bunches. Oh, wait, you're right. Not in Morganville, it isn't." God, Trent was hyper, which was weird for a guy consuming as many brews as he had. Maybe he was just naturally that way. Maybe his Ritalin had worn off. Anyway, it was bugging me.

"Boo-ha-ha. Is that funny at all in other vans in town?" Jane asked. "Because it's not so funny in here, ass pirate."

"You should know, princess; you've been on your back in every van in town," Trent shot back.

"Hey, bitch!" Jane tossed an empty bottle at him; Trent caught it and threw it in the plastic bin in the corner. Which, I had to admit, meant that despite the jittering, Trent could hold his liquor, because he led the field in ounces consumed by a wide margin. "Seriously, Eve—what are you going to do?"

I hadn't thought about it. Or, actually, I had, but in that *what if* kind of way that was really just bullshit bravado . . . but now it was down to do-or-don't, or it would be when the sun came up in the morning. I was going to have to choose, and that choice would rule the rest of my life.

Maybe I shouldn't have gotten quite so trashed, given the circumstances.

"Well, I'm not signing with Brandon," I said slowly. "Maybe I'll shop around for another patron."

"You really think anybody else is going to stand up and volunteer if Brandon's got you marked?" Guy asked. "Girl, you got yourself a death wish."

"Yeah, like *that's* news," Jane said. "Look how she dresses!"

Nothing wrong with how I was dressed. A skull T-shirt, a spiked belt low on my hips, bike shorts, fishnets, black and red Mary Janes. Oh, maybe she was talking about my makeup. I'd done the Full-On Goth today—white face powder, big black rings around my eyes, blue lips. It was sort of a joke.

And also, sort of not.

"It doesn't matter," said a small, quiet voice that somehow cut right through the music.

I'd almost forgotten about Miranda—the kid was sitting in the corner of the van, her knees drawn up, staring off into the distance.

"It speaks," Trent said, and laughed maniacally. "I was starting to think you'd just brought the kid along to protect your virtue, Jane." He gave her a comical flutter of his long, lush eyelashes.

Miranda was still talking, or at least her lips were moving, but her words were lost in a particularly loud guitar crunch. "What?" I yelled, and leaned closer. "What do you mean?"

Miranda's pale blue gaze moved and fixed on me, and I wished it hadn't. There was something really strange about the girl, all right, even if her rep as the town Cassandra was exaggerated. She'd supposedly known about the fire last year that burned the Collins family out; people even said she predicted that Alyssa Collins would die in the fire. Jane said Miranda made it all up after the fact, but who knew? The girl had a double helping of weird, with creepy little sprinkles on top.

"It doesn't matter what you decide to do," she said louder. "Really. It doesn't."

"Yeah?" Trent asked, and leaned over to snag another beer from the Coleman cooler in the center of the van floor. He twisted off the cap and turned it over in his black-polished fingers. "Why's that, o Madame Doom? Is one of us going to die tonight?" They all made hilariously drunken *ooooooooo* sounds, and Trent upended the bottle and chugged.

"Yes," Miranda whispered. Nobody else heard her but me.

And then her eyes rolled up in her skull, and she collapsed flat out on the filthy shag carpet on the floor of the van.

"Jesus," Guy blurted, and crawled over to her. He checked her pulse and breathed a sigh of relief. "I think she's alive."

Jane hadn't moved at all. She looked more annoyed than concerned. "It's okay," she said. "She had some kind of vision. It happens. She'll come out of it."

Trent said, "Damn, I was starting to get worried it was the beer."

"She didn't have any, moron."

"See? Serious beer deficiency. No wonder she's out."

"Shouldn't we do something?" Guy asked anxiously. He was cradling Miranda in his arms, and she was as limp as a rag doll, her head lolling against his head. Her eyes were closed now, moving frantically behind the lids like she was trying to look all directions at once, in the dark. "Like, take her to the hospital?"

The Morganville hospital was neutral ground—no vampires could hunt there. So it was the safest place for anybody who was, well, not working at full power. But Jane just shook her head.

"I told you, this happens all the time. She'll be okay in a couple of minutes. It's like an epileptic seizure or something." Jane looked at me curiously. "What did she say to you?"

I couldn't figure out how to tell her, so I just drank my beer and said nothing.

Probably a mistake.

Jane was right, it took a couple of minutes, but Miranda's eyes fluttered open, blank and unfocused, and she struggled to sit up in Guy's arms. He held on for a second, then let go. She scrambled away and sat in the far corner of the van, next to the empty bottles, with her hands over her head. Jane sighed, handed me her beer, and crawled over to whisper with her sister and stroke her hair.

"Well," Trent said. "Guess the emergency's over. Beer?"

"No," I said, and drained my last bottle. I was feeling loose and sparkly, and I was going to be seriously sorry in the morning—oh, it was morning. Like, nearly 2 a.m. Great. "I need to get home, Trent."

"But the night's barely late–middle age!"

"Trent. Man, I have to go."

"Party pooper. Okay, fine." Trent shot me a resentful look and jerked his head to Guy. "Help me drive, okay?"

"You're driving?" Guy looked alarmed. Trent had downed lots of beer. *Lots.* He didn't seem to be feeling it, and it wasn't like we had far to go, but . . . yeah. Still, I didn't feel capable, and Guy looked even more bleary. Jane . . . well, she hadn't been far behind Trent in the Drunk-Ass Sweepstakes either. And letting a fourteen-year-old epileptic have the wheel wasn't a better solution.

"Not like we can walk," I said reluctantly. "Look, drive slow, okay? Slow and careful."

Trent shot me a crisp OK sign and saluted. He didn't *look* drunk. I swallowed hard and crawled back to sit with Jane and Miranda. "We're going home," I said. "Guess you guys get dropped off first, right? Then me?"

Miranda nodded. "Sit here," she said. "Right here." She patted the carpet next to her.

I rolled my eyes. "Comfy here, thanks."

"No! Sit *here*!"

I looked at Jane and frowned. "Are you sure she's okay?" And made a little not-so-subtle loopy-loop at my temple.

"Yeah, she's fine," Jane sighed. "She's been getting these visions again. Most of the time they're bullshit, though. I think she just does it for the attention."

Jane was looking put out, and I guess she had reason. If Miranda was this much fun at parties, I could only imagine what a barrel of laughs she was at home.

Miranda was getting more and more upset. Jane gave her a ferocious frown and said, "Oh, God. Just do it, Eve. I don't want her having another fit or something."

I crawled across Miranda and wedged myself uncomfortably into the corner where she indicated. Yeah, this was great. At least it was going to be a short drive.

It was what was waiting at the end of it that I was afraid of. Brandon. Decisions. The beginning of my adult life.

Trent started the van and pulled a tight U-turn out of the high school parking lot. There were no side windows, but out of the back windows I saw the big, hulking '30s-era building with its Greek columns fading away like a ghost into the night. Morganville wasn't big on streetlights, although there were a crapload of surveillance cameras. The cops knew where we'd been. They knew everything in Morganville, and half of them were vampires.

God, I wanted to apply for the paperwork to get the hell out, but it was a waste of time. I needed an acceptance letter to an out-of-state university or waivers from the mayor's office. I wasn't likely to get either one with my grades and 'tude. No, I had to face facts: I was a lifer, stuck in Morganville, watching the world go by.

At least, until somebody cut me out of the herd and I became a snack pack.

Trent was driving faster than we'd agreed. Not only that, the van was veering a little to the side of the road. "Yo, T!" I yelled. "Eyes front, man!"

He turned to look back at me, and his pupils were huge and dark, and he giggled, and I had time to think, *Oh shit, he's not drunk; he's high,* and then he hit the gas.

Miranda's hand closed over my arm. I looked at her, and she was crying. "I don't want them to die," she said. "I don't."

"Oh, *Jesus*, Mir, would you stop?" Jane said, and smacked her hand away. "Drama princess."

But I was looking at Miranda, and she was staring at me, and she slowly nodded her head.

"Here it comes," she said, and transferred the stare to her sister. "I'm sorry. I love you."

And then something bad happened, and the world ended.

I walked away from the smoking wreckage. Staggered, actually, coughing and carrying the limp body of Miranda; she was alive, bleeding from the head but still alive.

My brain wouldn't bring up anything about Trent, Jane, or Guy. Nothing. It just . . . refused.

I walked until I heard sirens and saw flashing lights, and dropped to my knees, with Miranda in my lap.

The first cop on the scene was Richard Morrell, the son of the mayor. I'd always thought that even though his family was poisonous, he was kind of a nice guy. He'd been kind to me when I'd had to testify against my brother, after Jason . . . did what he did. Richard proved it again now by easing Miranda out of my arms and to the ground, cushioning her head gently to keep it from bumping against the pavement. His warm hand pressed on my shoulder. "Eve. *Eve.* Anybody else in there?"

I nodded slowly. "Jane. Trent. Guy." Maybe I'd been wrong. Maybe I'd imagined all of that. Maybe they were about to crawl out of that twisted mass of metal and laugh and high five. . . .

Too much imagination. I imagined dead, bloody bodies crawling out of the wreck and swayed. Nearly collapsed. Richard steadied me. "Easy," he said. "Easy, kid. Stay with me."

I did. Somehow, I stayed conscious even when the ambulance drivers wheeled the gurneys past me. Miranda was taken first, of course, and rushed off to the hospital with flashers and sirens.

They didn't bother hurrying for the others. They just loaded the black zippered bags into one ambulance, and it drove away. They wanted me to go with them, but I told them no, I was fine, because no way was I getting in there with the bodies of my friends. I couldn't.

The fire department hosed down the wreck, and it smelled like burned metal and reeking plastic, alcohol, blood. . . .

I was still kneeling there on the pavement, pretty much forgotten, when Richard finally came back, did a double take, and looked grim. "Nobody came to get you? From your family?"

"You called them?"

"Yeah, I called," he said. "Come on. I'll take you home."

I wiped my face. The white makeup was almost gone, and my skin was wet; I hadn't even known I was crying.

Not a mark on me.

Sit here, Miranda had told me. *Right here.* Like she'd known. Like she'd picked me over her own sister.

I couldn't stop shaking. Officer Morrell found a blanket in his patrol car and threw it around my shoulders, and then he bundled me in the back and drove me the five miles home. All the lights were on at my parents' house, but it didn't look welcoming. I checked the time on my cell phone. Three a.m.

"Hey," Richard said. "This is the big day, right? I'm sorry about your friends, but you need to focus now. Make the right choices, Eve. You understand?"

He was trying to be kind, as much as he knew how to be; must have been hard, considering the asshole genes he'd been given. I tried to think what his sister Monica would have said in the same situation. *What a bunch of trashed-out losers. They shouldn't be in our cemetery. We've got a perfectly good landfill.*

I knew Monica too well, but that wasn't Richard's fault. I nodded to him numbly, gave back the blanket, and walked up the ten steps from the curb to my parents' front door.

It opened before I reached for the knob, and I was facing Brandon, the family's vampire Protector.

"I've been waiting for you, Eve," he said, and stepped back. "Come in."

I swallowed whatever smart-ass remark I might normally have given him and looked back over my shoulder. Richard Morrell was looking through the window of the police cruiser at me, and he gave a friendly wave and drove off. Like I was in good hands.

You know every stereotype of the romantic, brooding vampire? Well, that's Brandon. Dark, broody, bedroom eyes, wears a lot of black leather. Liked to think he was badass, and what the hell did I know? Maybe he was. He was badass enough to scare kids, anyway, with those sweet eyes and those cruel hands. Psycho bastard.

I hated his guts, and he knew it.

"Honey?" Mom. She was hovering behind Brandon, looking timid and nervous. "Better come inside. You know you shouldn't be out there in the dark."

Dad was nowhere to be seen. I bit my tongue and crossed the threshold, and when Brandon closed the door behind me, it was like the cell slamming shut.

"I was in an accident," I said. Mom looked at me. We didn't seem much alike, even when I wasn't Gothed up. . . . She had fading brown hair and green eyes, and I took after Dad's darker looks.

"Oh, yes, Officer Morrell called," she said. "But he said you weren't hurt. And you know, we had a guest, we couldn't just *leave.*" She smiled at Brandon. My skin tried to crawl off my bones at the sight of that sick, eager-to-please look on her face.

"Three of my friends were killed," I said. I don't know why I bothered to say it; not like anyone here really cared. But just for once, I wanted to see my mother *feel* something for me.

And once again, I was disappointed. "Oh, dear," Mom said. "That must have been terrible."

Yeah, once more with feeling, Mom. I sometimes thought maybe this was some kind of play, and Mom was an actress, not a very good one. If that was true, she really phoned in her performance.

"Any of mine?" Brandon asked casually. I gritted my teeth, because I wanted to scream and hit him, and that wouldn't have done me any good at all.

"N-no," I managed to stammer over the fury. "Jane Blunt, Trent Garvey, and Guy—" What the hell was Guy's last name? I wanted to cry now. Or keep on crying, because I wasn't sure I'd ever stopped. "Guy Finelli."

Brandon smiled. "Sounds as if Charles had a bad night." Charles being a rival vamp. I knew he was the Protector for Jane's family. I hadn't known he'd been responsible for one or both of the others. Charles was just the opposite of Brandon—a bookish little man, soft-spoken and mild until you pushed him. Not a bad choice, if I had to go shopping for Protectors, I supposed.

God, I hated this. I wanted this *over.*

"Let's just do it," I said, and walked down the hallway to the living room. Predictably, Dad was parked in his recliner with an open beer, probably working on his usual six-pack. He was a bloated vision of my future—two hundred and fifty pounds, sallow and grim and full of rage and resentment he couldn't fling anywhere but around here, in the house. He managed the biggest local bar, which of course was owned by Brandon. All nice and tidy. Brandon owned the mortgage on the house. Brandon owned the notes on our cars.

Brandon owned us.

And now Brandon was smiling at me, all sleek and horrible with those hungry, hungry eyes, and he was taking a folded, thin sheaf of papers out of the pocket of his long black coat.

"You only wear that thing because you saw it on *Angel*," I said, and snatched the paperwork from him. I read the first few sentences. *I, Eve Evangeline Walker Rosser, swear my life, my blood, and my service to my Protector, Brandon, now and for my lifetime, that my Protector may command me in all things.*

This was it. I was holding my future in my hands, right here.

Brandon held out a pen. My father tore his attention away from the glowing escape of the television and took a sip of beer, watching me with angry intensity. My mother looked nervous, fluttering her hands as I stared without blinking at the black Montblanc the vampire was holding out.

"Happy birthday, by the way," Brandon said. "There's a signing bonus. Ten thousand dollars."

"Guess I could bury my friends in style with that," I said.

"You don't have to worry about that." Brandon shrugged. "Their family contracts cover that sort of thing."

Mom sensed what I was thinking, I guess, because she blurted, "Eve, honey, let's hurry. Brandon does have places to go." She encouraged me with little vague motions of her hands, and her eyes were desperate.

I took a deep breath, held the crisp paper in both hands, and ripped it in half. The sound was almost drowned out by my mother's horrified gasp and the sound of the beer can crushing in my father's hand.

"You ungrateful little—" Dad said. "You disrespect your Protector like that? To his face?"

"Yeah," I said. "Pretty much just like that." I ripped the contract in quarters and threw it at him. The paper fluttered like huge confetti, one piece landing on his shoulder until Brandon calmly brushed it off. "Fuck off, Brandon. I'm not signing with you."

"No one else will take you," he said. "And you're mine, Eve. You've always been mine. Don't forget it."

My dad got out of his recliner and grabbed my arm. "You're signing that paper," he said, and shook me like a terrier shaking a rat. "Don't be stupid! Don't you know what you're doing? What you could cost your family if you do this?"

"I'm not signing *anything*!" I screamed, right in his face, and took Brandon's expensive pen and stomped on it with my Mary Janes until it was a leaking black stain on the floor. "You can be slaves if you want, but *not me*! *Not ever again!*"

Brandon didn't look angry. He looked amused. That was bad.

Dad shoved me and sent me reeling. "Then you're gone," he said. "I won't have you in my house, eating my food, stealing my money. If you want to go out there bare, then do it. See how long you last." He turned to Brandon. "Our Protection stays intact if she leaves, right?"

Brandon inclined his head and smiled.

I was stunned, at least a little; Dad had never even threatened a thing like that before. I backed away from him, into Mom. She got out of the way, but then, she always did, didn't she? She had all the backbone of a balloon.

She avoided my eyes completely. "You'd better go, honey," she said. "You made your choice."

I turned and ran down the hall to my room, slammed the door, and dragged my biggest suitcase out from under the bed. I couldn't take much, I knew that; even taking a suitcase was risky, because it slowed me down. But I couldn't wait for dawn; I had to get out of here now, before Brandon stopped me. He wasn't supposed to use compulsion on me, but that didn't mean he wouldn't.

I filled up the bag with underwear, shoes, clothes, and a few mementos that I couldn't leave, just in case Dad decided to fill up the barbecue with my belongings the minute I was out the door. I left the family photos, even the good ones, the ones from when I was a little kid and our family wasn't a total freak show. I didn't want those memories, and I didn't want pictures of my brother Jason, who was better off in jail, where he was currently rotting. Seeing his face made me feel sick.

I went out the back door, since Brandon was still talking to Mom and Dad in the front, and dragged the suitcase as quietly as possible across the backyard to the alley. Alleys in Morganville are freaky at night and wildly dangerous, but I didn't have much choice. I hurried, bouncing my suitcase over rough, rutted ground and past foul-smelling trash bins, until I was on the street.

And I realized I had no idea where to go. No idea at all. All the friends I'd had were dead—dead *tonight*—and I couldn't even really grieve about that; I didn't have time. Life-saving had to come first, right? That's what I kept telling myself.

Didn't help me carry that giant boulder of guilt.

Cabs didn't run at night, because cabbies knew better, and besides, there were only two in the whole town. No bus service. At night, you either drove or you stayed home, and even driving was dangerous if you were unProtected.

I could go to the local motel for the night, the Sagebrush, but it was a good twenty-minute walk, and I didn't think I had twenty minutes. Not tonight. I'd officially forfeited Brandon's Protection when I'd ripped up that paper, and that meant I was an all-you-can-suck buffet until I got somebody to take me in. Houses had automatic Protection. Any house.

Michael. Michael Glass.

Michael lived only a few blocks away. I'd gone to school with Michael, crushed hard on Michael from a distance, and semistalked him after he graduated, attending every single guitar-playing gig he'd landed in Morganville. He was really good, you see. And a sweetheart. And little baby Jesus, he was wicked hot. And he *had his own house.*

I knew the Glass House. It was one of the historical homes of Morganville, all gently decaying Gothic elegance, and Michael's parents had moved out of Morganville on waivers two years ago. Michael lived there all alone, as far as I knew.

And it was only three blocks away.

I had no idea if he was home, or if he'd be stupid enough to let me in when I was running for my life, but it was worth a try, right? I broke into a jog, the wheels of my suitcase making a whirring, grating hiss on the sidewalk. The night felt deep and dark, no moon, only starlight, and it smelled like cold dust. Like a graveyard. Like *my* graveyard.

I thought of Trent, Guy, and Jane, in their silent black bags. Maybe they were in cold metal drawers by now, filed away. Lives over.

I didn't want to be dead. I *didn't.*

So I ran, bumping my suitcase behind me.

I didn't see a soul on the streets. No cars, no lights in windows, no shadows trailing me. It was eerily quiet outside, and my heart was racing. I wished I had weapons, but those were hard to come by in Morganville, and besides, I had nosy parents who trashed my room regularly looking for contraband of all kinds. Being under eighteen sucked.

Being over eighteen wasn't looking so great, either.

I heard the hiss of tires behind me, over the puffing of my breath, and the low growl of a car engine. I looked back, hoping to see Richard Morrell following me in the police car, but no such luck; it was a nondescript black sports car with dark-tinted windows.

Vampire car. No question.

Two more blocks.

The car seemed content to creep along behind me, tires crunching over pavement, and I had plenty of panic-time to wonder who was inside. Brandon, in the back, almost certainly; he'd be cruising with his friends, and when he took me, he'd do it in front of an audience.

The suitcase hit a crack in the sidewalk and tipped over, dragging me to an off-balance halt. I saw a light go on in one of the houses I was passing, and a curtain twitch aside, and then the blinds snapped shut and the lights flicked off. No help there. But then, in Morganville, that wasn't unusual.

I wasn't crying, but it was close; I could feel tears burning in my throat, right above the terror twisting my guts. *This was your choice,* I told myself. *You couldn't do anything else.*

Right now, that wasn't much comfort.

Up ahead, I saw the looming bulk of the Glass House—one more block to go. I could make it, I could. I had to. Jane and Trent and Guy were gone. I owed it to them to live through this.

The car sped up behind me as I crossed the street to the next corner. Four houses to go, all still and lightless.

There was a porch light on in front of 716, and it cast a glow on the pillars framing the porch, picked out the boards in the white fence in front. There were lights on inside, and I saw someone pass in front of a window.

"Michael!" I screamed it and put everything into one last sprint. The car eased ahead of me and pulled in at the curb with a squeal of brakes, tires bumping concrete. A door flew open to block the sidewalk, and I gasped, picked up my suitcase, and tossed it over the fence. It weighed about fifty pounds, but I managed to pick it up and throw it. I grabbed the rough whitewashed boards with their sharp tops and vaulted over, got my shirt caught on the way and ripped it open. No time to worry about that. I grabbed my suitcase and started dragging it over the night-damp grass toward the pool of light. I yelled again, with even more of an edge of panic. "Michael! It's Eve! Open the door!"

They were behind me. They were *right* behind me. I knew it, even though I didn't dare look back and they made no sound. I could feel it. I felt something grab the suitcase, nearly twisting my arm out of the socket, and I let go, stumbling against the porch stairs. The house stretched above me, gray and ghostly in the dark, but that porch light, that was life.

Something caught my foot. I screamed and kicked, fighting to get free, but I went down to my hands and knees, then flat as whoever had me pulled. My searching fingers scratched at the closed wood of the door, and I tasted dust again. I'd been close, so close. . . .

The door opened, and warm yellow light spilled out over me. Too late. I tried to grab for a handhold but I was being yanked backward . . . and I could feel breath on the back of my neck. Cold, rancid breath.

Something flew over my head and slammed into the vampire pulling on me, knocking him backward. I crawled back toward the door and got a hand over the threshold.

Michael Glass grabbed my fingers and dragged me inside with one long pull. My feet made it over the line just a fraction of a second before another vampire slammed into the invisible barrier there.

That vampire was Brandon. Oh, damn, he was angry. *Really* angry. Our vampires were all about fitting in, but right now he clearly didn't care what we saw. His eyes had turned bloodred, and his face was whiter than I'd ever made mine. And I could see fangs, fangs a viper would have envied, flicking down from their hiding place to flash in menace.

And Michael Glass didn't flinch. In fact . . . he smiled. "You're not coming in, Brandon, so save it," he said. "Leave."

He looked like I remembered him from high school, from the concerts, only . . . better, somehow. Stronger. Tall, built, golden hair that waved and curled surfer-style. He had blue eyes, and they were fixed on Brandon. Wary, but definitely not afraid.

"You okay?" he asked me. I nodded, unable to say anything that would really cover how I felt. "Then get out of the way."

"Huh?"

"Your legs. Please."

I pulled them toward me, and he calmly shut the door in Brandon's face. I sat there on the wooden floor, knees pulled in to my chest, and tried to slow my heart down from triple digits. "God," I whispered, and rested my forehead on my knees. "That was close."

I heard the rustle of fabric. Michael had crouched down across from me, back to the opposite wall. He was wearing some comfortable old jeans, a faded green cotton shirt, and his feet were long and narrow and bare. "Eve Rosser, right?" he asked. "Hi."

"Hi, Michael." I was having trouble getting my breath.

"How have you been?"

"Good. You?"

"Fine. What the hell is going on?"

"Um . . . my eighteenth birthday." I was shivering, and I realized my skull shirt was displaying a whole lot more bra than I'd ever intended. Kind of a plunge bra. Victoria's Secret. Not so much of a secret right now. "Brandon's kind of pissed. I didn't sign."

Michael rested his head against the wall and looked at me with narrowed eyes. "You didn't sign. Oh, man."

I shook my head, unable to say much more about that. I knew what he was thinking, and he was right: I'd brought trouble right to his door. Some friend. Acquaintance. Whatever. My cousin Bob always used to say *No good deed goes unpunished.* In Morganville, Bob was damn sure right.

Michael said, "You got someplace to go? Relatives, maybe?"

I just looked at him miserably, and I felt tears starting to bubble up again. What had I been hoping for? Some white knight hottie to save me? Well, I wasn't going to get it from Michael. He hadn't even come outside to get me, he'd just thrown a chair or something.

Still, he'd opened the door. Nobody else on this street had or would have.

"Okay," Michael said softly. He stretched out a hand and awkwardly patted me on the knee. "Hey. You're okay, right? You're safe in here now. Don't cry."

I didn't want to cry, but that was how I vented, and boy, did I need to vent. All the fury and grief and rage and confusion just boiled up inside and forced their way out. I was sobbing like a punk, and after a couple of shaking breaths I felt Michael move across to sit next to me. His arm went around me, and I turned toward his warmth, soaking his shirt with tears. I would have told him everything then, all the bad stuff . . . the van, my friends, Brandon. I would have told him how Brandon gave my dad a pay raise when I was fifteen in return for unrestricted access to me and Jason. I would have told him *everything.*

Lucky for him I couldn't get my breath.

Michael was good at soothing; he knew not to talk, and he knew just how to touch my hair and how to hold me. It wasn't until the storm became more like occasional showers, and I was able to hiccup steady breaths, that I realized he had a clear view down my bra.

"Hey!" I said, and tried to artfully tuck the torn edges of my shirt under the strap. Michael had an odd look on his face. "Free show's over, Glass."

Trent would have snapped back some snazzy insult, but not Michael. Michael just looked uncomfortable and edged away from me. "Sorry," he said. "I wasn't—"

Well, if he wasn't, I was offended. I gave good bra: 34B.

He must have seen it in my expression, because Michael held up his hands in surrender. "Okay, yeah. I was. That makes me an asshole, right?"

"No, that makes you male and straight," I said. Was it wrong I felt relieved? "I just need to change my— Oh, damn. My suitcase! It's still out there—"

"Come on." Michael got up and walked down the polished wooden hallway. The house felt warm but strange—old, and despite the big open rooms, kind of claustrophobic. Like it was . . . watching. I loved it. I had no idea why, but it just felt . . . right. Strange and odd and right.

The living room was normal stuff—couch, chairs, bookcases, throw rugs. A guitar case lying open on a small dining table, and the acoustic was abandoned on the couch as if he'd put it down to see what the trouble was out in the yard. I'd heard Michael play before, though not recently. People had said he'd given it up . . . but I guessed he hadn't. Maybe he'd just given up performing.

Michael pulled the blinds and looked out. "It's on the lawn," he said. "They're going through it."

"What?" I pushed him out of the way and tried to see for myself, but it was all just a black blur. "They're going through my stuff? *Bastards!*" Because I had some lingerie in there that I seriously wanted to keep private. Well, maybe share with one other person. But privately. I yanked the cord on the blinds and moved them up, then unlocked the window and threw up the sash. I leaned out and yelled, "Hey, assholes, you touch my underwear and—"

Michael yanked me back by my belt and slammed the window shut about one second before Brandon's face appeared there. "Let's not taunt the angry vampires," he said. "I have to live here."

Deep breaths, Eve. Right. Suitcase not as important as jugular. I sat down in one of the chairs, trying to get hold of myself and not even sure who that was anymore. Myself, I mean. So much had changed in five hours, right? I was an adult now. I was on my own in a town where being alone was a death sentence. I'd made a very bad enemy, and I'd done it deliberately. I'd been disowned by my own family, not that they'd been much of a family in the first place.

"I am so screwed," I said. Michael didn't say anything to that; it was kind of rhetorical. "So. You look like a nice, nonpsycho kind of guy. Need an unstable roommate with lots of enemies?" I asked, and tried for a mocking smile. Michael hesitated in the act of reaching for his guitar, then settled in on the couch with the instrument cradled in his lap like a favorite pet. He picked out random notes, pure and cool, and bent his head. "Sorry. Bad joke."

"No, it's not," he said. "Actually—I might consider it."

"What?"

"I didn't sign, either," he said.

Oh, man. No, I hadn't known that; I couldn't remember who his family's Protector had been, but it couldn't have been Brandon. Michael wasn't wearing a symbol bracelet, so no clues there.

"I was thinking," he continued, "that maybe we ought to stick together. Those of us who don't have contracts. Besides, you and me, we always got along in school. I mean, we didn't know each other that well, but—" Nobody had known Michael really well, except his buddy Shane Collins, but Shane had bugged out of Morganville with his parents after his sister's death. Everybody had *wanted* to know Michael, but he was private. Shy, maybe. "It's a big house. Four bedrooms, two baths. Hard to manage it by myself. Bills and crap."

Was he offering? Really? I swallowed and leaned forward. My shirt was coming loose again, but I left it that way. I needed every advantage I could get. "I swear, I'm good for rent. I'll get a job somewhere, at one of the neutral places. And I clean stuff. I'm a demon with the cleaning."

"Cook?" He looked hopeful, but I had to shake my head. "Damn. I'm not so great at it."

"You'd have to be better than me. I can screw up the recipe for water."

He smiled. He had one of *those* smiles. You know the ones—the kind that unleashes lethal force on girls in the vicinity. I couldn't remember him smiling in high school. He was probably aware that it might cause girls to faint or unbutton clothes or something.

"We'll think about it until tomorrow night," he said. "Pick any room but the first one; that's mine. Sheets are in the closet. Towels are in the bathroom."

"My suitcase—"

"After dawn." He was looking down again, picking out a sweet, quiet melody from the strings. "Look, I've got someplace I have to go before then, but you'll be safe enough if you just go out to get it and come right back inside. I don't think Brandon's pissed enough to hang around in the sun."

"But you can't go out in the dark! He could—"

"Brandon? No, he couldn't. Trust me."

Oh, no. Alarm bells went off. "You're not—"

He looked up sharply. "I'm not what?"

I mimed fangs.

Michael sighed. "No, I'm not."

"Well, you know, the whole gone-during-daylight thing . . ."

"I have a job; maybe you've heard of it. You leave the house, make money . . . ? Any other questions?"

"Yeah. Then how come you're up so late if you have to get up so early?"

He looked at me for a second blankly, like he couldn't believe I'd asked. "Well," he said slowly, "I *do* get up to eat, shower, that kind of thing before work. Why? Don't you?"

Oh. Put like that, it didn't sound quite as suspiciously vampiric. I swallowed hard, wondering if I could trust him. If I should. *Well, idiot, what choices do you have?*

I pulled the silver chain around my neck and flipped the tiny silver cross out to hang over the tattered rags of my shirt. "Touch it," I said.

"What?" He now clearly thought I was crazy.

"Touch the cross, Michael."

"Oh, for Christ's sake—"

"I have to be sure."

He reached out and put a fingertip squarely on the cross, then spread his whole hand over it.

That came comfortably close to the top of my breasts. Not what I'd intended, but . . . wow. Bonus.

We sat there for a long second, and then Michael cleared his throat and sat back. "Satisfied?" He seemed to realize it was a trick question and didn't wait for an answer. "I'll be back by dark. We'll talk about the rent then. But for now, you should—" He looked up. His gaze reached the level of my chest, stopped, and then lowered again. The smile this time was directed at the guitar. "Put on a new shirt or something."

"Well, I would, but all my shirts are in my suitcase, getting molested by Brandon and his funboys." I flipped a finger at the window, in case they were watching.

"Get something out of my closet," he said. I thought he was playing something from Coldplay's catalog now, something soft and contemplative. "Sorry about the, uh, staring. I know you've had a tough night."

There was something so damn *sweet* about that, it made me want to cry. Again. I swallowed the impulse. "You don't know the half of it," I said.

This time, when he looked up, his gaze actually made it to my face. And stayed there. "I'm guessing that means bad."

"Oh, whole new definitions of bad. But you don't want to hear about that."

"You'd tell me if I was a friend, right? And not just some guy whose door you randomly knocked on in the middle of the night?"

I thought about Jane, poor sweet Jane, my best and only real friend. Trent and Guy, who probably had been destined for nothing but still had been, for tonight at least, my buds. "I'm not so good for my friends," I said. "Maybe we ought to just call you a really nice stranger." I took a deep breath. "I lost three people tonight, and it was my fault."

He kept looking at me. Really looking. It was a little bit hot, and a little bit disconcerting. "Then would you talk to a really nice stranger about it? For—" He checked his watch. "Forty minutes? I need to leave, but I want you to be okay before I do."

It only took thirty minutes to tell him about the Life and Times of Me, actually. Michael didn't say very much, and I felt so tired afterward that I hardly knew it when he got up and went into the kitchen. I must have dozed off a little, because when I woke up, he was kneeling next to my chair, and he had a chocolate brownie on a plate. With a semimelted pink candle sputtering away on top.

"It's a leftover," he warned me. "It was crap in the first place, so I don't know how good it is. But happy birthday, anyway. I promise you, things will get better."

I had news for him. They just had.

When the sun came up, I'd have a whole new set of problems. Not the least of which would be finding a workplace not afraid to hire a girl with serious vampire relations issues and a wardrobe that leaned toward the macabre.

But for now?

I took a bite of brownie, smiled at my new housemate, and celebrated my freedom.

The Witch and the Wicked

Jeanne C. Stein

Jeanne C. Stein is the author of the Anna Strong series, the first of which, The Becoming, *was released in December 2006. The second book,* Blood Drive, *was published in July. She lives in Colorado, where, when not working on her novels, she edits a newsletter for a beer importer and takes kickboxing classes to stay in shape. She can be reached through her website, www.jeannestein.com.*

The idea came to Sophie during Jonathon Deveraux's one hundred fiftieth birthday party.

She was not there as a guest, of course. Witches are seldom invited to vampire functions, their magics dismissed as parlor tricks to amuse the masses. No, she was catering the event. Her business, Weird and Wonderful Catering (voted number one in the latest Supernatural Hot Ticket poll as *the* caterer for that special event), made her the only choice for a party of this scope and magnitude. For the moment, at least, her questionable heritage as a witch was forgotten.

Sophie blew on the tip of her finger and muttered, "Extinguishé."

The small lick of flame sputtered and died. She waved her hand in the air in a vaguely distracted way, looking down at the cake and its many candles.

"Damn vamps," she said to no one in particular. Well, to no one at all, really, since she was alone in the room. Still, that didn't stop her from rambling on. "Why did I agree to this? I almost burned my finger off lighting all those damned candles."

She turned from the table with a rustle of silk, her long burgundy skirt swirling around her legs. She wasn't an old witch, as witches go. Only eighty years. Her back was still straight, her dark hair barely touched with gray. She didn't look a day over forty, really. Good genes. And even better cosmetics, most of her own making.

She blew again on her smarting fingertip. She ought to pursue that—marketing her own line of fine cosmetics—instead of this thankless occupation. Caterers were underpaid, overworked, and generally ignored. Unless something went wrong. Then they became the center of unwanted and often perilous attention.

Especially with her unique clientele.

The door to the kitchen swung open. "Are you ready with the cake, Sophie?"

The question was asked in an eager, breathless way by a woman who looked twenty but whom Sophie suspected might be a little older, though certainly not by much. With vampires it was hard to tell. The woman standing in front of Sophie was confident, beautiful, and wife to a distinguished vampire. She was dressed to the nines in a designer gown with jewels that flashed at her neck and ears. Rumor had it that Mr. Deveraux turned her on their wedding night, and that was only six months ago. Now here she was, acting every bit the mistress of the manor.

Sophie swallowed a wave of envy and said, "Yes, ma'am. Would you like me to bring it in?"

"Oh, I want to do it." The woman's face glowed with anticipation. "Jonathon will be so surprised."

Sophie frowned. "You must be careful, Mrs. Deveraux," she said. "There are one hundred fifty burning candles on this cake. If your dress brushes against even one of them—"

Her concern was flicked away with the back of a bejeweled hand. "Don't worry. I know how to be careful around fire. This is my surprise and I want to deliver it."

Sophie stepped back from the table. "As you wish."

The woman took her place behind a tea cart bearing the huge tower of a cake. Sophie held open the door, careful to keep her own dress and hair out of the path of the blazing birthday tribute. The air fairly shimmered from the heat and glare of the candles. Why a vampire, especially such an old one, wanted candles on his cake was a mystery to her. One spark and he would burst into flame like an old Christmas tree.

Sophie hadn't met Jonathon Deveraux, tonight's guest of honor, but she had seen a picture of him, a portrait hanging over the fireplace, when she came to finalize the party arrangements. He was a tall, good-looking man who must have been turned in his thirties because his face was unlined, his hair dark and thick. That it was a contemporary portrait was borne out by his clothing, a casual shirt and linen slacks, and a backdrop of the stables here on the property. It was just an impression, the feeling that this was not a man who would have indulged in such a pretentious birthday display as one hundred fifty burning candles. No, Sophie thought, this must have been the idea of his vacuous new wife, too recently turned to know the danger.

Oh, well. Sophie looked at the mountain of cake pans and utensils stacked in the sink. Not her problem. Time to clean up.

She waved a hand. "Lavàto."

The dishes arranged and rearranged themselves, moving from a sink of soapy water to another of clear running water and then onto a rack to be dried by a gentle stream of warm air. From the rack, they floated to the proper shelves in the cupboard or into silverware drawers. All done in the whisk of a cat's tail.

For the first time this evening, Sophie could relax. The cake was done, the kitchen in order. She had nothing to do now but wait for the festivities to be over. In reality, a vampire party was the easiest of all supernatural functions to cater. Vampires didn't require food. But they did like to impress each other with flashy displays, like the birthday cake. She found her biggest challenge for a vampire party was coming up with novel ways to serve blood. Like *real* Bloody Marys (finding thirty women named Mary to donate blood was no easy feat!). Tonight she had gone to great lengths to find something really special—a case of vintage Rothschild taken from actual Rothschilds. She hoped the guest of honor appreciated the effort, since he was paying for it. But like most rich vampires, and their condescending wives, he would most likely take the gesture for granted along with the witch who provided it.

Thankless. This job was thankless.

Sophie took a seat on a stool and leaned her elbows on a granite countertop. She let her thoughts wander again to her favorite subject of late—starting her own cosmetics firm. She was facing the shiny surface of a chrome toaster and she scooted down to examine her reflection.

Clear skin. Tiny wrinkles touching the corners of wide blue eyes. Generous mouth with none of the telltale crinkles that caused lipstick to smear and marked the lips of the middle-aged woman. She truly did not look her age. Not in the way of vampires who not only physically stopped the aging process but reversed it. But nearly as good. Her creams slowed it to a crawl. And her cosmetics transformed the plain into . . . She examined her features. Her mascara made pale lashes long and dark, and her blush gave cheeks the definition that nature hadn't.

She touched the tip of her nose. Nothing short of surgery would fix something like that, of course. But artfully applied foundation, dark at the sides of her nose and light at the tip, diminished the contour.

She wasn't beautiful by any means. But she *was* good at this. She could show others how to be good at it, too.

She'd made a success of the catering business; why not try her hand at cosmetics?

The screech and howl came simultaneously and Sophie jumped off the stool.

Ye gods, she thought. The idiot has caught herself on fire.

This was exactly what she feared might happen. Sophie knew in spite of her warnings to Mrs. Deveraux, *she* would be blamed for the accident.

For a second, she considered fleeing. But that would be a waste of time. Mr. Deveraux knew his wife had hired Sophie to cater his party. Unless she planned to transport herself to an alternate universe, he would find her.

She might as well face the music now. Teleportation would be a last resort. She listened as the din of the crowd gradually faded from shock and horror to mumbled condolences to the new widower. Sophie waited for the kitchen door to open and for the bereaved to storm in to exact his revenge.

It took much longer than she anticipated. The crowd was slow to leave, evidently, and Mr. Deveraux in no hurry to show them out. This puzzled Sophie but again, the antics of vampires were a constant source of puzzlement to her. They never did what was expected or what decorum dictated. She guessed that's what came from living hundreds of years and not being tied to the laws of god or man.

Sophie began to relax. Obviously, Mr. Deveraux was not devastated by the loss of his wife. Perhaps he had grown tired of her already. After all, what could he have had in common with such a young woman? In the manner of adolescents today (for to Sophie, anyone under the age of thirty was an adolescent), she would neither know nor care anything about recent history, let alone events from her husband's distant past.

Sophie took the fact that Deveraux had not yet made an attempt on her life as a sign from the gods that it was indeed time to switch careers.

When it became obvious that the party was proceeding, Sophie took a seat again at the counter. She pulled a small notebook from the pocket of her tunic and opened it. On the inside cover was clipped a pen which she pulled free. With a careful, precise hand, she started making notations. She thought a night cream would be a good introductory product. When women saw the results, they would naturally want something for the daytime, too. Following that, she would launch cosmetics: foundation, blushers, mascaras. All with the same miraculous base guaranteed to slow the ravages of age.

Hmmmm. Ravishing. That might be an appropriate name for the line. A play on words. Ravaged to Ravishing. Voilà. A slogan.

Sophie felt the excitement build. She would do this. While the catering business was basically a one-woman show, this would be different. Her lotions were made the old-fashioned way, by hand. She would need to find a suitable place to make the cosmetics in batches large enough to accommodate what was sure to be a huge demand. And there was packaging and marketing to consider. She knew a warlock in advertising. He could help her find the right people to handle—

The kitchen door flew open. Sophie, caught unaware and deep in her own musings, nearly fell off the stool. She scrambled to regain her footing and steeled herself to meet Mr. Deveraux.

"I'm so sorry, sir," she began, turning to face what would surely be her angry host.

The words died on her lips. *Mrs.* Deveraux stood smiling at her from the doorway. "Not to worry, Sophie," she said. "Mr. Deveraux had a long, full life. He went out in a blaze of glory befitting a vampire of his age and stature."

Sophie was too stunned to reply. How could a vampire as old as Mr. Deveraux let himself be caught on fire? Her candles were magic. One puff on one candle and the rest extinguished themselves. It was a safety feature of her own invention designed exclusively for vampires. The only danger would have come when the cake was presented.

She narrowed her eyes. "I don't understand."

Mrs. Deveraux waved a hand. "It's nothing for you to worry about. I have no intention of seeking retribution." She bent her head and examined her carefully manicured fingernails. "It was entirely my fault. I tripped on the rug and the cart bumped Mr. Deveraux. When he turned around, poof. His jacket caught. It was an unfortunate accident."

She looked up at Sophie then, her own eyes tightening a little at the corners. "I'm sure you must be relieved to know I don't hold you responsible in any way."

Sophie was smart enough to recognize the threat. She shrugged. "I am relieved, yes."

The bright smile returned. "Then please come and do a quick cleanup, will you? There is ash on the cake, but I think if you work your magic, you can re-frost it or something and we can enjoy it. After all, my guests and I have heard so much about your wonderful cakes. It would be a shame to throw this one away. Will you fix it? Please?"

Sophie waved a hand, and a spatula flew from a drawer and into her grasp. She followed Mrs. Deveraux into the living room, barely drawing so much as a glance from anyone at the party. In fact, everyone seemed to have recovered quite nicely from the recent tragedy, thank you. The laughter and chatter and clink of glassware went on as if Sophie were here to clean up a small culinary accident instead of disposing of the host's mortal remains.

Sophie examined the cake. A dusting of ash did indeed cover one side, and a small mound of the stuff sparkled on the floor. Vampire dust was like diamond dust, hard and bright and the consistency of fine beach sand. Wouldn't do to bite into it. She started to smooth dust and icing away from the base of the candles when Mrs. Deveraux stopped her with a butterfly touch to the arm.

"Get rid of those candles, too, won't you? It's a gruesome reminder of—well, you know."

Sophie nodded. Yes, she did know. Mrs. Deveraux showed no more grief for her dearly departed than any of her guests. Maybe it was a good thing Sophie hadn't met Mr. Deveraux. He must have been a thoroughly disagreeable individual to have his passing marked with such ambivalence.

Sophie invoked a spell and the candles disappeared. It made patching the icing much easier. When she was finished with the cake, she muttered another spell and a small dustpan and whisk broom materialized. She scooped up the ash from the floor and the small mound of dust-embedded icing and, with a nod to Mrs. Deveraux, retreated with relief back to the kitchen.

Sophie scraped the gritty icing into the garbage disposal. She stared at the sandy residue left sparkling in the dustpan. This was the first time anything like this had happened at one of her parties. She'd heard the stories of vampires accidentally immolating themselves through drunken or careless behavior. It happened more often than people realized, actually. Vampires took their immortality for granted and didn't follow basic principles of common sense. Falling asleep with a lighted cigarette, for instance, was as fatal to vampires as humans.

Sophie shook the remains of the late Mr. Deveraux into the palm of her hand and let him—it—sift through her fingers. The ash felt surprisingly silky to the touch. She thought of the portrait hanging over the fireplace. Mr. Deveraux died the second death on his one hundred fiftieth birthday, and yet he passed among humans as a thirty-year-old. Now *that* was the ultimate age defyer.

She sat up straight. How did vampires do it? How did they remain physically ageless regardless of the passing of time?

They drank blood, for one.

Sophie's brow wrinkled in concentration. She reviewed what she knew about vampire physiology. It wasn't a lot. She did remember reading somewhere that the blood thing was to supply energy needed to replace what could no longer be derived from normal food sources. Vampires had all the internal organs of an ordinary human. They just no longer functioned, frozen in their bodies, Sophie guessed, to preserve the outward physical appearance of a normal human being.

So was that what made them immortal? Organs that did not atrophy with age or disease? Was that what stopped the aging process?

She had no idea. Nor did she have anyone she could ask. Witches and vampires avoided each other. She was an exception, as were other witches who supplied services that vampires were unable or unwilling to perform for themselves.

She looked again at the ash, winking like starlight in the glare of the kitchen's bright incandescence. This was the essence of a vampire.

What would happen if she mixed some of the ash into her lotions?

She felt a thrill as the idea took shape. Why not try it? What if adding the ash to her moisturizer, instead of merely slowing or decreasing the signs of age was, in fact, able to reverse them? It would be a revolutionary breakthrough. And it would be hers.

Sophie carefully emptied the ash into a ziplock bag and tucked it into a pocket in her tunic. She grew restless, impatient to get out of here and eager to experiment with this new ingredient. Glancing at her watch, she saw that it was just a little before 1 a.m. Drat. Since vampires had adapted to sunlight, the constraint of getting home before dawn was no longer an issue. This party could drag on well into midday.

How to get around that?

What could she say to get Mrs. Deveraux to allow her leave early? The obvious answer would be that she was devastated by the accident. She could offer to come back tomorrow and clean up, maybe even throw in a free cocktail party to be given at Mrs. Deveraux's time of choosing.

Vampires, for all their accumulated wealth, were notoriously tightfisted. The free party might just do it.

Sophie closed her eyes and willed Mrs. Deveraux to come into the kitchen. She had only to wait a minute before the woman appeared at the door, looking slightly puzzled.

She frowned at Sophie. "Now this is strange. A second ago I had a reason to come into the kitchen but now I seem to have forgotten it completely." She laughed a little self-consciously. "The events of this evening must have unnerved me more than I realized."

Sophie assumed a properly downcast expression. She even began to clasp and unclasp her hands like an anxious schoolgirl facing a stern headmistress, making sure her distress transmitted itself through the air and into Mrs. Deveraux's consciousness.

Mrs. Deveraux immediately picked up on Sophie's angst. She reached out a hand but stopped just short of touching her. Sophie was, after all, the help and a witch to boot. "Please, Sophie," she said. "I can see how upset you are. I assure you there will be no repercussions from tonight's accident."

Sophie let a single tear trail down her cheek. "I just feel so awful. The whole thing is making me physically ill." For added emphasis, she brought a fist up and pressed it against her mouth.

Mrs. Deveraux backed away in alarm. "Perhaps you should go home," she said quickly. "I didn't consider how this might affect a woman of your age. I can have my own staff clean up tomorrow. There is no need for you to stay." She caught herself then and gave Sophie a sideways glance. "Naturally, I would expect a credit on the bill. . . ."

Vampires were so predictable. Sophie kept her face a mask of unhappiness. "Naturally."

After that impudent crack about "a woman of her age" (for Mrs. Deveraux had no way of knowing how old Sophie was), Sophie was tempted to forget about the party offer. But she didn't have that many vampire contacts and if the ash worked . . . She acknowledged Mrs. Deveraux's permission to leave with a nod. "And for your consideration, I would be happy to cater a small cocktail party for you in the future. No charge."

That clinched it. Mrs. Deveraux practically pushed Sophie out the door with admonitions to take care going home and to put the unfortunate event of the evening out of her mind.

Sophie waited until the door was firmly latched behind her to allow a smile. She summoned her transport telepathically. She didn't drive. Often she teleported herself, a trick she learned from her big sister. Not many witches could do it. It took concentration, though, and she found when she was distracted or excited the results were sometimes spotty. She might end up in a different county or a different state. Tonight she was both distracted *and* excited. Better to be safe than sorry.

Besides, she liked to support local business. The company she used was owned by a warlock with a driving service that provided after-hours transportation for supernaturals at reduced rates. Sometimes that meant waiting awhile for a car to appear. But tonight Sophie was lucky.

In a matter of minutes, the cab materialized in the driveway. Sophie climbed in, greeted the driver, and gave her address. The cabbie neither acknowledged the greeting nor the address. In fact, he hardly waited for her to pull shut the door before the car lurched away. Sophie's head banged against the headrest.

Had a bad day, have we?, she thought grumpily, wondering if she should make it worse by giving him warts.

But happier thoughts soon prevailed. She couldn't wait to get home and mix up a batch of moisturizer, this time with a pinch of Mr. Deveraux. How much to use would be a serious consideration. She pulled the baggie out of her pocket. There wasn't a lot of ash. Even considering what little she scraped off the cake, the amount left would maybe fill a half-cup measure. It must be terrifically concentrated.

The driver screeched to a stop in front of her house the same abrupt way he had pulled away from the Deveraux mansion. Again, Sophie's head bounced. Her temper flared and she raised a hand to plant a great big hairy wart on the tip of his nose when he turned around for the first time.

She let her hand fall. Great. Of all the drivers in the city I get the troll, she thought. His hairy face was already covered with warts. And trolls were notoriously bad drivers.

His guttural voice barked at her. "Here you be, ma'am. That'll be twenty bucks."

She clicked her tongue and forked over the cash, adding a five-dollar tip even though she knew he didn't deserve it. She had a soft spot for trolls. They couldn't help how they looked or their thorny temperaments. It was genetic.

At least this time, he waited for her to get all the way out of the cab before gunning away from the curb.

Sophie started up the path to her house. She lived on the outskirts of the city, a place close enough to allow access to the museums and theaters she loved, but far enough removed to allow the kind of outdoor activity witches enjoyed without attracting the curiosity or attention of neighbors. Her cottage was small but comfortable and she filled it with beautiful earthly objects—rocks, seashells, flowers, and plants. It was a place of refuge and light.

And best of all, it was a place with a basement.

Which is where Sophie headed now, pausing only to switch on a light upstairs before heading down. Her workshop was here. Her tools, her cauldrons, her herbs. She'd had an industrial sink and stove installed and shelving to hold the basic ingredients of her cosmetic line. Everything was neat and orderly and stored in a way to make her work easy.

Sophie was nothing if not organized.

She tied her hair back and an apron around her slender frame and got right to work. In forty minutes, she had a batch of moisturizer brewing on the stove. It was time to add the new ingredient; time to add Mr. Deveraux and see what he brought to the mix. Her hand was shaking with excitement as she measured out a teaspoon, then reduced it by one half. After all, she had no idea what the effect of the ash would be. And since she was going to be the guinea pig in this experiment, she felt it prudent to proceed cautiously. She could always add more to a later batch if need be.

Sophie stirred in the ash. It dissolved into the cream base instantly. Now all she had to do was wait for the mixture to cool. She could hardly stand still, her excitement and impatience bubbled up inside her like champagne waiting to be uncorked. She stuck her finger into the pan, testing, again and again only to snatch it back and dance around waving her burned digit. Why was it taking so long for the damned stuff to cool? She had spells to make things hot as fire but none that did the opposite. She'd have to work on that.

Later.

At last, the mixture was cool enough to allow Sophie to spoon a portion onto a glass plate. She swirled it a bit, approving of the texture—not too greasy, not too dry. She lifted the plate and sniffed. A nice citrusy bouquet . . . with just a slight undercurrent of musk. She wrinkled her nose and sniffed again. The citrus was supposed to be there. The musk? She wasn't too thrilled but realized that the musk was Mr. Deveraux. He was male, after all. Perhaps in the next batch she would add a stronger fragrance—essence of jasmine, maybe, or frangipani—to counteract it.

In any case, the scent was not important. It was time to sample the cream, to see if what she hoped was true.

Her hand shook a little as she scooped a portion onto two fingers. She crossed the room to watch in the mirror as she smoothed the moisturizer onto her face. It felt rich and luxurious on her skin. That was a good thing. It was absorbed quickly into her skin, leaving no greasy residue. Good, again. It tingled just a little. Sophie's inspiration for when she took the stuff public. It gave the impression that there were active ingredients in the lotion, that it was *doing* something. An attribute of her original formula.

They were all attributes of her original formula.

So far, she saw and felt nothing new. No flush of rejuvenation. No tightening of the skin to signal a return to youthful firmness and texture.

Maybe she needed to give it more time.

She stared at her reflection. And waited.

And waited.

Finally, after fifteen minutes, she gave up. With a shrug, she turned away from the mirror. She wouldn't let herself be too disappointed. This was only a first attempt, after all. She stared at the pan on the stove, wondering if she should give it another try tonight. But her tired feet and tight shoulders intervened, begging to be put to bed.

Sophie acquiesced with a sigh. She *was* exhausted. She locked the baggie with the remains of Mr. Deveraux in a drawer, flipped off the light, and went upstairs to lay her weary bones to rest.

When she awoke the next morning, the first thing Sophie did was rush into the bathroom to examine her face in the mirror. She'd had a dream that the cream worked. Her dreams were often portents of things to come and she believed in them.

But she could see nothing changed in the heart-shaped face that stared back at her. The tiny wrinkles still radiated out from the corners of her eyes. Her hair was still touched with gray at the temples, though she hadn't really expected the cream would change her hair. Not unless she rubbed the stuff into it. She scolded herself in impatience for thinking such ridiculous thoughts. If she wanted to change her hair, there were plenty of conventional human products on the market to take care of it. No, she was looking for something different. Something to take the years away, not just cover them up.

She got dressed and went directly back down to the basement. This time she added a full teaspoon of the ash to a new batch of moisturizer. She applied it liberally and went about her day.

There were always lots of chores for a practicing witch. Besides her catering business, Sophie had clientele who came for readings or spells. There were herbs to gather, earth summonings to perform. She was an important witch in her part of the country, and a great deal of her time was spent in correspondence with others of similar station all around the world. Generally, the time passed quickly and she was content.

Today, however, Sophie felt restless and ill at ease. She couldn't concentrate on her readings, had no interest in her spells. She ignored the weeds in her garden and cut short her correspondence on the Worldwide Witches Web, even though one of the messages was from her sister and marked "important."

When at last evening arrived, she allowed herself to look in the mirror. She saw no remarkable changes. Actually, she saw no changes at all. She stared at her reflection and frowned bitterly.

Then she grew angry with herself. She recognized why her day had been unproductive and knew very well what was at the root of her restlessness. She had been self-indulgent, selfish, something very out of character. She had gotten caught up in a foolish daydream. She knew there was nothing (short of becoming vampire) that could reverse the signs of age. What had possessed her to even consider it? Especially since her own formulas worked a kind of magic in themselves and didn't rely on immolated vampire dust to work.

No, better to proceed with her original formulas. They were pretty darned good when you thought about it. Look at her. She was eighty, for goodness sake, and no one ever believed it when she told them. Besides, even if the formula had worked, how did she think she'd get her hands on more vampire ash? More birthday candle accidents? How likely was that?

She hurried down to the basement, determined to throw Mr. Deveraux right into the trash. She opened the drawer and pulled out the baggie, even had her foot on the pedal that levitated the lid of the trash can, when something stayed her hand.

The dream.

The dream she'd had last night. She closed her eyes and conjured the image. In the dream, she had been standing right in this very place, at this very counter, and when her eyes had risen to the mirror, the face and body reflected there were hers but younger, prettier. Her lashes were long and luxurious, her lips full, her body lush. She was perfect. She was beautiful. The cream had not only transformed her face but had altered her entirely.

For a woman who had always been considered "plain" (though not unattractive, she was quick to amend), it was a captivating and alluring dream. And one she was, in reality, loathe to abandon.

And so Sophie made the decision to give it one more try. This time, she would add all that was left of Mr. Deveraux's mortal remains to the cream in the bottom of her kettle. She did it quickly before she could change her mind. Then she scooped the mixture onto her fingers and smoothed it thickly onto her skin.

She didn't stand around this time and wait for something to happen. She went straight to bed. If when she awoke in the morning, there was still no change, she would give it not one more thought. No, she'd proceed with her original plan and contact a witch she knew in real estate to start looking for an industrial site where she could manufacture her night cream. *Her* night cream. No more thoughts of adding vampire dust to a perfectly good product.

Sophie first heard the voice at 2:30 a.m. At least she thought it was a voice. It—something—made her sit straight up in bed, heart pounding. She looked around, wild-eyed and gasping. She was so frightened she dove back under the covers and waved her hand to illuminate every light in the house. Only when the cottage was aglow did she again peek out, eyes darting into every corner.

She was alone.

Sophie crept out of bed. She tiptoed from one room to the other, finding nothing amiss, no one (or thing) lurking anywhere. Just to be certain, she looked in every closet and peeked under the bed and under every large piece of furniture. She went from being frightened to embarrassed and then to feeling more than a little foolish.

What was wrong with her?

Sophie trudged into the basement. She was wide-awake now. Might as well clean up the mess she'd left after her unsuccessful experiments with Mr. Deveraux. As she moved around, sending pots and utensils into the sink to be scoured, she thought how fortunate it was that none of her witch friends had been here to see that mortifying display of cowardice. She would have been drummed out of the Witches' Benevolent Society whose sole purpose was to come to the aid of fellow witches in times of peril. No one would have entrusted her safety to a witch that showed such a lack of courage, and because of what? An imagined whisper in a stupid dream.

Sophie looked around once the chores were done. She was keenly aware that deep inside her heart of hearts disappointment coiled like a serpent ready to pump its deadly poison into her psyche if she let it. Despite her best efforts to contain her optimism, she had wanted the cream to work. It would have elevated her in the human world, something from which Sophie had always felt separate and apart. It would have been her entrée into a world of celebrity and acceptance. She would have been welcomed and sought after because she could offer what no one else had ever been able to—a veritable fountain of youth. It would—

"My god, how long am I going to have to listen to this drivel?"

The voice was right at Sophie's ear. She started and yelped in surprise and shock. She whirled around, fists at the ready, a curse of protection on her lips.

She was alone.

How could that be?

Her heart seemed ready to burst from her chest. "Who's there?" she yelled, adrenaline making her voice fierce and harsh. "I am a powerful witch. If you don't show yourself, I'll send you to Hades in a million broken pieces."

There was a chuckle. Once again, right at her ear. "I'm afraid you've fixed it so I can't show myself. However, if you look in that mirror over there, we might be able to figure this out."

The voice was masculine, authoritative, with a hint of a British accent.

Sophie didn't move. She was afraid it might be a trick. There were, after all, lots of invisible beings in the spirit world and not all of them were friendly. In order to battle one, however, she had to know what she was dealing with.

"I have no idea what I am now," the voice replied rather snippily, as if divining her thoughts. "You've fixed that, too. Now go over to the mirror. I'd like to know even if you don't."

Then, through no effort or will on Sophie's part, her feet moved toward the mirror. She tried to stop, digging in her heels, grasping at the counter with both hands. It did no good. Her feet trudged onward, and some invisible force broke her grip. She was being inexorably drawn to the mirror like a puppet responding to a master's tug on her strings. Her temper flared. Whatever this was might get her to the damned mirror but it couldn't make her look.

She squeezed her eyes shut, even pressed the palms of her hands against her eyelids, refusing to give in.

"Oh, for the love of everything evil and unnatural in this world and the next, will you stop behaving like a child? You're the one who did this. At least allow me to see what kind of hell you've trapped me in."

Sophie began to panic. The voice was right. Whatever it was had taken up residence in her body. How is that possible? She knew of possession. But whatever *this* was did not feel like a devil, exactly. And she wasn't levitating or spewing invective—

"Not yet anyway," the voice said. "But if you don't open your eyes in ten seconds, you'll be spewing more than invective, I promise you."

Sophie swallowed hard and took a deep breath. Okay. Let's get this over with.

She opened one eye.

The other flew open all on its own.

Ye gods. What was she seeing?

She rubbed her eyes and raised them again to the mirror.

"What the—"

The voice managed to sound both amused and horrified at the same time.

Sophie's right hand reached up and grasped her chin. It turned her head to the left and right and back again.

"You're a girl." This time the voice held only horror.

A girl.

Sophie couldn't ignore the thrill that swept over her. The face in the mirror was hers. But not exactly. She looked twenty again, but not the twenty that had been her reality. This young woman's perfect skin stretched smooth and unwrinkled over high cheekbones. Her lashes were long and luxurious, her lips full.

She stepped back a bit, to see the rest. A body that was lush, perfect. A body she had seen before. The body in her dream.

Sophie gasped. The cream had worked!

"Cream? What cream? What is going on?"

Sophie's excitement morphed into irritation. The voice's intrusion into her thoughts brought with it a wave of emotion different from her own. The voice had its own power over her feelings. She had two separate and distinct personalities inhabiting this one perfect body. And she knew who the second personality belonged to.

"Mr. Deveraux?" she whispered.

"You know who I am?"

She nodded at the mirror. "I think this is my fault."

"Think?" This time the voice thundered. "What did you do, witch?"

Sophie's shoulders slumped a little as she told him. She felt his anger and frustration and they flooded her with guilt. When she finished explaining, though, a shift occurred. His fury dissipated to be replaced by cold amusement at the absurdity of his predicament.

"So this is the result of a science experiment gone wrong?"

Sophie bristled. "Not gone wrong. Gone right, actually."

"Oh? I am trapped inside the body of a girl witch. This is the way it was supposed to be?"

Sophie shrugged. "Well. Not entirely. You see, you were supposed to make me . . ." She pirouetted in front of the mirror. "Like this. But *you* weren't supposed to come back. I mean, the mental part of you."

Mr. Deveraux snorted. "How like a woman. Only wants a man for his body."

Sophie felt color creep into her cheeks. "That's not what I meant. I thought your ash—"

"Which is another thing you have to answer for," he interrupted with an impatient huff. "What did you think you were doing, letting my wife handle such a dangerous thing as a blazing cake? What kind of caterer are you? Was this your first vampire affair?"

It was Sophie's turn to interrupt with an indignant huff of her own. "Now just a minute. I warned her about the danger. Even offered to bring the cake in myself. She wouldn't hear of it. In fact, she insisted it was her surprise and she wanted to present it."

As soon as the words were spoken, Sophie and Mr. Deveraux were hit by the same thought. While Sophie's reaction was shock, Mr. Deveraux's was something quite different. Rage scorched through Sophie like an inferno.

"It was no accident."

They spoke the words as one, not aloud but like an echo that bounced from one consciousness to the other.

Sophie was half afraid to ask the next question but felt she owed it to herself as well as Mr. Deveraux to find the answer.

"Why would she do such a thing?"

Mr. Deveraux did not answer. Sophie could sense a tornado of emotion emanating from him and ripping through her. A deep sadness gave way to disappointment and then surged again to fury before settling into an ominous sense of betrayal.

Through her memories of the night, Mr. Deveraux saw and interpreted his wife's actions, and through his, Sophie felt the cart being thrust deliberately and firmly into his back. Mrs. Deveraux had not tripped, and when her husband turned, his coat on fire and fear stark on his face, she had smiled and turned away to stand in the shelter of the arms of a young man who had reached out to her.

Now another emotion, the desire for retribution, made bile rise in the back of Sophie's throat.

"What are you going to do?" she asked.

That brought a chuckle that sent gooseflesh racing up Sophie's arms. "You mean what are *we* going to do, don't you?"

She shook her head. "I can't be a part of malefic evil," she said firmly. "I am a good witch."

Mr. Deveraux grew quiet, Sophie grew uneasy. At last, Mr. Deveraux said, "Where are we anyway?"

His abrupt change of subject made Sophie suspicious but she decided to give him the benefit of the doubt. She turned so that her eyes swept the area. "This is my home."

"You live in a—" He groped for the right word. "Warehouse?"

She shook her head. "This is the basement. Where I make my—" She stopped. Maybe she shouldn't go into what she made. It might lead back to why they found themselves in this predicament to begin with.

It didn't seem to matter to Mr. Deveraux anyway because he didn't pursue it. "So show me the rest of the place," he said. "I hope it's nicer than this."

Sophie bridled at his condescending tone. "It's a very nice home. I happen to love it."

"Then show me."

Sophie started upstairs. Slowly. Even though she had been quick to snap at his insult, she was fully aware that Mr. Deveraux, until very recently, had lived in a mansion in the best part of the city. She, on the other hand, lived in a cottage on the edge of town, and while she did love it, he might not recognize its charm or appreciate its character.

And he did not.

When she completed the tour (it took about a minute), he lapsed into stunned silence.

Then he said, "Well. We can do something about this right off. We're moving to the mansion. It does belong to me, after all."

"But what about Mrs. Deveraux?" Sophie asked, trying to point out the obvious.

He snickered. "What about her? It will give me great pleasure to throw my wife out on her pretty butt. She and her boyfriend can find their own place to live."

Sophie felt a chill. She didn't ask how he planned to accomplish such a thing because she knew. Mr. Deveraux had no intention of throwing his wife out. He had something much more sinister in mind for her, and for the boyfriend. "I won't be a party to murder," she said.

She expected an outburst. Instead Mr. Deveraux changed tack again. "I think I'm hungry," he said, his voice reflecting confusion and awe. "For food. Human food."

Sophie panicked. Was he hungry *for* humans? Had he gone from drinking blood to actually craving the corporeal body? Was that a result of the melding of their species? She hadn't had time to consider all the ramifications of a vampire and human commingling of the flesh. This one was pretty awful.

Mr. Deveraux started to laugh. "No, silly. I mean I'm hungry for steak. Steak and French fries. Maybe a beer."

Sophie shook her head "I don't have steak or beer," she said. "I'm a vegetarian and I don't drink alcohol. I could bake a potato for you though."

A long, exasperated sigh escaped Mr. Deveraux's lips. "For the first time in a century and a half, I can enjoy real food, and I get trapped inside a teetotaling vegetarian? Well, let's get one thing straight right now, missy. If I have to live life as a woman, you are going to have to make a few concessions, too. And the first is finding me a steak and a beer."

"I'm afraid I can't do that," Sophie said. "I told you I don't eat meat. I can't even bear to touch it. You'll have to learn to—"

Sophie didn't finish the sentence. She couldn't. Her breath was cut off. Pressure built in her chest. It felt as if Mr. Deveraux had inflated a balloon that squeezed against her heart and cut off her oxygen. Gasping, she fell to her knees. The pain got worse and her vision began to fade. She was losing consciousness, darkness closing in until it surrounded her, beat her down, and she knew what it felt like to be dying.

And then it was over.

Sophie rolled onto her back, panting and clutching at her chest.

Mr. Deveraux's voice cut through her fear. "We have to coexist, Sophie. Let's try to make the best of it."

It was the first time he had used her name. Somehow it chilled her as nothing else before. She gathered her wits about her and sat up. Her nightgown had bunched up around her waist and she tugged it into place, embarrassed that she had so exposed herself. Mr. Deveraux seemed strangely absent from her mind, as if he was giving her time to compose herself. It did not comfort her. This demonstration had made it plain that he was in charge. He had given her physical beauty and taken away free will.

"Are you all right now?"

Sophie pushed herself into a standing position. "What do you think?"

He ignored the sarcasm. "Do you live alone?"

Another abrupt change of subject that sent ice through Sophie's veins. "Yes."

"No boyfriend? Husband?"

Sophie shrugged, "No."

"Widowed, then?"

"No."

Sophie felt a gentle probing of her mind and, more disturbingly, of her body. Then she felt Mr. Deveraux's startled reaction. "You're a virgin? You lived eighty human years and never had sex?"

He said it as if it was a terrible failing on Sophie's part, as if she had somehow let him down.

"Oh, this gets better and better," he moaned. "No red meat, no alcohol, and no sex. What fresh hell is this?"

Sophie squared her shoulders. "I wanted to save myself," she said with great dignity. "For the man I loved."

"Oh? How'd that work out for you?"

His disdain cut like a whip. It also triggered a flash of temper. "At least my wife didn't set me on fire to get rid of me," she snapped.

Mr. Deveraux lapsed again into silence. Sophie congratulated herself on the tiny victory and went into the kitchen. She could use a cup of tea.

"Coffee," Mr. Deveraux corrected.

"No," Sophie responded. "Tea."

She waited for something to happen, for Mr. Deveraux to hurt her again, but he didn't. Once again, he was strangely absent. He seemed to feel the same things she did. Perhaps his display of cruelty backfired because the pain inflicted on her came back to torture him.

She fixed the tea and sat down at the kitchen table. Her head spun with confusion and anxiety. She had no idea what she should do. On the one hand, she could live her dream. She was sitting here in the body of a beautiful twenty-year-old with the unlimited possibilities that offered. On the other hand, she shared that body with a man who could inflict pain. A man who was not very nice. Who might even be—she gulped at the thought—wicked.

She wished she could talk to someone about her dilemma. Her sister, maybe. But Belinda lived in San Diego and was caught up in some intrigue of her own. Besides, to Sophie's dismay, Belinda teetered on the knife-edge of white and black magic. Sophie couldn't always trust her advice.

Sophie sipped at her tea. She watched herself, her reflection caught in the window over the sink. Her hair fell in a straight, shiny sweep to her shoulders. Her eyes shone with bright expectation. If she saw this woman in a café or restaurant, she would be envious. Wonderful things happened for beautiful women. Boyfriends and husbands, families who showered them with love. Beautiful women learned early what they could get with a dazzling smile.

Sophie had never before possessed a dazzling smile.

Mr. Deveraux made fun of her when she said she had not had sex because she had saved herself. Sophie realized he probably knew the truth. No opportunities had ever presented themselves. She had never had a boyfriend.

"We're going to do something about that."

Mr. Deveraux was back. His tone this time was not caustic but actually cheerful. "I've been taking a test drive thorough the neighborhood," he said brightly. "It's not too bad in here. You've got a brain, a fairly good one for a female. Business sense. A knockout body. Sophie, you've got potential."

Sophie was almost afraid to ask. "Potential for what?"

"Why, for just about anything. This night cream, for instance. Great idea. We can do something with it."

Sophie shook her head. "I've been thinking about that. Look what happened to me—to us. If we started going around setting vampires on fire, it would certainly attract unwelcome attention from the community. Once or twice is an accident; more than that is war."

He clucked his tongue. "No. You don't understand. We're not going to use ash."

"What then?"

"We're going to use blood."

"Blood?"

"Yes. I've been thinking about it, too. You were correct in assuming the ash was the concentrated essence of a vampire. *Concentrated* being the key word. You got the whole enchilada. Something else I'd like to try, by the way. Blood, on the other hand, is a vampire's source of *physical* energy. Blood keeps a vampire strong and controls the outward signs of aging. Get it?"

Sophie nodded. The way Mr. Deveraux explained it made perfect sense. If they added blood to her cream, the user would get the benefit of youthful beauty without—

What was she thinking?

Sophie squeaked in protest. "If we thought setting vampires on fire would be a problem," she said, "what do you think will happen if we start *bleeding* them?"

"Well, I admit there are some wrinkles to iron out."

He said it in an offhand, casual way that made Sophie wary. "What are you up to?" she asked.

He chuckled. "Well, conjoined less than a day and you have me figured out. All right. I'll confess. We need a test subject, right?"

Sophie nodded.

"I have the perfect person in mind."

Since it happened to be her mind, too, Sophie knew exactly who that perfect person was. "How do you expect to get Mrs. Deveraux to agree?"

A hush settled deep in Sophie's consciousness. It was neither peaceful nor serene but heavy with foreboding. She shivered involuntarily.

"I cannot be a party to evil," she said, for what seemed the thousandth time.

A flare of indignation burned through her. "You have already been a party to evil," Mr. Deveraux answered with contempt. "You made the damned cake that murdered me."

Sophie squirmed in the heat of his accusation. "Well, we won't have to kill her, will we?"

In a flash the indignation was gone. "Of course not. What good would it do to kill her? We need to keep her alive to use her blood, don't we? And if it works, we'll pick only the most wicked vampires to drain. The gods know there are plenty of them around. Think about it, Sophie. We'll be performing a public service. Ridding the world of bad vampires and offering mortal women the gift of beauty. It's perfect."

Sophie sighed. She couldn't believe she was actually considering Mr. Deveraux's plan. But some of what he said made sense. Mrs. Deveraux was not exactly an innocent. She had murdered her husband. On his birthday, no less. And there were lots of bad vampires around wreaking havoc and taking innocent lives. This would get them out of circulation.

Besides, she was a partner in this enterprise. She would use her good influence to counterbalance any evil Mr. Deveraux tried to sneak by her. Like exacting revenge on the guests at his party who carried on as if nothing had happened after his death.

Sophie knew Mr. Deveraux was sensing the shift in her thinking. She could feel it in the shifting of his own disposition. Warmth flooded her system.

"How are we going to approach her?" Sophie asked at last.

Mr. Deveraux greeted her question with a mental clap of approval. "That's my girl. Sophie, this is going to be the start of a great adventure, I promise. Now go get dressed and throw some things in a suitcase."

"Suitcase?"

"I told you we would be moving to the mansion."

Sophie stood up slowly from the counter and looked around. "I've lived here a long time. Do we have to move?"

He released a snort of impatience. "You've *seen* the mansion. You can't possibly expect me to live here."

But when he sensed the spark of anger his remark provoked in Sophie, he added, "But we'll keep this place. You can come visit anytime you want. How's that?"

Sophie thought about it a minute. She *had* seen the mansion. And the grounds. And the cars. What would it hurt to experience them, too?

She moved toward her bedroom. "You didn't answer my question," she said. "How are we going to approach Mrs. Deveraux?"

Mr. Deveraux remained silent for the time it took Sophie to throw some things into a battered valise. She felt timid, at first, getting dressed with Mr. Deveraux here. But she did it by standing away from mirrors and only stepping in front of one to comb her hair. Seeing her reflection sent a thrill once more along her spine. She was truly, wonderfully beautiful.

Her dress, however, looked like a rag on her youthful frame.

Mr. Deveraux clucked his tongue. "We need to go shopping. Your taste in clothes runs to the archaic."

Sophie didn't argue. He was right.

She smiled at her reflection. She couldn't help it. Just as she couldn't help the thrill of anticipation coursing through her. Mr. Deveraux had said they were embarking on a great adventure. She'd never had a great adventure.

She turned away from the mirror and snatched up the suitcase. "Okay. What's the plan?"

Mr. Deveraux was smiling, Sophie could feel it. "You promised my wife a party, right?"

Sophie nodded.

"Well, it just so happens that Mrs. Deveraux has a birthday of her own coming up. Next week, in fact."

"Do you think she'll recognize me?" Sophie asked, casting another approving glance at her reflection.

"Doesn't matter. You can tell her you're Sophie's granddaughter. Her business manager."

Sophie smiled. It could work.

"Of course it will work, Sophie," Mr. Deveraux said. "It's all going to work. Now let's go see a woman about a party."

Blood Wrapped

Tanya Huff

Tanya Huff lives and writes in the wilds of Southern Ontario. Her twenty-two books run the gamut from heroic fantasy to space opera although she is probably best known for the Vicki Nelson Blood books—recently adapted for television as Blood Ties *and showing on Lifetime in the United States and a CHUM affiliate in Canada. Her twenty-third book,* The Heart of Valor, *was a July 2007 release, and the sequel,* Valor's Trial, *will be out in the spring of 2008. The following story is in the world of the Smoke books—*Smoke and Shadows, Smoke and Mirrors, *and* Smoke and Ashes.

"What do you think of that?"

"The window display?"

"The shawl!"

Henry stepped closer to the Treasures of Thailand window and examined the lime green silk shawl draped more-or-less artistically over a papier-mâché mountain. "Nice," he said after a moment, "but not your color. If I were you, I'd wear the turquoise." A wave of his hand indicated a similar shawl hanging in the window's "sky."

"It's not for me!" Tony Foster shot a scathing look at his companion.

"Ah, for Lee then. In that case, you need a deeper green."

"It's for Vicki!"

"Vicki?" Henry turned, frowning slightly, to see Tony staring at him with an expression of horrified disbelief.

"You didn't forget. Don't tell me you forgot. You must have gotten Celluci's e-mail."

"E-mails." Over the last few weeks there had been a series of messages from Detective Sergeant Michael Celluci. Each of them had been as direct and to the point as the detective himself tended to be, falling somewhere between terse and rude, and each of them had been read and promptly deleted. "About Vicki's birthday."

"Right. So"—looking relieved, Tony nodded toward the shawl—"what do you think?"

"I think you're unnecessarily concerned," Henry told him. "It's just a birthday."

Tony stepped out into the middle of the sidewalk and stared at the bastard son of Henry VIII, once Duke of Richmond and Somerset, Marshal of the North, now vampire and romance writer, like he'd just grown another head. "Are you insane?"

Tony took a long drink of his latte, set the mug carefully back on the artfully distressed surface of the coffee shop's round wooden table, leaned forward, and looked Henry right in the eye. It was something not many people could or would do and not something he dared on a regular basis, but he needed to make sure Henry understood the seriousness of the situation. "She's turning forty."

"She's essentially immortal," Henry pointed out, keeping the Hunter carefully masked despite the other man's provocation.

"What difference does that make?"

He spread his hands. "An infinite number of birthdays."

"So?" Taking the opportunity to look away without backing down, Tony rolled his eyes. "She's still only going to turn forty once."

"And someday, God willing, she'll turn a hundred and forty, two hundred and forty . . ."

"You just don't get it, do you?"

"Apparently not." Taking a swallow from his bottle of water, a modern conceit he appreciated since it granted him an accepted public behavior—and there were many in Vancouver who drank neither caffeine nor alcohol—Henry studied Tony's reaction and shook his head. "Apparently not," he repeated. That Vicki Nelson, who had been the first child of his kind he'd created in almost four hundred and seventy years, would care about something so meaningless as a birthday was hard for him to believe. Granted, she'd been definitely human before the change: strong willed, opinionated, with a terrier-like determination. . . . No, not terrier. That implied something small and yappy and Vicki was neither. Pit bull then. Aggressive, yes, but more often badly handled and misunderstood. He grinned at the thought of anyone attempting to put a muzzle on Vicki Nelson.

"What? You're wearing one of your *I'm so clever* smiles," Tony told him as his thoughts returned to the coffee shop. "Have you thought of something to get her?"

Best not to mention the muzzle. Toronto, and Vicki, were three thousand odd miles away but the idea of that getting back to her gave him chills the way nothing had in the last four centuries.

"I've know her for years and I've never given her a birthday present."

"Forty, Henry."

"And why is that so different from thirty-nine?"

Tony sighed. "You write bodice rippers, Henry. I can't believe you know so little about women!"

"No woman in my books has ever approached forty." Grocery bills might be negligible but he still had condo fees and car insurance to pay and middle-aged heroines didn't sell books.

"Yeah, and your fans?"

From the mail he got, his fans were definitely closer to middle age. Given that they thought he was a thirty-five-year-old redhead named

Elizabeth Fitzroy, he declined all invitations to romance conventions. "We don't exactly converse, Tony."

"Maybe you should. Look"—elbows planted on the table, he leaned forward—"forty is a big deal for women. It's either the age where they have to stop pretending or have to start pretending a lot harder."

"Pretending what?"

"Youth, Henry."

"Vicki will be forever young."

"No." Tony shook his head. "You'll be forever young; you were changed at seventeen. Vicki was thirty-four when you drew her over to the dark side—you know, dark? Literally." As Henry frowned, Tony waved a hand at the coffee shop's window and the night sky just barely visible behind the lights of Davies Street. "Never mind. The point is, she was human twice as long as you were. And she was in her thirties. And she's a woman. Trust me, forty counts. And if you can't trust me, trust Celluci; he's living with her."

Vampires did not share territory. By changing her, Henry had lost her to his mortal rival. *And that sounded like a line from a bad romance.* He rubbed his forehead and wondered what had happened to make his life so complicated. Stupid question. Vicki Nelson, ex–Wonder Woman of the Metropolitan Toronto Police, had happened. Vicki had seen past the masks and gotten him involved in life in a way he hadn't been for hundreds of years. Vicki had pushed Tony into his life and had, with her change, been at least indirectly responsible for the two of them ending up in Vancouver. Forty years to such a woman should mean nothing.

"Look at it this way, Henry." Tony's voice interrupted his musing. "Vicki's essentially immortal; that's a long time for her to be pissed at you."

On the other hand, who was he to say what forty years should mean to such a woman? He moved his water bottle, creating concentric rings with the condensation. "What are you getting her?"

Tony, ex–street hustler, ex–police informant, third assistant director on the most popular vampire detective series on syndicated television and the only practicing wizard in the lower mainland, sagged against the wrought iron back of his chair. "I have no fucking idea."

There were two messages in Henry's voice mail when he woke the next evening. Both were from Tony. The first was, predictably, about Vicki's birthday. According to the script supervisor working on *Darkest Night*, women of her age appreciated gifts that made them feel young without reminding them of their advancing years. Given that Vicki's years weren't exactly advancing, Henry had no idea of what that meant.

Assuming it contained more of the same, Henry intended to delete the second message without listening to it but he hesitated a moment too long.

"Henry, there's a little girl missing from up by Lytton and someone called Kevin Groves about her."

Kevin Groves, who worked as a reporter for the *Western Star,* one of the local tabloids, had the uncomfortable ability of recognizing the truth. Given that his byline had once run under the headline OLYMPIC ORGANIZERS RELOCATE FAMILY OF SASQUATCH, this was occasionally more uncomfortable for those who knew about his skill than it was for him. Over the last year he'd become an indispensable way of keeping tabs on the growing metaphysical activity in Vancouver and the lower mainland.

Like attracted like. Henry had experienced this phenomenon over his long life, and as Tony gained more control over his considerable power, he was discovering it in spades. The difference was that while Henry would move heaven and earth for those he claimed as his own, he was generally willing to let the rest of humanity go its own way. But Tony had bought into the belief that with great power came great responsibility and become something of a local guardian for the entire lower mainland. A policeman, as it were, for the metaphysical.

Henry, because he considered Tony his, very often found himself acting as the young wizard's muscle. Vicki referred to them alternately as Batman and Robin or the new Jedi Knights, and for that alone deserved to have her birthday forgotten.

Occasionally, Henry wondered if he wasn't using Tony as an excuse to become involved. Celluci had called him a vampire vigilante once. He'd meant it as an insult, but when Henry thought of little girls gone missing, he also thought that the detective had been more perceptive than he'd been given credit for.

Moving quickly into the living room, Henry picked up the remote and turned on the TV.

". . . while playing in the backyard with her mother working in the garden only meters away. There is rising fear in this traumatized community that a bear or cougar or other large predator has come out of the mountains and is feeding upon their children."

Henry suspected the reporter had taken advantage of a live feed to get that last line on the air.

The young woman stared at the camera with wide-eyed intensity and the certain knowledge that this was her time in the spotlight. "Julie Martin's distraught father has declared his intention of 'taking care' of who or whatever has made off with his precious little girl. A spokesperson from the Ministry of Natural Resources has suggested that it would be dangerous for search parties to head into the wood unless accompanied by trained personnel but admits that their office is unable to provide trained personnel at this time."

She makes it sound like the Ministry should have grizzled trackers standing by. Henry waited until they cut back to the news anchor who solemnly reiterated that four-year-old Julie Martin had disappeared without a trace in broad daylight, then, as the screen filled with a crowd of angry and near-hysterical townspeople standing outside the RCMP office, berating two harassed-looking constables for not having found the child, he turned off the set.

If Kevin Groves had gotten a call about Julie Martin's disappearance and felt it had validity enough for him to call Tony, then the odds were good it wasn't a police matter. Or a matter for the Ministry of Natural Resources, as it was currently mandated.

At 6:47 p.m. Tony would likely still be on the sound stage, so rather than leave him a message Henry went straight to the source.

"*Western Star*; Kevin Groves."

"It's Henry."

Very faintly, Henry heard the reporter's heartbeat speed up. Everyone had a hindbrain reaction to vampires, the most primal part of them gibbering in terror in the presence of an equally primal predator. Kevin Groves knew why.

"So, are you . . . That is, I mean . . . You're calling about the missing Martin kid?"

"I am."

"Werewolves."

"I beg your pardon."

"I had a tip that there's werewolves in the mountains."

There was, in fact, a pack working an old mining claim just outside of Ashcroft. "And you believe that a werewolf took Julie Martin?" It wasn't unheard of for a were to go rogue; they were more or less human after all.

"No. Just that there's werewolves in the mountains, but if that's the case then . . ."

"Then?" Henry prodded when Kevin's voice trailed off.

"Well, you know. Werewolves!"

"Is that it?"

"One of the Martins' neighbors saw something large and hairy carrying a small body."

"In its mouth?"

"No, but . . ."

"Werewolves don't have an intermediate state. They look like wolves or they look human." Essentially like wolves and essentially like humans but close enough. "It's not werewolves."

"The old lady seemed pretty sure it wasn't a Sasquatch."

Even six months ago Henry would have believed *it wasn't a Sasquatch* went without saying. "Large and hairy?"

"That's what she said."

They couldn't save every child who went missing in British Columbia but large and hairy pointed toward something the police might not be able to handle. "Give me the witness's name and we'll check it out."

"So"—just past the Spuzzum exit, Henry pulled out and passed an empty logging truck then tucked his 1976 BMW back into the right lane—"where's Lee?"

"He's down in L.A. for a couple of days, auditioning for a movie of the week."

"He's leaving *Darkest Night*?" Lee Nicholas, Tony's partner, was one of the leads in the popular syndicated vampire detective show.

"What? No." That pulled Tony's attention off the screen of his PDA. "They'll be shooting in Vancouver; he figures he can do both. C.B.'s willing to adjust our shooting schedule if necessary."

"That doesn't sound like him." Chester Bane was notoriously inflexible when it came to situations that might cost him money.

"He's hoping he can scam some free publicity."

Henry snorted. "That does. What," he asked a few kilometers later when it became obvious Tony wasn't going to pick up the conversational ball, "are you finding so fascinating on that thing?"

"Sorry, I was just going over the list of possible . . . um, things."

"Things."

"Suspects who might have taken the kid. But they're not exactly people."

Eyes nearly closed in the glare of oncoming headlights, Henry sighed. "Let's hear the list."

"Well, there's Bugbears, a kind of a hairy giant goblin. Or Chimeras, because the lion and goat parts are hairy and that might have been all they saw. It could be any one of a number of different demons but then we need to find out who's calling them. Uh . . ." He squinted at the screen as he scrolled down. "Displacer Beasts look like cougars except they're black and have tentacles so it wouldn't necessarily be carrying the kid in its mouth. Ettins are two-headed giants that live in remote areas and—"

"Tony, where did you get this list?"

"Sort of from Kevin Groves."

"Sort of?"

"He lent me an RPG monster index. RPG: role playing game," Tony expanded when Henry's silence made it obvious he had no idea what that meant. "Like Dungeons and Dragons."

"I've never heard of it."

"Really? Because it's old. Well, oldish." When Henry replied with more silence, he sighed. "I wanted to go in with more information than hairy thing that eats children and hopefully isn't a werewolf."

"So you went to a game?"

It was Tony's turn to snort as he powered down and twisted around to slip the PDA into a side pocket on his backpack. "Yeah, well believe it or not, Googling *big hairy eats children* doesn't pull up anything useful."

"But imaginary . . ."

"Henry, whatever this is, I guarantee it'll be considered imaginary by most of the world. Hell, we're considered imaginary by most of the world."

"I'm sure more people than you expect believe in third assistant directors."

"You'd be surprised." Slouching down as far as the seat belt would allow, he propped his knees up on the dashboard. "Ninety-nine percent of the world's population is in denial about something. Take you, for instance."

That drew Henry's attention off the road. "Me?"

"You're still in denial about Vicki's birthday."

"I said I'd get her something."

"Yeah, but it has to be something good and I don't think you're giving it much thought."

"There's a child missing. . . ."

"You want to talk about that all the way to Lytton? Because I don't."

"Fine." Henry pulled out and passed a pair of trucks. "What about a gift certificate?"

"Dude, it's a good thing you're hard to kill."

The village of Lytton was about a two-hour drive from Vancouver. Henry had picked Tony up at his apartment in Burnaby at twenty to eight, and it was a quarter to ten when Henry left the highway and steered the BMW down Main Street.

"You think they usually roll the sidewalks up this early," Tony wondered, staring out at the dark windows, "or is this a reaction to the Martin kid getting grabbed?"

"Bit of both, I expect."

"I feel like we're being watched from behind lace curtains."

"Why lace?" Henry asked.

"I don't know." Tony waggled the fingers of his left hand in front of his face, sketching in the air lacy lines of power that dissipated almost instantly. "It's creepier I guess."

"I don't know about the lace, but we're definitely being watched." Henry could feel the fear and anger roiling through the town. Could feel some it directed toward them. With a child missing in a village of only three hundred and eight souls, any and all strangers would be suspect. "It might be best if we were . . . unnoticed."

"Do you have to use such cheesy setup lines?" Tony muttered, laying two fingers against the metal strip between the front and back windows. In the last few months, he'd gotten enough practice in with the Notice-me-not spell that he no longer needed to consult the instructions on the laptop. Of course, there were still one hell of a lot of spells he wasn't as adept at, so the laptop remained close at hand.

From their perspective within the car, nothing changed but Henry felt the watcher's attention drift away.

"Could be a troll under the railway bridge."

"Julia Martin wasn't anywhere near the bridge," Henry reminded him. "And a troll would never hunt that far from home. They're creatures of habit."

Grace Alton, the witness who'd spoken to Kevin Groves, lived out past Eighth Street where Main began to curve toward Cache Creek, three houses closer to town than the Martins'. Old enough to be part of the original settlement, the small, white frame house was set back from the road at the end of a long, gravel driveway.

Henry pulled in behind an aged Buick and parked. "There's lights on in the front room. She's still up."

"It's just ten. Why wouldn't she be?" When Henry turned and lifted a red gold brow, Tony shrugged. "Right. Country."

Standing on the front porch, Tony fingered the ball bearing that anchored his personal Notice-me-not and glanced back toward the car.

Because he knew exactly where the BMW had been parked, he could almost see a shadowy outline—anyone else would have to bump into it to find it. Which was how he'd found it the first couple of times, although it had been more *slam into it* than bump. His right knee ached remembering.

"One heartbeat. She's alone."

"Does it matter?"

"Makes it simpler," Henry said as he opened the door.

"The door's not . . . Right. Country," Tony said again as he followed Henry into the house. By the time he reached the living room, Henry was on one knee beside an ancient recliner holding the hand of an elderly woman who was staring at him like he was . . . something elderly women really got into. Tony had no idea of what that might be although from the décor, crocheted doilies and African violets figured prominently. The place smelled like cat piss and the fat black-and-white cat staring disdainfully at Henry from the sofa seemed the most likely culprit.

Unlike dogs, cats had no issues with vampires.

Or wizards, Tony noted as the cat turned that same unblinking green stare on him, and if there was a spell they deigned to acknowledge, he hadn't found it yet.

"Just tell me what you saw," Henry said softly, and by the way the old lady leaned toward him, Tony knew his eyes had gone dark and compelling.

"I was out back, wasn't I, checking to see how the trellis at the end of the old summer kitchen had come through the winter. I have roses in the summer, pink ones; they climb right up to the roof. I saw something moving down by the river. There's nothing wrong with my eyes." Her upper lip curled. "I don't care what that constable says. I can see at a distance as well as I ever could. All right, fine, up close maybe I should wear my glasses, but at a distance I know what I saw."

"What did you see, Grace?"

She preened a little, an involuntary response to Henry's attentions, which, given the visible as opposed to actual age difference, was kind of creeping Tony out. "It was passing between those two clumps of lilac bushes. They're nothing much now, but you should see them in the spring. Lovely. And the smell. Snotty young pup from the Ministry wanted to tear them out. I tore him a new one, that's what I did. Those lilacs are older than he is."

Tony wasn't without sympathy for the guy from the Ministry, whichever ministry it happened to be.

"What did you see passing between the lilacs, Grace?"

"I saw something bigger than a man but hunched over. And it had a big, hairy hump. The shape looked wrong. It looked . . . evil!" She drew out the final word with obvious enjoyment, and Tony, who'd seen some terrifying things over the last few years, suppressed a shudder. "It was moving fast but I saw, I saw clear as anything, that it was holding a child. I saw the leg kick and the poor little thing had on a red rubber boot. Julie Martin was wearing red rubber boots when she disappeared, you know. I yelled for it to stop but then it was gone, so I came inside and I called the Mounties and they didn't believe me. Oh, they were polite enough, those young men, but they didn't believe me not for one minute. 'Are you sure the boot was red?' they said. Like I couldn't see a little red boot against a big, hairy creature. Not like a Sasquatch, I told them. They're just misunderstood, poor dears. This was ungroomed, ratty. I don't like to judge but it was *clearly* a creature of evil appetites come down out of the mountains to feed. He asked me what kind of creature, and I said how would I know; did I look like I knew creatures? And he said maybe the light was playing tricks so I said it was a lot better back when I saw it because they hadn't exactly hustled to get here, you know. When they left, I said to Alexander"—she gestured toward the cat, who looked bored—"I said, we'll involve the fifth estate, that's what we'll do, and I called the paper."

A messy pile of tabloids, topped by a copy of the *Western Star*, had a place of prominence beside her chair. The only visible headline screamed, IT'S NOT A RACCOON! Tony rubbed at a healing bite on his calf. It had actually been a Pekinese with a really bad temper.

"The man at the paper, he believed me."

"I believe you, Grace."

She patted Henry's cheek with her free hand. "I know, dear."

As amusing as it was to see Henry Fitzroy, vampire, treated in such a way, Tony couldn't see how this was getting them any closer to finding Julie Martin. They'd gotten as much information from Kevin.

Then Henry leaned closer. "What did you hear, Grace?"

Her eyes widened. "Hear?"

"What did you hear?"

She frowned, slightly, and cocked her head to one side. "I heard rustling through the bushes, but that might have been the wind. I heard the river, of course. I heard . . ." She looked surprised. "I heard a car door slam."

"Werewolves drive."

"Some of them," Henry admitted as they crossed the backyard. "But not very well."

"It's been a long winter and kids are easier to hunt than elk. Maybe they're taking food back to the pack."

"It's possible but unlikely that there'd be enough rogue were around to form a pack."

"You just don't want it to be were," Tony muttered, staring into the gap between the lilac bushes. The gap was only minimally less dark than the bushes themselves. The sky had clouded over and he could barely see his hand in front of his face. "You'll have to guide me through to the other side. I don't want to risk a light until I'm blocked from the road. There's only so much a Notice-me-not can cover.

"Guide me," he repeated a moment later as Henry set him down. "Not carry me."

"This was faster. You need to put more work into that Nightsight spell."

"Yeah." Tony snapped on his flashlight, beam pointed carefully at the ground. "I'll get right on that in my copious amount of spare time between working and saving the world. You got anything?"

Crouched, Henry brushed a palm over the crushed grass. "Unfortunately, the police believed Grace enough to check this out. There's no scent here now but theirs."

The tracks—the mess the police had made visible even to Tony—followed a path behind the lilacs probably created by deer or some other non-small-child-eating animal. The police appeared to have reached a set of tire tracks that lead up between two houses and back to the road and stopped their search.

"Do you think Ms. Alton told the Mounties about the car door?"

"No. She didn't remember it until I asked her specifically what she heard. I think because this"—Henry indicated the tracks—"is the obvious place for a car but the tracks just as obviously haven't been used this spring, the police assumed Grace was . . ."

"Making things up to get attention?" Tony offered diplomatically.

"Possibly. And you can't exactly blame them; there'd be no reason to bring an abducted child down here unless you had a car and this"—he waved at the unused tracks again—"this says there was no car. But because we know there was a car involved we need to find another place you can bring in a vehicle. Wait here."

"Why—"

"Because I'll be moving quickly and I don't want you to fall in the river."

Tony sighed and turned off the flashlight. He couldn't see the river, about three meters away and down a steep bank, but the sound of rushing water filled the night, drowning out every other sound.

Five minutes. The scar on his left palm itched and he thought about conjuring a Wizard lamp. Ten minutes. When he got his first decent job in Vancouver, he'd bought a cheap watch with a luminescent dial, tired of spending unacknowledged time in the dark. Fifteen minutes. He yawned and nearly swallowed his tongue as Henry's pale face appeared suddenly out of the shadows.

"Just past those cedars, it's all bare rock. It wouldn't be impossible to get something with four-wheel drive and a high clearance along the edge of the river and then back up to Highway Twelve right at the bridge."

"Just because it 'wouldn't be impossible' doesn't mean there was a car there," Tony pointed out as they headed for Grace Alton's driveway and the car. "I doubt Ms. Alton heard anything over the sound of the river, Henry. That track's likely got nothing to do with—"

Henry held up a small red boot.

Boot in one hand, laptop balanced on his knees, Tony scrolled through his spell directory. "Here it is. Pairbonding: joining two halves back into a whole. I cast the spell on the boot and it acts like a compass leading us to its mate." He pulled a black marker from the pack between his feet and slowly drew a rune on the instep of the boot.

"Whatever has the child reeks of old blood, old kills," Henry growled, driving up onto the bridge. "The stench hides its nature."

"If it isn't rogue were, there's nothing that says some of the smaller giants couldn't drive. I mean, as long as the car was big enough." Rummaging in the pack, Tony pulled out a plastic grocery bag of herbs, removed a spray of small red berries almost the same color as the rubber, and dropped it in the boot. "Belladonna," he explained. "To clear the way. I'm working the sympathetic magic angle. It's a diuretic, makes you piss, and that's clearing that way anyway."

"I didn't ask."

Boot balanced on his palm, Tony reached for power and carefully read the words of the spell.

The boot slammed against the middle of the inside of the windshield.

Henry's nostril's flared.

Tony sighed, powered down the laptop, and performed a quick Clean Cantrip. "Yes, I pissed myself," he muttered defensively, cheeks burning. "Like I said, it's a diuretic but at least the boot didn't blow up. Or melt. Or break your windshield."

"But you're still using too much power."

"Am not. New spells always need a bit of fine-tuning."

"Fine-tuning? My car—"

"Is clean. Fresh. All taken care of." He slouched down in the seat. "Whether they believed Ms. Alton or not, the cops had to have searched the riverbank. How come they didn't find the boot?"

"I found it by scent down deep within a crack in the rock. The RCMP would have needed to go over the riverbank with a fine-tooth comb to find it, and I doubt they have sufficient manpower even for this given the foolishness of the recent budget cuts."

"You sound like Vicki. Only with less profanity."

Although she hadn't been a police officer for some years before Henry changed her, Vicki continued to take government underfunding of law enforcement personally.

"Speaking of Vicki"—because speaking of the boot or the child or the thing that had taken her would only feed his anger and that would make it dangerous for Tony to remain enclosed with him in the car—"do you think she'd like one of those purple plants?"

"Purple plants?"

"Like all those plants Grace owns."

"Would Vicki like an African violet? For Christ's sake, Henry, she's turning forty, not eighty."

Reaching across the front seat, Henry smacked him on the back of the head. "Don't blaspheme."

Just before the sign for the Nohomeen Reserve, a gravel road led off to the east, into the mountains. The boot swung around so quickly to the passenger window, it nearly smacked Tony in the head. As Henry turned off the highway, it centered itself on the windshield again, bouncing a time or two for emphasis.

"Not exactly a BMW kind of road," Tony pointed out as a pothole nearly slammed his teeth through his tongue.

"We'll manage."

The road ran nearly due north, past the east edge of the Keetlecut Reserve and farther up into the wild. They passed a clear-cut on the right—the scar on the mountainside appallingly visible even by moon and starlight—then three kilometers later the boot slid hard to the left, the rubber sole squeaking against the glass.

Leaning out past Henry, Tony stared into the darkness. "I don't see a road."

"There's a forestry track."

"Yeah." Tony clutched at the seat as the car bounced through ruts. "Remember what you said earlier about a high road clearance and four-wheel drive? And hey!" he nearly shrieked as they lost even the dubious help from the headlights. "Lights!"

"We don't want them to see us coming."

"You don't think the engine roar will give us away? Or the sound of my teeth slamming together?"

A moment later, Tony was wishing he hadn't said that as Henry stopped the car. Except that he *didn't* want the engine to give them away. He didn't want to walk for miles up a mountain through the woods in the dark either but then again Julie Martin hadn't wanted to be snatched out of her backyard so, in comparison, he really had nothing he could justify complaining about.

He crammed handfuls of herbs into an outside pocket on his backpack and wrestled the red rubber boot into the plastic bag. When he held the handles, it was like a red rubber divining rod . . . bag, pulling with enough force that it seemed safest to wrap the handles around his wrist. As he leaned back into the front seat for his backpack, it started to rain. "Wonderful," he muttered, straightening and carefully closing the door. "Welcome to March in British Columbia. Henry, it's almost one and sunrise is at six oh six. Unless you want to spend the day wrapped in a blackout curtain and locked in your trunk, we need to be back at the car by three. Do we have time . . ."

"Yes."

That single syllable held almost five hundred years of certainty. Tony sighed. "I don't want to leave her out here either but . . ."

"We have time."

The flash of teeth, too white in the darkness, suggested Tony stop arguing. That was fine with him except he wasn't the one who spontaneously combusted in sunlight or bitched and complained for months after he spent the day wrapped around his spare tire and jack. And it wasn't like camping out was an option. He skipped the Brokeback Vampire reference in favor of suggesting Henry head for his sanctuary and he go on alone. "I'm not entirely helpless, you know."

"You're wasting time," Henry snarled.

The evil that had taken the child was close. The drumming of the rain kept him from hearing heartbeats—if these things had hearts—and the sheets of water had washed away any chance of a scent trail, but Henry knew they were close nevertheless. Vicki would have called it a hunch and followed it for no reason she could articulate so he would do the same.

For twenty minutes they moved up the forestry track, his hand around Tony's elbow both to hurry his pace and to keep him from the worst of the trail invisible to mortal eyes in the dark and the rain. The white bag pulled straight out from Tony's outstretched arm, a bloodhound made of boot and belladonna. A step farther and the bag pulled so hard to the right Tony stumbled and would have fallen had Henry's grip not kept him on his feet.

The track became two lines in the grass that led to a light just visible through the trees. Not an electric light, but not fire either. A lantern. Behind a window.

"Were build shelters," Tony muttered, ducking under a sodden evergreen branch. "Or the pack could be squatting in a hunting cabin."

"I hear nothing that says these are were." But also nothing that said they weren't. The rain continued to mask sound and scent but its tone and timbre changed as they drew closer to the building and a pair of large, black SUVs. The cabin, crudely built and listing to the left, did not match the cars.

Lips drawn back off his teeth, Henry plucked a bit of sodden fur from where it had been caught in one of the doors. "Dog. And the stink of old death I caught by the river lingers still."

"It was wearing dog? Okay." A moment while Tony assimilated that. "Still could be giants then. These things"—a nod toward the SUVs—"are fucking huge. Hang on." Releasing one handle, Tony reached into the bag and used the ball of his thumb to smudge out the rune. With the boot now no more than a reminder that a child's life hung in the balance, he wrapped the plastic tight and shoved it into his jacket pocket. "I'll likely need both hands."

The rune in his left hand throbbed with the beat of his heart.

As they stepped under the eaves of the roof and out of the pounding distraction of the rain, Henry felt something die. Not the child—he could hear her heartbeat now, too slow but steady, probably drugged—but an animal who had died terrified and in great pain. Growling deep in his throat, he looked in through the filthy window.

Half a dozen kerosene lanterns hung from the rafters of the single room. One lantern alone made shadows, mystery. Six together threw a light that was almost clinical.

There were two men, middle-aged and well-fed, standing at each end of a wooden table stained with blood. Henry saw nails and a hammer and didn't need to see any more. Over the centuries he had seen enough torture to recognize it in the set of a torturer's shoulders, in the glitter in the eye. Both these men were smiling, breathing heavily, and gazing down on their work with satisfaction.

He had seen their expressions on priests of the Inquisition.

They might have started by accident, inflicting pain on a hunting trophy wounded but not killed. Over time, they had come to need more reaction than an animal could provide, and to answer that need Julie Martin lay curled in the corner of an overstuffed sofa wearing one red rubber boot and one filthy pink sock. Her face was dirty but she seemed unharmed. From what he knew of men like these, Henry suspected the drugs that had kept her quiet had kept her safe. There was no point in inflicting pain on the unaware.

The raw pelts draped over the back of a chair had probably been worn when they took the girl. Perhaps as disguise. Perhaps as a way of working themselves up to the deed, reminding themselves of pleasures to come. Grace Alton had seen the evil. Had seen clearer than anyone had believed.

"They're just men." But not even Tony sounded surprised.

"There is no such thing as *just* men," Henry growled, barely holding the Hunter in check. "Angels and demons both come of men. To say these two are *just* men is to deny that. Is to deny this. I want the girl safe first."

"I've got her. Just open the door."

Henry didn't so much open the door as rip it off its hinges, rusted nails screaming as they were torn from the wood, the blood scent roiling out to engulf him.

He sensed rather than saw Tony hold out his scarred hand and call. A heartbeat later the young wizard staggered back under the weight of the child and grunted, "Go."

Henry smiled.

And the two men at the table learned what terror meant.

Tony slid the boot onto Julia's foot and lifted the sleeping child off the backseat of the car, settling her against his shoulder. As they drove back to Lytton, the drugs had begun to release their hold and, to keep her from waking, he'd sung her a lullaby from his laptop. It hadn't seemed to matter that the words were in a language she'd never heard nor would probably hear again. She'd sighed, smiled, and slipped her thumb into her mouth. Now he wrapped them both in a Notice-me-not and carried her up the road to her parents' house. Although it was just past two in the morning, all the lights were still on when he laid her gently on the mat and rang the bell.

Rolling the ball bearing between his thumb and forefinger, he walked back to the car, listening to the crying and the laughing and wishing he could bottle it. The sound of hearts mending and innocence saved: that would make the perfect present for Vicki.

"You think she'll remember anything?"

With the Notice-me-not wrapped around the car, Henry drove back toward Vancouver at considerably more than the legal speed, racing the sunrise. "I hope not."

"You think they'll ever find the bodies?"

He shrugged, not caring. "I expect someone will stumble over them eventually."

"You didn't leave anything that would lead the cops back to you? I mean"—Tony slouched against the seat belt strap—"these were men."

Henry turned just far enough that Tony could see the Hunter in his eyes. "Would you have preferred we left them to the law?"

"Hell, no." He scraped a bit of mud off his damp jeans. "They hadn't done anything to that kid yet but they were going to. It's just, monsters are one thing, but those—"

"Were also monsters. Do you have to throw up again?"

It had been a reaction not to what Henry had done but to suddenly realizing just what they'd prevented. It had also been incredibly embarrassing, but the rain had washed the stink off his boots.

"No."

"Good. It doesn't matter if or when they find the bodies, Tony. There's nothing that can link them back to us. To me." His teeth were too white in the headlights of a passing transport and his eyes were too dark. "No one believes in vampires."

Tony stared at the face of the Hunter unmasked and shuddered. "Dude, we're doing a hundred and fifty-five k. Could you maybe watch the road?"

"All right, I still don't understand how forty is any more important than one hundred and forty, but I think I've got Vicki's birthday covered." Henry pulled a jeweler's box from his jacket pocket and opened it. "One pair half-carat diamond earrings."

Tony stepped aside to let Henry into his apartment, peered down at the stones, and nodded. "Good choice. Diamonds are forever and so is she."

"Now read the card."

"Ah, you've included a newspaper clipping about the miraculous return of Julie Martin. Very smart. Almost makes up for the pink, sparkly roses on the front of this thing. Blah, blah, blah, as you approach the most wonderful years of your life, blah, blah, young as you ever were, blah, in your name a pair of evil men have been sent to hell where they belong." Tony looked up and grinned. "Man, they really do make a card for every occasion."

"I added the last bit."

"No shit? Seriously, Henry, it's perfect. You don't have to wrap it, she doesn't have to find space for it, and you can't beat the sentiment."

"You think she'll like it?"

"Like it?" Tony snorted as he tossed the card onto his kitchen table. "I think she'll want to collect the whole set. You should start thinking about what you're going to do when she turns fifty."

"Fifty." Halfway across the apartment, Henry froze.

"Fifty. Sixty-five. Seventy-five. Ninety. One hundred. One hundred and twenty-seven."

"One hundred and twenty-seven?"

"Kidding. You get her something really fine at one hundred and you're probably good until at least one-fifty . . ."

The Wish

Carolyn Haines

Carolyn Haines has written more than fifty books. The latest in her Mississippi Delta series is Ham Bones. *She also writes single titles.* Hallowed Bones *and* Penumbra *were named one of the top five mysteries of 2004 and 2006, respectively, by* Library Journal, *and Carolyn received an Alabama State Council on the Arts fellowship. An avid animal-rights supporter, she shares her home with nine cats, six dogs, and eight horses. Because no minute should go unused, Carolyn also teaches fiction at the University of South Alabama. Her website is www.carolynhaines.com.*

It hasn't rained for weeks, longer than anyone remembers. Each gust of wind carries tiny particles of dirt—soil shifting from place to place, fleeing across the borders of lawns, counties, and states. The land is on the move, as if it's given up hope for America and is headed vaguely north, aiming to cross the border. It's a long way to Canada from Mobile, Alabama.

The weather is all the talk in the grocery and feed stores, the nurseries and post office, places where I carry on the business of my life. Old men, as weathered and crinkly as the grass, study the sky that looks like spring and feels like Minnesota as they stand outside the Hickory Pit and the tractor dealership. They see nothing good. The climate is changing, and the farmers are catching the brunt of it. Gamblers at heart, they have no clue where to lay the odds in this New South of hard drought and hurricane.

Sitting in my pickup, waiting for a load of mulch and fertilizer while the heater blows ineffectually, I watch the dirt fly down Highway 45 in an orange cloud. Across the road, at the Stovalls' abandoned nursery, a tulip tree sways purple against the clear blue sky of another cold, dry, windy day.

The late February winds, unusually strong for south Alabama, pick up the fallen petals of the tulip tree, and suddenly I see her shape against grass that glistens with melting frost. The coffee cup I hold slips from my nerveless fingers and drops to the floorboard. I never hear the crockery shatter, nor the tinkling of the wind chimes abandoned at the nursery. My world goes mute. Again.

She stands beneath the tree, beside barren hydrangeas and glossy green miniature gardenias that will permeate the April air with a scent as delicious as taste. How easily I'd assumed that spring was a season I'd experience—waiting has become my only game. I haven't been to a doctor for fifteen years, but I feel healthy enough. Illness isn't my destiny. She's taught me that.

She nods at me, an acknowledgment of our pact, and then she's gone. The bruised petals fall softly to the thawing ground. Bosco, my old coonhound, breaks into a long, low howl in the backseat of the truck. He understands who and what she is. The enemy.

Mobile isn't the center of anything, merely a small port city on a bay where lazy rivers meet in one of the last untainted habitats in the Southeast. It's a sleepy place with smiling, crocodile politicians one step removed from the horse thieves and slave traders who first took the land from the Choctaw Nation. While the town is physically beautiful, it lacks the sophistication of New Orleans, or at least pre-Katrina New Orleans. The Moral Majority holds sway in Mobile, those prunelike faces set against the joie de vivre that made New Orleans so special.

I should have left Mobile, but it's because of her that I've remained here for so many years. Her and a certain ship's captain who finds the empty downtown of old Mobile to his liking. No Disney creation, this pirate holds the answer to my dilemma.

Anxious in my grief and unable to sleep one long night, I walked the empty streets. By happenstance that evening, I saw him plying his trade in a dark alley, and I made it my business to learn his haunts and habits. He is my field of expertise, the most important element of my future. The cobblestone alleys of old Mobile are a perfect hunting ground for him, and one he returns to regularly, because in the dark of the moon, anything that's truly desired can be found in old Mobile.

Once I deliver the mulch and fertilizer, I'll put my plan into action. By moonrise, I'll find him, the man, or some would call it a thing, who will help me.

To fully explain my story, I have to go back in time twenty years to a hot August day. Sometimes I forget that once I was another person. A wife and mother. A woman with dreams and expectations. To understand how I came to this point, the past has to be pulled out like so many wrinkled snapshots and examined.

It's an irony, really, because I hate remembering. In memory, the images are so sharply focused they slice through the layers of alcohol I've used to pad my pain. People tell me that I live in the past, like that's an accusation of moral degeneracy. "You live in the past" in their mind equates with "You killed your children." Hardly. We all have a past. We all have a present. But not all of us have a future.

Once upon a time, I had a future. I had the family and job, the normal, boring things that Middle America takes so for granted. I also had a mortgage and a car note and nights when my husband and I made passionate love and forgot the dirty dishes in the sink, the piles of laundry waiting, and the spats about bills and babies. Today, none of those things trouble me. They're all in the past, along with my heart.

On a too-hot August morning twenty years ago, I woke up plagued with a fever of unexplainable origin. The day was sweltering, even for south Alabama, and the humidity lay on my skin like a wool suit. We were in dog days, when it rains each afternoon and Mobile takes on the foliage of the tropics, thick and lush and green. Dennis had a breakfast meeting, and even though I felt terrible, I took Kala and Kevin to day care. My intention was to return home, shower, and go to work. I had a client meeting that couldn't be missed, a big account, a cash bonus.

The antihistamine I'd taken in an effort to dry up my sniffles had left me feeling dizzy and disoriented. The twins, identical even in their moods, were quiet as I buckled them into the car seats and headed out, a cup of hot tea in my hand. The day care was only eight blocks away. Eight short blocks in a residential neighborhood shaded by live oaks that buckled sections of the sidewalk with gnarled roots.

I was almost there—I could see the day care sign with the happy alphabet letters spelling the name—when I saw her in the Darcy yard. I thought I was hallucinating, and I slowed the car for a better look. Some would call her a wind wraith, a substanceless creature of twigs and leaves, but she isn't. Nor is she a sprite or fairy or gremlin. I stopped the car, completely stunned at this creature formed of debris and spinning air currents who beckoned to me from the shade of the Darcys' yard. I didn't know it then, but I know now what she is. She's an angel. A dark angel with a list of names. At the top of her list were Kevin and Kala.

I never saw the Ozark Water delivery truck that hit me from behind. I never even had a chance to glance at my children in the rearview mirror. My seat belt stopped me from impaling myself on the steering column, but my forehead cracked the wheel, and I was knocked unconscious, or so they told me at the emergency room when I tried to tell the doctor what I'd seen. No one believed me, but it doesn't stop it from being true.

From far away I heard sticks and sand pelting the windshield. Semiconscious, I fought to wake up, to protect my babies. A man yelled at my window, but I didn't pay any attention to him. I watched her, standing at the passenger side of the car. Her hands reached through the car, lovely hands, fine boned and delicate. Kala took her hand first, then Kevin. Each one so trusting.

"No! No! Kala! Kevin!" I tried to call them back to me. "Don't leave me. Don't go."

She held my children's hands and shook her head at me. "I'll be back for you," she said.

"Don't take them," I begged. "Please. They're only children. Take me instead."

"It isn't your time."

Such a matter-of-fact answer for an event that would make me wish for death a million times over.

"Take me. Let my children have a chance to grow up. Kala wants to be a veterinarian. She wants to make animals well. And Kevin—" My voice broke and I couldn't continue. "Dennis will be a good father. They'll be fine without me. Take me." I held out my wrists, offering the veins to the broken windshield for a slashing.

"It isn't your time." Her face was pale, the eyes dark and sad.

"Make it my time. Trade me for them." Panic had begun to build beneath my ribs. My heart squeezed, and I hoped it was the first sign that a deal had been struck.

"You can't bargain with death," she said. "It's either your time or not. This isn't your time."

Against the pain in my chest, I struggled to free myself from the seat belt that held me. "No!" I fought, but the belt was tight. "No!"

They backed away from the car. A shaft of sunlight touched Kala's chestnut curls. Tears hung in her lashes. "Mama." She held out her arms to me. Kevin bit his lip.

"Please!" I ignored the man tugging at the driver's door, his face showing horror and panic. "Please don't take them."

"It's their time."

"That's supposed to bring me comfort?" I wanted to kill her. I wanted to tear her fleshless body with my teeth, rending her apart. Anything to protect my children.

"Their purpose is done. Let them move forward."

The pressure in my chest became unbearable, and I knew it wasn't a heart attack. Grief had set up lodging. My new boarder had brought his full accommodation of pain. "For God's sake, I'd rather be dead. Please, take me!"

She shook her head. "When your time comes, I'll be back."

They stepped out of the sunshine and slowly dissipated in the shade cast by the oaks.

"Please!"

I was still shrieking when the man got the door open and Mrs. Darcy reached in to grasp my hands that clawed at the air. She tried to calm me until the ambulance came, but I could tell by the tears on her face that my children were gone. Just like that, gone. As quick as snuffing out a match.

There was a funeral, which I don't remember. For a year, Dennis tried to make a go of it, but he lost not only his children but his wife. No man should have to live with a zombie, and though Dennis tried, there was nothing he could do to bring life back to the husk of my body. I ate what I was forced to eat. I sat in the sun if someone led me there. I bathed if a bath was drawn. Mostly I sat in a rocker by the front window and watched for her. I knew I'd see her again.

After Dennis left me, I cut my wrists in a bathtub of warm water. It's a funny thing, but I'd always expected it to be painless. Bleeding to death is excruciating. The body demands to live, no matter what the mind or spirit says. My lungs burned for oxygen. My starving heart suffered anguish. I felt agony, but I knew soon it would be over.

That's when I saw her again. She stood in the doorway of the bathroom, a vague creature of swirling air currents and energy and bath powder. For a moment I saw the terrible beauty of her face as she shook her head.

"It isn't your time, Sandra." She held out a scroll, and for a split second, I thought I saw names written in blood. "Your name isn't here."

"Fuck you." It's hard to be witty while bleeding to death.

"You can't cheat death," she whispered. "And you can't hurry it."

"Where are my children?"

"Their destiny is no longer your concern. They're where they're supposed to be."

With those words, I knew Kala and Kevin were forever lost to me. Death would not resolve my loss. "I hate you! You won't win! I'll do whatever is necessary." My voice weakened.

She slipped closer and looked into the tub that was bright with warm blood. "It isn't your time."

She disappeared and I heard footsteps pounding up the staircase. Dennis to the rescue. Why couldn't he leave it be? He could've collected the insurance money and been done with the guilt. But no, he'd come back to check on me. I hadn't looked good. He'd been worried, had a bad feeling. Feeling guilty over the divorce, he'd come back to make sure I was okay. But, of course, I wasn't. I was far from okay.

Two years later, the wounds on my wrists were hard to find. My new attitude—one of self-sufficient acceptance—had won my freedom from West Briar Estates, the place where crazies can get twenty-four-hour surveillance and legal pharmaceuticals to blur reality. Never make the mistake of telling a psychiatrist that you've had a conversation with Death; it's a surefire ticket to involuntary incarceration. While under the watchful eye of the medical staff, I began to formulate my revenge.

I learned to smile and pretend an interest in the news and the visits of my nieces and nephews. Actually, I was interested in the news. I'd begun to catch glimpses of her in the newscast footage of violent slums, on the dusty roads of the Middle East, and in the mud villages of Central America as a flood swept houses away. She was always there, a half-formed face in the shuddering palm fronds or in a dust devil shifting across the desert. She was there, the Pied Piper of the dying. She'd always been there, but no one looked for her. Except me. I sought her out, gathering the tidbits that would become my arsenal.

When the doors of West Briar closed behind me, I moved into a lovely old home with screened porches and an acre of yard that Dennis bought for me. He'd remarried and his wife was pregnant. They both came to visit, to include me in the growth of their baby. No two people could have worked harder. So I feigned an interest and began to garden with spectacular results. I had a green thumb. Imagine that. Someone who watched for death could grow anything.

As the years passed and I waited to see her, my plan took shape. She'd sentenced me to a half life. When she took my children, she took my joy. She wouldn't let me die. She said it wasn't my time, as if she could dictate the end of a person's life by a timetable worked up like a train schedule. Good. I've been waiting. I've arranged for a little surprise.

It begins tonight, symbolically enough, on my birthday. I saw his ship in the harbor last night while I walked the midnight streets, unafraid of harm because it "isn't my time."

Tonight I'll be forty-three, a mother of dead children, a divorcée, a failed suicide. A winner.

The winter days are short, and I've watched the sun wane and the timid appearance of the gibbous moon. Somehow, I thought it might be full—too many superstitions and legends, I suppose.

My home isn't far from downtown, which is my destination. Thank goodness it's a weeknight. On weekends young people crowd Dauphin Street to drink and party and listen to music. Tonight, a Tuesday, the downtown will be quiet. The hunters will be out.

By the time I park my Volvo beside a meter, which I deliberately don't feed, dusk has fallen like the soft kiss on a child's sleeping brow. The

Mobile River is only a few blocks away, and I can smell the water. The last, lingering businessmen and -women are hurrying out of downtown. Hurrying home, as out of control of their lives as I used to be.

Neon lights a few bars, and I go to Barnacle Bill's. I've watched my pirate often enough to know this is where he'll be. Just as I step to the doorway, a rustle of wind reveals her image. She's in Bienville Square, a vague outline among the squirrels and homeless people who sleep on the park benches. She walks beside an old man, and he never senses her. I know exactly what she'd say. It isn't his time.

I never considered that she might read my mind. Can she squeeze my heart at a distance? Can she send a blood clot streaming through my lungs? I'd always assumed she has to touch me, but I might be wrong. Now that would be a fatal mistake, so to speak.

I step into the darkness of Barnacle Bill's and inhale the smell of stale smoke and spilled beer. Old men slouch at the bar, hovering over mugs of beer. I'm the only woman in the place, and that draws interest, for about ten seconds. One look at my face, and all the men turn back to the drinks they're nursing. I'm not there for company.

A puff of smoke spirals from a corner so dark I can't make out the features of the smoker. That's where I want to be. I walk to the booth and sit, uninvited.

"I'm Sandra, and it's my birthday," I say. "I have a wish."

"Fascinating." The accent is impossible to place, a blend of French and Spanish and old South. Beautiful. Seductive. I hadn't expected to feel that.

"Will you grant me a wish?" I have to clear my throat twice before I get the question out. I'm afraid. Fancy that. After all this time, all the planning, I'm afraid.

"Depends."

"I know who you are. I know about you. I've done my homework. Mobile Bay, 1823, the ship *Esmeralda*. You were walking along the docks late one night. You felt a tap on your shoulder and then a bite on your neck. You come back to Mobile to commemorate your making, and to hunt."

He leaned forward, his eyes so black I felt as if I were being pulled into bottomless darkness. "And what else do you think you know, *cher?*"

"I know you can give me peace. You can take my life and give me immortality."

His hand, the fingers chill, brushes my cheek. His touch is sensual and also terrifying. This is the hand of Death that I've sought for the last half of my life, but death on my terms.

"It doesn't always work that way, *cher.* This immortality you request comes in degrees and always with a price."

When he smiles, I see the points of his fangs. His face is dark-hued, the color of coffee or a nut. His teeth are white and his hair jet-black, long and beautiful. He's no older than forty-five, or maybe two hundred and forty-five.

"Death has come for me. She *says* it's my time. After twenty years of begging to die, I refuse to do it on her schedule. She took my children. She took my life." The anger hardens my words into rocks that I hurl at him. "She has her little list with my name at the top, but she won't win this time."

His laughter is sucked into the beer-sodden wood of the bar. I've amused him.

"You think to best Death."

"I do." I don't hesitate. I stretch out my wrists. "I've wanted to die for a long time. Now I refuse—because it suits *her.*"

"So you want the bite of immortality. To what end?"

"You hold the power of life and death. You are her rival. I want you to win."

His smile looks haunted, and he doesn't answer immediately.

From the table beside us a pile of napkins whirl into the air. She's here. She's standing right beside me, her hand reaching out for mine.

"Help me. Please." I ignore her and focus all of my powers of persuasion on him. I think that I shouldn't have waited until the last minute. I should've come sooner.

Before I can blink, he's swept me into his arms. In a blur of speed we're out the back door and into the alley.

"Happy birthday, Sandra," he says just before his teeth sink into my neck. This time the blood loss is erotic instead of painful. I feel my body grow limp. Soon I will sleep and awaken to a world where Death has no hold on me.

Fire and Ice and Linguini for Two

Tate Hallaway

Tate Hallaway is the author of other works featuring the main characters in this story: Tall, Dark & Dead, *published in May 2006, and* Dead Sexy, *published in May 2007. She's intimately familiar with Midwest winters, having grown up in LaCrosse, Wisconsin. Tate currently lives in Saint Paul, Minnesota, with five monochromatic cats and her adorable four-year-old son, Mason.*

Sebastian told me several times that his birthday was cursed. I didn't really believe him, but when I found myself standing ankle deep in exhaust-smudged snow on the shoulder of County Highway 5 while Sebastian stared glumly at the engine block of our stalled car, I started to reconsider.

We were stuck. A broken broomstick handle propped open the hood of the '90 Honda Civic. Sebastian usually drove a mint-condition classic car, but since it had no heater, it wasn't especially suitable for Wisconsin winters. The Honda was a beater from Jensen's, the garage where Sebastian worked. He had it on loan for as long as the bad weather lasted.

Sebastian held the distributor cap in his hands and was doing something to it with a fingernail file he had borrowed from my purse. The way he was dressed, it could be twenty degrees, instead of twenty below—no hat, no scarf, no gloves. In fact, all he had on as protection against the wind was one of those shapeless parkas, broken-in, loose-fitting jeans, and cowboy boots. He looked much more like a car mechanic than a vampire. Of course, he *was* a car mechanic—it was his day job. That's right, you heard me, *day* job. Sebastian had been made by magic instead of by blood, and he could walk in the sunshine.

Not that there was much of that left.

The sunset threw pink and blue shadows over the frozen cornfields. In the fading light, icicles glittered from the eaves of a nearby abandoned barn. A dog howled in the distance. It would have been beautiful if it wasn't so damned cold.

Despite the below-zero breeze pulling at his long black hair, Sebastian worked unhurriedly, impervious to the cold. The tips of his ears weren't even red; I could feel mine burning under the fake fur of my hat. His composure in the bitter cold made him seem especially supernatural. When I took in a deep breath of icy air, my jaw clenched in a way that made my teeth actually chatter.

It must be nice to be dead.

Meanwhile, I was freezing my butt off. I looked great in my estate sale–find Harris Tweed wool coat, fluffy Russian hat, and fake-fur lined boots, but the skimpy little black number I had underneath everything let the cold seep in to the bone. Normally, a forecast of subzero temperatures suppressed my fashionista tendencies, but it was Sebastian's birthday, and I'd wanted to glam things up. No doubt I looked absolutely fabulous underneath my winter layers, but a fat lot of good that did me right now. I was shivering so hard that my knees literally knocked together.

The deep blue shadows stretched in the fading rose-colored light, and above us, a highway light snapped on. Sebastian glanced up in the sudden illumination, and then glared at me for a short moment before going back to the distributor cap.

Sebastian hadn't said much since the car sputtered and died twenty minutes ago, and I knew he was brooding. He hadn't wanted to come out for his birthday. He said he'd never celebrated it in all the thousand-odd years of his life, and he hardly wanted to start now. It had never been a happy occasion for him.

He believed his birthday caused him to become a vampire.

Today was Christmas.

Apparently, the superstition at the time Sebastian was born was that sharing a birthday with Jesus was extremely bad juju—something about your parents engaging in earthly pleasures at the same time of year that the Virgin Mary had been divinely conceiving. Whatever. It made no sense at all to me, not being of a religious persuasion that concerned itself with Jesus' birthday, but it was important to Sebastian. Plus, he had been reminded of this wickedness every single birthday. He told me once that the curse had become a kind of self-fulfilling prophecy, since he had pursued the "dark arts" of alchemy and witchcraft partly because people expected him to. If he hadn't, he would never have discovered the formula that made him a vampire.

"Try it now, Garnet," Sebastian shouted from somewhere under the hood. I slipped and slid over the frozen slush to the driver's side. I scooted into the driver's seat and shut the door to the wind. Depressing the clutch, I put my hand on the key and made a quick appeal to Pele, the Hawaiian goddess of fire. I closed my eyes and whispered, *Give us a spark. Please.*

When the engine turned over, I almost thought my prayers were answered. Then the noise stopped again, and this time, I had the distinct impression that something died—a metal-on-metal, grinding, final death.

"Nothing," I shouted back as if he couldn't tell. Having grown up with Midwestern winters, I couldn't help but complete the traditional call-and-response of injured vehicles.

I waited for another word from Sebastian. Instead, he shut the hood with a firm finality, like closing the lid of a coffin.

I cranked down the window as he came around. I gave him a hopeful smile, but he shook his head. "It's dead."

I tried to remain perky. "It's still early," I said. "We could call a cab."

Sebastian leaned against the driver's side door, looking away from me. Crossing his arms in front of his chest despite the bulk of his parka, he stared out into the darkening fields. "Is anyone going to be working today?"

"The restaurant is open," I reminded him. "As is the movie theater." Despite being moderately sized, Madison—a left-leaning, radical, college town—had a large contingent of people for whom Christmas is just another day. In fact, I'd debated long and hard about whether or not to keep open the occult bookstore I managed but had decided to close it in deference to Sebastian's birthday. It was winter break and my college-age staff was all at home enjoying roast turkey right about now, and I'd have had to staff the store myself. I'd wanted the day off to spend with Sebastian.

Sebastian fished through his pockets for his cell phone, but came up empty-handed. "Figures," he sighed as we searched the car. "Benjamin must have walked off with it again."

Benjamin was Sebastian's resident house-ghost—well, poltergeist, really, since he had a tendency to toss things around when riled up. Still, it wasn't like him to run off with Sebastian's things. Benjamin was usually very loyal to Sebastian to the point of "defending" the house from all interlopers, even me. "What did you do to piss him off?"

"I've been thinking about rewallpapering Vivian's room."

"Are you insane?" Vivian was Benjamin's wife, whom we suspected Benjamin had axe-murdered in that very room. Benjamin got especially crazy if anything in her bedroom was altered. In fact, Benjamin was so obsessed with keeping things precisely as they were, Sebastian could sometimes trick him into cleaning the place by moving some of Vivian's things to other parts of the house.

Sebastian lifted his shoulders in a shrug barely visible through the thick down of his parka. "Why don't we just go home?"

I would have been more excited about his suggestion if he'd sounded more "in the mood." But I could hear the defeatism oozing from each syllable. Even so, part of me did want to just give up—the exact part being my frozen toes—but I was on a personal crusade to shake Sebastian of his birthday melancholia. He'd been carrying around this hatred of his birthday for a millennium. It was time for an attitude adjustment.

Sebastian's farm was just about as far away from us now as Portobello Restaurant, where we had reservations in twenty minutes. We could still make it.

"I'm sure there's a farmhouse nearby," I said, rearranging my hat so it covered more of my ears. "We can call a cab from there."

"For home."

"For the restaurant."

We got into one of those stare-downs where a normal person would just let the vampire win. The look of fierce intensity in those chestnut brown eyes with their eerie golden starburst pattern around the pupil said *Back off*. I, however, am a pigheaded Witch, and I'm somewhat careless with my sense of self-preservation.

"Come on." I pasted a cheery smile on my face, despite the skin-numbing chill. Swinging the car door open, I strolled out into the frozen wasteland with a jaunty step. "It'll be an adventure."

For several steps I wondered if Sebastian was going to let me have this so-called adventure on my own. Then, in that silent way he had, he was suddenly beside me.

"You're incorrigible," he grunted, but there was the hint of a smile in his voice. Victory.

It didn't take long for me to regret my pluckiness. Minus twenty was dangerously cold, and I was just not dressed for it. My face felt raw, and my toes had gone way past the tingly phase. I was seriously entertaining the idea of asking Sebastian to turn me into one of the living dead so that I didn't have to deal with the prospect of freezing to death when we spotted a pickup truck heading in our direction.

Actually, at first, all I saw were two points of light, like the eyes of some huge animal. Through the still night air, I heard the snarl and spit of a working engine. I waved frantically, hoping to flag the vehicle down. My only thought was: heater.

Miraculously, it stopped.

Behind the wheel of the shiny black Ford was a woman in her mid to late fifties. The curls of hair that stuck out from an Elmer Fudd earflap hat were the color of steel wool. Her cheeks were burned red by the wind and cold. One look at her REI arctic-ready parka, insulated gloves, snow pants, and heavy-duty boots, and I knew she was a farmer.

The interior of the cab was blessedly hot and smelled faintly of stale coffee and wet dog. "Thanks for stopping," I said, climbing in gingerly.

She nodded in that rural way that implied *You're-welcome* and *I-should-have-my-head-examined-for-this-act-of-kindness* all at once.

"You should really stay with your car on a night like this," the driver said as I wedged myself into the center of the bench seat. She was right, of course. Beyond the actual temperature, there was the wind chill, which could be considerably lower. A car protected you from that. Plus, out in the elements the cold hemorrhaged heat from your body. Inside a car, at least, you could build up a bit of warmth just from your own breathing. Not to mention the fact that I had no idea how far I would have had to walk to find another farm, and there's always the risk of getting lost. Cops and snowplow drivers are trained to stop for cars with red flags tied to the antenna to look for people trapped inside.

As a native Minnesotan, I knew all that. I was about to acknowledge my failure in winter safety rules when she added, "Don't either of you two have a phone?"

"No," I said miserably.

Sebastian just shook his head. "I don't suppose you do?"

She flashed a thin smile that held only a hint of self-righteousness. "Of course." She pulled a sequin-studded flip case from the interior pocket of her parka. I raised my eyes at the shiny appliqués as I handed it to Sebastian.

He snapped it open and frowned. "No signal." Then, "And . . . now your battery is dead." Handing it back to me, he mouthed, "Cursed."

"That's strange," she said when I gave it back to her. "It was working a half hour ago."

"I'm cursed," Sebastian said out loud this time, matter-of-factly.

The woman gave us a crook of a snow-white eyebrow and pulled back on to the road. "So," she said, sounding anxious to get rid of us, "where are you headed?"

I didn't take it personally. I was sure we made a strange pair—me, bundled up like some kind of accident between a Russian babushka and a Goth supermodel, and him, grumpily cryptic and ridiculously underdressed.

I looked to Sebastian for an answer to her question, but he stared out at the graying sky. I had to snap him out of this. He was being downright antisocial and rude.

"If you're headed to town," I tried hopefully, and when she didn't deny it, I added, "Anywhere close to State Street would do us."

She nodded, her eyes on the black strip of asphalt. Wind threw streaks of powdery snow across the road where it slithered like snakes, twisting and turning before merging with the drifts on the opposite side. "You kids off on a date?"

"His birthday."

She nodded as if considering something. I braced myself for a Christmas comment or joke. Finally, she simply said dryly, "Nice day for it."

Thunder rolled outside, strangely synchronous with her tone.

Sebastian roused himself from his brood enough to inquire, "Was there supposed to be a storm coming in?"

"Oh yeah," said the driver, in a pitch-perfect Minnesotan accent. "National Weather Service issued a winter storm warning."

"This just gets better and better," Sebastian grumbled.

I gave him a punch in the arm, as if to say, "Be nice!"

"I feel terrible," I said. "I should really have introduced myself. I'm Garnet Lacey, and my delightful companion here is my boyfriend, Sebastian Von Traum."

She nodded her greeting. "Fonn Hyrokkin." In the flash of a passing car's headlight, something sparkled in her eyes like ice.

Hyrokkin sounded a lot like the Finnish surnames I'd grown up with in northern Minnesota, but something about the way she said it, as though it were more of a title, made me pause.

I looked with my magical vision, but it was too dark to get a good read of her aura. Auras are like halos of refracted light around a person or an object, and they can't be seen without some kind of illumination. I've found artificial fluorescents work best, but light of some kind is an absolute must. The glow of the dashboard just wasn't cutting it.

Despite my growing unease about our driver, we fell into a silence.

You can't live in the upper Midwest without having to deal with quietness. I grew up in Minnesota, so I should be used to it: but I'm a chronic chatterer. I even commit the cardinal sin of enticing strangers into conversation in elevators. When I can't talk, I tap my toes and drum my fingers. It was strange, but one of the things I like about my adoptive state of Wisconsin is that people around here seem to be much more willing to engage in copious amounts of small talk. Just my luck, the one Norwegian in all of Wisconsin would have to pick us up.

I glanced at Sebastian for support as my feet started their nervousness dance. He just glumly watched the darkness roll past the window.

Pulling at the fingers of my gloves, I looked back at Fonn. She stared resolutely ahead. Our shoulders touched when the truck bounced over uneven patches in the road, and each time they did I would have sworn I could smell dog more sharply. I told myself that maybe her golden retriever liked to nap on her coat. I mean, I was sure some of my clothes smelled of cat. Barney snoozed in my dresser drawer any time I accidentally left it open. Anyway, why should that make me so nervous? As someone who kept a pet, I tended to see animal ownership as a positive personality trait. The people who didn't have animals when they could always seemed a little suspect. So what bothered me? Was it that the dog wasn't anywhere in sight?

I listened to the sound of the engine growling as we continued to bump along the deserted county road. I wanted to ask Fonn about the dog I could smell but couldn't think of a polite way to bring it up. "Say, I notice your truck stinks of wet pooch. So what kind is it, and where is it anyway?! Oh, that's actually your body odor? My bad," seemed just a little bit tactless.

On the side of the road, Christmas lights festooned a one-story ranch whose lawn was littered with illuminated and motorized reindeer, elves, snowmen, and a glow-in-the-dark plastic crèche. Three pairs of eyes turned to watch the extravaganza disappear behind us, but, in true Midwestern fashion, we kept our own counsel.

Lightning flashed across the sky. Snow sprinkled the windshield.

"What the heck?" I said, looking at tiny kernels of snow that the wiper brushed away. "It's far too cold to snow." I might have failed winter safety, but I knew that there were temperatures at which snow couldn't form. It was simply not possible.

Something very strange was happening outside. Something unnatural.

"Storm," Fonn whispered reverently. "It's going to be a big one."

Deep in my belly, Lilith grumbled.

Sharing a body with the Goddess Lilith meant that sometimes She felt free to editorialize. The snarl surprised me, however. It struck me as threatened . . . or even territorial. Though I knew it wasn't audible to anyone else, I put my hand over my stomach.

I glanced over at Sebastian to see if he registered Lilith's complaint. Thanks to a blood-bonding spell, Sebastian could sense Lilith's moods.

He inspected Fonn with sudden interest. I followed his gaze to see what it was about her that suddenly fascinated him and concerned Lilith. In the bluish glow of the dashboard lights, her facial features were sharp, yet broad, and her skin stretched tightly across high cheekbones. She had a certain regalness about her, but nothing I hadn't seen in countless faces of the farmers in Finlayson, Minnesota, where I grew up.

The only thing that struck me as particularly odd was the faint hint of a smile. She stared out at the wind and snow like something about it tickled her fancy . . . or made her proud. Yeah, that was it. She was staring at the growing storm like a mother would watch a baby taking its first steps.

Creepy.

Sebastian and I shared a look that said, *Something here isn't right.* After all the silence, I was grateful to be communicating with Sebastian again, even if it was only about the bizarreness of our situation. He flashed me a crooked smile which seemed to say, *Isn't this just our luck?* I nodded in quiet agreement.

Wind pushed against the truck hard enough to cause us to coast slightly toward the center line. Fonn corrected for it with a twinkle in her eye.

So, my first thought was that Fonn was some kind of demented storm chaser, except that Lilith rarely gave me the nudge when people were just plain odd. If She did, I'd be getting poked a lot, given the type I tended to attract. No, there had to be something supernatural going on here, but what?

If Fonn wasn't a deranged meteorologist, what else could she be? Severe weather made her ecstatic, she was out on a cold night alone, and her truck smelled like dog. Seemed to me it was time to play twenty questions. Yet how to interrogate her without raising suspicion? "So, Fonn," I said, trying to affect the vaguely disinterested conversation style of a church basement social gathering. "You from around here?"

"Nope."

Argh! Foiled by a yes-no question and a wily yet taciturn respondent.

"Where *are* you from?" Sebastian asked, picking up the dropped ball.

"Came over from the Old Country."

"Me, too," Sebastian said. "I was born in Austria. You?"

"Norway."

Okay, we had something on her. Not that it helped much. I looked to Sebastian, but he just shrugged. He didn't have a clue what sort of magical being she might be, either.

The wind howled around the truck. Sheets of snow spattered against the windows. That was another oddity. The snow had changed from tiny ice pellets into large, fluffy flakes. The temperature must have shifted dramatically. It was just plain strange to see that kind of snow transformation so quickly. Normally, you saw one kind of flake or another, or if they changed at all, it was gradual, like over the course of several hours. Not minutes.

This storm challenged all my well-honed Midwestern senses. It was seriously freaking me out. Somehow Fonn was behind it, I was certain.

So, okay, maybe Fonn wielded some kind of weather magic. Did I know any Old Norse otherworldly beings in charge of snow? To be honest, the only Norwegian female baddie I could think of was a Valkyrie, and somehow I sensed that wasn't right. It seemed to me that you had to die in battle to meet one of those—oh, and you should probably also be a Viking. Unless something really weird had happened without my knowledge, neither Sebastian nor I fit that particular bill. Well, okay, Sebastian was dead. And he had died in a battle, like the Crusades or against the Huns or something, but that was a long time ago and he definitely wasn't Norse.

Fonn turned the truck onto a major thoroughfare. The snow became a blur of fast-falling, large flakes. Despite the wider, well-traveled road, all I could see ahead of us was a vague sense of the center line and ice crystals glistening in the headlights. The truck barreled ahead confidently, but I snaked a hand over to Sebastian's and squeezed tightly.

Lilith rippled across my abdomen—a warning.

Okay, so Fonn was crazy magical, but what was Lilith saying? Was Fonn dangerous, too? How?

Despite the Ford's heater going full blast, I felt an icy breeze on the back of my neck. My muscles tensed involuntarily. I snuggled a bit closer to Sebastian, who seemed to be feeling the chill also. The arm he wrapped around my shoulder shuddered slightly.

"Cold?" I asked him.

"Yeah," he said, raising his shoulders as if to ward off a wind. "Just now."

"The storm is picking up," Fonn said, as if that explained why the temperature suddenly affected my undead vampire lover. "We might need to find shelter," she added, using her gloved hand to turn the wipers up a notch. They beat furiously against the glass.

"We've got to be getting closer to town," I muttered to myself. Sebastian's farm was no more than ten minutes from the edges of Madison's suburbs. It seemed like we'd been driving twice that long, especially given that when we'd broken down we were almost halfway to the edge of town.

"I may have missed a turnoff," Fonn said. "Visibility sucks. I think I might have gotten turned around. We're a bit lost."

We're not lost, I thought. *We're being taken somewhere.* Madison wasn't exactly a bustling metropolis. Okay, sure, it was the capital city of Wisconsin, but there weren't that many roads that led in and out of it. Provided you stayed pointed in the same direction, getting lost was actually kind of difficult. Fonn knew where we were, I was sure of it, especially when I noticed that slight, malicious smile twitched across her lips again. I was just about to call her on it when Sebastian piped up.

"A bit lost? Isn't that like being a little pregnant?" Sebastian asked, though his question was clearly rhetorical and sarcastic. "Lost. That's fantastic."

I rolled my eyes and shrugged out from under his arm. "This is not your curse," I said with a long-suffering sigh.

"Are you kidding me?" Sebastian snapped out of his funk long enough to let out a rant. "We're stuck in an ice storm with the creature from the black lagoon, and you don't think it's because my parents are sinners and I practiced the dark arts on the holy days?"

"No, I don't. You're suffering because your parents had sex on a night they weren't supposed to? Do you even realize how insane that sounds?" I asked, giving him the *she-can-hear-you* glare.

"I'm from Norway," Fonn added, sounding only a little put out. I started to giggle at the absurdity of her correction, when she continued, "And I'm not a 'creature'; I'm a demon."

"Oh, well," Sebastian said dryly. "That makes things *much* better."

I gave Sebastian a little nudge to say *Go ahead, idiot, poke the demon.*

The wipers smeared ice and slush uselessly across the windshield. We were surrounded in whiteness. The storm had become a full-on blizzard.

Pulling off to the side, Fonn slowed to a stop. "We need to wait this out."

"Yeah, great," Sebastian muttered.

Even though she'd identified herself as a demon, I still figured a little common courtesy could go a long way. "Thanks for picking us up," I said, staring out into the shifting white. "We'd be dead otherwise."

Fonn smiled.

Lilith tightened the muscles in my abdomen.

The chill crept along my spine again, like fingers of frost.

"Jesus, it's cold in here," Sebastian said, reaching for the heater.

Sebastian huddled near the vent, hugging himself for warmth. I looked at Fonn and the gleam in her eye.

Fonn pushed a button on her dash, and suddenly the cabin was filled with the droning voice of some announcer on Wisconsin Public Radio talking about the stock market and Bulgarian politics or some other esoteric subject. I didn't really listen. I was too busy freaking out. Sebastian looked miserable. He shivered pathetically. I ran my hand along the back of his neck lightly to comfort him. His skin felt cold.

Cold? That wasn't right. Yeah, okay, he was a vampire, and most vampires have cold skin. Not my boy. His magic made him hot-blooded. I pulled my fingers away in surprise.

"Sebastian," I said. "You're cold."

"Damn right. I'm freezing." He rubbed his arms in the classic style, trying to get some heat from the friction.

Wind rattled the windows of the truck. Everywhere was white on night, and where the headlights beamed, it reminded me a bit of the image of hyperspace from *Star Wars*. Sebastian shouldn't be cold; this storm shouldn't be so strong, so soon.

"You're sucking the life from us to make this storm, aren't you?" I demanded of Fonn, who sat smugly watching the snow pile up on the windshield.

Midshiver, Sebastian glanced up at Fonn. "Hey, I don't have any life," he pointed out.

"Energy," Fonn interjected. "And, if I may say so, you're both loaded."

That would explain why Lilith didn't like Fonn much. An energy-snarfing demon would probably consider a goddess an all-you-can-eat-buffet.

"That's fan-fucking-tastic," Sebastian said. "Happy birthday to me."

A knock on the driver's side window made everybody jump, even Fonn. She powered-down the window, letting in an arctic blast of wind and snow. I noticed the faint flash of blue lights behind us and the reflective paint at the tip of a snowplow's blade.

"Everyone all right in here?" a male voice asked. I had the impression of a mustache underneath the fake fur of a parka hood wrapped tightly around his head.

Fonn eyed the newcomer in a way that could only be described as hungry.

"We could use some help," Fonn said, her voice abruptly shifting to that of a feeble older woman's. Fonn was going to eat this unsuspecting stranger, too! I suddenly realized she'd been out trolling for victims and anyone would do. Of course, she'd lucked out and got a goddess-toting Witch and her supernatural vampire boyfriend. Good day for Fonn; bad day for us.

Lilith pushed against my stomach, like a snake uncoiling. But before I could react, Sebastian spoke up.

"Actually, we're fine. Just waiting out the storm a bit." Sebastian's voice was liquid glamour. For a moment, I swore the cab of the truck smelled faintly of cinnamon toast and hot cocoa—very comforting smells, very homey. In fact, even I was feeling pretty safe and a little bit sleepy.

The snowplow driver nodded, completely duped by vampire charm. "Yeah, this weather sure is a doozie. You take care now."

He disappeared into the snow, and I let out my breath when I heard the plow's engine spring to life behind us.

Fonn did not look happy with either of us.

The temperature inside the cab dropped ten degrees. I could see my breath come out in white puffs. Sebastian took in a ragged breath at the same time, as if he also felt the shift. The snowy wind coming through the open window tossed Fonn's curls about wildly. Her eyes flashed a stormy gray. Wind howled around the truck like a wolf.

Heat leeched from me in waves. I could see steam lifting from my body, rising to curl around Fonn like smoke. Fonn's expression was pure triumph. She was going to suck the heat from us and make the mother of all blizzards.

So I kicked her.

I'm not usually a big proponent of violence, but I found her self-satisfied grin too annoying to bear.

I'd like to pretend that after my swift kick to the shin Fonn crumpled over in abject pain and suffering, we overpowered her, and that was the end of things, but in reality she gave me a *do-that-again-and-I-will-squash-you-like-a-bug* frown and continued stealing our life force.

Undaunted, I kicked her again. Harder. With both feet this time.

I must have gotten the angle just right, because she fell backward onto the door latch. Unexpectedly, the door swung open, causing her to lose her balance. She flailed around gracelessly for a second, groping for something to hold on to. Finding nothing, Fonn fell with a whump out of the cab.

I slid into her seat and shut the door.

"Go!" shouted Sebastian, despite the fact that the only thing I could see out of the window was white, white, and more white. "Let's get out of here."

"We can't," I explained. "You saw what she was like with the snowplow driver. She'll just find another person to suck." Rolling up the window, I cranked up the heater a notch.

"Garnet," Sebastian said, "she's clearly some kind of elemental. We're not going to be able to stop her. I'm not even sure Lilith could. Forces of nature are just that. . . . Part of the natural order of things. You can't just wipe out the one in charge of winter."

Why not? Couldn't I just back the truck up and run over her a few times? Bump-bump, no more winter! I mean, come on, in Wisconsin winter generally sucks. Here in America's Dairyland it was cold and miserable for nearly half the year. Sure, the first snowstorm with those fluffy, storybook flakes was beautiful, but it took less than a week for all the snow to get dirty from exhaust and other urban detritus.

But I supposed Sebastian had a point. Global warming was already a problem. If we stopped having winter altogether, we'd probably ruin some endangered ecological niche. Walleye population would explode from a lack of ice fishing. There'd be no annual mosquito die-off and they'd take over the world. So not cool, as it were.

Especially since I try to be so low-impact, you know? I even recycle my toilet paper rolls.

"We have to do something," I insisted. I was starting to feel a bit warmer, more like myself, but not quite. My hands shook where I gripped the steering wheel.

"Yeah, drive," said Sebastian. "Away. Fast."

The snow flurries lessened enough to give me a tad more visibility. I glanced down out the side window, hoping to see Fonn unconscious on the snow. No luck. She was out there somewhere. Lurking.

I waved my hands in the direction of the sheets of snow still coming down thick and wet. "If I hit the gas right now, Sebastian, we'd ram into a light pole or another car. I can't see a damn thing."

"Except that," Sebastian said dryly, pointing.

I gasped. Fonn pressed her face against the windshield. Rows of sharklike teeth lined an open, hungry mouth. Her hair whipped like snakes in the wind, blending into the sleet. Claws raked at the glass.

"Oh, great," I said.

"Did you have a plan to get rid of her?" Sebastian asked as the safety glass began to show spiderweb cracks. "Because now would be a great time to let me know."

"So, what do you think?" I asked, jumping in my seat at each slam of her claws on the windshield. "Could you take her? You've got super-vamp strength, right? How about you jump her?"

"How about I not? For one, I don't think I could take her down, and secondly, what do I do once I have her? I can't bite her; she might have antifreeze in her veins. How about you unleash Lilith?"

The windshield was completely cracked and starting to buckle in places. Safety glass, my ass.

Lilith was more than ready for the fight. It would not be a difficult thing to let Her out; but, She was Queen of Hell, Mother of Destruction. What if Lilith not only killed Fonn but also showed her usual lack of discretion and killed Sebastian, too? Then we'd have all that environmental disaster or Ragnarok or Goddess-knows-what-end-of-the-universe kind of stuff, *and* I'd be out one boyfriend.

Coldness began to seep in. I knew Fonn would be inside in a second.

I hit the gas hard and then slammed on the brakes. She slid off the hood and disappeared into the whiteout.

"Oh," said Sebastian, a little startled. "Good job."

"She'll be back," I reminded him. "We need to think of something slightly more permanent, but not too permanent."

"Not to be unmanly, but I still think running away is a good option."

"Well, it may come to that," I admitted, hating the idea of leaving the next poor sap who happened to be out on Christmas to the fate of getting chomped by a heat-munching demon. "Are you sure you can't bite her?"

"I could," Sebastian said thoughtfully, then added, "if I want to die. Magical blood will kill me dead. And, like I said, God knows what's coursing through those veins. You saw her, right? Did she look even vaguely human?"

"No," I agreed. "So, if she eats energy, how do we counter that? She can't be too affected by cold. I mean, she clearly controls it."

"What about antifreeze?" Sebastian asked. "What if we blasted her with hot water and antifreeze straight from the radiator? Maybe, if nothing else, we could overload her. . . . Yeah, this could work. Turn off the engine. I've got an idea."

Switching the ignition off meant no more heat. In the dangerous snowfall, it made no sense. As I hesitated, I felt someone pull at the truck's door. I had to twist in my seat to double-check that it was locked. Sebastian reached across the seat and pulled out the keys.

"Distract her," he said, opening the passenger's side door and disappearing into the snow.

"Distract her? With what, my good looks?" I shouted at the open door. Two seconds later it registered: there was an open door.

Slowly taking form, Fonn materialized out of the snow. First, I noticed the black pits of eyes. Next I saw snow-white hair slashing wildly around her inhuman face. She crawled across the seat toward me, slowly, like a cat stalking its prey. Bitter wind blasted me, freezing the tips of my nose and ears.

Okay, I'll admit it. I screamed. Screeched, really—all high-pitched and useless. I even started fumbling with the locks, slipping and scrabbling like a classic horror-film babe, until I remembered my purse. I made a snatch for it, and in a second, my fingers found the Mace where it always hung on the chain next to my keys.

Pulling out the tiny canister, I pointed the nozzle at those razor-sharp teeth. I let rip a big, nasty blast of the stuff.

Fonn reared back with a painful shriek. She pawed at her face.

I didn't wait to see how quickly she might recover. Besides, discharging the pepper spray in an enclosed space had unintended consequences, like my own eyes starting to water. This time deftly flipping the lock, I scrambled out of the truck. Once outside, I slammed the door. I hadn't really meant to shut it quite so hard, but the wind propelled it out of my hand.

Snow raged around me in blinding swirls. Momentarily, I lost sight of the truck even though I was standing right beside it. For a second, I thought maybe I'd blinded myself with the Mace. Then the truck reappeared in a gust of wind. I slapped my hands on to the metal frame so as not to lose it again.

"Sebastian," I shouted into the squall. "Where are you?"

I strained to hear anything beyond the rush of air, and I inched forward toward the hood of the vehicle. Oh, it would so not be good to lose my boyfriend on his birthday. I started to feel a real quiver of panic as the storm continued to bluster. I couldn't see anything. Snow slid into the tops of my boots as I sank knee-deep with each step. I felt like I was climbing forward into empty space.

"Sebastian!"

At this point, I might even have been grateful to see Fonn. Any sign that I wasn't completely swept away into nothingness would have been welcome.

As if on cue, claws snipped at my back. Talons pierced my coat and scratched skin.

I tried to run. I tripped over something and lost my grip on the truck. My entire world became snow. There was snow in my mouth, my eyes, my nose, covering my face, and surrounding my body. I felt suffocated by cold. I started really screaming—deep, terrified-for-your-life bawling.

Hands griped my shoulders with a familiar strength and pulled me under the truck. The space between the undercarriage and the road was like a little cave. Heat from the engine had carved a no-snow zone, and I lay on my belly on warm, wet road. Sebastian stretched out beside me with a long hose in his hand. The hose was attached to something above us, and his fingers rested on a tiny spigot.

"Radiator drain," Sebastian explained. "Is she coming?"

I started to explain that Fonn had been at my back a second ago when we noticed the digging. Claws scooped out huge chunks of snow, like a demonic prairie dog. Plus, I could feel her magic leeching the heat from me. Cold seeped in from the ground. My body felt heavy with ice, as if I were freezing solid.

Teeth were the first things I saw. I swore they'd grown. They now extended into grotesque spikes, like something you might see on a deep-sea creature or in your nightmares. Her face, too, was distended, almost fishlike, so she seemed to be one human-sized, extended gullet.

Sebastian's hand began to quake. Ice rimmed his eye lashes and coated his hair. I hadn't noticed that his fingers crimped together the hose; as the magic started to immobilize him, his fingers slipped off. A blast of heated liquid shot forward. Steam billowed everywhere. The smell of antifreeze filled the air, and I coughed, gagging.

Neon green splashed down Fonn's gaping throat. When she startled and closed her mouth with a snap, the hot stuff squirted her right between her eyes.

Fonn yelped like a wounded dog, but there was so much steam in the cramped space I had a hard time seeing what was happening. But I certainly *heard* the gnashing of teeth, the snarling (which might have been Sebastian, come to think of it), and then a howl like a wounded hound of hell that nearly split my eardrums. The wind lifted the tires of the truck off the ground unevenly, so it seemed to bounce.

Then everything was quiet. Dead quiet.

Sebastian crimped the hose again. When the steam cleared, all I could see was a huge melted hole of toxic-green slush. From the front bumper, icicles dripped to sharp points like teeth.

There was no sign of Fonn. I held my breath hopefully and strained to hear anything. Sebastian scanned all around us, his fangs still bared.

I almost didn't dare hope, but I felt the difference immediately. I still felt cold, but my limbs lightened. I no longer thought I might become a block of ice.

Sebastian put his hand on the spigot. "Do you think we got her?" he asked.

I wedged my hand between the ground and my belly. Closing my eyes, I let my consciousness rise out of my body. With Lilith's eyes, I scanned the storm. When I didn't sense Fonn in the immediate area, I reached my mind out further. Far off, on Highway 169, I caught the image of a woman riding bareback on a giant wolf. The vision blurred at the edges, melting into the snow, and steam streamed out of her like blood. She was running wounded. "We got her," I said confidently.

Then I sneezed. The antifreeze smog and the cold plugged up my nose. Dirt was slowly freezing itself into the fabric of my ripped coat and dress. Sebastian screwed tight the spigot and looked over at me. Perhaps in reaction to my miserable expression, he laughed.

"I'm clearly not cursed." He smiled.

"Oh, yeah, why not?" Although, when I said it, the words sounded a bit more like "Hi, what?"

"For one, we're not dead," he said, pulling the hose from the radiator drain. "Second, you've got a smudge of dirt on your nose that's absolutely adorable." He leaned over and kissed said nose, and I had to scrunch my face to hold back another wet sneeze.

I shook my head. "No, you are cursed. This was insane."

"Come on," he said with a laugh. "Once I get the hose back in place, we can get this baby running again."

I guess defeating an ice demon can brighten a vampire's day, or night, as the case may be. Feeling gross, exhausted, and tired of the cold, I wasn't nearly as chipper as I had been at the start of our trip.

As he popped the hood, I started to wonder. I supposed the truck now could be considered a stolen vehicle. What is it when you borrow an abandoned one? Still a crime, no doubt. And, honestly, I had to wonder about whether or not Fonn owned this truck to begin with. What if, somewhere out in the snow drifts, there was a heat-sucked corpse waiting to be found and somehow linked back to us? "Are you sure that's a good idea?"

"Be practical," Sebastian said as he slid me out of our warmish, wet cave under the truck. "You'll freeze to death without the heat."

He had a point. I was already chilled to the bone. "What about all the antifreeze?"

"The truck can run on water for a little while."

I tried to remember if I'd seen a bottle of water anywhere in the cab. "Where are we going to get that?"

Sebastian looked around at the piles of snow and gestured with his open hands. "We seem to have an abundance of the frozen kind right here."

I nodded. He got to work with a grin and a whistle. He seemed genuinely pleased to be fixing up the truck. I left him to it. The storm had abated to the point where I could see where I was going, so I stumbled my way back and threw myself into the passenger side of the truck. The interior stank of pepper spray, and, while I waited for Sebastian to finish, I coughed and sneezed until I had to open a window. Sebastian worked by the light of the headlights, while I sat there glumly.

In the fifteen minutes it took him to reconnect the hose and refill the radiator with snow water, the storm quit enough that I could see the occasional star through breaks in the clouds.

The truck ran hot all the way into town, but, luckily, Sebastian told me that the best way to contain that problem was to keep the heaters on full-blast.

My toes were toasty again by the time we pulled up to the darkened restaurant. "Oh, no," I said, noticing the absence of any lights.

Sebastian just shook his head, a trace of his earlier sullenness returning. Even so, he pulled the truck into a parking spot and killed the engine. "We might as well go check it out."

Despite myself, I felt a deep stab of desolation. The one thing I'd been fighting for—a decent night out for Sebastian's birthday—now seemed ruined. I could feel a tear hovering at the corner of my eye. I wiped at it with a knuckle. "Yeah," I said, trying to sound hopeful, but failing even to my ears. "Let's go check it out."

I trudged through the courtyard, one of my favorite features of Portobello during the summer. Snow draped the barren Virginia creeper vines that twined around the walls like white-frosted lace. Where they poked through the drifts, black-eyed Susan seed heads wore dots of snow. Dried husks of milkweed and mullein stood sentry over sleeping garden beds. The cobblestone walkway had been recently shoveled, and Sebastian and I made our way quickly to the heavy wooden door. A pull on the brass handle confirmed my worst fears. It was locked. Closed.

"I'm sorry," I blubbered. Despite my best efforts, a hot tear ran down my chill-burned cheek.

Sebastian wrapped his arms around me, and I smelled that comforting scent of cinnamon again. I breathed in deeply. "It's okay," he lied smoothly. "I'm just glad we're both alive."

Yeah, and it's my fault we were out in the first place, I wanted to say, but I was too choked up to make my throat work. I was just about to suggest we turn around and head for my apartment, when the door swung open, nearly knocking us off our feet. A round-faced older man wrapped in a shapeless parka and a stocking hat raised his eyebrows at us hugging on the restaurant doorstep.

"Von Traum party?" he asked.

"Yes," I said, wiping at my tears. "How did you know?"

"You were our only reservation tonight," he said. "When the blizzard hit, everyone cleared out. The storm only now just let up enough for me to get out and shovel. I was just about to head home."

I wanted to beg him to stay, but I couldn't blame the guy for wanting to get home after a storm like this one. "Please don't let us stop you. I'm so sorry you waited for us. We forgot our cell phone."

"No, no problem. If you're happy to pay, I'm happy to stay!"

"Seriously?" I brightened.

He waved a mitten dismissively. "I've seen worse storms. Besides, it's your birthday," he said to Sebastian. "You should do something nice. I know how it is; my birthday is on Thanksgiving. Do you even know how sick of turkey I am?"

We all laughed.

Then, to Sebastian I asked, "Are you up for it? Really? I'd understand if you just wanted to go home, too."

Sebastian smiled. "Let's stay. I'm starving."

Though my dress had claw marks down the back, we had wine and pasta by candlelight and the place to ourselves. The cook pampered us with special sauces, fresh breadsticks and garlic butter, and tiramisu for two. Sebastian's kisses tasted of fresh whipped cream and chocolate.

We walked to my apartment in the quiet, peaceful snow, hand in hand. At home, I gave him his birthday present—ironically, a part for his antique car that he'd been searching for—and a lot more.

"Still think you're cursed?" I asked him, after.

Sebastian thought for a moment. "Let's see, today we had our car break down, met some kind of storm demon who tried to kill us, and had fantastic pasta. Yes, I'm cursed," he said. When I was about to protest, he put a finger on my lips. "But I also have you. That makes the whole thing bearable."

And then he called me incorrigible again, and we laughed and kissed until dawn.

Vampire Hours

Elaine Viets

Elaine Viets is the author of two mystery series. Murder with Reservations *is her sixth Dead-End Job novel. Her third Josie Marcus Mystery Shopper book,* Accessory to Murder, *will be out this fall. Elaine has won both the Anthony and Agatha Awards for her short stories. "Vampire Hours" is her first vampire story. She lives in Fort Lauderdale, across the water from a condo whose occupants were the inspiration for this story.*

"It's three o'clock in the morning, Katherine. Go to sleep."

My husband, the surgeon. Eric barked orders even in the middle of the night.

"I can't sleep," I said.

"I have to be at the hospital in three hours. Turn off the light. And go see a doctor, will you? You're a pain in the ass."

Eric rolled away from me and pulled the pillow over his face.

I turned off the light. I felt like a disobedient child in my own home, as I listened to my husband of twenty-five years snore into his pillow. Eric could fall asleep anywhere, any time. Especially when he was in bed with me.

If I pushed his face into the pillow, could I smother him?

Probably not. Years of late-night emergency calls had given Eric an instant, unnatural alertness.

I lay alone on my side of the vast bed, stiff as a corpse in a coffin. My white negligee seemed more like a shroud than sexy sleepwear. My marriage to Eric was dead, and I knew it. I wanted him to love me, and hated myself for wanting a man so cold.

He wasn't like that when we were first married. Then, he'd ripped off so many of my nightgowns, he'd bought me a thousand-dollar gift certificate at Victoria's Secret. I'd model the latest addition and he'd rip it off again. Back then, he didn't care if he had early surgery. We'd had wild, all-night sex.

A tear slipped down my cheek, and I cursed it. Tears came too easily these days, ever since menopause. "The change," my mother had called it. Once, before I knew what those changes were, I'd looked forward to menopause. I wanted the monthly flow of blood to stop. I was tired of the bloat, the cramps, and the pain.

But the change was infinitely worse. Oh, the blood stopped, as promised. But nobody told me what would start: the weight gain, no matter how hard I dieted. How could I get fat on rice cakes and lettuce?

The change brought other changes. My skin started to sag along the jaw. The lines from my nose to my lips deepened into trenches. My neck looked like it belonged on a stewing hen.

And my husband, the old rooster, was chasing young chicks. I knew it, but I didn't dare confront him. I'd seen what happened to my friends when they'd faced down their rich, powerful husbands. Elizabeth, courageous, I-won't-stand-for-this Elizabeth, had been destroyed. She'd caught Zack, her husband of thirty years, groping some not-so-sweet young thing in the dim lights of the local bar. Elizabeth had fearlessly confronted Zack on the spot. She'd embarrassed him in front of his backslapping cronies.

Good old Zack hired a pinstriped shark—one of his bar buddies. Now the elegant Elizabeth lived in a cramped hotbox of an apartment, with a cat and a rattling air conditioner. She worked as a checker at the supermarket and barely made the rent. Elizabeth was on her feet all day and had the varicose veins to prove it.

I'd taken her out to a dreary lunch last month. I'd wanted to do something nice. We went to the club, where we'd always lunched in the old days, when she was still a member. Some of our friends didn't recognize her. Poor Elizabeth, with her home-permed hair and unwaxed eyebrows, looked older than her mother. She was so exhausted, she could hardly keep up a conversation.

That same fate awaited me. I had to stall as long as I could, until I could figure out what to do with my life. If Eric dumped me now, I'd be at the supermarket asking my former friends, "Would you like paper or plastic?"

I'd be one more useless, used-up, middle-aged woman.

I was already. In seven days, I'll be fifty-five years old. My future had never looked bleaker. I had no money and no job skills. My husband didn't love me anymore. Happy birthday, Katherine.

"Lie still," Eric snarled. "Quit twitching."

I didn't think I'd moved. Maybe Eric felt my inner restlessness. Maybe we were still connected enough for that.

But I couldn't lie there another moment. Not even to save myself. I slid out of bed.

"Now what? Where are you going at this hour?" Eric demanded.

"I thought I'd get some fresh air. I'm going for a walk."

Eric sat straight up, his gray hair wild, his long surgeon's hands clutching the sheet to his hairy chest. "Are you crazy? You want to go outside in the middle of the night? After that woman was murdered two streets away?"

"People get murdered all the time in Fort Lauderdale," I said.

"Not like that. Some freak drained her blood. They didn't put that little detail in the papers. The city commission wants to avoid scaring the tourists. Dave at the medical examiner's office told me. That woman hardly had a drop of blood left in her. She went for a walk at three in the morning and turned up drained dry. For Chrissakes, use your head."

"All right," I said. "I'll sit on the balcony. I didn't want to wake you."

I put on my peignoir and padded into the living room. I never tired of the view from our condo. To the east was the dark, endless expanse of the Atlantic Ocean, lit by ancient stars. Straight down were the black waters of the Intracoastal. Across the little canal that ran alongside our building were the Dark Harbor condos. Those places started at three million dollars. But it wasn't the money that fascinated me. Florida had lots of expensive condos. There was something about Dark Harbor. Something mysterious. Exciting. Exotic. Even at three in the morning.

I slid open the glass doors, careful not to make a sound. The warm night air caressed my cheek. I loved the night. Always had. Moon glow was kinder than the harsh Florida sun. I could hear the water softly lapping at the pilings on the dock, seven stories below.

Laughter drifted across the water, and the faint sounds of a chanteuse singing something in French. It was an old Édith Piaf song of love and loss.

There was a party in the Dark Harbor penthouse. Such a glamorous party. The men wore black tie. The women wore sleek black. They looked like me, only better, smoother, thinner. These were people in charge of their futures. They didn't have my half-life as the soon-to-be-shed wife. They were more alive than I would ever be.

I sighed and turned away from my beautiful neighbors. I drifted back into our bedroom like a lost soul, crawled in next to my unloving husband, and fell into a fitful sleep.

Eric woke me up at five-thirty when he left for the hospital.

"Good-bye," I said.

His only answer was a slammed door.

That night, while getting ready for bed, I looked in my dressing room mirror and panicked. I'd always had a cute figure, but now it had thickened. I had love handles. Where did those come from? I swear I didn't have them two days ago. I burst into tears. I couldn't help it.

I ran into the bathroom to stifle the sobs I knew would irritate Eric. But it was too late. "Now what?" he snarled. "I can't take these mood swings. Get hormone replacement therapy or something."

He was definitely getting something. I'd found the Viagra bottle in his drawer when I put away his socks. It was half empty. He wasn't popping those pills for me. We hadn't made love in months.

No pill would cure my problem. Not unless I took a whole bunch at once and drifted into the long sleep. That prospect was looking more attractive every day. Didn't someone say, "The idea is to die young as late as possible"? Time was running out for me.

I spent another restless night, haunting the balcony like a ghost, watching another party across the way at Dark Harbour. Once again, I drifted off to sleep as Eric was getting ready for work.

Tuesday was a brilliant, sunlit day. Even I couldn't feel gloomy. I was living in paradise. I put on my new Escada outfit—tight black jeans and a white jacket so soft, it was pettable. I smiled into the mirror. I looked good, thanks to top-notch tailoring and a body shaper that nearly strangled my middle.

I didn't care. It nipped in my waist, lifted my behind, and thrust out my boobs. I sashayed out to the condo garage like a model on a catwalk. A sexy, young model.

I had a charity lunch at the Aldritch Hotel. I was eating—or rather, not eating—lunch to support the Drexal School. I didn't have any children, but everyone in our circle supported the Drex. As a Drexal Angel, I paid one hundred dollars for a limp chicken Caesar salad and stale rolls.

My silver Jaguar roared up under the hotel portico. A hunky valet raced out to take my keys. The muscular valet ogled my long legs and sensational spike heels, and I felt that little frisson a woman gets when a handsome man thinks she's hot.

Then his eyes reached my face and I saw his disappointment. The valet didn't bother to hide it. I was old.

I handed him my keys. The valet tore off my ticket without another glance at me. I felt like he'd ripped my heart in half. I used to be a beauty. Heads would turn when I strutted into a room. Now if anyone stared at me, it was because I had a soup stain on my suit or toilet paper stuck on my shoe. I was becoming invisible.

I caught a glimpse of myself in the hotel's automatic doors. Who was I kidding in my overpriced, overdressed outfit? I was losing my looks—and my husband.

I stopped in the ladies room to check my makeup. My lipstick had a nasty habit of creeping into the cracks at the lip line. I used my liner pencil, then stopped in a stall, grateful it had a floor-to-ceiling louvered door. I needed extra privacy to wriggle out of the body shaper.

I heard the restroom door open. Two women were talking. One sounded like my best friend, Margaret. The other was my neighbor, Patricia. I'd known them for years. I nearly called out, but they were deep in conversation and I didn't want to interrupt.

". . . such a cliché," Margaret said, in her rich-girl drawl.

"I can't believe it," Patricia said. Her voice was a New York honk. "Eric is boinking his secretary?"

Eric. My husband, Eric? Panic squeezed me tighter than any body shaper. There were lots of Erics.

"Office manager," Margaret said. "But it's the same thing. She's twenty-five, blond, and desperate to catch a doctor. It looks like Eric will let himself get caught."

"Can you blame him?" Patricia honked. "Katherine's let herself go."

Katherine. No, there weren't many Erics with Katherines. I felt sick. I sat down on the toilet seat and listened.

"She won't even get an eye job," Patricia said. "And her own husband is a plastic surgeon. How rejecting is that? Eric did my eyes. Then he did the rest of me." Her words filled the room. I couldn't escape them.

"You slept with him?" Margaret sounded mildly shocked.

"Everyone does," Patricia said.

I could almost hear her shrug. I wanted to rush out and strangle her. I wanted to blacken her stretched eyelids. But I was half-dressed, and my jiggly middle would prove she was right.

"It's part of the package," Patricia said. "My skin never looked better than when I was getting Dr. Eric's special injections."

"You're awful," Margaret said. Then my best friend laughed.

"It's part of my charm," Patricia said. "But someone better clue in Katherine, so she can line up a good divorce lawyer before it's too late."

"It's already too late," Margaret said. "Eric's already seen the best lawyer in Lauderdale, Jack Kellern."

"And you didn't tell Katherine that Eric hired Jack the Ripper?"

"How could I? He's my husband."

And you, Margaret, are my best friend. Or rather, you were. Margaret had also had her eyes done by Jack. Did she get the full package, too?

I waited until my faithless friends shut the restroom door. I rocked back and forth on the toilet in stunned misery. It was one thing to suspect your husband was playing around. It was another to learn of his betrayal—and your best friend's. I was a joke, a laughingstock. I had even less time than I thought.

I pulled my clothes together, pasted on a smile, and found my table. A waitress set my salad in front of me. I studied the woman. She was about my age, with a weary face, limp brown hair, and thick, sensible shoes. This time next year, would I be serving salads to the ladies who lunched?

Only if I were lucky. I didn't even have the skills to be a waitress. I picked at my salad but couldn't eat a bite. No one noticed. Well-bred women didn't have appetites.

A polite clink of silverware on glasses signaled that the headmaster was at the podium. He was a lean man with a good suit and a sycophantic smile.

"You've heard that Drexal has one of the finest academic records . . ." he began. My thoughts soon drifted away.

Menopause had killed my marriage, but it had been dying for a long time. I knew exactly when it had received the fatal wound: the day my husband asked to cut on me.

I was thirty-five, but looked ten years younger. Eric was itching to get out his scalpel and work on my face.

"Just let me do your eyes," he said, "and take a few tucks. If you start early, you'll look younger longer."

"I look fine," I said.

"You don't trust me," he said.

"Of course I do," I said. "You're the most successful plastic surgeon in Broward County."

But not the most skilled. Eric was right. I didn't trust him. He'd never killed anyone, unlike some Florida face sculptors. But I saw his work everywhere. I could recognize his patients: Caucasian women of a certain age with the telltale Chinese eyes and stretched skin.

Eric gave them face-lifts when no other doctor would. He'd give them as many as seven or eight, until their skin was so tight they could bikini wax their upper lip.

I pleaded fear of anesthesia. I invented an aunt who died from minor surgery when I was a child. But Eric knew the truth: I was afraid to let him touch me. I was his in every way, except one. I would not surrender to his knife.

For ten years, he never stopped trying. He nagged me for a full facelift at forty. At forty-five, I knew I could probably use one, but still I wouldn't submit.

"Nothing can make me twenty-five again," I said. "I'll take my chances with wrinkles."

It was the worst rejection a plastic surgeon could have. I made him look bad. Everyone could see my lines and wrinkles. These normal signs of aging became an accusation. They said every woman but his wife believed Eric was a fine surgeon.

When I turned fifty, Eric quit asking. That's when our hot nights together cooled. I suspected there were other women, but knew the affairs weren't serious. Now things had changed. Eric was going to marry a twenty-five-year-old blonde. In another five years, she'd submit to his knife.

Suddenly, I was back in the hotel ballroom. The headmaster's speech had reached its crescendo. "We have almost everything we need to make the Drexal School the finest educational institution in Broward County. Only one thing is missing. After today, we'll have it all. I'm pleased to announce the creation of the Drexal Panthers—our own football team. Your donations have made it possible."

The lunching mothers cheered wildly.

I looked down at my plate and realized I'd eaten an entire slice of chocolate cheesecake with raspberry sauce.

Worse, I hadn't tasted one bite.

No wonder I was fat.

On the way home, I picked up some college catalogues. I made myself a stiff drink and settled into my favorite chair in the great room to study the glossy catalogues. I looked at careers for legal aides, dental assistants, and licensed practical nurses. One choice seemed more depressing than the other.

What had I wanted to be before I met Eric?

An English teacher. Back then, I saw myself teaching poetry to eager young minds, watching them open like flowers with the beauty of the written word. Now, I knew I couldn't cope with the young ruffians at the public schools. Would the Drexal School hire an Angel down on her luck? Would the headmaster remember how often I'd lunched to make his dream team possible?

If I went back to college, how many years would I need to complete my degree? Would my life experience count for anything? What had I done in fifty-five years?

I fell asleep on the pile of catalogues. I woke up at midnight when I heard Eric unlock the door. I hid the catalogues with my arms, but he never noticed them. Or me. He went straight to bed without even saying good night.

I woke up at three. I couldn't sleep through the night anymore. I kept vampire hours now. I drifted into the living room and watched the condo across the way. There was another party tonight. This time, the music seemed livelier, the guests more keyed up, more dramatically dressed, as if they were at some special ceremony.

Our condo walls seemed to close in on me. I slipped on my jeans and a cotton shirt. I was going for a walk along the water, even if it killed me. I'd rather risk death than suffocate inside.

The night air was delicious, cool but not cold. I was drawn to the lights of the Dark Harbor party, and picked my way along the docks until I was almost underneath its windows. I couldn't see anything, but I could feel the contained excitement inside. The walls seemed to pulse with life.

"Wish you were here?"

I jumped at the voice—very rich, very male.

The man who came out of the shadows wore evening dress. His skin looked luminous in the moonlight. His hair was black with a slight curl. There was strength in his face, and a hint of cruelty. I couldn't tell his age. He seemed beyond such ordinary measures.

"I'm sorry. I didn't mean to trespass," I said.

"You aren't trespassing, Katherine," he said. "You spend a lot of time watching us, don't you?"

"Am I that obvious?" I said.

"No," he said. "But I feel your yearning. It makes you very beautiful—and very vulnerable."

Inside the condo, there was a shriek of triumph, followed by polite tennis-match applause.

"Excuse me," he said. "I must return to my guests. My name is Michael, by the way."

"Will I see you again?" I said.

"If you want to," he said.

He was gone. Only then did I wonder how he knew my name.

I floated back to my condo wrapped in soft, warm clouds of fantasy. How long had it been since any man had called me beautiful?

I was beautiful. Michael made me feel that way. I crawled into bed beside my husband and dreamed of another man.

In the morning, I woke up smiling and refreshed. For the first time in months, I didn't check my mirror for more ravages. I didn't need to. I was beautiful. Michael had said so. I was dreamy as a lovesick teenager, until the phone shattered the sweet silence at eleven a.m.

"Katherine, it's Patricia." Of course it was. She'd slept with my husband and confessed it in a public restroom. I'd know her honking voice anywhere. Except today it had a different note. She sounded subdued, even frightened. "Have you heard about Jack?"

"Jack who?" I said.

"Margaret's Jack. They found his body in the parking lot of his law office early this morning."

"What happened?" I said. "Was he mugged?"

"They don't think so," Patricia said. "The police say the murder didn't take place there. They think he was abducted."

"Kidnapped and murdered? But why?" Which wife killed him, I wondered. How many deserted women wished him dead?

"No one knows. But it gets worse. Jack's body was drained of blood. Completely dry."

"That's awful," I said. "I'll go see Margaret immediately."

I hung up the phone quickly, hoping to hide my elation. Jack the Ripper was dead—horribly dead. My husband no longer had a divorce lawyer. I felt a brief stab of shame for my selfish thoughts, but Jack's death was poetic justice. Someone had sucked the blood out of the city's biggest bloodsucker. Someone had given me more time.

I put on a navy pantsuit and a long face, and stopped by a smart specialty shop for a cheese tray and a bottle of wine. My long-dead mother would be proud. She'd taught me to bring food to a house of mourning.

There were other cars in Margaret's driveway, including what looked like unmarked police cars and three silver Lexuses. Lawyers' cars.

Margaret was a wreck. Her eyes were deeply bagged and swollen. Her jawline sagged nearly as badly as mine. All my husband's fine work was undone. I felt petty for noticing. She's a new widow, I told myself. Show some pity.

"Katherine!" Margaret ran weeping into my arms, smearing my jacket with makeup.

"I'm sorry," I said, patting her nearly fleshless back. I could feel her thin bones. It wasn't a lie. I was sorry for so many things, including the death of our friendship. Women need the sympathy of our own kind. Margaret had destroyed even that small comfort for me.

"Come into the garden where we can talk," she said. "The police are searching Jack's home office. Three lawyers from his firm and a court-appointed guardian are arguing over what papers they can take."

We sat at an umbrella table near a bubbling fountain. Palms rustled overhead. Impatiens bloomed at our feet. It looked like every other garden in Florida. A Hispanic maid brought iced tea, lemon slices, and two kinds of artificial sweetener.

"May I have sugar, please?" I asked.

"Sugar?" the maid said, as if she'd never heard the word.

"You use sugar?" Margaret might be dazed with grief, but she was still surprised by my request. In our crowd, sleeping with a friend's husband was a faux pas. Taking sugar in your tea was a serious sin.

"Doctor's orders," I said. "Sweeteners are out. Cancer in the family."

Actually, I liked real sugar. And it was only eighteen calories a spoonful.

"How are you?" I asked.

"I don't know," Margaret said. Two more tears escaped her swollen eyelids. "I thought Jack was seeing someone, and that's why he worked late so often these last few weeks. I was furious, but I couldn't say anything. I was too afraid."

"I understand," I said.

She flushed with guilt.

"My husband went to see Jack," I said. "So I know how you feel."

Margaret had the grace to say nothing. I appreciated that.

"Do you think Jack's lover killed him?" I said.

"I don't know. I don't even know now if he had a lover. One of the firm's associates found Jack in the parking lot when she came to work at six this morning. Maybe he really had been working late. I had to identify him. Jack didn't look dead so much as . . . empty. Someone took all his blood. It wasn't some slashing attack. Just two holes in the side of his neck. There were bruises, too. Terrible bruises on his wrists, legs, and shoulders."

"Was he beaten?" I asked.

"No. They think someone—or maybe more than one person—held him down while he was—while they—" Margaret couldn't go on.

"Do the police think it was a serial killer?" I asked.

"They won't say. But the way they're acting, I know it's strange. There were other attacks like this in Lauderdale. Jack wasn't the only person to die like this."

"No," I said. "Eric told me that the woman found off of Bayview had been drained dry, too. He heard that from the medical examiner's office. The police kept it out of the papers."

"It's like some nightmare," Margaret said, "except I can't wake up. Mindy is flying home this afternoon from college. This will be so hard for our daughter. Mindy idolized her father." Margaret started weeping again.

I wasn't sure what to do. If we'd still been friends, I would have folded Margaret in my arms. But she had betrayed me. I knew it, and she knew it.

I was saved by a homicide detective and a lawyer.

"Margaret," the lawyer said, "I'm sorry to disturb you, but we have some more questions about your husband."

"I'd better go," I said. "I'll let myself out." I air-kissed her cheek. It took all my self-control to keep from running for my car.

Once, I would have called my husband and told him the awful news. Now I didn't. What could I say? *You know that lawyer you hired to strip me of my last dime? The son of a bitch was murdered. Couldn't happen to a nicer guy.*

I suspected Eric already knew about Jack's death. He was probably looking for a new bloodsucker.

I spent the afternoon taking calls from Margaret's shocked friends, pretending to be sad and concerned and hating myself because I couldn't feel any of it. Instead, I felt oddly excited. I broiled a skinless chicken breast, steamed some broccoli, and waited for my husband to come home.

At eleven o'clock, there was still no sign of Eric. He didn't bother to phone me. I didn't humiliate myself by calling around asking for him.

What if he turned up dead, like Jack? I wondered. Then my troubles would be over. I felt guilty even thinking that. But it was true.

At three in the morning, I woke up alone and drenched in sweat. Night sweats, another menopausal delight. I punched my soggy pillow and tried to settle back to sleep. At three-thirty, I gave up. I reached for my jeans, then abandoned that idea. Instead, I pulled out a long, nearly sheer hostess gown that looked glamorous in the soft moonlight.

I wasn't going for a walk. I was going hunting. For Michael.

There was no party tonight. His condo was dark except for flickering candles in the living room and the opalescent light of a television. Michael was alone, like me. He couldn't sleep, either.

He was waiting for me down by the Dark Harbor docks. At first, I heard nothing but the gentle slap of the water and the clinking of the halyards as the boats rocked back and forth. It was a peaceful sound. A light breeze ruffled my hair and pressed my gown against my body.

"You dressed for me, didn't you?" he said.

Michael seemed to appear from nowhere. His white shirt, open at the throat and rolled at the sleeves, glowed in the moonlight. His hair was black as onyx, but so soft. I longed to run my fingers through it.

"Yes," I said.

His hand touched my hair and traced the line of my neck. I stepped back. It wouldn't do to seem too eager too soon.

Michael smiled, as if he could read my mind. "You don't have to play games," he said.

"I'm not playing games," I said. "I'm being cautious. I don't know anything about you. Are you married?"

"My wife has been dead for many years. I live alone."

"You have such lovely parties." I couldn't keep the wistful note out of my voice.

"I have many friends. We enjoy the night."

"I do, too," I said. "I'm tired of the Florida sun. It burns the life out of everything."

"You may be one of us," Michael said. "I'd like to see more of you, before I go."

"Go?" The word clutched at my heart. "Where are you going?"

"I'm selling the condo. Nobody stays long in Florida. You know that. Will you be here tomorrow night? May I see you again?"

"Three o'clock," I said. "Same time, same place."

There. I'd done it. I'd made a date with another man. My marriage was over, except for the legalities. It was time to face the future. Maybe, if I was lucky, I'd have Michael in my life. If not, I'd find someone else. He'd shown me that I was still attractive. I was grateful for that. I'd let Eric destroy my confidence.

I turned around for one last look, but Michael was gone. Only then did I realize he hadn't asked if I was married. I wondered if he knew. Or cared.

Eric was waiting for me when I returned, tapping his foot like an impatient parent.

"Where were you?" he said.

"I could ask you the same question," I said.

"I was with a patient," he said.

"Administering more special injections?" I said. "Patricia says they're wonderful for the complexion. I wouldn't know. It's been so long I've forgotten."

"You're certifiable." Eric turned the attack back on me. He was good at that. "Jack is dead. Murdered! Some freak drank his blood. And you're roaming the streets at night like an Alzheimer's patient. I should hire a keeper."

I should hire a hit man, I thought. But I held in my harsh words. I didn't need Eric now. I had Michael.

"Good night," I said. "I'm sleeping in the guest room."

"You can't—"

I didn't stop to hear what I couldn't do. I locked the guest room door and put fresh sheets on the bed. What I am doing? I wondered. I have a three a.m. rendezvous with a man I don't know. There's a murderer running loose in my neighborhood. Yet I'd never felt safer or more at peace. I slept blissfully until ten in the morning. I woke up with just enough time to get ready for my literacy board meeting.

As I walked into the dark paneled board room, I caught snatches of conversation: "he was drained dry . . . don't know when they'll have a funeral . . . Margaret is devastated."

All anyone could talk about was Jack's murder, at least until the board meeting started. Then we had to listen to Nancy blather on about bylaws changes. She'd kept the board tied up with this pointless minutiae for the last eight months.

Once I saw myself as a philanthropist, dispensing our money to improve the lives of the disadvantaged. But I'd sat on too many charity boards. Now I knew how little was possible. Here I was in another endless meeting, listening to a debate about whether the organization's president should remain a figurehead or have a vote on the board.

How did this debate help one poor child learn to read? I wondered.

"Katherine?"

I looked up. The entire board was staring at me.

"How do you vote on the motion: yes or no?" Nancy asked.

"Yes." I wasn't saying yes to the motion, whatever it was. I was saying yes to a new life.

Mercifully, the board meeting was over at noon. I dodged any offers of lunch and went straight home. I spent three hours on the Internet, looking at my career options. Work couldn't be any worse than board meetings. Then I'd get ready for my date with Michael.

By four that afternoon, I'd decided to become a librarian. It would only take another three years of college. The pay was decent. The benefits were not bad. The job prospects were good. I'd be a useful member of society, which was more than I could say for myself now.

I pushed away the memory of Elizabeth's dreary apartment and made an appointment with a feminist lawyer. Tomorrow, we would discuss my divorce. Today, I wanted to think about my date with Michael.

I washed my hair, so it would have a soft curl. I applied a mango-honey face mask and swiped Eric's razor to de-fuzz my legs. Eric hated when I did that. I hoped the dull razor would rip his face off tomorrow morning. I sprayed his shaving cream on my long legs. I was now covered with goo from head to toe. Naturally, the doorbell rang.

Who was that?

I looked out the peephole. A young woman with a cheap blond dye job was on my doorstep. Her skirt was some bright, shiny material, and her tight halter top barely covered her massive breasts. I'd seen her before, at Eric's office.

"Just a minute," I called, and quickly wiped off the shaving cream and the mango mask.

When I opened the door, I was hit by a gust of perfume.

"Yes?" I said. "You're from Eric's office. Is there a problem?"

"There is." She boldly walked into my home and sat down on my couch. "My name is Dawn. I'm Eric's office manager."

And his lover. The recognition was a punch in the face. Eric was leaving me for this big-titted cliché. I stood there in silence, hoping to make this husband-stealing tramp squirm. She'd have to do the talking.

Dawn came right out with her request. "We want to get married," she said.

"We?"

"Eric and I."

"He's married to me," I said.

"That's the problem, isn't it?" Dawn smiled. She had small, feral teeth, and smooth skin. Eric would revel in that flawless skin. How my husband would love to put a knife into it. He had the gall to try to improve perfection.

"If you make it easy for me, I'll make it easy for you," Dawn said. "I'll make sure you get a nice allowance. You drag us through the courts, and I'll fight you every step of the way."

"You're threatening me in my own living room?" I said.

"It won't be yours for long," Dawn said. She looked around at my carefully decorated room. "No wonder Eric doesn't like to hang here. It's like a funeral parlor. White couches in Florida. Hello? Can you say corny? This place needs some life.

"Oh, dear, you've got some gunk on your forehead. Those do-it-yourself beauty treatments don't work. Should have gone to your husband for help. You might still have time. But maybe not. He can only do so much."

I sat there, speechless, while the little slut sauntered past me. I picked up the first thing I could find, a delicate gold-trimmed Limoges dish—a wedding present—and threw it at her. Too late. She'd already shut the door.

The dish shattered with a satisfying sound. Plates, glasses, candy dishes, even a soup tureen followed, until the hall's marble floor was crunchy with smashed crockery and broken glass. It took me an hour to sweep it up and drop it down the trash chute. I knew Eric wouldn't miss any of it. He wouldn't even notice anything was gone. These were the things I loved. I wondered if the slut would be dining off my best china and drinking from my remaining wedding crystal. Over my dead body. Better yet, over hers.

I cleaned off the remnants of the mango-honey mask and shaved my legs with a shaky hand. I had a date with a man at three o'clock in the morning. What kind of time was that? I nicked my leg and watched a small drop of blood well up. Blood.

Three a.m. was a good time for a vampire.

That's what Michael was, wasn't he? Who else had drained Jack dry but a vampire? What else could Michael and his sleek, night-loving friends be?

I expected to feel shocked and horrified, but I didn't. Michael and his friends did me a favor by killing Jack. If they'd killed Eric, I would have been the center of a murder investigation. Instead, they gave me a little more time to arrange my life before it self-destructed.

Was Michael a danger to me? I didn't think so. If he'd wanted to kill me, he'd had many opportunities. No, Michael wanted more than a quick kill. But what, exactly? His conversation was full of innuendoes, invitations, and explanations.

"I feel your yearning. It makes you very beautiful—and very vulnerable."

"My wife has been dead for many years. I live alone."

"I have many friends. We enjoy the night."

"You may be one of us."

Michael had told me what he was, if I had listened carefully. Did I want to be one of his beautiful friends? Could I kill other people?

Depends, I thought. I could kill lawyers like Jack, doctors like my husband, and that little bitch who waltzed into my house and claimed my husband like a piece of lost luggage.

I wondered about the other woman who'd been drained dry. Who was she? Did she deserve to die? I didn't have her name, but I knew the date she'd died and the street where she was found—Forty-seventh, off of Bayview.

A quick Internet search found the story in the *Sun-Sentinel.* The dead woman was forty-five, divorced, an IRS auditor. Another deserving victim. Another bloodsucker. Eric and I'd been audited one long, hot summer. The IRS found one small error, but the accountant and lawyer bills to defend ourselves were tremendous. We would have had more rights if we'd been accused of murder instead of cheating on our income tax.

Yes, I could kill an IRS auditor. I could hand out justice to the unjust. In my new life, I would punish the wicked. I would be superwoman—invisible by day, fearless by night. That beat being a divorced librarian living in a garden apartment.

I hardly tasted my dinner, I was so excited by my new life. Not that my dinner had much flavor: four ounces of boneless, skinless, joyless chicken and romaine with fat-free dressing.

For dessert, I treated myself to two ounces of dark chocolate and a delicious daydream of Michael. It had been a long time since any man had wanted me. And this man had so much to give me.

I watched the full moon rise and paced my condo. Eric didn't come home that night. I didn't expect him to. I was glad. I was in no mood to confront him.

I dug out my favorite black Armani dress. It was specially designed to cover my flaws. The high neck hid the crepe under my chin. The short sleeves disguised the unsightly wings under my arms that no workouts could eliminate. The short hem showed my legs at their best. I put on sexy high-heeled sandals. They were dangerous on the docks, but I was living dangerously these days.

Michael was waiting for me outside my condo. He'd come to me this time. His hair was black as a midnight ocean. His luminous skin was like moonlight on snow. He kissed me, and his lips were soft and surprisingly warm.

"You know who we are, don't you?" he said.

"Yes," I said. "I want to be like you."

"You must be sure. You must have no illusions before you adopt our way of life. You must ask me any questions tonight."

"Are you immortal?" I said.

"Almost," he said. "We can be killed by fire, by sunlight, and by wooden stakes through the heart. All natural elements."

"What about crosses and holy water?"

He laughed. "There were vampires long before there were Christians."

"What will happen to me? How will I become one of you?"

"I will make you a vampire by giving you my blood. I will take yours. Don't be frightened. It's not painful. You'll find it quite exhilarating. Once the transference is complete, you must make your first kill."

"Will I change? Will I look different?"

"You'll look like yourself, only more beautiful. Any wrinkles will vanish. Any physical flaws will disappear. You'll quickly attain your ideal weight. Our people are never fat."

Vampirism—the ultimate low-fat diet. I wanted to smile. But suddenly, I couldn't joke. The changes were profound, and frightening. "I'll never be able to eat food again." I felt a sudden desperate pain at what I would have to give up.

"Do you eat now?" Michael said.

The question seemed ridiculous. "Of course," I said.

"But do you like what you eat? Do you actually hunger for carrot sticks? Do you long for steamed broccoli and romaine with diet dressing?" He put his warm lips next to my ear and whispered, "When was the last time you had food you really wanted?"

I thought of the meals of my youth, when I could eat anything: fried chicken and cheeseburgers, crispy French fries lightly sprinkled with salt, hot fudge sundaes with warm whipped cream, crusty bread and butter.

"You haven't had any of those in years, have you?" Michael said.

He could read my mind. I knew that now.

"You'll never experience the pain of dieting again," he said. "You will have no need for ordinary food. You will drink the food of the gods. Blood is offered to them as a sacrifice. You will take it for your own pleasure. It is a thrill you cannot imagine. You will still hunger, but now you will be satisfied. You are hungry, aren't you? Even now, after your supper of skinless chicken."

"Yes." The pale, pathetic hunk of bird nearly turned my stomach. "I can do good, too," I said. "I can feed on those who deserve to die."

His eyes were suddenly darker, and I realized he was angry. "No! You must embrace the dark side like a lover. Any good you do will be accidental."

"But Jack—" I began.

"When Rosette killed that bloodsucking lawyer, she made a lot of scorned wives happy. But Jack will be mourned by his daughter. Randall killed the IRS agent because she'd been auditing his books. She nearly drove him crazy, and he was innocent. But she was the sole support of her elderly mother. And, irritating though she was, the agent was an honest woman.

"You cannot fool yourself into believing that you will only feed on serial killers or child molesters. That is romantic nonsense.

"You are evil and you must choose it. Your killing will not make the world a better place. We kill for revenge, for sport, for reasons that are impossibly petty. Marissa once killed a dress shop clerk on Las Olas because she wouldn't wait on her."

"So you've killed more people in Fort Lauderdale than Jack and the IRS agent?" I said.

"Many more," Michael said. "The details about the other bodies being exsanguinated did not make the papers. The police try to hide that information. When it becomes public, then it's time for us to leave. That's why we're going tomorrow night."

"What happened to the other bodies?"

Michael said nothing. He didn't have to. I realized we were looking at the wide black ocean.

"Where will you go when you leave?" I said.

"The south of France," he said. "I have a cottage by the sea. The air smells of lavender and the sound of the waves is wonderfully soothing."

A small sigh escaped me. He was offering me such a beautiful life.

"Why me?" I asked. "There are millions of women like me, a little past our prime, abandoned by our husbands."

"Do you define yourself only by your husband?" he asked. "I don't think so. Americans have such boring ideas about age. Older cultures celebrate all aspects of a woman's life. Americans only want youth, which can be the dullest time. I prefer a woman who has lived.

"And you are not like the others. You are strong. You have resisted the lemminglike urge for plastic surgery. It's became a national obsession, but you fought it, even though it cost you your marriage and your comfortable life. You knew it wasn't the right choice for you. That takes courage. You know who you are. Do you know what you are?"

For the first time, I knew I was someone special.

He took my hand. "I'd like you to join us," he said. "I want you. Now that you know, you have only two choices: join us or die."

"May I have twenty-four hours? I have some loose ends to tie up."

"Yes. But, remember, no one will believe you if you go to the police. And we will be gone before they can get a search warrant."

"I would never betray you," I said. "You've already helped me. Did you encourage Rosette to kill Jack? For my sake?"

"I wish I could take credit," Michael said. "But Jack was her idea. Still, I'm glad it helped you."

Then he kissed my hand. "You have much to think about," he said. "I hope you make the right decision."

I left him feeling oddly lighthearted for a woman whose only choice was death: my real death, the living death of middle age, or the death-in-life of a vampire.

I slept well that night, or what was left of it. Then, at five-thirty, I was awakened by Eric slamming doors and opening drawers. He had four white shirts in plastic bags. I'd picked up those shirts for him from the best laundry in Lauderdale, prepared precisely the way he liked: hangers, no starch.

I sat up groggily in bed. "From now on," I said, "have your slut pick up your laundry. That's the last errand I'm running for you."

"Don't you dare call Dawn that," Eric said.

"Dawn! What kind of name is that? Has it dawned on you how trite you are?" My bitterness burst like a lanced boil, and I was screaming like a fishwife. My husband yelled right back.

Our argument was interrupted by a pounding on our front door. Marvin, our condo security guard, was standing on the doorstep. He looked embarrassed. "I'm sorry," he said. "But there have been complaints about the noise."

We both apologized to the guard. Now my humiliation was complete. Eric walked out a few minutes later, clutching his fresh shirts by the hangers. "You'll hear from my lawyer," he said.

That was it. That was how he ended our quarter-century marriage, the day before my birthday.

He'd forgotten that, of course. He couldn't even say, "I'm sorry, I've found someone else." Eric wasn't sorry, was he? But he would be.

I watched the sun rise on the last morning of my life. The new morning turned the air a pearlescent pink, and a shimmering fog drifted across the water. White birds skimmed along the Intracoastal.

I will never see this beauty again, I thought. But I didn't have time to wallow in regret. I had things to do. I stopped at a diner for a last, lavish breakfast. The young, busty waitress was too busy flirting with a table full of businessmen to pay any attention to me. I could hear the cook ringing the bell in the kitchen. When the waitress finally brought my breakfast, the eggs had congealed to rubber and the home fries were coated with grease.

"This food is cold," I said to the waitress.

"Huh?" she said, as if she'd just noticed me for the first time. Once again, I was the incredible, invisible middle-aged woman.

"I'll get the cook to warm it up," she said.

"Never mind," I said. "I'm not hungry after all."

I threw some money on the table and left. I'd lost my taste for food.

At ten o'clock, I was weeping in my lawyer's office. The tears came easily, and they weren't entirely false. Only the accusations were made up.

"Please help me," I sobbed. "My husband is divorcing me. He has a new girlfriend and he hates me. They're fighting about how soon they can get married. I'm in the way. I'm afraid Eric will harm me."

"Harm you how?" the lawyer said.

She would look perfect on the witness stand during Eric's murder trial, I thought. She was serious enough for the women to believe her, but sexy enough to get the men's attention. There was something about her tailored black suit, tightly pulled-back hair, and horn-rimmed glasses that made men wonder what she'd look like without them.

"K-kill me," I said. "Eric doesn't let anyone stand in his way."

"Have there been any threats?" the lawyer said.

"Nothing in front of witnesses," I said. "But we had a terrible fight this morning, and he said he'd kill me if I didn't give him a divorce and . . . I'm so embarrassed. Condo security had to knock on our door."

"That's good," the lawyer said. "I mean, it's not good, but it will help."

She made plans to get a restraining order and told me to change the locks. Of course, I would tragically disappear before I could carry out her instructions.

It was after noon when I left the lawyer's office, my least favorite time of day in Florida. The parking lot was baking in the harsh sun. It showed all the cracks in the buildings and the sidewalks—and in my lips and skin. I won't miss this, I thought. Not one bit.

I wanted to treat myself to a special dress for this evening, my coming out. I strolled along Las Olas Boulevard, where all the smart shops were. The windows glowed with dresses in dramatic black and fabulous colors.

Black, I thought. Black was the right choice when you're going to the dark side.

I entered a cool shop. A young saleswoman, who looked like a thinner version of Dawn, was talking to another clerk. They didn't look up when I came in. They didn't notice me.

"Excuse me," I said. "May I have some help?"

The two young women smirked and rolled their eyes, and I understood why Marissa had killed her salesclerk. If I had more time in Lauderdale, I'd come back for this one.

But I didn't. I bought the first dress I tried on. It didn't fit quite right. I could see my drooping back in the mirror, the little rolls of fat at my waist. But they would be gone soon. In my new life, this dress would be spectacular.

As I left, I knew I'd made the right decision. Not about the dress. About my life. I would be invisible, but it would be my choice.

I would be powerful.

I would be beautiful forever.

I would get the blood back. It would flow again. It would flow into me, and I would feel the ecstasy. I would not be young, but I didn't want to be young. The young were vulnerable, trusting, hurting. I never wanted to feel that way again.

I sat in my condo and thought about the rest of the night and the beginning of my new life.

When the sky began to bleed red, I walked once more through my condo, saying good-bye to all my things. It would be easy to give them up. I sat on the balcony until the sun set and the sky turned dark velvet. Then I dressed for my final night.

At midnight, I met Michael down by the docks. He was frighteningly beautiful.

"Have you made your choice?" he said.

"I choose you," I said.

He kissed me. "I'm so glad," he whispered. "Everyone is waiting for you. Who will be your first kill?"

"Dawn, Eric's office manager. The police will find her bloodless body outside his clinic."

"What about your husband?"

"I'll let him live. It will be fun to see how he explains his drained and dead girlfriend and his missing wife. I'll be gone, but I won't take anything with me—no money from our bank account, no stocks, not even my jewelry. I'll follow the trial on the Internet from the south of France."

Michael smiled. "I'm sure we'll all be entertained by the drama," he said. "Happy birthday, Katherine."

How Stella Got Her Grave Back

Toni L. P. Kelner

Toni L. P. Kelner is the author of the Laura Fleming Southern mystery series and the forthcoming Where Are They Now? series about a freelance entertainment writer who specializes in articles about the formerly famous. She has won the Agatha Award for best short story and the Romantic Times Career Achievement Award, and has been nominated for the Anthony, the Macavity and the Romantic Times Reviewers' Choice awards. She lives in Massachusetts with her husband, fellow author Stephen P. Kelner Jr., and two daughters. Though she's a longtime fan of vampire fiction, this is her first vampire story.

They stared at the tombstone. Or rather, Mark stared. Stella glared.

"Are you sure this is the right place?" Mark asked.

"Of course I'm sure!" she snapped.

"It's been a while since you've been here, right? And the circumstances that night were pretty much tailor-made for making you forget the exact location."

"I'm sure," she said. "A person doesn't just forget something like that!" She continued to glare at the tombstone, as if waiting for its current inhabitant to rise and answer her questions. "What I want to know is, who the hell is buried in my grave?"

"I told you this was morbid."

Almost exactly an hour earlier, Mark had asked, "Don't you think this is kind of morbid?"

"We're vampires," Stella replied. "It doesn't get much more morbid than that."

"Still, visiting your grave on your birthday? That kind of goes beyond the pale." He snickered. "Beyond the pale! That's good—I mean, we're nothing if not pale."

"It's not bad," Stella admitted. "Not that you're all that pale yet."

"True." He'd been a vampire for less than a year, so as long as he applied generous amounts of SPF 45, he could still go outside in the daylight, and his tan hadn't faded.

They drove down the North Carolina highway in silence for a few minutes, Stella handling the maroon Cadillac with the ease only decades of practice can bring, and the caution for which vampires were infamous. While they could walk away from most accidents, reckless driving could lead to overly curious medical personnel or jail cells with uncurtained windows, so vampires tended to obey the rules of the road. Mark hadn't had time to absorb that yet, which was why she was driving.

He asked, "Is this your actual birthday or the anniversary of your death?"

"Both," she said.

"You died on your birthday? That's harsh. How old were you?"

"You tell me."

"No way! I know better than to try to guess a woman's age."

"We vampires are proud of our age."

"Yeah, right. If I said you looked thirty-five when you stopped aging at twenty-five, I'd be walking home."

"You think I look thirty-five?"

"What I think is that you are a timeless beauty." There was something about becoming a vampire that enhanced a person's best traits, but Mark suspected Stella had been gorgeous even before death. Her hair was glossy chestnut, her eyes chocolate brown, her skin like porcelain, and her figure lush. "In fact, I think you've become even more beautiful since I've known you."

She smiled. "I'll accept that. But, for the record, I was eighteen."

"Really? I would have guessed thirty-five."

"Bastard," she said, still smiling.

They passed a few more exits before Mark went back to his original point. "Other vampires don't go to their graves on their birthdays, do they?"

"Other vampires don't put dirt into their beds, either."

"That's not fair! Ramon swore that I'd lose vitality if I didn't sleep in the earth of my homeland."

"I wonder how long you'd have kept doing it if I hadn't smelled it on your pillow."

"No telling," he said. "He bugs me about it every time he sees me, too."

"He tells everybody he sees about it."

"Damn it! How long will it take me to live that down? Die that down. Whatever."

"Until he plays the same trick on somebody else."

"Yeah, like he's going to find a sap as big as me anytime soon," he said glumly, looking out into the darkness of the countryside as they approached Allenville. "What counts as the dirt of my homeland anyway? Does it have to be from the town where I died or the town I was born in? Or buried in, for that matter? Or just the county? The state? The country?"

Stella flipped on her signal and turned off of the highway. "Well, the dirt in Allenville would have done the job nicely. I was born here, died here, and buried here."

"On your birthday. That sucks!" He resisted any number of potential vampire/sucking jokes, having been threatened with being locked inside a tanning booth the last time he made one.

"Are you kidding?" Stella said. "It was the best birthday ever!"

"I see you celebrated birthdays differently in your youth."

She flashed him a look. "Look around the town."

"Just let me know when we get there."

"We *are* there."

Mark looked out the window. The interstate had been better lit than the street they were driving down, which had just enough light for him to see the WELCOME TO ALLENVILLE sign put up by the local Jaycees. The existence of a few scattered houses was betrayed only by the flickering blue glow of TV screens. "Not exactly a happening place, is it?"

"Not unless you're into chicken farming. Have you ever smelled a chicken farm?"

"Wait! There're lights ahead." They crested a hill, but he saw nothing more exciting than a McDonald's, a gas station, and a Wal-Mart. "Never mind."

"At least there's a Wal-Mart now," Stella said. "If we'd had something like that here when I was growing up, I'd have been in hog heaven."

Mark realized that her usual sophisticated tones had been growing more and more countrified during the drive but decided it would be impolite to mention it, and perhaps dangerous as well, considering the strength and speed of a vampire Stella's age.

"You weren't happy here?" he asked as they left the oasis of neon behind.

"Mama used to say I started walking early, just so I could get away from here that much sooner."

"But you didn't."

"I wanted to, God I wanted to, but I had nowhere to go. No money, no schooling, nobody to stay with. I saved every penny I could, but I'd just about given up on ever getting a chance to leave when I met Vilmos. As soon as I saw him, I knew he was my ticket out of here."

"Just not quite in the way you expected."

"Not hardly," she said. "Anyway, I thought I was seducing him, and afterward, I poured out my heart to him. He offered me the Choice, and I accepted it."

"And you never looked back?"

"Not once."

Of course that begged the question of why they were there that evening, but he resisted asking until they reached an area with knee-high weeds that Stella insisted was the parking lot for the graveyard she'd abandoned. That was when he stepped into something he wouldn't have wanted to go near with his former sense of smell, let alone with the vampire upgrade.

"Why are we here again?" he groused

"Because it's my birthday," she said.

"That's a lousy reason."

"How about because I'm your sire and I say so?"

"Why are you my sire, anyway?"

"Because I bit you, bled you to the point of death, and gave you my blood. Or are you asking why I decided to bring you over?"

"No, I know you brought me over because you couldn't resist my manly wiles. I mean, why are you my sire? Shouldn't you be my dam?"

"Excuse me?"

"A sire is a male parent. A female is a dam. And damned if you're not female."

"Vampires always say sire," she said doubtfully.

"That's because vampire society is male chauvinist, and has been since Dracula developed a taste for Turks on a stick. Let's strike a blow for feminism! From now on, you can be my dam. My dam of the damned!"

As quickly as only a vampire could, Stella grabbed him by the neck and kissed him soundly. "That," she said, when she was done ravaging his mouth, "is why I brought you over." Then she went back to leading the way.

Though Mark had no false modesty about his manly wiles, which included jet-black hair, green eyes, and a swimmer's build, he knew part of the reason for the enthusiastic smooching was Stella's nervousness. He recognized it even though the only other time he'd seen it was when he'd first woken up after his death, and she was there to welcome him to vampirehood.

She'd been so afraid he wasn't going to like it, that he'd be angry at her. It had taken some effort to prove to her her that he considered the Choice to be better than a lifetime pass to Disney World, and one of his other manly wiles was showing the strain by the time she was convinced.

They reached the entrance, an open iron arch with the name "Spivey" overhead.

"Spivey was your name?" Like most vampires her age, Stella had changed her name more than once.

"No, Spivey was Mama's maiden name. I'm a Boyd. Mama didn't get along with Daddy's people, so she had me and him buried here." She hesitated.

"Are you sure you want to go in?"

"It would be right silly to come this far and not go in," she said.

"It's silly to go to monster truck rallies, too, but that never stopped me."

She smiled briefly, then stepped through the arch. Mark followed closely in case she needed him and because her night vision was considerably better than his own.

"Stella Boyd," he said experimentally. "Not bad."

"Try again. My old name was Estelle," she said, putting the emphasis on the first syllable. "But nobody calls me that now. Ever."

"Message received."

They kept on for a few minutes, Stella pausing now and then to read the words on tombstones that were nothing but black blocks to Mark. She finally stopped by a wide monument, with room for two names.

"Here's Mama and Daddy. I didn't find out about her dying until a long time afterward, but I figured she'd be buried here, with Daddy and me."

Mark moved close enough to make out the inscriptions. "Caleb Boyd. Beloved Husband and Father. Oveda Boyd. Beloved Wife and Mother."

"Mine is over by that tree."

"What tree?"

"Sorry, by that tree stump. It was a tree when I was here last. But there's my stone."

"I'm guessing your epitaph includes 'beloved.' "

"I don't know. It hadn't been put in when I left—there was just a big fieldstone marking the place. I imagine Mama had to save up to pay for a tombstone."

Stella walked over to the grave, then went as still as only a vampire can.

Mark, thinking she must be feeling like Scrooge had when confronted by the price of his sins, put an arm around her, but she didn't respond. He looked down at the stone, then blinked.

"It says 'Jane Doe,' " he said. There was no birth date, and the only date of death was the year.

"I know what it says."

"Then where's your grave?"

"You're standing on it."

"Are you sure this is the right place?"

"Of course I'm sure!"

"It's been a while since you've been here, right? And the circumstances that night were pretty much tailor-made for making you forget the exact location."

"I'm sure. A person doesn't just forget something like that!"

She stayed there while Mark wandered over toward the neighboring graves, hoping to find the correct one, but there was no Estelle Boyd. Eventually he came back to where she was still standing.

"Maybe your mother moved you somewhere . . ." He stopped before saying *nicer.* "To another cemetery."

"She wouldn't have moved me and left Daddy here. I was a Daddy's girl from the day I was born—she wouldn't have separated us."

"Well, maybe nobody realized you were already here. I mean, you said there was no tombstone."

"Are you saying my own mother didn't buy me a tombstone?" she said, an edge in her voice.

"No, I'm just saying— Hell, I don't know what I'm saying." He looked around helplessly, but there was no night watchman to bespell and question. "Let's go back to the hotel. I'll hit the web and see what I can Google about Jane. Okay? We'll find out what happened."

Fortunately they'd already fed, so they could go straight to their hotel, where Mark immediately booted up his laptop. By searching for "Allenville, NC" and "Jane Doe," he found a hit on the *Allenville Sentinel*'s website archives.

"Here we go," he said. "Story dated a year and a half ago. Jane Doe to be buried in Spivey family plot. Unknown murder victim. Believed to be between sixteen and nineteen years old. Found raped and strangled in Allenville six months previously. No funds in the budget for burial, so Officer Norcomb offered room in his family plot. He must be a relative of yours."

"I suppose so. The Spiveys always were a fertile bunch. Mama would have had a house full if Daddy hadn't died so early."

Mark continued reading. "Ongoing investigation. Norcomb still hopes he'll be able to identify her and her killer. There's a photo of the funeral, complete with locals paying their respects."

"Nothing about relocating the previous inhabitant of the grave?" she asked.

"Nope. Shouldn't they have found your coffin?"

"There wasn't much left of it when I broke out of it."

"Vilmos didn't dig you up?" he said, appalled. Stella had arranged it so that he'd never been buried, but sometimes it was necessary to placate the human world. In those cases, the vampire's sire dug up the coffin as promptly as possible.

"He was late. It took him longer than expected to find some men to bespell to do the digging. I could have waited, but I panicked."

"No wonder. Why didn't he dig for you himself? He could have done it faster than bespelled humans."

"Vilmos get his hands dirty? Please!"

Mark supposed it wasn't surprising that he disliked Stella's sire so intensely.

"At any rate," Stella said, "the coffin was broken up pretty thoroughly. Vilmos splintered the rest, tossed it back into the grave, and had it buried again. I don't know how long it takes wood and cloth to rot, but I don't expect they found anything when digging Jane's grave that would have told them I'd been buried there. Only there should have been a marker of some sort. Let me see that picture."

He moved the screen so it was aimed toward her.

"No tombstone, no fieldstone, no nothing," she said. "I don't understand. Why would Mama have moved the marker? Why didn't she get me a real tombstone? I know they're expensive—she had to save for a year to pay for Daddy's—but . . . I guess she decided not to bother."

"Hey, don't make assumptions! Tell you what—tomorrow I'll go back and see what the story is. There must be records of who's supposed to be where."

"Probably not. When Daddy died, Mama just picked a spot and buried him. I'm not even sure who owned the land then, let alone now."

"I bet Officer Norcomb will know. I'll track him down and ask him."

"It doesn't matter anyway. You were right. It was stupid to come back."

"I didn't say it was stupid—I said it was morbid. And I'm going to find that guy tomorrow and see what happened."

She shrugged, saying only, "I am a little curious." Then she reached for the TV remote control. "I wonder what they've got on pay-per-view."

They picked out something violent and mindless, and when it was over, Mark produced the birthday present he'd hidden in his suitcase. Stella demonstrated her appreciation for the sapphire pendant ardently, proving once again that her years had given her skills beyond safe driving. Still, Mark could tell her unbeating heart wasn't in it, though he certainly enjoyed her efforts on his behalf.

As the night ended, Stella got into bed, and after making sure the door was locked, the windows thoroughly curtained, and the DO NOT DISTURB sign was in place, Mark joined her. An instant before dawn arrived, he felt her start to cry. Then they both stiffened in death.

At some point, Mark shifted from a vampire's death-sleep to human sleep, and he woke when it was nearly eleven. Stella would remain cold and unmoving until dusk, but his body was still fighting off the vestiges of humanity.

Normally he stayed nearby while Stella rested, especially when they were away from home, but finding out about Stella's grave took priority. His first target was Officer Norcomb, the one who'd given permission for Jane Doe to be buried in the Spivey plot. While en route to Allenville, he used his cell phone to call the police station to find out if Officer Norcomb was in. According to the cop who answered the phone, Norcomb was on his lunch break, and he directed Mark to Benny's Truck Stop near the highway.

Mark had noticed Benny's the night before, admiring the glamor of the chubby neon chef and his flashing burger. In the daylight, it was less glamorous, but the gas and diesel islands were doing a brisk business. As Mark got out of the car, he tried for a deep breath of fresh country air but instead breathed in a horrible mix of ammonia and general nastiness coming from the buildings a field away. He stepped inside quickly.

As the only police officer in the place, Norcomb was easy to spot. A skinny man, despite the remains of gravy-soaked meat and mashed potatoes left on his plate, and as far as Mark could tell, he didn't bear the slightest family resemblance to Stella.

Mark approached his booth and, with his friendliest smile, said, "Officer Norcomb?"

Norcomb gave him such a suspicious look that Mark used his tongue to make sure his fangs weren't out. "You the one who called the station looking for me?" he said.

"That's me. Can I join you?"

"If this is about a traffic citation, don't bother. I don't fix nobody's tickets."

"Nothing like that," Mark assured him. "I'm here about Jane Doe."

Norcomb sat up straight, and before Mark could put rump to the sticky vinyl of the bench, the cop said, "Do you know who she is?"

"No, I'm afraid not, I just wanted to—"

"Are you a reporter?"

"Why don't we start over? My name is Mark Anderson." He offered his hand, and Norcomb reached over his late lunch to take it. As they shook, their eyes met, and Mark exerted the force of will a vampire used to bespell his victims.

A moment later, Norcomb said, "You going to let go of my hand anytime soon?"

"Sorry," Mark muttered. Stella assured him he'd develop the ability to bespell victims before too much longer, but so far, nothing. Since his compelling gaze hadn't worked, he'd have to rely on his backup plan. "I believe you and I are related," he said.

"Is that right?" Norcomb said skeptically. "I don't recall any Yankees in the family. No offense."

"None taken. If we are related, it's only by marriage. You see, my wife's great-aunt Estelle is from Allenville, and she's always said she wanted to be buried in the Spivey family cemetery. Since I'm in Raleigh on business, my wife asked me to confirm that it's still in use."

"I'd heard there were some Spiveys who moved up North, and I know old folks are big on coming back home to be buried."

"Exactly. Aunt Estelle is getting quite frail, so I don't think it will be too much longer."

"I'm sorry to hear that," Norcomb said with enough genuine sympathy to make Mark feel guilty.

"At least she's had a long life," Mark said, which was true enough. "I found the Spivey cemetery the other day, and while I was checking for recent burials, I noticed Jane Doe's grave. I was curious, so I did some research on the web, read that you gave permission for Ms. Doe to be buried there, and figured you were the one to talk to. Do we need to fill out any paperwork?"

"Shoot, we don't get that formal around here. If Aunt Estelle is family, she's welcome."

"My wife will be glad to hear that."

Norcomb seemed to be pulling himself together in preparation for leaving, so Mark hurriedly said, "I know you've got to go back on duty, but I did wonder how Jane Doe came to be buried with the Spiveys. Is there reason to suspect she's a relative?"

"We don't have any idea of who she is, bless her heart."

"Really? I realize it might not be proper to talk about an ongoing investigation . . ." He tried to bespell the man again, and was almost certain he felt *something*. Or maybe Norcomb just felt like talking.

He said, "The case is still open, but I wouldn't exactly call it ongoing. That poor girl's been dead over two years, and we don't know a bit more than we did a week after we found her. Wasn't far from where we are now, as a matter of fact. Just on the other side of that chicken barn you can see from the parking lot."

"So it's chickens in that building. What a stink!"

"You should smell then in the middle of summer. Anyway, some boys found the girl in a field, partially covered up with leaves and brush. She'd been stripped, and the killer bashed her face in so bad that she was unrecognizable, so we had no clue who she was. Nobody's ever claimed her."

"I read online that she was seen in Wal-Mart."

"That's right. The manager identified her from her hair, believe it or not. She had it dyed solid black and cut kind of funny. One of those Goths. We don't get many of those in Allenville, which is why the manager remembered her. Even though she bought some things, she paid cash, so that was no help, and she wasn't with anybody, either. I went through the store's security tapes and got some pictures of her to run in the newspaper, but nobody knows who she is."

"I take it that her purchases weren't helpful, either."

"Actually, that was kind of peculiar. She bought herself a whole outfit, and afterward, she went to the store's bathroom, changed into the clothes she'd just bought, and threw the old stuff into the trash can."

"That is peculiar."

"My take is that she was in trouble, maybe drug-related, and wanted to disguise herself. But whoever was looking for her found her anyway, and nobody in town saw anybody suspicious."

"Isn't that strange in a small town?" Mark said, tactfully not suggesting that a local could have been involved.

"Not as much as you might think. We get all kinds of people passing through: runaways, transients of every description. Plus Raleigh is a big city, with big city problems, and sometimes that causes us problems, too."

Having spent time in New York, Boston, and London, Mark didn't see Raleigh as big or dangerous, but perspective was everything. "I still don't understand how Ms. Doe came to be buried in the Spivey plot."

"We kept her in cold storage for a while, hoping something would turn up, but decided it would only be right to bury her. Bob Henry at the funeral home donated a coffin and tombstone and the florist sent flowers, but when nobody had a burial plot they were willing to part with, I offered her a place with my family."

"That was very decent of you."

The cop looked abashed. "We had plenty of space—that whole corner of the lot was nearly empty. Besides, I was the first officer on the scene, and I feel bad that we've never found out who she was. Not that I've given up, mind you. There's not enough time or money to keep an investigation moving indefinitely, but I'm like a bloodhound—I may not have a scent to go on now, but when I get one, I'll not give up." He started to rise again, and said, "Now I do need to get going. You have your wife give us a call, and we'll pick out a nice place for Aunt Estelle."

"I'd do that. Thank you very much for your time."

"Hey, what are families for?"

The two men shook hands, and Norcomb headed for the door. Mark was about to follow him when he noticed his stomach was growling. Stella no longer needed food, other than the occasional dose of dark chocolate she claimed vampires required, but he still ate one or two regular meals a day. So when the waitress came to clear off Norcomb's table, he ordered lunch.

On the way back to Raleigh, Mark speculated about how Stella would react. He honestly had no idea—Stella's unpredictability had been part of what had attracted him to her in the first place, even before she confessed her undead status. Some days she seemed as young as she'd been at death, while others she demonstrated every day she'd lived. Most of the time he was happy to go along, so even though he didn't understand why she'd wanted to make a birthday pilgrimage to her grave, he hadn't argued.

Now there was one thing he was sure of. Stella wanted her grave back.

Mark was in bed with Stella when she came back to life, and she responded immediately, if not in the way he'd hoped.

"You reek!" she said with a grimace.

"Damn it," he said, sliding out from under the covers. "All I had was a cheeseburger! No onions or mustard, and I brushed my teeth and used mouthwash. Twice!"

"It's not the food," she said, sniffing.

"I ate next door to a chicken farm," Mark said.

She shuddered. "Maybe that's it. After living near one all those years, I was ready to switch to blood just to make sure I never had to eat chicken again."

"Ready to hear about the body in your grave?"

"Not yet—I'm hungry." As long as he got regular food, Mark could go two or three days without blood feeding, but Stella could not. "Did you scout out a place for us to hunt? What should I wear?"

"Workout clothes. The desk clerk recommended a nearby jogging path. It's around a lake and includes numerous twists and turns."

"I'll hit the shower and get ready to go."

"I better shower again, too, to get that nasty smell off of me. And in the interest of conserving water . . ."

"By all means, let's conserve."

Oddly, taking a shower together took longer than two separate showers would have.

If it had been his grave, Mark would have been frothing at the mouth to find out more about the body buried there, but older vampires were annoyingly patient. Stella wanted to wait until after dinner.

Admittedly, it didn't take her long to pick out a healthy-looking man and bespell him into following her to a darkened patch of trees. She quickly sated herself, and then Mark took his turn. After that, Stella kept the man bespelled long enough for their saliva to heal the wounds, and fuzzed his memory before sending him on his way again. All he'd remember was that the run had taken more out of him than usual.

Mark could have tried to bespell his own donor, of course, but it would have taken longer, and he'd have had to spring for a nice dinner and a movie. Stella's methods were much more efficient.

Afterward, they headed back for the Caddy, and since he didn't have Stella's patience, Mark was about to explode with his news by the time she asked, "What did you find out?"

He told her everything Norcomb had told him but wasn't so distracted that he didn't notice that Stella was driving back toward the Spivey family plot. He finished as they arrived, and when she parked the car, he followed her to the grave.

She just looked at it. Though it was a much darker night, he had no doubt that she could read each letter of the tombstone's inscription.

"We could have her moved to a public cemetery," he said.

"How would we explain it to that cop?"

"We'll tell him Aunt Estelle doesn't like a stranger in here, that she wants this space. Hell, we've got enough lawyers and money that we don't have to explain anything. Or you can bespell him—that would be cheaper."

"I don't want to do that to her."

"It's not like she'd know. She's dead—really dead, I mean. It wouldn't hurt her feelings."

"How do you know?"

"Because there's no such thing as ghosts."

"A year ago, you'd have said that there's no such thing as vampires. A year from now, there's no telling what you'll be saying."

A chill ran down Mark's spine, but that was a conversation he wasn't ready for. "Well, if she is watching, she'll understand why you want your grave back."

But Stella shook her head. "I don't want to just dump her somewhere. At least here, she's got Norcomb looking after her. She won't be forgotten."

"Then we'll move her to another spot here in the Spivey plot."

"No. Why should I care if there's somebody buried here anyway? It's not like I'm planning to use the grave. And who knows? Maybe someday Norcomb will figure out who she is, and her people will take her home."

"Maybe," Mark said doubtfully, knowing that the majority of cold cases were never solved. What had Norcomb said? That there wasn't enough time or money to pursue an investigation forever. Mark considered it. Time wasn't a problem for him, thanks to the eternal life clause of vampirism, and neither was money. Stella was loaded and, as was customary, had settled a big chunk of change onto him when she brought him over.

"Stella, did you ever read the Nancy Drew books?"

"Why?" Before he could answer, she said, "Are you seriously suggesting we go snooping around like Nancy Drew to find out what happened to Jane?"

"Why not? We've got no plans for the next few days."

"And you believe you can solve a murder in a few days when the police haven't been able to in two years?"

"I don't think it's any more ridiculous than believing in vampires."

She gave him a look.

"Okay, maybe it is," he conceded. "But how about this? We snoop around for a few days, and if nothing comes of it, we'll hire a private investigator. How does that sound?"

"Ridiculous." Then she smiled. "Let's do it."

Mark still didn't believe Jane Doe's spirit was watching, but he sketched a salute toward her tombstone as they left, just in case.

"What first?" he said once they were in the car.

"Are you admitting that even though this was your idea, you have no plans about what we should do first?"

"I'm a big-picture guy. I leave the details to you."

"I see," Stella said dryly. "In that case, I think I'd like to meet my third-cousin once removed, or whatever relation Officer Norcomb is to me."

They decided making another call to the police station to track him down might provoke unwelcome attention, so rather than drive back to get to Mark's laptop in Raleigh, Stella called Ramon in Boston and asked him to find Norcomb's address and directions to his house.

After hanging up, she said, "By the way, Ramon said—"

"I know, he said to remind me to put dirt in my bed. Smug bastard! I'll come up with a way to get him back one of these days."

"Would it help if I mentioned that Ramon is afraid of snakes?"

"Is he?" Mark said with just the kind of fiendish grin a vampire was supposed to sport. He was happily plotting revenge when they passed by Norcomb's house. A squad car was parked in the driveway, making it a good bet that Stella's cousin was at home.

Stella drove a few blocks farther and parked outside a dark house. "Does he live alone?"

"No wedding band, so he's not married, and he mentioned calling his mother, so he doesn't live with her," Mark said.

"Good. I don't want to risk anybody seeing the car, so you take it and keep circling the area. I'll call you on the cell when I need you."

"Aye aye, captain."

"Don't get lost!" She scooted out and was gone in a blink, while Mark moved to the driver's seat to randomly drive up and down the streets of the housing development, hoping nobody would notice him. An hour and a half later, his cell rang.

"Stella?"

"No, it's dear old Aunt Estelle. Do you remember that big red house right after we turned onto Norcomb's street?"

"Having driven past it approximately twenty-eight times tonight, I doubt I'll ever forget it."

"Pick me up there."

"Aye aye—"

"Once was funny. After that it gets old."

"Yes, beloved."

"That one never gets old."

"Neither do we," Mark said, and broke the connection.

Stella wasn't in sight when he drove up but appeared at his window almost immediately. "Move over." She climbed in and, as she got the car moving, tossed a yellow legal pad and a videotape into his lap.

"What's this?" he asked.

"My notes from my talk with Norcomb and a copy of the Wal-Mart security tape. Or rather the copy of his copy that I had him make. If he'd had a photocopier, I'd have copied the case files, too."

"He had all that at his house?"

"For one, your talk today got him thinking about Jane again, and for another, I think he's a little obsessed with her."

"Clearly." Then a thought occurred to him. "He didn't kill her himself, did he?"

"Nancy Drew would be proud of you," she said approvingly, "but no, he did not. I asked."

"You're sure? How thoroughly did you bespell him?"

"Deeply enough that he won't remember me, you, or Aunt Estelle. I could have made him forget his own address while I was at it, but that seemed a bit excessive."

"You've got to teach me how to do that."

"It just takes practice," she said.

"What else did he tell you?"

"Everything he knows about the case, but there wasn't a lot more than what he told you, unless you count the forensic details: decomposition, tissue damage, lividity. I'd have been done half an hour sooner if I hadn't had to ask what all the terminology means."

"You'll have to watch more *CSI*. Any leads we can use?"

"Possibly. It turns out that Jane was at Benny's the day she went to Wal-Mart."

"That's where I met Norcomb. Kind of a coincidence, isn't it?"

"Not really. How many restaurants do you think there are in Allenville?"

"Good point. Was she there before or after her shopping spree?"

"Before, when her outfit was still noticeable. Black on black, with a skull ring."

"No wonder she threw it away."

"A good thing she did, or the murderer would have disposed of it along with the clothes she was wearing when he killed her."

"What difference does that make?"

"Well, it turns out my cousin is one devoted investigator. He went to the dump and found Jane's old clothes, still stuffed in the shopping bag."

"Don't tell me he had that at his house, too?"

"He did. Having a boy like that in the family does my heart proud."

"And well it might. Did you learn anything from the clothes?"

"I didn't want to handle them too much—I've watched enough *CSI* to know about contaminating evidence—but I did get a good whiff of them. Of course, I got a good whiff of garbage from the dump, too, but still, I've got Jane's scent."

"Stella, how good do you smell?"

"Sweet enough to make bees give up roses, according to the perfume bottle."

"Granted, even without the perfume, but I was referring to your sense of smell. Compared to, say, a bloodhound's."

"I've never made the comparison," she said, "but I am considered gifted, even for a vampire."

"Gifted enough that you'll be able to track her after two years?"

"It's a long shot, but since this whole idea is a long shot . . ."

"True enough."

It took a while for Stella to find a secluded parking place somewhat near where Jane's body had been found, though it was still a long enough walk that Mark was glad they were wearing running shoes. Even vampires got blisters on their feet from walking too far in dress shoes.

Finally they found the spot Stella was sure matched the description in the police report, just past a decrepit wooden fence. The neon of Benny's was visible as a glow above the tree line.

"Now I know why you reeked when you came to bed today," she said.

Mark inhaled deeply and regretted it. "I see what you mean about chicken farms. They're foul. Or fowl, if you'd rather."

"It's not the chicken," Stella said. "Yes, I smell them, and yes, they are foul, but there's something else."

He started to ask what she meant, but she was leaning over, sniffing at the ground. Mark decided further bloodhound references would not go over well, so concentrated on staying out of her way as she wandered this way and that, sometimes breaking into a run so fast that he'd have lost her if he weren't a vampire, too.

Finally, after he'd chased her over what seemed like half the state, Stella came to a dead stop. "Here."

"You actually tracked her?" he said incredulously.

"No, you were right. It's been too long. I caught a trace of Jane's scent back where the body was, but that's it."

"Then what are you talking about?"

"I smelled somebody else. There's another body here, Mark—we're standing on the grave."

"Are you sure?"

"Can't you smell it?"

"You know I'm new at this," he grumbled, but leaned over and tried again. She was right. The stench of death was there, though masked by the chickens' stink and several feet of earth between them and the corpse. "It's not fresh."

"No, but I think the one over there is." She pointed a little bit away.

"There's another?"

"More than that, I think."

"Jesus, Stella, what have we gotten ourselves into?"

Between their sense of self-preservation and the realization that dawn was coming, they made their way back to the car and drove back to the hotel, arguing as they went. Mark was in favor of an anonymous call to Norcomb about the bodies, along with another bout of bespelling him if necessary, but Stella wasn't willing to risk their involvement coming to light.

Or so she said, but Mark suspected that she just didn't want to give up their investigation, and when he said so, she pulled rank on him. He objected, and by the time they got back to the hotel, they were no longer speaking.

Mark was still angry when he woke the next day, and both ignored Stella and pretended he'd never heard of Jane Doe. It was only when he'd gone out for lunch, defiantly eating a large bowl of chili with onions on top, that his resolve weakened, as it always did with Stella. She was older, richer, stronger, and faster than he was, and had other vampiric abilities he was just beginning to discover, and he still felt protective of her. He had no idea if it was a man-woman thing, a vampire-sire thing, or just a Mark-Stella thing. Whatever it was, he went to buy something they were going to need, and nearly had it set up when Stella woke.

Her nose wrinkled, so he knew she smelled his lunch despite his using a whole bottle of mouthwash, but she refrained from comment. "What are you doing?" she asked.

"I got a VCR so we can watch the security tape." He made the last connection, turned on the TV and VCR, and reached for the tape.

Stella got to it first. "We don't have to do this," she said. "*You* don't have to do this."

"I know."

"All that 'I'm your sire and I say so!' stuff is bullshit!"

Mark blinked at that—Stella rarely swore—and repeated, "I know."

"Then why did you get the VCR?"

"Consider it a belated birthday gift."

She smiled. "Only if you come here and let me give you an early birthday gift."

He started to join her on the bed but then stopped. "My lunch was kind of smelly."

"So I won't kiss you. Not on the lips, anyway."

An hour later, they got around to watching the video. Norcomb had put together a greatest hits tape, with snippets from various camera views that showed Jane. The film quality was mediocre, but they got the general idea.

Jane arrived dressed in urban Goth glory—black cargo pants, a black T-shirt ripped at the neckline, scuffed black boots. Her hair was, of course, black with the flat look of a cheap dye job. It was short, but Mark couldn't tell if it had been styled to look asymmetrical or just hadn't been brushed recently. She must have used half a tube of mascara to ring her eyes so thoroughly, and she was wearing a fine selection of heavy-looking Goth adornments: a skull ring, a bat wing necklace, and other less visible chains and rings.

"She doesn't exactly blend in, does she?" Mark said.

"But she doesn't seem to mind being stared at," Stella commented.

Even though nearly everybody who saw her did a double-take, Jane strode through the store confidently, not seeming to notice them. She headed out of range of that camera, and the view switched to the juniors department. Jane went through the racks to pick out a pair of jeans and a light blue pullover sweater. After a trip to the dressing room, which was not documented, she went to the shoe department to try on sneakers in blinding white. She got socks, too—the ones she was wearing had holes in both big toes. Next she got panties and a bra.

"Granny panties," Stella said thoughtfully.

"Beg pardon," Mark said.

"The female equivalent of tighty whities. Waist-high briefs, instead of a bikini or a thong."

The next scene was of her standing next to a rack of hats, and she settled on a light blue sun hat, the kind of modified ball cap Mark saw girls wearing in the summer.

She went to the register with her gleanings, still ignoring the curious looks she was getting, and once it was all paid for, headed toward the bathroom. There was a break in the film, and it started up again with her coming out again. Now Jane was dressed in her new outfit, and with her face scrubbed clean, her hair hidden under the hat, and the jewelry gone, she looked like a new person. The people walking past her didn't give her a second glance, except a high school boy who flashed a grin.

Jane walked toward the front of the store, carrying the Wal-Mart bag that presumably carried her old things. But just before she stepped out, she looked at the bag, then stuffed it into a trash can by the door. She walked out the door, and after ten seconds more, the tape ended.

"Kudos to your cousin for spotting her," Mark said. "I wouldn't have known it was the same girl."

"I don't know that I would have, either," Stella said. "Not by sight anyway. So how did her killer recognize her?"

"He must have known her well."

"What about the other bodies?"

"Norcomb thinks drugs were involved," Mark said, "and drug dealers make lots of enemies. Though I have to say that Allenville doesn't seem like the place for that kind of activity, even with the big city nearby."

Stella rewound to the part where Jane emerged from the bathroom. "She looks a lot younger like that. Even her body language changed. Before she was so sure of herself—now she looks almost timid."

"Part of the disguise?"

"Maybe." Stella watched to the end again, shut it off, and announced, "I'm getting hungry."

They decided not to risk returning to the lakeside park from the previous night and instead went to the North Carolina State Fair, which was in full swing. After Mark won a stuffed version of Seasame Street's Count from the milk bottle throw, they started looking for a likely target.

"There," Stella said, nudging Mark in the side. A group of women who looked like college students was discussing what ride to go on next, and when they decided on the Ferris wheel, one of them begged off, saying she wanted to get something to drink. The others kidded her for being afraid of heights and joined the long line for the ride.

"Perfect," Mark said. They followed the acrophobic girl for a few minutes, then flanked her, and Stella made eye contact to bespell her instantly. It took only a few minutes to find a secluded spot between trailers, and Stella fed while Mark kept watch. Then they escorted the girl back, Mark bought her a Coke, and Stella implanted the idea that a very attractive man had flirted with her.

They were halfway back to the hotel when Stella said, "That's it!"

"That's what?"

"Why did we pick that girl to feed on?"

"Because she was temporarily alone."

"Because she was vulnerable. Now think about how Jane looked. Before she changed clothes, she looked tough and streetwise. People stared at her but nobody messed with her. Afterward, she looked vulnerable."

"Okay."

"Norcomb thought she changed clothes as a disguise, and that may be it, but maybe that's not why she was killed. What if she was killed because she was vulnerable? What if somebody saw that and marked her as his prey?"

"Another vampire?"

"No—the autopsy report had nothing about her being drained. But we're not the only predators around."

"Meaning what?" Mark said, thinking uncomfortably of those other *things* Stella had referred to before. "Werewolves? Zombies? Ghouls?"

"I'd have smelled any of them at the graves we found," Stella said matter-of-factly, and Mark didn't know if she was kidding or not. "I'm talking about a human monster."

"A serial killer," Mark said, momentarily relieved, "with a penchant for young girls."

Stella nodded. "We know Jane was at Benny's before she went to Wal-Mart, but we don't know where she went next. If she was passing through, wouldn't she go back to the truck stop to look for a ride? And if you lived in Allenville and wanted a steady supply of victims, wouldn't you hang around Benny's to find them?"

"May I point out that Benny's isn't far from where Jane's body was found and from where the other bodies still are."

"Right you are, Ned."

"Ned?"

"Ned Nickerson. Nancy Drew's boyfriend."

"So what would Nancy and Ned do in a case like this?"

"Set a trap for the killer."

"A trap requires bait."

"Who do we know who looks younger and more vulnerable than she really is?" Stella said, batting her eyelashes.

Despite his teasing before, Stella really did look older than the eighteen she'd been before making the Choice. Mark didn't understand how—something about the way she moved, or her clothes and makeup—but she looked like a woman, not a girl. At least, she always had until retreating into the bathroom with the bag of stuff she'd bought at Target on the way back to the hotel.

Mark was watching CNN when he heard, "Excuse me?" in a timid voice.

He looked up to see a girl in khaki crop pants with a peacock blue cami that did nothing to hide the pink bra strap beneath or her generous bosom. Her soft brown hair was held off from her face with a glittery headband, and her makeup was frosted pastels. Her necklace said "Princess," with a heart dotting the i.

"Stella?" he said wonderingly.

"How do I look?" She spun around.

"Like jailbait. If you were my daughter, I would order barbed wire for the fence and a chastity belt for you."

She dimpled—he hadn't known she could dimple—and said, "Do you think you could, you know, let me use your car?"

"Dear Lord, you even speak young! I'll drive—you don't look old enough to have a license."

Damned if she didn't dimple again.

Mark was still a bit unnerved when, halfway to Allenville, Stella reached over and stroked his thigh. "Do you want to, like, park somewhere before we go in?"

"God, no!"

"I beg your pardon?" she said as she drew her hand back, sounding like her old self.

"No offense, but I never cared for *Lolita*, and you're just too damned convincing."

"I thought all men fantasized about young girls."

"I prefer women."

"I see," she said, sounding more thoughtful than offended.

"Were you like this when you were eighteen?"

"Well, I probably would have dressed in comparable fashion, given the choice, but for one, we didn't have the money, and for another, Mama would never have allowed it."

"Good for her," Mark said self-righteously. "Now, if you could make yourself up as a coed, maybe midtwenties . . ."

"Pervert," she said amiably.

Mark exited at a rest area they'd seen a mile before the Allenville exit, and parked around back. Stella got out and, after checking to see that nobody was watching, slipped into the bushes to make her way to Benny's over land. Mark returned to the highway to drive the rest of the way.

The truck stop was bustling with vacationers, locals, and truckers. Mark snagged the last open booth and ordered a cheeseburger with no onions, fries, and a beer. Then he pulled out his laptop and a stack of paperwork so it wouldn't look suspicious if he stayed around for a while.

Mark knew Stella had arrived before he saw her, thanks to their sire-vampire, or dam-vampire, relationship. But he tried not to watch as she found a seat at the counter, made a show of counting out how little money she had, and asked for a burger and a small Coke. When he finally risked a glance in her direction, he saw that she'd let herself get a touch grubby during her trip through the woods, making the illusion of a runaway that much more convincing.

For the next hour and a half, Mark ate, sipped his beer, fiddled with papers, and watched as people wandered past Stella. She made eye contact with every lone man she saw, and some of the women, but while reactions included delight, disgust, and lust, nobody reacted like the predator they were looking for. She even asked a couple of the men for rides, but nobody took her up on it.

The crowd thinned, Mark was running out of things to do, and

Stella had been nursing the last quarter inch of her Coke for half an hour when Mark decided that their quarry hadn't come in that night. They might well have to stake out the place for weeks, especially if the killer was a trucker or commuter. Stella's repeated presence would be noticed, even if she changed her look, so he'd started considering other young-looking vampires they could enlist to play bait when he saw the cook coming out of the kitchen.

The man looked like he was in his midthirties, stocky, with greasy hair Mark hoped was caused by his own body chemistry and not the food he prepared. He slipped an order of fries in front of Stella along with another glass of Coke.

She tried to thank him, but he scurried away before the waitress could see him.

Stella, still in character as a hungry runaway, scarfed the fries down. Mark was impressed. She could still eat regular food, but her body gained no nutrition from it, and since her senses were so refined, she rarely enjoyed the taste. Eating the burger must have been a strain, and to add fries on top showed how seriously she was taking their investigation.

Another half an hour passed. Mark was about to gather his belongings and give Stella their prearranged signal to call it a night when the cook snuck back out of the kitchen and placed another full glass in front of Stella, again not meeting her eyes when she tried to thank him.

The hairs on the back of Mark's neck prickled. Random generosity wasn't unheard of, but something about the man's furtive movements bothered him. Besides which, the man was supposed to be working in the kitchen, not watching customers.

While Mark was trying to work it out, Stella drank down the Coke and left enough money on the counter to pay her check. Then she stood up and wobbled, as if she'd lost her balance. Mark's eyes narrowed. Vampires, at least vampires as old as Stella, didn't lose their balance.

Their plan had been to leave separately, with at least five minutes between their exits, so Mark stayed put, despite his consternation. What was Stella playing at anyway? Trying to look more available by pretending to be drunk, even though all she'd had was Coke? Cokes, he corrected. Two of which had been given for free by a man who was acting decidedly odd. "Jesus!" Mark whispered. The bastard had put something into Stella's drinks!

He shoved his things into his briefcase, threw money onto the table, and headed for the door. He stopped by the car, hoping Stella had used her key to get in, but when she wasn't there, he tossed the stuff into the trunk and grabbed a tire iron.

He slowly walked through the parking lot, checking for Stella's scent, and caught it leading out across the field in the direction of the chicken barn. There was another scent mingled with hers, the strong sweat from the truck stop cook.

They'd lured out their predator, and in normal circumstances, Mark would have had no doubts about Stella's safety, but the way she'd been weaving as she went out the door worried him. He couldn't have been too far behind, and he was moving with the speed even a young vampire could muster, but he couldn't see them, and he quickly lost the scent.

Had his nose misled him? Had the man gotten Stella into a car or even met up with a confederate? Where were they? He was alone in a field, with nothing in sight but the truck stop behind him and the chicken barn before him, when he realized where they had to be. He ran toward the barn.

As he got closer, he heard talking and recognized Stella's voice, even though it was slurred.

"Where are we? Who did you say you were anyway?"

"Just a friend," a man's voice said, and Mark guessed it was the cook. "I thought you might need a place to sleep. See, there's a bed here."

"It smells funny."

"That's just the chickens. If you lay down, you'll be asleep in no time, and it won't bother you anymore. Here, let me help you take your shoes off."

Stretching up, Mark could peer into the window of the room where Stella and the man were, and even from the outside, he knew the smells in that room had nothing to do with chickens. While he watched, he saw Stella's eyes drift shut, and she slumped to the floor.

"That's my girl," the cook said, and reached for her.

Mark had seen enough. He ran around the building until he found the door. It was locked, but he shoved his shoulder against it, splintering it. More chickens than Mark had ever seen at one time fluttered wildly, clucking and shrieking and making even more protesting noises as he ran through them to get to the door that lead to Stella. The man had heard him coming, of course, and was waiting behind the door as Mark burst in. Mark had been expecting it and dodged at the last minute, which was enough to deflect the knife thrust from his back to his arm.

Unfortunately it was the arm with the tire iron, which slipped from Mark's grasp as he whirled around to face his attacker.

It took Mark only an instant to take in the scene, the man standing in front of where Stella lay sprawled on the bed. He was about to launch himself when a hand moving so fast it seemed to appear from nowhere latched itself onto the killer. Between his legs. Gripping his genitals.

He crumpled with a sound that would have been a scream if he'd had enough breath for it.

Stella went down with him, still squeezing. The expression on her face had nothing to do with the nymphet she'd been pretending to be and everything to do with a vampire.

"All right, you son of of a bitch," she said. "Tell me who Jane Doe is before I rip your prick off!"

"I don't know," he wheezed.

"Are you telling me you don't know one of your victims is buried in the Spivey family plot?"

"I know she's there, but I don't know her name. I don't know any of their names."

"You lying sack of shit," Stella said, squeezing harder. "You kept her clothes, didn't you? I bet you jacked off in them. There must have been something."

"Nothing. I swear. Only a little money."

"Tell me!"

The man's face was starting to change colors.

"I don't think he knows," Mark said.

She didn't let up.

"Stella, he doesn't know. Trust me—no man is going to let you keep doing that if he has any way to stop you."

For a long moment she still didn't react; then, with a last squeeze, she let go. The man rolled into a ball and whimpered.

"Are you all right?" Mark asked.

"Of course. You know drugs can't affect me."

"I wasn't sure," Mark admitted. "You're a very good actress."

"What about you? That bastard stabbed you," Stella said, and Mark finally noticed that his arm was bleeding freely. "Does it hurt?"

"Quite a bit, actually."

Stella stepped over the killer, touched the blood with one finger, and brought the finger up to her mouth. Then she gave Mark a kiss that almost made him forget the pain.

"You're welcome," he said breathlessly. "What do we do now?"

"First we take care of your arm," she said, and leaned over to start lapping at his wound. Not only did it stop the bleeding, but it felt damned good, too.

With that done, Stella dragged the killer from the floor, grabbed his chin to make him look her in the eyes, and bespelled him so thoroughly he'd have laid still for her to finish squeezing his balls off, if she'd asked him to. Then she told him exactly what he was going to remember about this night. How he'd drugged the girl at the truck stop and brought her to his nest, meaning to rape and kill her the way he had the others. But the girl had fought back, gotten in a lucky blow, and left him unconscious on the floor. Meanwhile Mark did a bit of stage decoration, leaving threads from Stella's clothes on the bed and dropping the princess necklace on the floor. Then they picked up the tire iron and made their way out through the still-agitated flock in the barn.

Their next stop was the pay phone outside the truck stop, where Stella called the police to tell them who had attacked her and where. When they asked who she was, she hung up.

Mark already had the car running, and they lost no time in taking off, driving away just as the first police car arrived, siren blaring.

Despite the lingering pain in his arm, Mark was feeling pretty pleased with himself. "What do you know? We solved the case."

"No, we didn't. We still don't know who Jane Doe is."

"But we did catch a serial killer. Nancy Drew never did that, I bet. Not only will he not kill anymore, but now they'll find his other victims. Doesn't that count for something?"

"Of course it does. I've been thinking of all those mothers who must have been wondering what happened to their daughters. It's made my coming home worthwhile. I just wish we could have found out who Jane is. Her mother needs to know, too."

They were quiet for a few miles.

Then Mark said, "Stella, about coming home. Why now?"

"I told you. For my birthday."

"You've never come back for your birthday before, and eighty-two isn't a particularly meaningful birthday."

"No, but it's been a meaningful year. Because of you."

"I don't understand."

"You're the first vampire I've sired. Or damned. My first child."

"I'm not a child."

"No, but you are the closest thing I've got to a child. You're my bloodline. Is it any wonder that I've been thinking about my human bloodline?"

"And about your mother?" he guessed.

She nodded. "Granted that my feelings toward you aren't precisely maternal—"

"Thank God for that!"

"But it has made me think about being a mother and how I'd feel if anything happened to you. How Mama must have felt when I died. God, Mark, I was a terrible daughter!"

"Why would you say that?"

"I told you—when Vilmos gave me the Choice, I never looked back. Ever. I lived the high life in Europe for decades, and by the time I even thought to check on Mama, she'd been dead for years. I forgot she existed. And I guess she forgot me, too."

There was no way Mark could answer her, no way he could comfort her, so he didn't even try.

Only when they were in bed did he say, "If I'm your child, does this mean I've got to give you a Mother's Day present?"

Her smile was his reward. "Damned straight! I want breakfast in bed, flowers, and a bottle of perfume, too."

"It's a deal."

The results of the night's adventures were all over the news the next morning, and Mark spent most of the day watching the story unfold, as the newscasters put it. He was still watching when Stella woke for the night.

"Did it work?" she asked him.

In answer, he pointed to the TV screen, where the local news was discussing the case, complete with film of Officer Norcomb with the killer cook in cuffs. “They’ve found two bodies already. This guy has been working at the truck stop for several years, so there’s no telling how many more there are.”

“Has he said anything about Jane?”

“Only that he killed her but got interrupted by hunters before he could bury her, and she was found before he had another opportunity. Nothing about who she was.”

“Oh.”

“We did good, Stella. You did good.”

“I know.”

“Besides, with all the extra publicity, maybe somebody will come forward with new information. You know Norcomb isn’t going to give up now. And if he does, you can bespell him into changing his mind.”

“True enough. Are you hungry?”

“I am. Hey! I didn’t eat any food today—I didn’t even think of it.”

“My little boy is growing up.”

He gave her a determinedly Oedipal kiss and said, “There’s an NC State game this evening. Should be a good place to get a bite. I’ll hit the shower. Want to join me?”

“No, thanks. I want to get dinner before midnight this time.”

“Spoilsport.”

When Mark was done, he saw Stella was watching TV but not the news. Instead she was watching the security tape of Jane.

“Stella . . .”

“I’m not brooding. There’s just something about Jane that’s not right. Or rather about Norcomb’s explanation of what she was doing in Allenville.”

“How so?”

“He figured she was tied into drug dealing, but all we really know is that a girl who looked like a runaway came to Wal-Mart and bought new clothes. If she wasn’t disguising herself, why the makeover?”

Mark thought about it. "Could she have been doing the same thing you are?"

She cocked her head at him. "Meaning what?"

"You were sort of a runaway but eventually you wanted to come home. Right?"

"Yes, but—"

"Hear me out. When you came back to Allenville, suddenly you had an accent again. You kind of reverted to who you used to be. Maybe Jane was reverting, too. She'd been this Goth creature of the night, but now that she was coming home, she wanted to become a normal girl again. So she stopped at Wal-Mart, dressed like her old self, and threw the Goth identity away. She wanted to go home."

Stella looked at him, eyes wide. "You're a genius!"

Mark tried to look modest and pointed out, "Of course, that doesn't really help us figure out who she was."

"It might. Jane only bought one set of clothes, and she put them on right away. That means she expected to get home that night or the next day at the latest—otherwise the new clothes would have gotten dirty. She may not have been from Allenville, but she was local. This could narrow Norcomb's search enough to find her!"

"It must be hereditary—you're a genius, too! Shall we call in another anonymous tip?"

"I've got a better idea." Stella got ready in record time, and they took yet another trip to Allenville. It took a while to track down Norcomb, what with his working the biggest case of his career, but once they found him, it didn't take long for Stella to bespell him and plant both the idea about finding Jane and the conviction that he'd thought it up himself. As Stella put it, it was the least she could do for family.

They stuck around Raleigh for a while longer as the police continued to find bodies, celebrating when two of the victims were identified by personal effects kept by the killer. But the big celebration came when

Norcomb announced that Jane's real name was Leah and that her family lived in nearby Cary. They'd heard about Jane Doe, but between the poor quality of the Wal-Mart security tapes and the changes in Leah's appearance during the four years she was gone, they'd never made the connection between Jane and their daughter.

The next day, the newspaper reported that an anonymous donor was paying for Leah's body to be moved closer to her family and that a tasteful granite monument would be included. Mark was among the many who attended the funeral, making sure that Leah finally got back home.

Stella was ready to head back to Boston, maybe stopping in New York to see some shows, but Mark put her off, pointing out that the state fair was still going on, and they hadn't ridden all the rides. Though he knew that she knew he was up to something, she played along.

The next night, Mark drove them back to Allenville, and parked outside the Spivey family plot.

"Okay, why are we out here?" Stella asked.

"I want you to show you something."

He led her through the gate toward where her parents were buried, and she couldn't resist looking over toward Jane's, or rather Leah's, former grave. "Why did they leave the tombstone?"

"Let's look."

He was watching her face as she got closer and realized it was a different stone.

She turned to him. "You bought me a tombstone?"

"I was going to," he admitted, "but somebody beat me to it."

"I don't understand."

"I went to see Bob Henry. He's the man who donated Jane's tombstone, and I thought a little karmic payback was in order, so I was going to order one for you from him. When I told him where it was to be placed, he mentioned that his family had been in the business for several generations, and that they've done all the monuments in this plot. And when I told him the name to put on the stone, he told me the story."

"What story?"

"Do you remember the tree that used to be over your grave? Lightning hit it years after you were buried and knocked it down."

"So?"

"So it fell on the tombstone your mother had put up for you and broke it."

"Then she did get me a stone?"

He nodded. "She had Bob Henry Senior take it back to repair it, but she was already ill and died before she could finish paying for the work. It was still in the storeroom. All I did was pay the balance and a rush charge to get it out here tonight."

"Then Mama bought this?"

"It was her last gift to you."

Stella knelt down on the grave and ran her fingers over the stone's inscription. Not her name, or the dates of her birth and death, but the two words under her name:

Beloved Daughter

COPYRIGHTS